Hue & Cry

A Hew Cullan Mystery

SHIRLEY McKAY

First published in Great Britain in 2009

This edition first published in Great Britain in 2010 by
Polygon, an imprint of Birlinn Ltd
West Newington House
10 Newington Road
Edinburgh
EH9 1QS

www.birlinn.co.uk

9 8 7 6 5

ISBN 978 1 84697 152 5

British Library Cataloguing-in-Publication Data
A catalogue record for this book is available on
request from the British Library

Typeset in Bembo by Palimpsest Book Production Limited,
Falkirk, Stirlingshire
Printed and bound by Clays Ltd, St Ives plc

For Neil,
always
and only

Acknowledgements

Thank you to Caroline Knox and Lynn Curtis, who both provided invaluable editorial advice on early versions of the manuscript; to Caroline Oakley, for her careful and constructive reading; to Anita Joseph, for her shrewd and sympathetic editing; and to Neville Moir of Polygon, who caught a glimpse of sunshine in the haar.

Thanks also to Neil Rhodes, for advice (not always welcomed) and for his constant love and support; to Alice, for believing; and to Peter, for putting up with it, even though he wished I had a proper job.

And above all, to my agent John Beaton, without whose tireless guidance, patience and persistence, Hew Cullan and his friends would not have braved the world.

Historical note

In the year 1580, King James VI of Scotland turned fourteen. On his first royal progress he visited the town of St Andrews where he saw a play performed in the courtyard of the New Inn of the priory as part of the entertainments. The event was noted in the diary of James Melville, who left a record of his time at St Andrews University. This moment, snatched from history, underlies the fiction that is *Hue and Cry*. With the exception of King James and his retinue, the people in this book have had no previous lives.

Prologue

St Andrews, Scotland
1579

In the privacy of that small room, blanched yellow in the candle-light, Nicholas spoke to the boy in his own tongue, no longer accusing but low and soft like a girl. It was a mistake perhaps, because Alexander's eyes began to fill with tears. The kindness felt too clumsy and too intimate. He struggled to recover his authority.

'We will talk more of this tomorrow. In the meantime, please try to apply yourself. Study your text for an hour or so more. We'll go over the passage again.'

'Won't you just look at them?' The boy spoke in Scots, so quietly that Nicholas took a moment to hear him. He did not look up as he spoke, but stared hopelessly down at the paper between his fumbling hands. Nicholas forced down the impulse to hurt him, to say something childishly spiteful in reply.

'You would do better to spend more time with your books and less making verses, if you ever hope to matriculate. But yes, I will look at them when I return. Now read a little longer. And Alexander . . .'

Nicholas turned at the door, exasperation failing at the sight of the boy huddled miserably over his work in the guttering light, and spoke again, in Latin now, to mask the gentleness. 'Alexander, take the blanket from the cot. The evenings are too chill to sit in your shirt. And remember to blow out the candle.'

The boy's bright hair, he thought, was the only warmth in the sour and windowless room. It was a relief to escape down the narrow stair to the last of the late summer sun.

Hew

From the deck of the Dutch flieboat *Zeedraak* a young man looked out to shore. As the land unfurled before him like a map he began to feel less sick. For it was not the motion of the ship but the length of his absence that caused his soft belly to flutter and fall. The sight of the town reassured him. It looked as it had always done, fronted by the ramparts of its castle, etched on the horizon by the starkness of its rock. Perhaps it was a trick of the light, but the strip of land between the castle and the shore appeared to have diminished as it weathered the encroaching of the tide. And the cathedral, by the square-built tower and chapel of St Rule, had crumbled further into stone, allowing the sunlight to stream through its frame and illuminate the town that had grown up in its shade. Beyond, from east to west, were ranked the four main thoroughfares: the fair and leafy south street, with its colleges and kirk; the broad and bustling Mercatgait; the north street, with its college halls and chapel braced against the winds; the Swallowgait that opened on the Castlegait and cliffs, falling sheer into the water, sweeping west towards the links and eastwards to the harbour, where the shallow basin washed into the sea. These four streets converged on the cathedral, and with their rigs and gardens set the pattern of the town. Criss-crossed between them, from north to south, vennels, wynds and closes narrowed and made deep its inner life.

True to its name the flieboat had crossed the North Sea from Holland fiercely and swiftly and soon disgorged its contents in the sunlit bay. The young man, Hew Cullan, found little to detain him. Since he was no merchant he had nothing to declare. In fact he had nothing at all. He had travelled from France through Flanders to Campvere, where he was shown to one boat and his belongings inexplicably were thrown upon another bound for Leith. He had only a purse of French coin and the fine suit of French clothes he stood up in, which now seemed unfit for the drab Scottish soil. He felt a pleasing lightness as he scrambled from the boat, coming back as a stranger to find his old faith with the town.

St Andrews was constructed on parallel streets within and between which its business took place. He climbed from the harbour through the sea gate to the pends that opened out upon the south street. Behind him stood the old cathedral and the priory vaults and cloisters where the merchants thronged on fair days, to the right the grand houses, some in mid-construction, where they pawned their wealth. On his left – and here he paused – were the college and the chapel of St Leonard. This was where, as a boy of fourteen, he had first entered the university to begin the education that had taken him to France. For four years he had worked and dreamt behind these quiet walls. Since it was September now, the gates were closed. The term would not begin for several weeks, and the present crop of students had not yet arrived to straggle obediently from college to kirk, from lecture to links, snaking through the town.

A little further up the street he passed the Kirk of Holy Trinity, turning sharply at its corner to the Mercatgait. Here stood the tolbooth, house of law and commerce, the marketplace with its rows of shops and luckenbooths, the ancient well, the mercat cross and tron. The cross and the tron, where butter was weighed, hid a more sinister side. Hew shivered as he passed. It was a short step from the tolbooth to this place of persecution, to the pillories and whipping posts where the sins of the people were exposed to public shame. It was in part his horror of such things that had deflected his purpose in the study of the law. The closer he came to its practice the more acutely he considered its effects. Today he was relieved to find there were no jeering crowds, no victims to be vilified and branded in the street. The marketplace was empty. It was now past six o'clock and there was little passing trade.

Somewhere above him he heard a door close. A thin man

dressed in scholar's black hurried down a forestair and brushed past him, absently clutching his gown. Hew gave a wry smile. Once, and not so long ago, he had himself been so immersed, so preoccupied in study, he had failed to see the world. The stairway belonged to a shop, grander than most of those that flanked it and no doubt more recently built. Perhaps the scholar lodged above. Below was some sort of a workshop, at this late hour still open to the street. Intrigued, he looked inside.

The whitewashed walls were clean and the floor freshly swept. A row of new candles lit up the counter on which lay bolts of woollen cloth in varied natural shades of russet, ash and clay; blue-green and stiff grey Sunday plaids, lengths of woven leine flax and saffron-coloured shirtcloth. Behind lay rare imported wares on wooden shelves: slubbed silks and velvets, mohair, milk-white linens and Flanders lace in violet, primrose, straw and plunkett blue. And in the gloom beyond these riches were looms strung with yellow threads, skeins of dyed and undyed wool, a brace of spinsters' stools, spindles, shuttles, fleeces, reels and pins. A solitary black-haired boy swept up the fallen threads.

'Leave that the noo, Tom, and help load the cart!' A squat, bearded man in scarlet hose bustled in from the back of the shop. His cloak was a soft tawny brown, napped like velvet, brooched and belted in mulberry silk. A gold-tasselled purse clinked from his sleeve. 'We've an early start to market . . . ah, beg pardon, sir; I did not see you there.'

Hungrily, he gazed at Hew, who was trying to make a strategic retreat.

'In point of fact we're closed.' He took in Hew's clothes, the peascod coat and full round hose. 'But if there's something in the shop you care to see?'

'No, not at all. Some other time.'

'Oh, you *are* a Scot!' Clearly this had proved a disappointment. But the merchant was quick to recover. 'Though you're evidently used to more outlandish fashions. French, I would hazard? You're not from round here.'

'Aye, I was once.' Hew gave nothing away. He edged towards the door. 'Since you're closed, I will not keep you.'

The shopkeeper seemed torn between the wish to tempt his prey and his earlier concerns. The boy with the sweeping brush stood waiting patiently.

'Well,' he conceded, as Hew stepped outside, 'you may call again on Monday. Or, sir, if you care to go to Crail, we are there all day tomorrow for the Sunday market. You see, we have very fine cloths.'

'Thank you, I'll think on it,' Hew said politely.

'I am not, you see,' disconcertingly, the man had followed him into the street, 'your common cottage woolman. In addition to the house and shop I have a sizeable flock on the outskirts of the town. My wife and daughter spin the wool for my looms and the looms themselves are seldom still. And my brother is a merchant, sir, a most ambitious man.'

At this point a young girl appeared, barefoot on the forestair, calling 'Dadda! Mammie says she's finished with the wools.'

She was prettily dressed in a pale greenish-grey, like rivulets of water from the burn. She tossed her curls appraisingly at Hew while her father adjusted the scope of his pride.

'Ah, Isabel! My Tibbie! Bonny, is she not?'

But the woolman put his question to the wind, as Hew took the chance to escape. He hurried past the tron and out of sight. Moments later he was standing in the cookshop on the corner of the Fishergait and Castlegait, just as he remembered it.

'It's Saturday, so no hot meat. Will you leave your name?'

Hew found an old Scots merk at the bottom of his purse. 'No, I'll pay for it.'

His name still remained on the wall by the bar. He was re-assured to find the system was unchanged: the same yellowed debts on thin scraps of paper, the same smell of onions and old gravy stains. Yet he preferred to stay a stranger for a while, allowing old sensations to come upon him slowly. He was not ready to go home. He ordered herrings fried in oatmeal and a stoup of ale, taking his cup out to sit in the courtyard, where half an empty barrel had been set out as a stool. Presently the girl came with a plate of buttered oatcakes. 'We're full tonight with sailors. Did you want a room?'

Hew shook his head. He had recognised some of the crew from the *Zeedraak*, whose raucous shanties spilled into the street.

'And yet you're not from here?' the lass persisted.

'I lived here once. I have been gone a while.'

'You'll see some changes, then.'

Behind her he could see the castle and the cliffs sweeping to the sands, the gulls dipping out of the last of the sunlight. Reluctantly he answered: 'One or two.'

She sighed and gave him up. 'I'll fill your cup. We close at nine.'

At nine o'clock he crossed the street by the castle towards the east sands. It was too late to return to Kenly Green. Was this how he had planned it? The sky began to darken. He felt the first drops of rain. On the shore below he saw two huddled figures: a young man in a ragged gown hunched against the wind, a young lass dressed in green clutching at his arm. Some things did not change. He smiled. Turning into Swallowgait he hurried through the rain to St Salvator's College.

St Salvator's, oldest and grandest of the three university colleges, had already closed its doors upon the night. Hew found the north and west gates in darkness. At the main entrance beneath the bell tower of the old collegiate chapel someone had hung out a lantern, casting a grey light upon the wet cobblestones. Hew hammered on the great oak door until he heard the bolts shot back, a consummate grumbling and jangling of keys. He stepped back a little to allow the sullen lamplight to illuminate his face.

'What do you want there? The college is closed.'

'I've come to see your principal, Professor Giles Locke.'

'Wha's that then? The quacksalve?' the man enquired rudely.

In recent years the privy council had imposed, or tried to impose, a series of reforms upon the university, the latest of which was the appointment of a professor of medicine as principal of St Salvator's College. Clearly this had not been welcomed.

7

'I know him as your provost,' Hew persisted, frowning, 'and a friend.'

The porter remained unimpressed. 'What business ye have then is not with the college. I have not been told it, sir, nor warned I should admit a stranger. The man that you mention – I don't say he's here, mind – but if he *were* here then no doubt he'd have gone to his bed.'

'It's true, he's not expecting me, but he will wish to see me. If you would send up my name . . .'

The porter faced him squarely, with an ominous retraction of the keys. 'Aye for sure, in the morning. I'll tell him you called.'

Behind him a door in the courtyard had opened and closed. A serving man approached them, balancing a tall jug in the one hand and a wide shallow basin draped in a cloth in the other. The porter blocked his path. 'I hope you paid for that.'

'Tis accounted for.' The man winked cryptically at Hew. As he passed through the archway he shifted the bowl to the crook of his arm and tugged discreetly at his sleeve.

'Did I hear you ask for the doctor?' he murmured. 'Pray, sir, are you sick?'

The porter took advantage of the diversion to slam shut the door and make fast the bolts, muttering as he withdrew. Hew groaned. It occurred to him, fleetingly, that perhaps he *was* sick. For certain he was out of sorts, a sinking in his stomach that no bleeding, probe or purging could restore. He would never have confessed it. As robustly as he could he shook his head.

'No, not sick. I am an old friend of the doctor's, lately come from France. We shared rooms there.' To give credence he added, 'in the Rue des Fosses.'

The servant looked him up and down as if he weighed the probabilities. At length he seemed convinced, for he shifted the basin back into his hand and nodded.

'Aye, well, ye may follow me. His rooms are in the turret of the house across the wynd.'

West of the chapel, across Butt's Wynd, stood the provost's

lodging house. It seemed fitting that the college did not house him in its cloisters but kept him at arm's length. On the south side the chapel was flanked by two stone houses, each with a round turret tower. In the turret to the left Professor Locke was stationed. The servant led him to the door. 'Ye'd best wait here.'

Hew waited a moment and then slipped up behind him, climbing the narrow staircase to the tower. He heard his friend's familiar voice before he saw him, resonant and deep.

'What have you found, Paul?'

'A quart of new milk and a dish of green plums.'

Hew smiled to himself. His friend's stomach sat close to his heart.

Then came a muffled exclamation and the servant's voice rose sulkily. 'The first fruit of the season from the priory garden. They're ripe enough now, I'm sure of it, sir.'

There was no mistaking now the note of gloom. 'Aye, roasted, perhaps, and baked into custards, or bottled, or jellied, or candied, or dried. Eaten raw and green, they're sure to lead to colic, if not worse. I once did know a child . . . no matter, though,' the doctor broke off kindly, 'no doubt you did your best. I suppose there's nothing else? No fish or cheese?'

'Nothing,' said the servant shortly. 'Though there's *him*!'

He jabbed with his finger back towards Hew, who stepped through the doorway, lapped like a ghost in the light from the fire.

Lying on the floor of Giles Locke's tower, Hew felt at home for the first time since leaving France. Giles had dragged a feather mattress into the centre of the room, on which his friend lay sprawling, gazing at the walls. The room was filled with objects from the Rue des Fosses, no less familiar because they were strange: discoloured substances floating in jars (he always had avoided those), compasses, astrolabes, globes and nocturnals, pigs' feet and goats' teeth, the beak of a gull. Curious though they were these things were not collectibles but used and loved. Several of the books were

marked with crumbs of toasted cheese. Most comforting of all was
Giles himself, both broad and tall, perched upon his bedstead at
the flat side of the wall, his warmth and generosity enough to fill
a larger room than this. They had finished the milk. Hew, against
all advice, had sampled the plums and Giles had unearthed a flagon
of brandy, most of which had now been drunk.

'The truth is,' Hew said suddenly, 'I *could* have gone home. Tis
only four miles.'

'*But?*' Giles prodded helpfully.

'*But* I did not want to face my father. That's the truth.'

'Is he such a tyrant, then?'

'Tyrant, no. If he were, it would not be a problem, for then I
could thwart him and he could be damned. If he stormed and
raged it would be easy to defy him. It's his disappointment that's
so hard to bear.'

'Disappointment? Stuff and nonsense.' Giles felt a flood of affection, fuelled by the brandy, towards his young friend. 'Always been
exemplary.'

'Oh, aye,' Hew laughed dryly. 'Four years at St Andrews, passed
with distinction. Six years abroad with no indiscretions – apart
from the cook at the Auberge du Coq.'

'Whose *lapin à la moutarde* was beyond compare,' Giles recalled
fondly. 'That alone were enough to excuse it. So what's to dis-
appoint him, then?'

'Only after ten years spent in study, I have learned one thing.
I do not want to be the man my father was.'

'Ah. And is he set on that?'

'He was an advocate of some repute. At the height of his power
he abandoned the courts and retired to the country. Then his
ambitions were all turned towards me.'

'How singular. But why?'

'I was twelve years old and in the grammar school. I did not
ask him, Giles. I have thought since it was perhaps to do with
the queen, for he was of her camp and had hoped to be queen's
advocate. He saw the tide turn and disliked the change.'

'And yet he sent you to St Leonard's?' Giles remarked. 'For a man of his leanings, St Salvator's would seem the more obvious choice.'

'Twas politic. In his heart, he would rather I had come here to the Auld College; in his heart, he would rather I kept the old faith. Yet he had me schooled against it. My schoolmaster was a friend of George Buchanan and they both had more influence on my early education than my father did. I cannot blame him for that, for they were good men and I learned well from them. But I felt he sold my soul for something he did not believe in, and I have long resented it.'

'Perhaps,' Giles consoled him, 'you misunderstood. You were just a boy. Why don't you talk to him?'

Hew sighed. 'I shall, of course, and of course I will not say these things. The truth is I still want to please him. But the deeper I go into it the less I like the law.'

His friend shook his head 'This is humour, I think, and will pass. It pleased you well enough in Paris.'

'I will admit I like to win, and I find myself ashamed of it. Because this game of wits is always at someone's expense. Too often it ends at the end of the rope.'

'If you lacked such scruples I'd be more concerned,' said Giles. 'You merely want detachment, which will come with age. Besides, from what I have seen of the law, most of it concerns itself with property and debt, and in capital offences there is little to be done for the defence.'

'Aye, and there *should* be,' Hew proclaimed fiercely. 'No, I'm done with argument, and sickened to the stomach with the law. Dispute for its own sake no longer interests me. I have fallen out of love with my profession. And when I tell my father, it will break his heart.'

'Well,' said Giles judiciously, 'you may put off the telling. I prescribe a drink.'

Hew refused another cup, and fell back upon the mattress looking at the ceiling. 'What of *your* profession? Have you never had your doubts?'

'There have been moments, certainly. At times the puke can pall. But I flatter myself I may do some good in the world. The one thing I do regret is accepting this post, for I have not been welcomed here. The professors have been courteously lukewarm.'

'Perhaps it is your strange collections,' Hew observed ironically. 'Lights and livers sunk in pots.'

'The specimens? What piffle! There are worse things at the fleshmarkets.'

'Granted. But they don't like change.'

'That I can accept. But if the members of this college are suspicious, then the provost of St Leonard's has been downright rude. He makes allusions constantly to leeches, quacks and sawbones, though of course he will protest that he does not refer to *me*.'

'There has always been rivalry between the two colleges – who would win the golf, or the arrow at the butts – but I don't recall it ever was so personal,' reflected Hew. 'Perhaps things will improve when term begins. I have a friend who is regent at St Leonard's, a man called Nicholas Colp. We were students together. I should be sorry indeed if *he* were uncivil.'

Giles shook his head. 'I have not met the regents yet. But I have heard of Colp as a clever and devout man.'

'He is both. I cannot think he would subscribe to such rudeness. I must look him up and ask him how he goes on with the principal. Gilchrist, is it still? I do not know him well, for he came newly in my time. Nicholas and I were students under George Buchanan, who was a true friend. He left to take up post as tutor to the king.'

'Ah!' Giles interrupted, 'There's the real news! The king has had his thirteenth birthday and at last is to leave the confines of Stirling Castle and make his progress. Even now, as we speak, he comes into Edinburgh. And next year, in the spring, he is expected here.'

'The king left his castle? That's news indeed!'

'You cannot imagine the stir it has caused. And that, coupled with the anxiety over the new appointments – quacksalves and the like – has helped to fuel the tension in the college. The town and the university both are in uproar. King James has not been seen since infancy.'

'He has had a strange childhood,' Hew observed.

'And most of it behind closed doors. I am interested to see how he appears. Some say he is a cripple, suckled by a drunk, and that he cannot walk without support.'

'Poor boy! Rumour has made him a monster.'

'For certain. And also a wit. The story goes that he was last in public at the opening of the parliament, when he was five years old. He found a hole there in the tablecloth and all the while his lords were making speeches he explored it with his fingers. Then at length he asked, "What place is this?" "Why, sire," said the lords, "this is the parliament." To which the king answered, "Then there is a hole in this parliament!" Which the crowds did take for proof of his great wisdom.'

Hew laughed. 'As well they might! You seem to know a good deal about him.'

'Alas, I confess it. I have been charged to write his horoscope, for which I make a study of his early life. It is to be the college's gift to him. St Leonard's for their part are to put on a play, written by Nicholas Colp.'

'Then you will have stiff competition.' Hew looked across at the charts on the table. 'Where is this horoscope? May I not see it?'

'By no means,' Giles winked at him. ''Tis confidential to the king.'

'A hint, then,' Hew persisted, smiling. 'Will he take the English crown?'

'As to that old prediction,' Giles said severely, 'I could not possibly say. Besides, you know a horoscope does not foretell the future. I am a physician, not a necromancer. I can tell you merely whether he is prone to windy gout, or must beware the phases of the moon, or is disposed to toothache, or to jaundice or despair. In reality, of course, it will predict none of those things, but a long and healthy life, and go to great lengths in the proving that no illness shall befall him, because he is the king, you know, when all is said and done. The spheres themselves must shuffle to oblige him.'

'Then, Giles, you are nothing but a fraud!'

'Not at all,' his friend replied seriously. 'For hope is potent physic. An optimistic horoscope becomes its own effect.' He stifled a yawn. 'But no more of this now. I really must sleep. For if I don't appear at prayers first thing on Sunday morning it will confirm their worst suspicions: I'm the devil's man indeed. As for you, since no one knows you're here there's none to miss you. You may sleep the sleep of the righteous, and lie in as long as you please.'

Nicholas

Hew slept late into the morning. When at last he awoke he found himself alone, centred in the stillness of the tower. The light streaming in on motes of dust picked out the globe and astrolabe, the hourglass and the scales and measured out a world for him. He lay there for a while on his mattress, content to be still and remote at its heart, until the clamour of the kirk bell could no longer be ignored and the world outside began to reassert itself. The bell clock struck remorselessly. Eventually he gave in, threw open the high windows and looked out onto the street. A seagull strutting down below glanced up in contempt and plucked at the cobblestones, foraging for scraps. There was no one else in sight.

Giles had left butter and bread, and Hew took a book from the shelf to a small recess by the window where he ate his breakfast in the candour of the sun. Below the chapel doors swung open and St Salvator's scholars emerged from their prayers, blinking owlishly. Crowds were turning into the north street. Hew heard laughter in the cloisters on the north side of the tower. The door below stairs seemed to open and close but Giles himself did not return. It was some time later when the servant Paul appeared with a message from his master and a slab of mutton pie.

'Doctor Locke is detained at the New College; their principal is dying. Again.'

Hew suppressed a smile. It was the 'again' that had provoked it, for the servant's face and voice gave nothing away. The New College of St Mary had begun to consolidate its interests in the teaching of theology. Its principal, Professor Lamb, professed himself so close to God that he had hovered at His door for twenty years. Still, perhaps it had come true at last, and his bluff had finally been called.

As if he read his mind the servant went on, frowning, 'Doctor Locke has gone over there determined to cure him once and for all. It won't go down well. So he says to you, sir, he may not be home before supper, and please to make use of his books and whatever. That's if you're minded to stay?'

The proper thing to do would have been to take his leave politely and walk the four miles to his father's house at Kenly Green. It was a fair day, and warm, and he need not hire a horse. He would arrive before suppertime, and well before dark. Yet even as he thought this, he heard himself say, 'I'll stay another night here, if I may. I ought to go to church. Are there evening prayers still at St Leonard's?'

The servant seemed surprised. 'There is a service, sir. Master Gilchrist was made minister there last summer, and he has restored the old parish. Tis somewhat dreich, I doubt. Yon man at Holy Trinity puts on a better show.'

Hew laughed. 'I'm sure he does. But St Leonard's is my college and my parish kirk as well. I'll hear the sermon there.'

He paused only to exchange his coat of mustard-coloured silk for a scholar's gown he found hanging on a nail behind the door. Giles had asked him, after all, to make free with his things. His own clothes were too flamboyant. He preferred to break in quietly upon the past.

The college of St Leonard lay within the precincts of the old priory in the lee of the cathedral. As Hew approached the gate the chapel bell fell silent and the outer doors were closed. The congregation was already settled in the kirk. He found another doorway to the west, new since his last visit, open to a flight of wooden stairs. At the top he discovered a deep open loft, constructed to isolate the college from the commoners, and from this vantage point he had a clear view of both scholars and parishioners, and the minister himself, mounted on the stage. There were no seats on the bare earth below, but there were several benches for the scholars in the loft. Hew found a vacant one close to the door. A small clutch of scholars clustered in front. One or two had wives and children, in defiance of the rule. The masters, called regents, were responsible for the education and the moral welfare of their students through the four years of their course in philosophy and arts. Presiding over all, Hew recognised James Gilchrist, provost and principal master of St Leonard's College and minister of St Leonard's parish, theologian, scholar, and the scourge of Doctor Locke. He had embarked upon the lesson in a smooth, cultured voice that somehow still retained an undernote of peevishness, depressingly familiar from Hew's undergraduate days.

But the Lord said unto Samuel, Look not on his countenance, or on the height of his stature because I have refused him: for the Lord seeth not as man seeth; for man looketh on the outward appearance, but the Lord looketh on the heart.

The minister stood straighter as he spoke the verse, and his fingers strayed unconsciously towards his beard. He was a man to whom appearances were everything, to his fellow men as much as to God. He wore his hair perfumed and curled. When he had first come to St Leonard's it had caused quite a stir. The boy who had attended him each morning in his chamber reported that the master wore a strange contraption 'like a mousetrap' on his beard to keep the hairs neat while he slept. The beard was waxed black, cut sharp as a Spaniard's. There had been nothing of the sort with George Buchanan.

Smiling to himself, Hew allowed his eyes to drift towards the regents in the front row, looking for his old friend Nicholas Colp. He found him sitting with his head bowed, sober and devout.

God knoweth your hearts, for that which is highly esteemed among men is an abomination in the sight of God.

It was a sentiment that would appeal to Nicholas. Hew was leaning forward in the hope of catching his eye when the look on his friend's face stopped him cold. Nicholas was not composed. He did not smile or purse his lips at what was sheer hypocrisy but showed his own heart starkly in his face, a clear and striking horror that Hew barely recognised. He felt for a moment that he had seen into the dark place of his soul. A moment later, watching Nicholas discreetly as he closed his eyes to pray, he realised he had made a mistake. It was not horror he had seen in his friend's face, but something almost worse: Nicholas was weak from want of food. In prayer his face seemed crumpled like an old man's in repose. His skin was pale as water, and his shirt fell loosely round him, for he wore no coat or gown. Nicholas was sick. And the sickness, whatever it was, went deeper than the gloss of mere appearances.

After the service Hew waited for his friend to emerge. Nicholas looked blank for a moment, and then his smile returned a touch of its old sweetness to his face. He welcomed Hew's return. He spoke of past adventures and Hew's travels overseas, the visit of the king and the play that he was writing, and a textbook that he hoped would suit the grammar school. Still Hew sensed a lingering discomfort. At last he dared to ask, 'You are ill, I think?'

Nicholas shrugged. 'I had a chill. It passed. I find I do not sleep so well these warm nights.' He shifted a little, as though tired of standing.

'What happened to your leg?' Hew noticed blood on the hem of his shirt, an ominous blackness beginning to spread.

His friend laughed nervously. 'A foolish, childish thing. You remember how we used to steal the apples from the priory garden? Well, last night I was given some by the gardener. I peeled one with my knife, as we always used to do, and the blade slipped, cutting deep. Retribution at last! I had thought that the bleeding had stopped.'

Hew stared at him. The priory apples blossomed late, and would not be ripe by Michaelmas. He was astonished at the plainness of the lie.

Nicholas looked down. 'I ought to change my shirt.'

Several things went through Hew's mind, but he did not know how to broach them. In their place he ventured, 'Have you met my good friend Doctor Locke? He is the new provost at St Salvator's, and a fine physician. If you are unwell, I recommend him strongly.'

'I'm quite well, I assure you,' Nicholas said stiffly.

'Then I recommend him all the more.'

Nicholas relaxed into a smile. 'As a friend of yours I would be glad to meet him. I have no need of physic.'

'And no means of paying for it,' Hew thought shrewdly, 'yet we'll find a way.'

'All I know of Doctor Locke is that Gilchrist is afraid of him,' Nicholas continued, with a hint of his old self, 'and for *that* I am disposed to like him straight away.'

'*You there! Master Colp!*' They were interrupted by a college servant hurrying towards them. Hew shrank back a little, unwilling to be challenged as a stranger. But the man ignored him, calling out to Nicholas, 'You're wanted at the weaver's house, aye, now sir, straight away sir, for the lad has run away.'

'No, it is not possible.' It was not an exclamation but a statement of despair. The weariness was palpable.

'What is this about?' Hew inquired gently.

It was some moments before Nicholas could answer him. He struggled to express himself.

'It is a boy that I was teaching. They will say it is my fault.'

'How could it be your fault?'

'I will explain it. No,' he shook his head, 'I cannot explain it. Forgive me, I must go to them.' As though the resolution were enough he did not move. 'I'll go to them.'

Hew took his arm. 'We both will go,' he told him firmly. 'And you can tell me on the way.'

'The thing is,' Nicholas said miserably as they went by the cathedral, 'that yesterday I told them he was too young to start here next term. It was no fault of his.'

A haar from the sea had masked the frail sunshine. It clutched at Hew's chest. Nicholas looked chilled to the bone.

'Tell it plainly,' prompted Hew, 'and from the start.'

'There is not much to tell. I have been tutoring a young boy, Alexander Strachan. His father is a merchant from Perth, very rich, and a friend of our principal Gilchrist. His mother is dead. The boy has been staying with his uncle Archie Strachan who is a weaver in the town. The uncle's a bit of a bully.'

Hew gave an exclamation. 'I met him! Yesterday, on Mercatgait, I'm sure of it! In fact, now I think on it, I may have seen you there!'

'Really?' Nicholas looked taken aback. 'Well, if you have met him you will understand the sort of man he is. I have been teaching his nephew now for several weeks, because Gilchrist has promised him a place at the college, although he has no Latin, not to speak of. The boy is willing enough, but he is too young and badly schooled to matriculate this year. And yesterday, I told his uncle so. I told him that the boy was not to blame. Nonetheless, I think that he may have chastised him, and now we see the consequence. The lad has run away. Look, here we are at the house. That is Agnes Ford, Archie Strachan's wife.'

Hew sensed a rawness in the woman at the door. Her cheeks were blotched pink as if recently scrubbed. She spoke with a false note of brightness. 'Master Colp, I'm so glad you could come . . . and you have brought a friend.'

'Master Cullan from the college,' Nicholas said briefly.

Agnes smiled mechanically at Hew. 'Come into the house.'

'Has the boy not returned?' Nicholas asked anxiously. He hung back, reluctant to enter. Hew could understand why. Dull in the distance they heard her man grumble, voice rumbling dangerously into a roar. Agnes smiled again, that same deceptive brightness, masking features strained and worn. 'Whisht, Archie!' she called out, 'for we have company. Tibbie will see to the broth.'

'He only wants his dinner,' she excused him, as if he were the bad-tempered boggle in an ancient nursery tale. Hew suppressed a smile.

'No, he's not come home,' she replied to Nicholas. 'And I confess, I'm fearful. I have never known him stay away so long.'

'*How* long?' interjected Hew.

Agnes flushed a little. 'We have not seen him since last night. You see, Archie went to market down at Crail a little after five this morning, and I thought he had taken Alexander with him, so the boy was not missed until Archie's return. And then it turned out . . .' she paused to glance at Nicholas.

'Aye?' Hew persisted.

'Well, sir, it turned out, that after Master Colp had come to hear his lesson – that was yesterday, at six – his uncle reprimanded him for failing at his task.'

Nicholas hunched his shoulders, 'That was not what I said,' he protested.

'Nonetheless, Archie had words with him,' Agnes said apologetically. 'We have not seen him since.'

'Did your husband beat him?' Nicholas demanded. Hew heard him murmuring under his breath, '*Mea culpa, mihi ignosce*; for I did not know, forgive me.'

Agnes gazed at him curiously for a moment before she replied. 'You should know, Master Colp, that my husband does blame you. Don't take it ill. You see, sir,' she appealed to Hew, 'Archie's had a skinful at the market, and he's not himself. And Alexander left some letters. They're addressed to Master Colp.'

'Letters,' Nicholas echoed dully. 'Have you read them?'

'Archie said we weren't to open them, since they're addressed to you. Besides, they were in Latin,' Agnes added more convincingly. 'We left them in his room.'

Archie Strachan sat in his shirt tails, moodily poking the fire. A great pot of fragrant liquid bubbled on the hearth where his daughter Tibbie was setting out a cloth. She did not look up as they entered but began meekly to ladle pottage into bowls.

'Master Colp has come,' Agnes spoke out brightly, 'and a scholar from the college come to help him. This is Master Cullan.'

Hew was grateful for the borrowed gown. The weaver scarcely glanced at him.

'Ye bided your time, did ye no'?' he snarled at Nicholas. 'Did ye bring the bugger back?'

Strachan swayed dangerously as he rose to his feet, and Hew realised he was far too drunk to suffer rational argument. It was Agnes, surprisingly firm, who answered for them.

'Master Colp doesn't know where Alexander's gone any more than we do, Archie. Yet he has been good enough to come and help us look for him. Aye, and brought his friend. Now we're away upstairs. You drink your broth.'

She shivered as she spoke, clutching at her shawl. Hew could see Agnes was afraid of something. It was not her husband, slumping in his broth. Archie was a bully, to be sure, and Hew suspected he saw bruises darkening at her wrists. Still, he thought, it was not that, for Agnes could contain him; that much was apparent in the way she spoke to him. She allowed her husband the mere semblance of control. So there was something else, some new threat to the world she ordered and endured. Not her nephew, surely? Boys his age played truant all the time. Doubtless he'd come home again, none the worse for wear. But Agnes knit her fingers, plucking at her gown, as if she feared her whole world might unravel.

The loft room was airless, rank with candle fat, and Hew hung back a little in the shadow of the door. Agnes set the candle down and watched as Nicholas began to look around. The cot was well furnished with grey woollen blankets and surprisingly fresh linen sheets. Someone looked after the boy. At the bottom of the bed stood an ironbound chest, and to its side a writing table, stool and straight-backed chair. The ledge above the bed held a water pot and a pair of pewter candlesticks. The writing table had been neatly set out for the lesson. A grammar book, the *Ars minor* of

Donatus, sat next to inkhorn, pens and pocket knife, a tidy sheaf of papers and a lump of sealing wax. On top lay a slim bundle of what looked like letters; still tied with ribbon, though no longer sealed. Nicholas slit the ribbons with the penknife and glanced quickly down at the opening page. Frowning slightly, he turned towards Agnes: 'There's nothing here, mistress. Simply some verses he was turning into Latin for me.' He glanced across at Hew. 'It seems he has been working rather harder than his uncle gave him credit for. But don't you think it's odd he didn't take his knife with him, if he meant to run away? Did his father give him money, do you know?'

He hardly seemed to notice what he was doing as he slipped the packet of letters into the folds of his clothes.

Agnes was nodding. 'He looks after him well. It irritates Archie. He never felt that he deserved . . .'

Her words trailed away as Nicholas went on, 'I wonder if he took his cloak?'

Nicholas looked pale and grey in his shirt. He appeared to be shaking, from sickness or fear. 'Are you ill?' Hew asked again. But Nicholas seemed not to hear.

'May I look in the kist?' Without waiting for an answer, Nicholas lifted the lid of the dark oak chest where Alexander kept his clothes. Carefully he lifted out the contents and laid them one by one on the bed. Alexander had been well provided for with saffron yellow shirts, new and freshly dyed, dark velvet doublets and good leather shoes, a blue winter bonnet, caps and gloves and a length of blanket plaid. His cloak, a dark-green mantle cloth, had fallen on the floor. It lay crumpled by the bed, the only thing disturbed in the neatness of the room. Hew picked it up.

'Was this his?'

Agnes nodded. 'But he likes to go about without it, as boys will. I don't think he has much else.'

Nicholas had lifted out a little bundle from the bottom of the chest and placed it on the cot, where together they looked over the contents. It was a poignant collection: a couple of pieces of oddly shaped driftwood, childishly fashioned to form a crude boat, a handful of pebbles, smooth from the sea, a carved wooden whistle and a tiny painted horse, together with a purse of gold and silver coin. Nicholas picked this up and weighed it in his palm. It was a while before he spoke.

'He has not run away,' he concluded bleakly. 'Here are all his things. It almost looks as if . . .' He closed his eyes and whispered, *'Let it not be that.'*

Archibald Strachan, revived by his supper of barley and potherbs, sipped a cleansing cup of red wine as he stirred the embers of the fire. 'Mark my words, Colp, he'll have run away to sea. We won't be seeing him again. I'll have word sent to my brother in Perth and you can explain to Gilbert why you chose to be so hard on him that he'd rather be a cabin boy than pass into the university.'

'Hush, Archie,' Agnes interjected. 'No, you know he wasn't hard on him. And we've no reason to think he's gone to sea. You know he likes to walk upon the sands. No doubt he has forgot the time, and will be back by dark.'

'Did you beat him, sir?' cried Nicholas. Hew heard his voice rise hysterically high. He put out his hand to steady him. It was fear, no doubt. The castle cliffs were treacherous. A boy had fallen to his death in their first year at St Andrews. Hew had watched the parents arrive at the college to take home their dead son, just five weeks into the new term.

'Words, we had words, sir,' the weaver said smoothly. 'My brother wants him to do well, but for some reason bade me never raise a hand to him. It was *you*, sir, that did break his heart, and telt him that he would not make a scholar, and ye would not have him at your university.'

'I said none of that,' Nicholas protested, 'only at thirteen, he is still too young.'

'It's all the same,' the weaver said morosely, 'for the lad has gone.'

Before Nicholas could answer, the apprentice boy Tom came

running in from the workshop below, stammering out to his mistress, 'I cannot find that bolt of cloth we finished yesterday, the sea-blue wool. I wondered had you moved it? Will you help me look?'

'Oh Tom, do not fuss,' Agnes scolded. 'I swear I can't help you. I have not been down to the shop.'

'Please, mistress,' the boy whispered wretchedly. He glanced fearfully at Strachan. 'For if I cannot find it . . .'

'What can't ye find?' Strachan purred dangerously.

'Whisht,' Agnes softened. 'Whisht, let us look.' She reached for the lamp. 'Help us, will you, gentlemen? It will be dark below. She held out her hands to Hew, as if in supplication, holding out the light. Both of you, bring candles.'

Agnes looked pale. Hew took up the lamp and followed her, with Nicholas behind. It seemed the place unnerved her. No doubt there were rats. Together, they searched the back of the shop. Tom kept house effectively. The finished bolts of cloth were neatly racked or folded, the combs and cards were stacked against the walls. It seemed to Hew unlikely that anything here could go astray. The place was all too carefully ordered. Each bolt, each carded nap and scrap of thread, pretentiously fluffed and plumped, was held to account. Nonetheless he made a show of looking around him. There was little enough to see. In the rushlight the struts of the loom cast branching shadows on the walls. Like childhood puppetry, they made him ill at ease and fearful. He thought they sketched a plough, a tree, a gallows, then a gate. But there was nothing. Spindles, puppets, fire and shadows. Noise from the street and rooms above came dulled to him in the darkness. Archie Strachan maybe ranged his chair across the floor and called to Tibbie for a stoup of wine to fill his cup, or Alexander's footsteps crossed the cobblestones, coming home at last.

He became aware of Agnes by his side clutching her shawl around her shoulders. Did she feel it too, the sudden aching chill that gripped his bowels? She let her hand rest on his arm, as if to draw strength in the darkness. Then came her voice, unexpectedly clear: 'I haven't touched anything in here, Tom. Are you sure that's where you left it?'

'Aye.' The boy looked sullenly at her. 'Mebbe Alexander took it. They're both gone, aren't they?'

'What would Alexander want with it?'

'What's that over there at the back?' Nicholas had picked up a lamp. He motioned towards a dark outline in the shadows against the far wall.

'The closet? It pulls down into a bed,' answered Agnes. 'Tom lies there for warmth in the winter months. In summer he prefers to sleep beneath the counter.'

'I've my workday clothes in there, sir, nothing more,' Tom put in defensively. But Nicholas had made his way to the back of the room. He held up the light to the cupboard, and in its glare the others glimpsed a fragment of grey-blue cloth between the doors. Nicholas spoke bleakly, 'The doors are fast, Thomas, help me.' Together they tugged until the closet flew open, and out tumbled a bundle of soft sea-blue wool. Tom flushed, beginning to stammer, but Nicholas interrupted, 'No, Tom, mistress, go back.'

Nicholas' voice was low and cold. He had caught the bolt in his arms as it fell. He seemed to fall back with the weight of it, and now he moved very slowly and wearily. He laid the cloth on the ground and knelt stiffly down in front of it. He had placed the lamp beside him on the floor, and Hew, standing a little behind him, saw blood leach from his thigh as he began to open out the cloth. The plaid appeared mottled in the lamplight and at first Hew did not understand the layers unfolding. He saw but did not comprehend the strangeness of the patterning, a circle of bright flame above the drab storm-blue. He saw Nicholas unfold and gather in his arms a boy with ashen skin and flame-red hair. He saw him hold him there and touch his face, and stare down uncomprehending at his own hand bright with blood. And as Nicholas stared he let the boy's head drop so that Hew saw the splinter of bone, a ragged streak of pink beneath the hair.

Rites and Wrongs

After Alexander's death St Leonard's College closed its doors and Hew did not see Nicholas again for several days. Even Giles was unable to penetrate, for the college had closed in on itself, pulling in its horns like a snail inside a shell. Gilchrist responded to all whiff of scandal by holding his breath and turning his back to the world. Hew was called to the courtroom to make his report, where he established himself as a credible witness. The coroner advised him to remain in St Andrews until Gilbert Strachan had arrived and their statements could be sworn. It was clear he had no explanation for the crime. The murder of a child that had survived the storms of infancy was rare and cruel.

And so Hew was left without purpose, to renew his old acquaintance with the town. He walked the empty cloisters of the college to the once-familiar peal of Katherine's bell, and wandered through the vennels and the lanes. In search of solitude, he did not frequent the streets. He found himself exploring long-forgotten paths, across the windswept golf links to the Eden estuary, or on the cliff tops of the Swallowgait, gazing out to sea. He traced the course of the Kinness Burn down to the harbour and to the east sands, and wandered through the caves beneath the castle rock. Where the sea was wild, he took solace in the waves. When he grew tired, he read in Giles Locke's tower. In the evenings they drank claret and discussed philosophy. Once he stopped to watch the fishermen unloading their catch, until a dead fish tumbling from the nets brought the boy to mind so vividly he vomited, a thin spray that soaked his boots and caused the fisherman to stare and curse at him. Ashamed, he did not mention it to Giles. He climbed towards the castle, high upon the cliffs, and saw the fortress open and unfold its inner life. A clutch of boats were beached on the foreshore, and he watched a small procession turning through the gate that barred it from the sea. In the sunlight it displayed its workings like the glinting gears inside a clock; crates and kegs and vats of wine went winding up the steps, while sentries marked the process from the tower. The death of a boy, like a trough in the sand, made no impression here. He turned into the grounds of the cathedral. Already its walls had begun to decay, and the vaults of the pilgrims were quarried for stone. The hopeless courage of their ancient histories could not make sense of that small death, or overwhelm its poignancy for Hew. Centuries of magnitude and loss, antiquity itself, could not displace the image of the bruised and broken boy. Agnes, when she understood at last, had been inconsolable. Whatever she had feared most, in her worst imaginings, it had not been that. In the shrieking of the seabirds in the bay he heard her cry. Nothing in the vast and onward rush of tide threw back into perspective that one small and circling grief.

On the third day, Hew sensed a sea change. Returning to the harbour, he discovered that the ships were in, and his trunk and saddlebags were waiting in the customs house. The quayside thronged with merchants, all the noise and business of an international port, and he saw a channel open to the world, lost and found again amidst the dust and sunshine. The return of his possessions restored his sense of purpose. He felt a sudden longing to go home. He took the saddlebags to Giles Locke's turret room, where he changed into black satin peascod and hose, embroidered with fine silver thread. Thus fortified, he set off to the marketplace to purchase a flagon of whisky for Giles. He drank a stoup of watered ale and downed a rather dubious pie, receiving little change for his gold crown. Then he called in at the Mercatgait stables to arrange the carriage of his trunk. He felt recklessly light and refreshed.

'Do you know of a merchant will change my French coin?' he enquired of the man.

The ostler looked interested. 'How much do you have?'

'About three hundred livres, in crowns. Nothing small.'

'Ah, then that's the trouble,' said the ostler sympathetically. 'That much is hard to change. Now here at the inn, all currency is sound to us – your French ecus, your Dutch, your *English* even' – he spat superstitiously into the straw – 'all is sterling here. But still I could not change so large a sum.'

'Are Scots pounds worth so little now?'

The ostler tutted. 'Falling all the time. Still, your crowns are good.'

'Except I can't get change for them,' Hew observed ruefully.

'I see your point. But I'm afraid I cannot help you there. Unless . . .'

'Aye, then, what?' persisted Hew.

'Unless of course, you want to buy a horse. Then I could do you a deal and throw in a purse of Scots coin on the side. A man that's come from France will likely want a horse. It happens that I have one that I don't know what to do with, for he is too rare and brave to put out to hire. I had him from a gentleman, in payment of a debt, and he was loath to part with him, and he is called Dun Scottis. The horse,' he clarified, 'and not the gentleman.'

'What, Duns Scotus, like the schoolman?' Hew smiled. 'Then he must be a subtle and ingenious horse.'

'Most subtle and ingenious indeed. A most prodigious horse. Come, sir, come and look at him. Do not say yay or nay until you've seen him, now.'

It had not occurred to Hew, before the man suggested it, that he required a horse, and yet the thought immediately appealed to him. Though he could ride tolerably well, he had never possessed a mount of his own. As a student in St Andrews he had little need of one. In Paris he had hired a horse and wagon as required. Now the thought of riding home in his peascod coat and slops upon a brave new saddle horse was almost irresistible. The ostler broke into his reverie.

'Here he is. Dun is his colour, and Scottis for you know he is a Scots-bred horse, though I don't remember that gentleman's name. His mother was a Highland pony, stout and sure-footed as ever you saw, but his father was an Arab courser, fierce and swift and proud.'

Hew was a little disappointed. In his mind's eye he had seen a white horse or a grey, or a black with a blaze to set off his clothes. The horse that stared back was a mud-puddle brown.

'So if you want a courser, sir,' the ostler rambled on, 'Dun Scottis is your horse. But if you want an ambler, sir, Dun Scottis is your horse. But if you want to trot him, sir, or rack or leap or gallop him ...'

'Dun Scottis is your horse?' Hew ventured humorously.

'I see you have his measure, sir,' the ostler smiled. 'Look, he seems to like you. It is by no means common that he takes to you so well. In truth, I am amazed by it, for he is a gentleman's horse, and of a nervous temperament. Often have I seen him shake his ears at strangers. It's almost like he knows you! Here, give him some bread.'

Hew broke off a crumb of the coarse loaf of horsebread, and held it out to the dun-coloured horse. The animal received it with shy solemn grace, flashing a fine set of teeth. Its back was sleek and broad.

'Why is he fettered?' he wondered. The horse was tethered from a chain, with a cuff around its hind leg which had begun to rub the skin.

'The gentleman I had him from was none too happy with his loss, and would have stolen him away if I had not secured him,' replied the ostler smoothly. 'But he is long since gone; the danger's past.'

'Then you could let him loose now,' Hew suggested.

'Aye, I could,' the man agreed. He made no move to do so.

The horse swallowed the crumbs and nuzzled Hew's hand, and he heard himself asking impulsively, 'What do you want for him?'

'A hundred French crowns, and I'll throw in a pocket of change.'

Hew shook his head. 'It's too much.'

'I won't sell him cheaper, for he is a prince,' the ostler declared. 'But you shall have a saddle and a saddlebag besides. And look, here's a couple of Spanish doubloons,' he offered generously. 'Left in a bed by a Spaniard, no less. The wench didn't know what to do with them. And, if you like, take the rest of the horsebread, in case he feels hungry on the way home!'

Hew held out for four new shoes, stirrups and a halter, and the deal was done.

'He will not wear a bit,' the ostler warned. 'He has the softest mouth. But do not be alarmed. For I can tell he likes you; he'll handle like a lamb. Come back for him tomorrow, sir, and he will be waiting, saddled and shod.'

Hew left in high spirits, pleased with his purchase, and continued to the tolbooth to inform the coroner that he was leaving town. The coroner sat busy at his desk, scratching his signature onto a writ, to which he applied the chief justice's seal. He waved aside Hew's explanations.

'I thank you for your patience, sir. It is of little consequence, for you will not be needed now. The case is closed.'

'*Closed?*' Hew echoed, startled. 'Is the matter solved?'

The coroner chuckled. 'Solved, sir, aye. And this afternoon to be *resolved*, if you understand me.' He rewarded his pet witness with a teasing smile. 'I have the paper here. The libel is to be served. And if, sir, you attend the lykewake at the weaver's house this afternoon, then you may *see* it served.'

'Whatever has happened? Has someone confessed?'

'I don't say he has, sir. I don't say he hasn't. I say to you, *go* there. Pay your respects.'

It was Agnes, once again, who met him at the door and led him by the hand into the stifling room. There were no courtesies between them, for they had gone deeper than that, yet she seemed touched to see him there. Her anguish had subdued into a mute and heavy sense of loss. She took him to the curtained bed where Alexander's corpse lay freshly washed and dressed. The blood had been cleaned from his hair and the red curls damped down to conceal the split edges of bone. Beside the bed the Strachan family paid their last respects: Alexander's father breathing deep into his handkerchief, Tibbie softly weeping, Archie scowling at the corpse. Between them, Agnes flitted like a ghost, touching Gilbert's hand and face. He glanced warily at Hew.

'Gilbert, this is Master Cullan, from St Leonard's College,' Agnes murmured.

Gilbert stared at him. 'Have you come alone?'

Agnes answered for him. 'Master Colp is indisposed.'

'And my good friend Master Gilchrist. Is he likewise indisposed?' Hew swallowed hard. 'He offers his condolences.'

Gilbert turned abruptly, acknowledging the slight. Agnes shook her head. 'He is distraught. Excuse us.' She spoke again to Gilbert in a low and urgent voice. Hew began to find the room oppressive. Though the evenings were cool the days were still long and the corpse lay exposed to the heat of the sun. The air became thick with the scent of decay and the sweet overlay of dead petals and smoke. Choking, he forced his way back to the door. A thin man in black stood blocking his path.

'Excuse me, sir. Are you the minister?' Politely, Hew held out his hand. Though the man did not accept it he seemed pleased at the unwitting compliment.

'I, sir? No. The minister will no' be coming, for he doesna approve of feasting and dancing in the wake of the dead. The lad should slip quietly into the ground, without all this. Tis wrong, sir. I am an elder of the kirk, and I think ill of it mysel'.'

'And yet he sends you in his place?'

The kirk elder shifted a little. 'I am come, sir, in my other role, for I am master of the gild of dyers, and a family friend.'

Unconsciously, he put his hands behind his back, as though he was ashamed of them. It was why he would not shake, for dyeing was a dirty trade.

'*You*, I think, are not a cleric, but from the university,' he said aggressively.

It was simplest to continue the deception. Hew confirmed it.

'I thought as much.' The man leaned towards him, and forgetful of his inky fingers gestured with his hands as if he meant to prod him or grasp him by the cloak. Hew stepped back, alarmed, as the dyer raised his voice. 'Then you would do well, sir, to keep a check upon your students. Several of them were up before the kirk session last term for debauchery and drunkenness. And worse, though I blush to mention it here. That boy – I mean, Alexander Strachan – would not be dead now if his father had not got it in his mind to put him to the university.'

Hew was astonished. 'You surely don't believe that!'

'I do not say it was the college that killed him, understand me, sir, I do not say that. But if his father and uncle had not exposed him to such lewd influences, who knows what might not have become of him.'

'I can assure you that the students of St Leonard's lead a sheltered life,' insisted Hew, 'and are subject to most rigorous discipline.'

'Aye? If you say so, sir.' The dyer changed his track. 'But I cannot help but think that if his friends had taken better care of him, then this would not have happened. Where was his uncle when the boy was killed? Gone to market, on the Sabbath, which were profanation of the Lord's day, when he should have been at kirk. And his nephew is struck down. Now what does that tell you?'

'Did I hear you say you were a family friend, sir?' Hew enquired coldly. He turned his back on the dyer and moved a little closer to the centre of room. Archie was attempting to discuss the funeral expenses.

'I bought the candles, Gilbert, at considerable expense. You wanted five and twenty.'

'Candles? Aye. There must be candles,' Gilbert answered vaguely. 'He's feart of the dark, did you know? And we put him to sleep in such darkness, Agnes. My boy dead?' His voice rose to a wail. 'How can he be dead?'

'Hush, Gilbert,' Agnes soothed him like a child. 'We shall sit with him tonight. I'll take the turn with you.'

33

'Then there's the question of the mortcloth,' Archie went on doggedly. 'The kirk session's best one is cut to the middle size, most useful of course and well suited to your boy, but in truth it's much muddied and darned. Or the gild has for hire a fine piece of Genoa velvet, newly lined in black silk. It may be on the large side, though. Would it drag, do you think? The infant cloth is almost new, and lined in white silk, right enough, but it may yet be too small.'

'Archie, please.' His wife caught at his sleeve. But Gilbert rallied, 'Aye, the velvet.'

'Of course. And I think we can have it for a very fair price.'

'I care nothing to that. And I should say, Archie, that I mean to have justice for this.'

'Justice? And you shall, so you shall. If we only knew where to look . . .'

'Ah, but we do,' Gilbert said coldly. 'Did you think, brother, to have kept it from me? The culprit is plain. I have informed the coroner, and he will be here presently to serve the writ. But I want him brought here first. You have him down below, I doubt? If he declares his innocence, then let him touch my boy.'

Agnes shivered, 'Gilbert, *who?*'

'The prentice lad. Tom Begbie.'

Archie looked aghast, began to protest, then thought better of it and muttered his retreat. A few moments later he returned with his apprentice, pushing him wordlessly into the room. The boy looked about in confusion. At the far side of the bed, Gilbert Strachan was watching. He stroked back the hair from his dead son's head, exposing the cracked crevice of the skull, all the while staring at Tom.

Hew stiffened. He had not expected this. As Tom was brought forward he tried to move towards him but the crowd had formed a phalanx stretching to the corpse and he could not break through. The room was unbearably hot. He saw the boy stumble as they passed him hand to hand, the weaver urging onwards, looking round a little nervously as if to say, 'A shame, but what's to do?'

Bewildered, the boy was delivered to the bedside where they waited: Gilbert, Agnes, Tibbie, muffled in her plaids, and Alexander, waxen, waiting to accuse.

'You haven't touched him, Tom.' Gilbert's voice broke through the silence, strangely intimate. 'We all of us have touched him. Tibbie kissed him, Agnes laid him out; Archie and the tutor brought him here. I wish for all his friends to say goodbye to him. They say the spirit knows its killer, that the dead man's wound bursts open at the murderer's touch. Have you heard that, Tom? All that blood that was spilled, on your master's fine cloth. Look at his face! Look, see how pale he is! Will he bleed now, Tom? Can there be more?'

'Come, Gilbert, surely now, you don't believe that nonsense. And besides you know, I haven't touched him. Colp carried him up here himself,' Archie put in briskly.

'Haven't you, brother?' Gilbert scrutinised him. 'I'd be grateful if you would.'

'Godless nonsense.' And yet Archie touched his fingers to the wound, and let them brush the surface of the dead boy's broken head. Shuddering, he forced a smile at Tom. 'Nothing to it. Dry as dust. Do it, to be sure, it does no harm.'

'Aye, do it, Tom,' urged Agnes. 'See, there are no tricks here. Touch him, and you may be saved.'

But the sight of the waxen figure that that had tumbled out of the closet bed where Tom had kept his work clothes, where on winter nights he slept, had become too much for him. His hands fell useless by his sides. He could not touch the corpse, and he was damned.

'Would ye no' like to confess it, though? You would, you know.' Gilbert's voice came kindly, like light through a fog. Hew willed him not to follow it. It was the kindness that disarmed them. Hew had seen its force before, its treachery in court, that lulled men to confession when they longed for sleep. It was a sort of torture and it showed Strachan's ruthlessness.

'Don't take it, Tom,' he whispered desperately, 'don't grasp the light.'

35

But Tom Begbie, glancing right and left among the crowd that gaped and gawked at him, knew that they would drag him out and drown him like a kitten in the burn. He understood it plainly, though it made no sense. Tom did not confess. He opened his mouth and let slip, '*Katrin*,' like a prayer. Then there was nothing more.

The room was full of people now. Hew heard the voice of the dyer who had somehow pushed his way through to Archie, distilling his poison. 'Tell the truth before God, boy, and all will be well. Don't say I didna warn ye, Archie, that he was a bad one . . . an eye for a lass . . . we know where that leads.'

Agnes was staring, her eyes blank with fear. Tom gave a shriek, a high fluting wail that unsettled the crowd, until someone shook him by the shoulders and forced him to down a cup of cold ale.

Then came the coroner, on cue like a conjurer, waiting to pounce. 'You killed him, Tom, you know you did. Was it over Tibbie? Come, then, who could blame you? She's a bonny lass.' He looked across at Tibbie, crying by the bed, and shook his head indulgently. 'You broke his head with a shuttle from your master's loom and then concealed the corpse in a bolt of blue cloth . . .'

'For shame,' broke in a voice indignantly. 'I ordered that myself!'

The coroner scowled at the interruption. '*Then*,' he spoke a little louder, 'did you conceal the corpus in a closet where you slept and kept your clothes. Thomas Begbie, you are indict and accusit for the foul and cruel slaughter of one Alexander Strachan, that you did strike him on the head to his injury and death, wherefore you are to be delivered into ward until you come to trial at the next justice ayres, or else your friends stand surety on your behalf.'

He looked askance at Archie Strachan, who cleared his throat: 'His father died some years ago. I fear he has no friends.'

'He's contracted to you is he not? Indentured? He must be of good birth. Did his parents not make terms?' the coroner demanded.

'Aye, well, there's an awkwardness, you see. It's my nephew lies dead, after all.'

'Then I'll take him to the tolbooth. Come, lad, easy now.'

'Confess, Tom, do, you know you want to,' Gilbert whispered at his side.

'That's right.' Archie gave the boy an encouraging smile, and clumsily patted his shoulder. 'Tell the truth.'

The coroner winked at Hew as he marched the boy out. 'I telt ye we would see the thing resolved. Did ye not enjoy the show?'

Behind him, Gilbert Strachan fell back on the bed as though the effort of interrogation had exhausted him. Agnes sat beside him stroking down the dead boy's hair. Archie rubbed his hands and began to light the candles. Someone brought a fiddle. The party had begun.

Hew slept fitfully. He rose at dawn, intending to collect his horse and ride to Kenly Green. A dark gloom had descended that he hoped a change of air might soon dispel. It was a fine, chill morning, a little damp still from the haar. As he came to the harbour it occurred to him that at that hour he might find Nicholas at prayer. Since the college was deserted, he resolved to storm the gate. The students had removed a dozen stones as footholds on the far side of the wall, and a tree grew close enough to form a bridge. And so a little after half past five he scrambled down into the courtyard opposite the chapel, where he found his friend. Nicholas was kneeling in the dust. As he struggled to his feet he clutched at Hew.

'Is there news? Pray God, you bring me news! Gilchrist locks us in, and I hear nothing. I can think of nothing else. I have not slept.'

He looked grey in the half-light, his eyes moist and blank with exhaustion.

'The prentice boy Tom Begbie has been taken for the slaughter of your pupil,' Hew reported. 'Since I am going home today, I came to let you know.'

'The prentice lad,' Nicholas echoed wildly. 'Why? Has he confessed? What does he say?'

'He has not confessed. And yet he dared not touch the corpse, which some will say is tantamount to his confession.'

'Can that be enough?'

'To satisfy the law? By God, I hope not. He is taken to the tolbooth to await his trial. They say that it was jealousy, over Tibbie Strachan.'

'Surely, it could not be that!'

'Why not?' Hew looked at him curiously. 'Do you know something more?'

Nicholas cried fervently, 'I know nothing. But, God help me, Hew, I can think of nothing but that poor boy and his death. I cannot wash the blood clean from my thoughts. And I am starved of news. I need to have an answer.'

'Well then, you have one: Tom Begbie.'

'Aye, but *is* it, though? For he has not confessed. Do you think he did it? Was it Tom?'

'I confess, I do not know,' Hew answered evenly. 'I do not know these people as you do. The boy was found in Tom's bed. In truth, it was *you* that found him there. What do you think?'

Nicholas did not reply. He muttered, almost to himself. 'I will go and see Tom, aye, I'll see him, and find out. For there must be a reason to it. Aye, there must be something more.'

'I cannot think that wise,' objected Hew. 'There is a curfew on the college, and your interest must seem strange. And you are far from well. I wish you would make yourself known to my friend, Giles Locke. He is expecting you.'

Nicholas wiped his hand across his face, and Hew saw that he was sweating, on this chill September morning in the coolness of the kirk. 'I have no need of physic,' he demurred. 'It is my mind that is in flux, without I know the truth. This horror has polluted all my dreams. I may not be at peace until the matter is resolved. I thank you for the news; now leave me to pursue it as I will.'

'When did you last eat?' Hew demanded suddenly.

Nicholas stared at the ground. 'I find that these events depress the appetite,' he replied at last.

Hew persisted, 'Aye, but before? You will forgive my bluntness; we were friends as boys, and I know your circumstances. For the sake of that friendship, would you accept a small purse of coin?'

Nicholas coloured. 'I would not be in your debt.'

'No, and I protest there would not be a debt. Have they paid you for your teaching yet?'

His friend conceded in a whisper. 'We are paid only in termtime. As for Alexander, I can scarcely ask it now.'

'Then take the money, as a token of our friendship.'

'I cannot think it worth much,' Nicholas said oddly.

'Why do you say that?'

'Ah, tis nothing. I confess, I am in a sad darkness, and cannot see clearly. But I accept your money, and I thank you. Understand, I do not want it for myself, but to buy the way to Tom.'

Hew handed him his purse. 'If you won't be dissuaded, then I shall come with you,' he offered reluctantly. He was relieved when Nicholas refused. His baggage had been taken on to Kenly Green, his family was expecting him, and restless at the ostler's stood a sleek, dun saddle horse, itching to be ridden. The mists were clearing as they spoke. The day promised to break fair.

Dyeing

Nicholas bought a bannock from a baker in the street, still warm and crumbling in his hands. He walked along the south street to avoid the Strachans' shop. The bustle of the markets drifted through the lanes. Carts rumbled over cobbles. Hawkers cried their wares before a flux of people streaming in and out of church, but Nicholas remained oblivious to all. He passed the New College of St Mary and the house of the Dominicans, then crossed towards the Holy Trinity and on to the tolbooth through the Burgher Close. There was a gaol of sorts below, a narrow chamber open through a grating to the street. He walked over it now without looking down. Two Flemish merchants argued in the courtroom over confiscated goods. A clerk sat in the doorway scratching minutes in a ledger. Nicholas approached him cautiously. 'I've come to see Tom Begbie in the gaol.'

Squabbling broke out in the room behind him. A group of Dutch sailors had started a fight. He had to shout to be heard.

'You've surety for him?' The town clerk reached hopefully for his cash box. 'Indict and accusit of murderous slaughter. I'll just compute the cost. What did you say your name was? Are you his friend?'

'I am a friend. But I don't have enough for his bail. I'd simply like to talk to him.'

The town clerk sighed. 'Can't be done, friend. He's accused of murder. If you were his brother now—'

'Then I am his brother. Here's something for his keep.' He emptied all Hew's shillings on the desk in front of him. The burgess scooped them up with expert hand.

'Why did ye no' say? He's in the black hole. There's a man watches over the top of the stair. Tell him Davie Meldrum said to take you down. Bid him lend his candle, for you'll find it dark down there.'

The gaoler, such as he was, led him moodily down to the vault. 'He's in there. I'll be back for ye.' He slammed the door.

Nicholas held out the flame. Little daylight filtered through from the street. He heard a rustling in the straw, and gradually, a face emerged.

'Do you see me, Tom? I brought you bread.' He spoke softly, to disguise the tremor in his voice. His hands were shaking too.

'Are you the dempster, sir?'

The dempster read the *doom* or sentence of the court. The clerks had had their fun with Tom. His cheeks were black with tears.

'No, I'm not the dempster. It hasn't come to judgement yet. There'll be a trial. Don't you know me, Tom? I was Alexander's tutor.'

'Master Colp?' Tom emerged from the shadows, blinking in surprise, to squint into his face.

'I didn't kill him, sir,' he pleaded.

Nicholas said carefully, 'Why do they think it, then?'

Tom took the bread and nibbled at the corner. After a while he began. 'Because . . . because I couldn't touch the body. I was feart. And because we found him in my bed. And because they say that no one else was in the shop that night. But I swear it isn't true. I wasn't even there.'

Nicholas sighed in the darkness. 'Did you not tell them?' he asked.

The boy dropped his eyes. 'I *cannot*, sir. It's where I *was*.' He swallowed the bread and spoke thickly. 'My master keeps a flock at Kincaple, two or three miles to the west of the town. He sometimes sends me out to help if we're quiet in the shop. There's a lass there, Katrin. Her father Davie Fyffe's the drover. You'll have seen him in the town on market day. They have a cottage in the fields, scarcely even that, but a roof for their heads. And Katrin . . . well, her mother's dead. She lives a bit wild, I suppose. She helps out with the sheep. She doesn't like to come to town. My mistress Ford is kind to her. She sends them things – a pair of pigeons from the doocot or old clothes of Tibbie's. Katrin brings us herbs and brambles in return, perhaps some butter if the ewes have milk to spare. She's proud. I bought her ribbons from the market once.'

'You're saying that you passed the night with her?' Nicholas said shrewdly.

'We're handfast,' the boy flushed, 'so she does not count it wrong. I intend to wed her. Only no one knows. The Strachans think I mean to marry Tibbie, but I won't.' His tone was petulant. 'Tibbie's just a child. On Saturday I walked out to the fields and made my tryst with Katrin. We met in the lane after dark. My master trusts me to lock up the shop, but instead I leave it open, take him up the keys and slip out to the farm till dawn. In the morning he comes down through the house with the keys and asks me to open up again. You see, he never knows it has been left unlocked.'

'Then anyone might enter from the street?'

'Aye, and someone did. I knew it when we came back from the fair on market day. I feared they'd stolen Master Strachan's cloth and it would all come out, but it was worse than that. For there was Alexander lying killed. I couldn't touch him then. How could I? It's my fault. I'm to blame for his death. They call it art and part slaughter, the coroner says, as sure as if I'd done it myself. But, sir, I didn't kill him. I would never wish him dead. I wasn't there.'

Nicholas considered this. 'If what you say is true, it is not art and part. You were derelict in duty, to be sure. And your master may discharge you from your bonds. Yet you cannot be committed for the slaughter, if you did not mean to let the killer in.'

'Then you believe me, sir?' the boy asked tearfully.

'You give a plausible account. And Katrin will confirm it, I suppose?'

Tom slumped further to the ground. 'I fear that I'm a dead man, sir.'

'You don't think she will back you?'

'I will tell them it's a lie. I'll not see them shave her head and set her on the cutty stool for all the folks to gawp. She wouldn't understand, she thinks we're wed. She hasn't been brought up to fear the kirk.'

'Well then, Tom, she need not fear, if you're prepared to take her part. But you know you ought to marry her?'

'Aye. And so I will. But do you think the likes of George Dyer will leave it at that?'

'Who is George Dyer?' Nicholas asked cautiously. 'What is this to do with him?'

'A most officious elder of the kirk,' the boy said miserably. 'He's always watching us.'

'Then do you think he knew of this affair?'

Tom shook his head. 'I cannot think he did, else the wrath of Hell were already wrought upon us. We have ay been careful. For certain, he would like to know. And when he does, he'll have us both before the kirk for the sin of fornication. The session will demand it, handfast or not, for there's none to defend us. I'll never make a burgess now; we're nothing in the town. I care little for myself, but I won't see Katrin shamed.'

Nicholas nodded. 'Aye, I understand. Have courage now. I hear the turnkey's footsteps on the stair. But I'll come back tonight. I will speak to the girl – patience, for I will not fright her. And if she will confirm your tale, then something may be done to help you both.'

'Why, sir, would you help us?' The boy gazed at him doubt-fully, a faint light of hope through the tears.

Nicholas said softly, 'For Alexander's sake.'

The long walk to the cottage sapped his strength, for Nicholas was worn and hungry, and the poison in his thigh began to spread. The drover's daughter brought him oatmeal and a bowl of broth, thickly blackened with brambles and prune. He drank it grate-fully. She was birdlike, slighter than Tibbie, light on her feet with grey solemn eyes. She opened them wide as he tried to explain about Tom. 'To be sure he was here. I'm his wife. For why should he not be?'

She listened gravely as he told her, warming broth and water, flitting through the lamplight. She asked no questions, but quietly wept.

'Do you know George Dyer?' he concluded.

'Aye,' she stared into the fire. Her voice came oddly through the smoke. 'He watches us.'

'How so, does he watch you?' Nicholas demanded. 'Did he know what you were doing?'

Katrin shook her head. 'I know not, sir. He *watches* us.' She whispered, 'I did not know what we did was wrong.'

'I understand. Do not fear the dyer, Katrin, I will speak with him.' He tried to force a smile.

'And for myself, I do not think that what you did was wrong.' He winced a little. 'I am weary. May I rest awhile?'

The lass was standing at his side with a basin of warm water, watching him curiously. She had scrubbed away the tears with her fists.

'I think you are not well, sir. Are you wounded? May I see?'

He could not lift his shirt to her, and so he shook his head. 'I am a little tired,' he murmured, 'Aye, tis all.'

'My father won't be back before dusk. You may stay until then.' She put down the bowl. 'But I must go to him now to help with the sheep. He expects me. I'll leave you, sir. There's feverfew here for the pain.'

He seemed not to have heard her, for his eyes had closed. Katrin wrapped a woollen plaid around her shoulders. It had once belonged to Tibbie, heather grey with scarlet trim. A fold of grey wool cowled her face. Softly she closed the cottage door behind her, leaving Nicholas to sleep. She did not join her father in the fields among the ewes but turned instead to walk the narrow lane towards the town.

It was almost four o'clock when Nicholas awoke. Katrin had blown out the lamp and the house was in darkness, acrid with smoke. He pushed open the door. Outside he heard only the voice of the wind, the farm boys at work preparing for harvest, an occasional whistle or cry from the gulls. The sheep roamed wild among the barley. Circling, black crows scoured the skies. Of Davie Fyffe or Katrin he could see no sign.

The Dyers lived apart, by the Kinness Burn south of the town, close to the edge of the water. Their cottage was marked by a barrel of piss, a great tub of lye left out by the door, thickly putrid and rank. On summer days it hummed with flies. The townspeople seldom came by. When they did, plaids muffled round their mouths, with a faded Sunday shirt, a fleece or length of cloth to colour for their lass, the menfolk held their breath and pissed into the bucket as they left. It was the proper, the politest thing to do. It helped the litster make the mordants for his dyes. The women sometimes took a vessel in the house and voided more discreetly where the stench was fouler still. Rotting cakes of lichen, piss-soaked, smouldered by the fire. For weeks on end they hung there drying into dyes or painters' colours, mouldering in the damp or gently crumbling into dust according to the season. The children played outside in the air by the burn. They came indoors to hold their breath and use the pot. At night they never slept beside the fire.

No one used the house by day. The dyer simmered his pots on smoke piles at the back. He had three vats, almost four feet deep, copper-bottomed, rimmed with iron. They had been left to him by his father. Because of them, his hair and clothes were perfumed like a piss pot, his children were despised and his fingernails were blue. His eldest boy Will had a feel for the work, knowing just how much would give the deepest hue, when best to gather lichens, squeezing out the sap, which dyestuffs should be bought in from abroad. He chased the most elusive shades of yellow, red and purple, the most fugitive of colours, fading from the light. But George Dyer loathed the trade. He struggled for a place upon the burgh council and a voice within the gilds. He was an elder of the kirk who tirelessly bore witness against his neighbours at the sessions and spent his Sabbath rooting out delinquents from the alehouse, chasing truant farmers into church. Yet still he knew the merchants sniggered at his clothes. He bit his nails and tried to hide his hands.

He was working now on a great vat of purple, stirring up the embers of the fire. This was a delicate shade; based on violet orchil. He was afraid a little lye left in the yarn might turn it crimson or a spot of oil would stain it dirty blue. He ought to have left it to Will, but for once he was working alone. He had sent both his sons to help at the Strachans' shop, for it was well to keep in there. With Tom in the gaol he hoped for a place for his younger boy James. His wife and bairns were by the river, scraping grease from sheepskin, laying out fleeces to dry in the sun. They would be gone for several hours, the baby asleep by their side in her crib. Far off he heard the laughter of his favourite daughter Jennie as she danced on the stones. The afternoon was clear. The pelts should be dry before dawn.

He picked up a stick to stir the dark depths of the pot. Though the waters looked black the hooked strand of yarn that emerged was a deep speckled plum. He draped a little on a frame to test for fastness to the light. The deepest shades fled from the glare of the sun. There was room in the pot for more yarn. He had a stack in the cottage, newly spun, from tawny grey sheep that should take the shade well. Collecting it, he thought he heard steps and called out, but there was no reply. Perhaps the children played outside the house, or a passer-by felt the need to make use of the piss pot. It had happened once or twice. They did not like to be disturbed. He shrugged and returned to his work. The liquor had begun to cool. It was time to stoke up the fire. Lifting the yarn, he knelt over the pot. The waters lay still, like blackberry wine, lichens crusting round the edge.

The crust was the last thing he saw before the blow fell. He staggered forwards, falling, flailing in the vat. As he opened his mouth to cry out, the lye stripped the voice from his throat. Purple dye streamed through his lungs.

The killer stepped aside and wiped his fingers on his cloak.

A pity, he had spoiled the dye. But a presumptuous colour nonetheless.

It was Will, the dyer's son, who found the body. On his way home he stopped by the burn. His mother looked weary and hot, and he offered to fetch her a cup of fresh milk. Janet was heavy with child. He skimmed a stone or two with Jennie across the surface of the water and tickled the baby, dangling her legs in the stream. His brother James was still in Strachan's shop, but Will had left early to test out the strength of his dye. He had been working on the violet shade for several days. He hoped that it might please the king. Returning to the house, he found the door wide open. Beside it, on the ground by the great stinking pot, as if caught short and overtaken by the fumes, lay the figure of a man. Will dropped down beside him, lifting the hair that shrouded the face. The features were narrow and pale below a light shadow of beard. He'd met the man before in Strachan's house, where he had tutored the dead boy. His name was Nicholas Colp. He could not take him into the house, where the air was even fouler, so he dragged him clear onto the grass and called to his father for help. When the dyer did not come he returned to the burn to send his sister Jennie running into town. His mother brought cold water from the well. They waited for some time, until the college servants grumbled down the bank and made a cot to carry him. The children watched wide-eyed. It was only then that Will remembered to tend to his pots. He frowned to see the colour splashed around the sides. And in the bramble-coloured dye he found his father drowned, his face grotesque and swollen, bobbing like a plum. He was mauve to the roots of his hair and the whites of his eyes.

The hue and cry came slowly, distant as the weeping of the gulls as word began to whisper in the street. It began to grow dark in the town. On the Mercatgait, the weaver dimmed the lamps and closed the shutters of his shop. He settled in a chair to count his coins. Business had been brisk. Women came to stare but left with handkerchiefs and scarves. A woollen shawl was worth a glimpse, a mantle cloth a banquet with the corpse. He had even had enquiries for that shade of bluish-grey and had sold off half a length to make a dress. He could market it as Alexander Blue. He slipped the purse into his sleeve and hugged it close, alone among his profits and his thoughts.

In the darkness of the gaol a little further down the street, Tom Begbie wept. Nicholas had not returned. Outside he heard the bailies turn the locks, debtors calling down through open windows, footsteps running through the court. He did not see the small procession passing through the town. There was not enough light to look out through the grating. By night the streets were almost still. A woman's voice came coarse across the passage, then the sound of laughter dying back; a man said 'shush!' He crouched down in the straw and waited for the dawn.

In St Leonard's College too the light began to fail as Nicholas came home. They brought him dreamless from the west towards the abbey, through the gardens to the chapel where they laid him in the shade. His roommate Robert Black heard the proctors raise the cry but did not go to look. He was acting on the orders of his principal. Gilchrist had instructed him to read the play that Colp was writing. Robert had found the play and read the opening act. Tomorrow he would show it to Gilchrist. It seemed to him harmless enough. But at the bottom of the box where Nicholas had left his papers he had discovered something else. They looked like private letters and he had not meant to read them, but a brown encrusted leaf had caught his eye. They were wrapped in a torn college gown, blackened with blood. The ink on the pages was smeared. There were several letters and a poem. The poem was written in Latin, in the neat, open hand of a child. The Latin was crude and filled with mistakes, but the meaning behind it was clear. It was written to the master from the boy.

Alexander to Nicholas Colp:
Domine adiuva me tranquillare
Master, help me still
And steer this ship.
Your presence calms the ill,
The raging of the seas that rise,
This vessel cast adrift,
Amidst the foam and spawn.
Steer me, hold me, lash and force
Me steadfast to the climax of my course.
Becalm my swell, for thou art both the seaman
And the storm.

Robert let the paper fall as he heard footsteps on the stair.

Kenly Green

Released from his fetters, Dun Scottis took to the road with a will and alacrity that pleased his owner greatly, and for a mile or more he handled well. But two miles down the track, where the path curved to the left with a slight incline, the horse ground its hooves in the dust and came to a halt so abrupt that it was all that Hew could do to keep his seat. He righted himself and shook the reins crossly, and in no uncertain language urged it to go on. The animal ignored him. It stared impassively ahead, as though it confronted an invisible wall, or heard a distant voice of immutable command, of more authority and influence than Hew's. Hew struck it with his rod between the shoulder blades, just smartly enough to point out his frustration. Dun Scottis still did not walk on, but turned his head to gaze at him with such a look of sad reproach he did not have the heart to strike again. Puzzled, he dismounted. There was nothing on the ground or in the air to fright the horse; the birds were singing still, and Hew sensed nothing of that change of wind to which the nervous horse is tuned. Nor did Dun Scottis seem to be afraid. He showed no agitation, for he did not move at all, but stood placid and implacable as stone. Patiently, he waited still while Hew examined him. He was not overheated, and his hooves were free from nails. Hew took him by the halter and tried to lead him on. Dun Scottis failed to budge. Hew broached him from the other side, rapping at his rear end with a sharp tap of conviction; Dun Scottis merely flicked his tail against the hum of flies. Then, shoulder to rump, Hew tried to force the horse on from behind, while a passing farmhand gaped in frank astonishment. Dun Scottis stood his ground. Alone on the track, Hew's options were few. He walked on a little, whistling carelessly, and hoped the horse would follow him. Dun Scottis watched unmoved.

Hew had resolved to abandon him, full saddled in the middle of the track, when he recalled the horsebread in the ostler's saddlebag. He broke off a corner and wafted it just out of reach. Dun Scottis considered the offer. At length he shuffled forward in a spirit of concession. Hew took a small step backwards and by degrees, by this sole means, he coaxed the dun horse home to Kenly Green.

In the woodlands surrounding her father's house some four miles south-east of the town a young woman gathered watercress, trailing her arms through the stream. She laid the dark green tresses streaming on a square of linen, wrapped them carefully and placed the whole in a shallow rush basket, taking pains not to crush them. Then, wiping her hands on the front of her dress, she set off through the woods to the house. Her father's lands spilled outwards in the lee of Kenly Water through fields of oats and bere and straggled sheep towards the stonewalled gardens of a country tower-house. They had lived here for almost twelve years, since her father Matthew Cullan had given up the law to return to the land. His pale young wife had died in childbirth, and he liked his daughter to keep close to the house. She rarely strayed beyond these woods, planted many years before when the rowan, the holly, the elder and ash had protective and magical powers. Now winter threatened, the trees were beginning to fruit. Hard little apples and cobs freckled the leaves of the hazel and crab. The holly leaf curled on the branch, the elder and ash fell bruised by the wind, and close to the house the rowan trees bowed, veins bleeding darkly to crimson, small crops of berries blistering red. Below the trees the last of the late summer harebells drooped, dropping their flowers. The young woman passed on through the gate. From the hedgerow she chose a posy of pungent wild garlic to add to the basket. Among the thorns were brambles blackening, yellow rosehips flecked with pink. She picked a few and placed them gently on top of the herbs. Already the muslin dripped green. Then, from her garden by the house, she gathered tender nettles, sorrel and sweet cicely, wild leek and the roots of the white carrot flower.

Hew saw her pass through the gate and followed her at some distance through the woods, for he did not wish to be seen. He set loose his horse in the field by the stream. While it drank he rinsed the dust from his own eyes and mouth and waited, watching her disappear within the garden walls. Then he walked the path she made among the trees, the holly, the rowan, the elder and the ash. The pattern of the land remained the same. He recognised the scent of smoke and garlic flowers, the honeysuckle dying back, the distant chanter of the gulls. And by the garden wall he leant awhile to watch her through the gate as she gathered the herbs, a girl of eighteen, dressed in moss green with ragged black hair. From time to time she paused to push the strands out of her eyes. Gradually she became aware of him, though for a long moment she seemed to gaze into the distance, pale-lipped, and he wondered if she saw him after all, until he called out to her, 'Margret? Meg? Is it you?' and she smiled. She was running towards him, shaking the leaves from her dress, laughing as she took his hand.

'Here you are at last, Hew, and after all these years. You must be the grand scholar now.'

She was not as he remembered her. He recalled her trundling through the fields behind him, singing aloud to her doll. He realised he had half expected he would find her still a child, placid and trusting, or a country lass at least whose eyes would open bright to see his fine French clothes. He felt suddenly clouded and drab from the dust of the road.

'You've changed, Meg. Quite the woman. Eighteen years old and still at home? And you so fair,' he teased.

She tossed her dark head to look into his face, considering. 'While you've a lass or two in France no doubt. It's not so easy for me, Hew. I'll not leave Father while he lives. He needs someone here to take care of him. He's grown quite frail of late – it's as if he went to bed one night himself and woke up the next day an old man. He'll be glad to see you, right enough; he's been looking out for you for days, since first we had your letter. But you'll see a difference in him. We live alone here now. We have

52

the house and the lands are let out in feu; the steward takes care of the farm. We're done with the town and the court. But Father still finds solace in the old faith, and more and more he will not hold his peace in company. He dwells on Mother's death.'

'He doesn't hold mass here, does he, Meg?'

'Och, no.' She did not look at him. 'But he never goes to kirk. And he'll set the dogs on the session if they come by the house.'

'Has he really become such a fool?'

'No, Hew, he has not. Which is why he needs me here to tell the world that's all he is.' She laughed at his concern. 'I do it well enough. I'm off to kirk with my gossips every Sunday like the best of them, bonnet and plaid: "My faither's o'er frail to come today. He sends his steward and a dollar for the plate to help to feed the poor."'

He felt uncomfortable with this sharp young woman, not quite a stranger, and looked round for a safer subject. 'Is this your garden, then? I never saw such herbs. How do you grow them in this barren place? Are you a witch?'

'Hush!' she shushed him fearfully. 'Not even in jest. I spend my days out here. There's little else to do. I grow enough for our needs, a few roots and salads, potherbs for waters and simples. There's not much ails us here that can't be cured, except,' she sighed, 'for Father's age. But help me gather in the carrots and we'll go indoors – no, not that,' she brushed his hand away from a feathery fern, 'it's this one here, they're very like, you see.' She scooped up the wild roots with her hand.

They ate the leaves boiled in a salad with plump pigeon dumplings simmered in broth. It was as good, Hew protested, as anything he had eaten in France. The liquor was heady and fragrant. He wiped out the bowl with his bread.

'I brought you chanterelles from Paris, Meg – they're mushrooms, Father, good with meat and broth.'

'We don't eat mushrooms here,' protested Matthew Cullan. 'Your sister already throws all manner of things into the pot; I never know quite what I'll find, barley, berry or plum. Though by the bitterness of the broth I doubt she gives me physic on the sly.'

'Father's teasing,' Meg replied. 'He likes my cooking well enough. And I'll be glad to try the mushrooms, Hew. I've cooked them once or twice before,' her father pulled a face, 'with pottage or a pullet, but I don't feel safe enough to pick them from the woods. If I'd a mind to poison you, sir,' she told her father tartly, 'I'd have done so long before now.'

'You see how she treats me!' Matthew complained.

They talked into the evening hours, when someone lit the fire, and Matthew's eyes began to close. A servant entered with a jug of wine.

'If you please, sir, it appears your horse has broke loose, and has made free in Mistress Meg's garden,' she whispered to Hew as she passed. 'We thought it right to let you know.'

With a cry of alarm, Meg leapt from the fireside and fled from the room. As Hew began to follow her he was intercepted by his father's groom.

'Peace, we have secured him, sir. He's safe and well. But,' the man appeared to hesitate, 'you will not mind me asking, did ye buy him from the ostler in the marketplace?'

Hew answered grimly, 'Aye, and if I did?'

'I kent as much!' the groom exclaimed. ''Tis nothing, sir,' he grinned. 'A wee bit wager in the stable. Is yon horse Dun Scottis?'

Hew cast a nervous glance back at his father, who sat dozing by the fire. He had a notion he would not like what was coming, and did not care to have it overheard. He nodded, dropping low his voice. 'Aye, go on then, tell the worst,' he groaned.

The groom's expression mingled pity and amusement. 'Dun Scottis is well known here in the town. The bairns call him *Dung* Scottis, because . . .'

'Aye,' Hew interrupted quickly, 'I can guess the cause.'

'Well, sir, yon's a limmar. And a limmar too that sold him. Aye, sir, he's a rogue. And since you are a stranger here . . .'

'He must have seen you coming,' his expression said, too clearly. In deference, or compassion, he did not go on.

'I thank you,' Hew said firmly, 'For this intelligence. You may tell your friends you won the bet. Now tend him well.'

'You do not mean to keep him, sir?' The servant looked incredulous.

'Indeed I do. So give him food and water. Keep him well secured.'

'That's easier said than done,' the servant grinned.

Meg returned, a little flushed but smiling. 'All is well.'

'I fear your herbs are ruined, I'm sorry for it, Meg,' her brother told her earnestly.

'He only had the carrot tops. I think you mistake me, Hew, for it was not the garden I was feared for. Never mind, let's drink some wine.'

'What's the matter?' Matthew murmured. 'Did I hear the door?'

'Hew's horse was in my garden. But there is no harm.'

Matthew looked vexed. 'How careless of the groom.'

'In truth,' Hew confessed, 'it wasn't his fault.'

His father gave him a long look, and he felt himself grow hot.

'I have a dozen horses,' Matthew observed, 'that grow dull from want of riding. You are welcome, of course, to take any one.'

'Thank you, but I have a horse,' Hew insisted. His father smiled indulgently.

'Well then, home at last!' Matthew let the subject drop. 'And now that you are here we must make plans for your future. I have found you a place as an advocate's clerk. Tomorrow I will write to my old pupil Richard Cunningham, to tell him to expect you. He will be your master at the bar.'

'I wish you would not,' Hew blurted out. His father stared at him.

'Well,' he said after a moment, 'if you want a holiday then we can wait a little. I'll be glad to have you here. But we must not put it off too long. You want to be in Edinburgh by Martinmas.'

'I do not want it, there's the point.' Hew took a gulp of wine. 'Sir, I am resolved. I cannot proceed to the bar. I do not want to be an advocate.'

'I see.' Matthew raised his eyebrows. He looked at Hew for a long time without comment, and then enquired pleasantly, 'Have you thought what you might do instead? I know you well enough to think you will not be content without some occupation.'

'I might teach, perhaps,' Hew replied, grasping at straws. 'Or go into the church.'

His father gave a small dry smile. 'My son, a minister of the reformed kirk.'

'You had me schooled too well,' the son said somewhat grimly.

'Somehow, you know, I do not see it,' Matthew answered lightly. 'No matter, we will let it rest. I will not quarrel with you on your first night home. Peace, now!' He waved his hand as Hew began to argue. 'We shall speak of it another time. You are vexed, my child. Let me pour another cup of wine.'

They fell into an uncomfortable silence. For six years, Hew had been abroad, and Matthew had not seen him grow into a man. Now he observed the change in his son. Hew was a little more assertive and assured, though he had kept his boyish looks, for like his father he was fair, and struggled to maintain a beard. He had an open manner that would serve him well in court. It was Matthew's dearest wish to see his son become an advocate. And yet he had misgivings. Though he did not doubt the sharpness of Hew's mind, he sensed an underlying softness that appeared to be at odds with it. Hew gave his heart too easily, which threatened to distract him from the rigours of the law. He was too compassionate, too easily drawn in. When advocates were painting black as white, Hew would be distracted by the grey. And always, from a child, he recognised the *pity* of the thing, the human side. He was wary and fanciful, given to nightmares, dismayed by the cruelties of everyday life. The thoroughness of his schooling, where he had excelled, had not subdued or satisfied him. Always he had seemed to search for something else. Now the boy sat brooding, in a dark place. Matthew did not like to see him there. He cleared his throat. 'I notice that your things were here before you,' he remarked. 'Where did you sleep last night?'

Miserably, Hew downed his cup. 'With my friend, Giles Locke.'

'*Giles Locke*,' Matthew tried it like a claret on his tongue. 'Do I know the name?'

'He was my friend in Paris,' Hew explained. 'He's a physician, an anatomist of sorts, who lectures in philosophy. We shared rooms at the College d'Ecossais. The new foundation requires the university to elect a mediciner as principal of the Auld College, though physic is not taught there in the schools. Giles came hoping to persuade them to reform, but both were disappointed, for the college is dismayed by his keenness and his youth.'

'How old is he?' asked Meg.

'No more than eight and twenty. You would like him, I think,' Hew looked across at Matthew. 'He's a closet papist like yourself.'

His father feigned astonishment. 'I don't know what you mean.'

'He came a month or two ago to St Salvator's,' continued Hew. 'But he's unhappy there.'

'And he a closet papist?' Matthew teased.

Hew sighed. 'There have been problems at the university. And I don't know if you heard, there has been trouble in the town. A boy was killed.'

In Giles Locke's north street tower a sleeping figure stirred. Nicholas felt something tighten its grip round his forearm as another sharp blade sank deep in his flesh. He thought that he could fight it, but the grip was too strong. His lips moved soundlessly as the blood began to flow. Someone was whispering '*Nicholas*', watching his life slip away. He knew he was in Hell, and that his blood would ebb and flow forever, constant as the tides. But God had allowed him the solace of quietness. God was kind; he allowed him to sleep. He could hear only a far muffled drum, growing fainter, feeling it echoing slow in his heart.

The doctor stemmed the flow and sniffed the contents of

the bowl, rich as a thick Gascon wine. Satisfied, he set the cup aside and tied the linen strip more tightly round the vein. He touched a little water to his sleeping patient's lips, wiping away a strand of green bile. The stomach was empty, the waters ran clear and he had drawn off a quart of steaming black blood. He hoped the patient's humours were restored. Though privately he doubted it, for the limb below the sheet stank putrid and hot. He laced the room with a wreath of sweet herbs to counter the smell. He ate his dinner by the patient's bedside, a bad piece of mutton floating in broth, and longed for the cookshops of France. There was blood on his sleeve. It spotted the page of his book as he settled to read in the light of the lamp. When the patient lay quiet at last, he set down his book and took his pulse. He sat through the night while Nicholas slept, composing a letter to Hew. At daybreak he sent Paul upon a fat grey mare to deliver it to Kenly Green. Hew set off at once, leaving Paul behind to eat his breakfast. He waited only to collect and saddle up his horse.

'Will you take him back, then?' asked the groom.

'Thank you, no, I mean to keep him.'

'Sir,' the groom lowered his voice, 'that horse has had a hard life, though he's sleek and healthy now. Sometimes, when a horse has been ill used it makes him stupid. Yon's a useless horse. It can't be helped.'

'Might not kindness mend him?' Hew said softly.

'No, sir. Take him back.'

'Nonetheless . . .' Hew slipped the halter over his arm and led the horse out of the yard. He did not wish to mount in front of the groom. The stable lad stared after him.

'Why'd he buy the shit horse?' he wondered aloud.

'Whisht,' the groom told him sternly. 'He's your master's son.'

'But why would he keep it?' persisted the boy.

The groom shrugged. 'Soft in the head,' he conceded, 'doubtless due to being schooled in France.'

★ ★ ★

'Nicholas is charged with sodomie and slaughter,' Doctor Locke said tersely. He splashed his face with a jug of cold water and spat out the dregs. Hew stared at him in disbelief. 'It's madness, Giles. I lived with him for four years at St Leonard's. We shared a bed. If he lusted after boys, I would have known.'

They were standing in the turret, where they were not over-looked. Still Giles had fastened and bolted the door. Hew had left Dun Scottis in the street below. He found a boy to hold him, for payment of two shillings and another kept on promise. The first lad he approached had refused. 'Shit Scottis? Not likely!' did not augur well. But the next boy, though small, had proved willing, and Hew had accepted his offer, with more pressing things on his mind.

Giles was explaining: 'I only report what I heard. The coroner was here this morning to set out the case against him, though he is still too sick to be disturbed. He is supposed to have been in love with Alexander Strachan, and to have killed him in the throes of their unnatural converse.'

'*That* is very likely,' Hew said dryly. 'What about the dyer?'

'He had wind of their love and was blackmailing Colp. Don't scowl at me so. I only report what I heard.'

'Is there evidence of this?' demanded Hew.

Giles inclined his head. 'A regent, Robert Black, found in-criminating letters in the room he shared with Nicholas.'

'I saw Nicholas take letters,' Hew admitted reluctantly, 'from the boy's room in the Strachan house. He hid them in his clothes.'

The doctor sighed. 'It's possible that they will drop the charge of sodomie, since neither Gilchrist nor the boy's father is anxious to have it come out. The murders are a different matter.'

'It was Nicholas who found Alexander's body. But what about the dyer?' Hew persisted.

'He was drowned in a vat of his own dye. An unpleasant death,' Giles observed. 'The lye had stripped away his lungs, like vitriol. Nicholas was found beside him, overcome by fumes. And that is all I know.'

'I should never have left him,' Hew whispered. 'This is my fault.'

Giles regarded him curiously. 'I cannot see how it was *your* fault,' he reasoned. 'But come in and see him. He may be awake.'

He opened a door on the straight side of the tower room. Hew had not noticed it before.

'It's really just a closet,' Giles explained. 'You may find the air a little stale. Cover your mouth, if you will.'

On a low pallet mattress Nicholas stirred, wrapped in a damp linen sheet. It smelled like a shroud. He seemed to dream in conversations, shifting and endless, for as he slept he grumbled, frowned and sighed. Hew watched the doctor place a cooling hand upon his pulse.

'He's coming round. It's time to draw a little more blood. If you wouldn't mind holding him up?'

He flicked open the case of the lancet and wiped the blade on his sleeve. Hew shuddered:

'Giles, must you?'

'It seems that I must, for the college won't pay for a surgeon. I grant you it's hardly my place.'

'That's not what I meant. He looks so pale and lifeless.'

In his years as a student Hew had been routinely bled and purged as prophylactic against the plague. He did not think it ever did him good.

'Hew, do I tell you how to practick in the courts? The cup now, quickly. If he spews it's a good sign. Dammit, man, you've got blood on my hands.'

Suddenly faint, Hew had let the bowl slip, splashing the physician with blood. He turned away from the bed. Giles began to mop up. 'You may be right, though,' he conceded, 'we could blister him instead. There now, that's enough. He's out of it.'

Hew was standing with his back to them, looking out into the tower room, breathing heavily. His shoulders were hunched. Giles set down the cup and came to his side.

'Is he dead?' Hew asked, trembling.

60

'He's unconscious. It's a blessing, you know. It won't be for long. Don't take it amiss, Hew. Many men sicken at blood. You should have said.'

Hew excused himself quickly. 'No, it's the smell. What is it, Giles? It stinks like rotting kale.'

'Putrefaction. It could be his leg or my dinner; they both have been equally foul. Oh, my dear friend,' the doctor caught sight of Hew's stricken face, 'forgive me, I forget myself. Come in and look at him now. You'll find him at peace.'

Hew returned to the cot, his handkerchief pressed to his face. Giles had changed the splattered sheet and Nicholas looked pale and clean, resting neatly on his side. He made no movement or sound.

'In your letter you mentioned a flesh wound. How come he's so sick?'

'It's a small cut, but deep,' explained Giles. 'The wound has grown putrid. The poison's corrupting his blood. You see how black it streams?' Hew looked away quickly. 'And there's increasing stiffness in the limb. I am afraid it may be lockjaw. Hush now, we'll leave him to sleep.' He hung the soiled towel on a nail in the wall and motioned Hew out of the room. His friend took a gulp of clean air.

'Is there nothing more that you can do?'

Giles regarded him thoughtfully. 'There's nothing more I am prepared to do, though I have not cast his horoscope. Like you, I rather thought I'd done enough. You could pay a surgeon to take off his leg. True, the wound's high, but skilfully done it might help stop the spread of the poison. But don't look to me to assist.'

Hew swallowed. 'Could it save his life?'

'It could. But for what? His leg will roast with the rest of him. On or off.'

'You think he did it then? You think he killed the boy?'

The doctor shook his head. 'It scarcely signifies. I think that it's better to die in a clean college bed than to swing on the scaffold. Don't you?'

'But you're a man of physic, Giles. You cannot choose to let him die,' Hew pleaded.

'God will choose,' Giles answered patiently. 'I've done what I can. I've poulticed and bled him to balance the humours. Hypericum to cleanse the wound, milk of white rose – it's very expensive – and a little neat brandy to deaden the pain. He's comfortable here.'

'And there's nothing more to be done?'

'If you will, call the surgeon. They'll hang him in parts.'

Hew searched around for an answer. 'Might perhaps my sister nurse him?' he suggested. 'She has grown up on the farm, and is skilled in natural physic.'

'Is she past fifty?' Giles asked dryly.

'What?'

'I'm sorry, Hew. I don't mean to make light of it. The college frowns on women under fifty years of age. Still, I think we can get round that, at least until the term begins. Professor Herbert has installed a wife who can't be more than twenty-three. Though she is extremely plain, that is a mitigating factor. Your sister, though. Will she come?'

'I'm sure of it. She'll cook for you. She's a grand cook, you'll like her.' He forced out a smile.

'Then she must come at once.' The doctor brightened. 'I'd give my new plum doublet for a piece of roasted meat. Everything I've eaten since I came here has been boiled in mutton fat. And if Nicholas recovers, then I hope you'll make a case for him. He has few enough friends. In the depths of his fever he calls out for the boy, no one else. He's deeply disturbed in his mind.'

'But he hasn't confessed?' Hew asked anxiously.

'Oddly enough, he has not. But listen! Have they come for him? There's some sort of commotion outside!'

Hew made his way to the window and drew back the shutters. 'It's nothing. Someone has upturned his cart, a fruitman on his way to market. It looks like some sort of . . . *Oh!*'

A cartload of apples and plums were bowling like boules down the north street. In the midst of it all, freed from his tethers, cavorted a dun-coloured horse.

Hew returned by the shore, with the horse in disgrace at his heels. He walked in the swell of the wind; it helped him to focus his thoughts. Salt from the sea washed out the sharp taste, like a tooth turning bad, from his mouth. It was dark when he opened the gate. In the warmth of the hall, over supper of oatmeal and cheese, he told them about Nicholas. His plans for his sister were met with dismay. He could see that she was willing, for she spoke of herbs and medicines, but a glance towards her father held her back. Matthew shook his head. 'You don't understand what you ask, Hew. She isn't as strong as she looks.'

'There's no danger she'll fall sick, or I wouldn't take her,' argued Hew. 'It's a putrefying wound. I know she's cleansed them often on the farm. The steward's wife will feed you for a day or two, I'm sure. You cannot keep her here forever, sir; she's young, she needs to see the world. I swear I'll look after her. If you could see him you'd realise. He's too ill to be moved.' He tried not to remember the vomit, the stream of black blood.

'And what of your mediciner?'

'He's done what he can.'

Matthew nodded. 'I remember your friend. A sweet boy; a scholar. Tell me again of the charge.'

He sat silent for a long time quiet after Hew had told him. Finally he spoke.

'Then as I see it, it amounts to this. He may have killed the dyer or the boy, or neither, or both. He may also, or only, be a sodomite, but if he did not kill the boy that may not signify; the Strachans will not wish to press the charge. If you are to speak for him, Hew, you must find out the truth. Take Meg if you will, but take care of her. Trust me when I say she is not as strong as she seems. But, you're right of course. She has to go out in the world. I won't always be here to protect her.'

63

'Does she really need protection, Father? Or does she stay for your sake?'

'Perhaps.' His father smiled at him. 'Your sister knows her mind. She's determined to go with you. Consider, though, that if she saves his life, it may be to condemn him to another, crueller death.'

Hew nodded. 'Aye, I know. Giles said the same.'

'Then he's a better man than medic. I should like to meet him. But if you mean to find the truth, then you must learn to open your mind and close your heart. If it does come out as sodomie . . . God love him, Hew,' he ended quietly. 'I saw a young boy burned alive on Castle Hill for something of the sort.'

Salvator

They set off for the town at first light. Meg brought a basket of herbs, still wet, and a fresh sheep's cheese for Giles Locke. They had broken their fast in the darkness, sharing a loaf by the side of the fire. Matthew Cullan grumbled out of bed to take his leave of them. He whispered awhile in the corner with Meg. Hew stood apart like a stranger.

'We'll be back before nightfall,' Hew promised. 'Come, Meg. It will take us an hour if we go by the cliffs. And since it looks warm, shall we walk?'

They did so, for the day broke hot and fair. At Kinkell Braes they turned off from the road and made their way towards the shore. For a while the path led them through thick swathes of thistle and thorn, where leafy fern and marram grass obscured the water's edge. Meg filled her basket with brambles and rosehips, and as they fought their way through clumps of weed they feasted on blackberries, and were children again, forgetting their shyness, chasing through the nettles and the gorse. Presently, as they came closer to the cliffs, they saw the ragged outline of the maiden rock, and beyond it the outcrop of shoreline, black against the smoothness of the sea. A thousand seabirds flecked the rocks, from the stillness of the water to the pallid wash of cloud, forming layers of muted colours to the hills beyond. The landscape rose in strips of undulating flatness, the rocks a streak of blackness in the grey rush of the water, and the sea a streak of darkness in the whiteness of the sky. Then, as the light changed, they saw the pale arc of the bay, the curvature of windswept sand, coloured like the harvest, ripe against the perfect blue of the sea. The beach circled round to the pier, where the waters broke and scattered freely, sending spray like sleet above the harbour wall. And rising from the bay, they saw the town.

Meg caught her brother's hand. 'It's beautiful, Hew!'

'Had you not seen it before?' he teased.

'For sure, I never tire of it.'

Far above the harbour stretched the spires of the cathedral, its east gable window striking dark against the clouds. Behind it stood the sombre square-cut tower of St Rule, while the steeple of the town kirk and the weather vane and spire of St Salvator's chapel flanked it in the distance, high above the north and market streets. As they approached, the darkness of the stone gave way to grey and yellow walls, echoing the warm tones of the sand.

'The central tower has crumbled since I saw it last,' Hew observed.

Meg nodded sadly. 'Father will no longer come to town, for he cannot bear to see it. He says that it had weathered storms for nigh four hundred years, when in twenty the reformers stripped it to the bone. And when he was a lad, the roof was made of copper, that when the sun came slanting through the haar did wink and cast its burnished glow upon the town.'

Hew snorted, 'Aye, the glint of gold the fat priests fleeced from pilgrims. I do not think our father ever saw its glow; that is pure stuff and sentiment. The destruction of that church is no bad thing, for it was built on falsehood, and a heap of broken bones.'

'How could it not be bad, Hew?' she challenged him. 'The cathedral was our heart. And all the town that grew up in its shade, in the absence of its warmth must wither up and die.'

'Come with me through the Sea Yett,' he replied, 'on to the south street, or up the harbour steps towards the Swallowgait, and I will shown you fine new houses, with lintels and forestairs, and Dutch craw-stepped gables, quarried from your dead cathedral.'

'I have seen them, and admire them,' she admitted. 'Yet I fear the change.'

'This is my father's fault, for he has kept you cloistered far too long. The town reforms, but does not perish.'

They passed through the sea gate and turned on to the north

street, where a clutch of shrieking gulls swept round the fisher cross. 'It's market day,' said Meg, wrinkling up her nose. The cobblestones were wet with slime. Hurriedly, they crossed to St Salvator's College. Doctor Locke sat reading in his rooms, oblivious to haddie criers and their stink of fish.

'I had not thought to see you here so soon,' he welcomed them. 'Mistress, I am glad to meet you. Thank you, you may go now.' This last was to his servant, who was watching them curiously. 'My friends will stay till dinner, so I shan't eat in the hall. Can you bring us something different, Paul?'

'I brought you some cheese,' Meg ventured timidly. 'It's fresh from the farm.'

'Is it?' He sniffed at the parcel. 'Child, you're a saint. But you've come to see Nicholas. I've been to the chapel to pray for him, Hew. I'm afraid he grows worse. He's too weak to countenance loss of more blood. Nonetheless, come on in.'

Hew preferred to stay outside. In deference to his sister he hovered at the far side of the door. Meg had no such qualms. She walked in at once to the bed and looked over the patient. 'May I touch him?' she asked, folding back the sheet.

Giles gave a cough, looking on in amusement. 'Indeed, child, go on.' She was feeling through the bandages for Nicholas' thigh.

'What are you doing?' her brother objected.

'Be still, will you, Hew! I'm taking his pulse.'

'In the groin?'

'I don't hear him complain.' She flushed a little under his gaze but continued to probe for stiffness in the limb. 'It's in spasm. It's the lockjaw,' she concluded at last, carefully wiping her hands on the sheet.

The doctor nodded gravely. 'I felt it there this morning. If it spreads to the throat he will die.'

'I've seen it happen so. Pray God it will not spread. But, sir,' she seemed to hesitate, and then continued rather quickly, 'as for the putrefaction, I have had some success with spaghnum moss and oil of hypericum flower. I have both in my basket. I could dress the wound now if you hold the leg still?'

'Indeed?' The doctor stared at her. 'I've a compress of hypericum applied, but no moss. A good battle salve. Where do you find it?'

'I grow it at home for use on the farm. It will draw out the worst of the rot and you may cut the rest out with a knife. Can you hold him, Hew?' Her brother nodded weakly. 'Then when he comes round we'll give him a little beef broth. If we clean out the wound you won't have to bleed him again.'

Giles looked at her now with respect as she laid out her bottles and leaves, trimming a dense clump of moss. She took the open lancet from his hand and set the blade to glow white-hot upon the fire. 'It must be clean.'

'I grant you,' he said, 'but what of the cramps? He may die after all, in the end.'

'I know a herb that will release the limbs from spasm,' she dropped her voice, 'if we use it sparingly. I tried it on my father's mare. She suffered cruel convulsions in the spring. It started with that same raw heat and stiffness in the shank. I have the seed at home.'

'He isn't a horse, you would kill him for sure,' Giles hissed at her. 'And even if he lived, do you think the university would thank you? If it's hemlock you give him, then they'll have you for witchcraft. Don't start so, girl! I'm not a fool.'

'Why are you whispering?' Hew called out nervously. 'Please Meg, can't we be done?'

'We're careful not to frighten him. By the way,' Giles winked at Meg. 'What happened to the horse?'

'She lived. But she's still a bit lame.'

Together they opened the wound. Hew managed it well. His sister made the dressing, gathered up the dirty rags and threw them on the fire. 'He could do with some air. Never mind. We'll leave the door ajar. Do you have money, Hew? If there's a flesher in the market we'll buy beef to make the broth. I fear it's slow to cook,' she smiled at Doctor Locke, who had brightened visibly, 'but what Nicholas can't swallow will do well enough for you.'

Some twenty or thirty small booths and stalls had opened on the market street between the port and mercat cross. In the north street at the fisher cross the fishwives called their wares, their cries of 'callour herrin' drifting through the marketplace. By the butter tron stood troughs of milk and cheese, flanked by sacks of grain and oatmeal. Baxters cried loaves by the dozen, and fruit men sold apples and flowers. To the left of the flower stall, a rack of small songbirds shuddered in cages, while a thin clutch of poultry fowl strutted and squawked.

Meg purchased a posy to sweeten the sickroom before turning her attention to the meat. Among the stalls were several fleshers, their wooden slats and boards already clogged with blood. A calf's head on a spike poked out its blue tongue comically, and winked a bleary bloodshot eye at Hew. Meg tugged at his sleeve. 'The flesh is washed in brine to flush the maggots out, can you not smell it? And the meat is blawn out, full of air.' Hew felt his gorge rise. A bowl of steaming entrails slopped onto the ground. The law did not permit full slaughter in the street, in deference to existing filth and stench, but carcasses came whole to be dismembered there, and the scattered straw and sawdust did not dissipate the stew. This waste itself was wrung and sold, for not a scrap was wasted. Blood dripped onto oatmeal to produce a pudding, or was caught in cups to flavour scalded milk.

Meg had found another butcher, who employed a child to whisk away the flies. Satisfied, she made her choice, and the fleshmonger struck a great slab with his cleaver, sheer through the bone. He made the meat into a parcel of white linen, scented with the sweet metallic taint of blood. Meg handed it to Hew.

'I feel a little faint,' she murmured. 'It's the noise and dust.'

The beef had begun to seep through its bandages. Hew pulled a face. He wanted to escape the stench, the sweet foul stew of grease and blood, the drum and cry of hawkers and the bleating of the crowd.

'In truth, the stink is overpowering. But we are outside Strachan's house. His shop is cool and quiet. Let's go in.' Taking Meg's arm, he pushed open the door.

With a cry of alarm, Tom Begbie emerged. 'We're closed, sir. That door should be locked.'

Hew stared at him curiously. 'Is your master not here?'

'No, sir, at church.'

'On market day? How singular,' Hew commented. 'Then may we sit and rest awhile? My sister's feeling faint. We need not trouble you.'

'She mustn't, no, she can't. My master wouldn't like it, sir. We're closed.' There was a note of desperation in Tom's voice. 'And I was meant to lock the door, and if he knew I had not locked the door . . . twas only that I hoped that she might come . . .' The voice had trailed away. Without another word, he slammed the door and shot the bolt.

'How strange.' Hew glanced at Meg. 'You look quite pale. Let's try next door. Now here we have a souter.' Suddenly, he grinned. 'And I feel I need some shoes.'

The shoemaker sat in the light of the door, stitching a boot from a pile of bright hides. He looked up and smiled, watching Hew finger the shoes on the counter, plain, laced and buckled, blue-black and grey. One pair was fashioned of silk, outlandishly coloured and stiffly embroidered, too fine for the mire and the stew of the streets.

'You'll not find finer work than that, sir. Was it something for the court that you required?'

Hew had begun to regret the modish French cut of his clothes. He would not repeat the error of his horse.

'I'm looking for a pair of boots – no beads; perhaps a fringe. Something stout and plain enough,' he lifted up the hem of his cloak and sniffed at it fastidiously, 'to weather the pollution of the town. But my sister's feeling faint. It's come over rather warm, I think.'

'There's a steuch from the sea doesn't help. Ellie, a stool for the lass! Fetch her some ale! I'll measure you up while she rests.' The shoemaker rose from his last. 'Would you sit, sir? Black leather or brown?'

'Brown would seem appropriate. The streets are caked in filth. Your wife is most kind, sir. We called at the weaver's next door but the lad turned us out. An ill-mannered lout,' Hew observed idly.

'Who, Tom?' the shoemaker rose to the bait. 'He'll be feart of Archie Strachan. He's been caught without his breeches and his master's not best pleased. Beg pardon to the lady, there.' He winked across at Meg.

'Tsk, the young today!' Hew shook his head. 'He claims his shop's closed, on market day, besides. Don't you count that strange? I think I'll have the black pair too. We don't often come to town.'

The souter nodded greedily. 'They've closed up for the funeral. They're burying George Dyer. If you're not from town I suppose you haven't heard. We have had two murders, sir, and one of them next door, was Archie Strachan's nephew. But they have the man, thank God.'

'Indeed? How tragic. And you do not go yourself?'

'To the burial?' The cobbler pursed his lips. 'Yon wisna that well liked, though it were wrang to say it. For all he was devout, a mean-mindit sort of man. We went to the wake, as was proper, but there was nothing there to drink,' he said dismissively.

'Do you know the Strachans well?'

Hew knew at once that he'd been over-keen in his interest. The cobbler stood up with a glint in his eye.

'So that's the brown and black, sir, to be ready for you Tuesday, if you'd like to leave your name. Since the lady seems recovered, I will say good day to you. Or was there something else you wanted? Pockets? Purses? Belts?'

Meg expressed an interest in a pocket, coloured a soft shade of grey. As the souter closed in for the sale, Hew renewed his questioning. 'That lad seemed scared almost out of his wits. His master's a cruel one, I doubt.'

The souter chuckled. 'I'll warrant he has made his feelings known. But Tom has more to fear than him. For *one*, there is the kirk, where he'll be called to account for his lewdness. Ah, beg pardon, lass,' he winked again at Meg.

'He'll not be the first,' supposed Hew.

'Aye, sir, nor the last.' The man was warming to his theme. 'For *two*, he was arrested for the murder of his master's nephew, and was thrown in gaol, and all but hanged.'

'You don't say!' Hew whistled. 'The limmar!'

'Aye. He did not do it, though,' the souter said reluctantly.

'Then how was it resolved?'

'Well, sir, like I say, they have the man. And Tom was with his lass, which was how it all came out. For when she heard that Tom was taken, she came straight to Agnes Ford, that is the weaver's wife you know, and did confess it all.'

'*What* did she confess?'

'Why, that they were shafting, when the boy was killed.' He glanced at Meg and cleared his throat. 'I mean the lad had *steered the pot*, if you will understand me. So Agnes told the coroner, and Tom was freed from gaol, to answer for his rudeness to the kirk.'

'Better than the gallows,' Hew observed judiciously.

The souter snorted. 'Aye. And they say purgatory's no as bad as Hell. Now, sir, do you want the purse? That's fifteen shillings, then.'

'Ah, no thank you. Just the shoes, for which I'll call on Tuesday,' Hew said hurriedly. 'Come, Meg, are you well?'

'I never saw a lad more scared,' he muttered as they left the shop. 'I'd like to question him.'

'I cannot think what for. He has an answer to the charge,' Meg pointed out.

Hew answered, mock severely, 'Aye, and one I hoped you could not comprehend. You seem a little vexed, Meg. Did you want the pocket?'

''Tis only that I'm tired. But I think I *might* have had one.'

He laughed at her. 'You're sulking! You're a woman after all! Peace now, do not fret. If I can talk to Tom, then you shall have a gown.'

Meg retorted crossly, 'It may cost you more than that before you're done.'

They ate dinner with Giles, a cold mutton pie with a hard yellow crust, and a smear of Meg's cheese on good barley bread. The servant was touchingly proud of the pie. 'I bought it from the castle cookshop as a change from salt herring and kale. I'll clear the plates, Master Locke. I met Professor Herbert in the courtyard. He asks would you mind looking in on his wife? She's had the bloody flux a week now and he'd like to have your thoughts.'

'I must go, I suppose,' grumbled Giles. 'But you should say, Paul, I shall charge her. I'm a faculty professor, not a quacksalver brought from abroad to cure the college strumpets of their ills. They haven't offered me a penny for the care I've given Nicholas. I've not been paid yet for the term, Hew, which is why we're eating college kale and pies.'

'I could give you something for him if you liked? I'm sure my father wouldn't mind.'

'No, I do not grudge him. But I'll not give Herbert's mistress free advice upon her bowels. Can you stay with Nicholas? I know that Paul has other work to do.'

'You will, won't you, Meg?' His sister looked up from the fire. She had already begun to prepare a great cauldron of broth, roasting off onions and garlic, slicing the beef from the bone. She issued instructions to Paul. 'If you keep the flame low, you may lift out the meat for Master Locke's supper, then dampen it down and let the rest stew overnight. If there's ale or wine left, you can stir in the dregs. Then when it's quite dark, pour it through muslin and thicken it with herbs and barley. Or if you prefer it you can cook a capon in the liquor, like the French. The herbs here are for Master Colp.' She glanced across at Giles. 'There's marigold, mugwort and thyme, Doctor Locke, nothing more. Infuse them in a cupful of the broth and give it to him in drops on a spoon, as often and as much as you can. Of course I shall stay. I'm not wanted home before dark. But are you going out, Hew? Where?'

'To St Leonard's College. I sent word that I would like to call this afternoon. The principal expects me shortly after two.'

'You won't learn anything from him,' insisted Giles. 'He's forever on his guard, and keeps his secrets closely. And he'll remember you and Nicholas were friends.'

'Indeed, I don't intend to quiz him. Meg knows I have no flair for it. And I would hope he does remember me,' Hew pretended to look hurt, 'for as far as he's concerned, I've heard nothing of the news. I've just returned from France. I'm out of work. In fact,' he added thoughtfully, 'that's not a bad idea. For while I hold an opening there for Nicholas, the little I may earn will help to meet the cost of his defence. Come, if you're about to leave we'll make our way together to the street.'

The servant followed close behind them, fearful of a woman in the house. Meg was left alone to stir the broth. Absently, she nibbled on a leaf. At length she set the pot to bubble gently on the hearth and went to look at Nicholas.

The air in the room was already more sweet, but she was alarmed to find him lying twisted on the bed, his back in a curious arch. His breathing was rattled and low. Hurriedly she felt into her sleeve for a pocket, and opening it out, uncovered a handful of seeds. She knelt by the top of the bed and gripped his head hard, holding it tight with her knees. Then with all of her strength she forced open the jaw. She dropped the seeds into his mouth, pushing them down to the back of his throat. She continued to hold him, as well as she could, till the spasm began to die down, and his face lay rigid and grey, like a cracked mask of clay in the clamp of her hands. The mouth grinned bloody and frothing, gaping wide in pain. He was conscious for a moment; she saw it in his eyes, before they locked again and lost their focus. His body gave a great and noiseless sigh. His fingers began to uncurl.

74

She cupped his whole head in her hands and gently turned it. For a long time she sat by the bed, watching the tautness subside. When at last she was sure, she rose to her feet and steadied her hand on the wall. She had grown deathly pale. Shaking, she reached for the jug, and poured out a half cup of wine, which she drank with the rest of the seeds. She lay down among the rushes on the floor and fell into deep dreamless sleep.

Hew found it strange to be back in the college. It was just as he remembered it, the lecture hall and schools across the courtyard from the chapel, the kitchens and refectory, the washroom and latrines. He saw the window of the room that he had shared with Nicholas. Nicholas had been a pauper scholar, forced to lay the fires and fetch the water from the well, yet they became good friends. There had shared their hopes and fears, and worked together on responsions late into the night. At their last examination, both of them excelled. Nicholas obtained his licence and remained behind to teach while Hew had gone abroad to study for the law. He had written to Hew for a while, odd little satires, verses and squibs. But as Hew moved from Toulouse to Leuven, to Padua and back again to Paris, they had fallen out of touch. With a sense of nostalgia, Hew knocked on Gilchrist's door.

'Master Cullan? Do come in. I've been expecting you.'

'It's good of you to see me, Master Gilchrist. Strange to see the college so empty.'

'We expect the students very soon. I'm always glad to welcome back a graduate. It's Hew? Hew Cullan? I believe you had a brother here? No? Then let me see. Weren't you here with George Buchanan?'

'For a time, sir. I was beginning on my second year when you came to take his place.'

'Quite so. I remember it now. You acquitted yourself well, I recall. You took distinction, did you not? You and another from your class.' He frowned a little. 'Tell me, why are you here?'

Hew was taken aback by the directness of the question. He decided to be equally direct in his reply.

'I had hoped to ask you, sir, if you might recommend me to a place. I've been out of Scotland for six years, and I find I am forgotten by my friends. As you recall I took my licence here before continuing abroad to read the law. The pity is I find I have no calling for the bar. My mind's fixed on a readership, for I lectured both in Paris and Leuven and find it suits me very well. I believe there is a vacancy to teach the civil laws in Edinburgh, in the gift of Mary of Guise. But my father's set against it. He was an advocate himself of some repute.'

'Edinburgh? Oh, that would be a pity, Hew.' Gilchrist seized the bait. 'You are aware, I suppose, that there's no university there? We have professors in the civil laws here at St Andrews, within the higher faculties. Perhaps you did not know? There's the king's man at St Mary's now, a most prodigious man. We're growing all the while. And in a year or two, I'm sure we'll have a place for you.'

'Truly, principal, I wish I could be here for it. But unless I go in for the bar my father will withdraw his support. I can't afford to wait.'

'I can see that that's a problem. *Unless . . .*' he pretended to consider, furrowing his brow, '. . . I think I see a way, if you're prepared to take a lesser post until a readership comes up. Do you recall enough to teach the magistrands? They're well ahead this year.' Hew detected an odd note, almost regret. 'You need only read the metaphysics and the spheres, and take them through their disputations at the end. You'll no doubt recall it's a lucrative time. Presents of gloves, and feasts and the like.' He waved his arms, suggesting vague largesse. 'Term begins next month, so there's time to prepare. Might you consider it?'

'It's true, I could do it,' Hew capitulated. 'I still have the texts. But what has become of their regent? Surely he expects to take them through?'

'Alas,' the principal sighed, composing a small smile of disappointment. 'He's fallen sick. In confidence, I tell you, we don't expect him to survive. It has all been rather sad. But we must make of our loss what we can. I have no doubt that you will make an excellent replacement. The college has come under close scrutiny by the king's commissioners this last year, and some of our oldest traditions have been called into question. It has even been suggested that the regents should not teach the same class of students throughout their four years, lest they became too partial and intimate. As a graduate, you see how absurd that is.' Hew nodded sympathetically. 'And with our present difficulties . . .' Gilchrist went on, encouraged, 'well, it is enough to say we will be glad to have you back. Someone who has understood our ways. We'll call it settled, then. If you'll send for your books and arrange your affairs, I'll have them prepare you a room.'

In the closet room of Giles Locke's tower Meg Cullan was opening her eyes. At first she forgot where she was, until she turned to see Nicholas, stretched at her side. She lifted his hand. It was limp. Gently she arranged his limbs into a semblance of repose. The rigor had gone. His face hung grey and slack, lightly flecked with blood. She was changing the sheet when the doctor returned. He went at once to tend to Nicholas, feeling for a pulse, examining his eyes. At last he turned to Meg. 'Oh, my dear child! What have you done?'

'He's still alive,' she answered faintly. She could barely shape the words. 'He's in a deep sleep now. There's nothing that will rouse him. He has had convulsions. I think his jaw is broken. Please, may I go home?'

For a moment Giles seemed lost for words, then he recovered briskly. 'I'll send Paul for Hew. I suppose he was not here? You have been alone?'

'No one else was here.'

'Then you gave him nothing, *nothing*, do you understand? Shush, I'll take care of it now. Go down to the chapel and wait there for Hew.'

St Leonard's

To Hew's consternation, Meg slept for the whole of the following day. She had spoken barely a word on the journey from town and simply nodded when he told her of his triumph at St Leonard's. Their father was more sanguine. 'She'll be well enough by night-fall, Hew, don't fret. I did warn you she was frailer than she seems.'

'Is there no physic she can take?'

'She won't be any use to you today. When you come back from town you can tell us the news. She'll be glad enough to hear it when she wakes.'

It was a clear dismissal. Hew felt deflated. His news had gone flat, like a bladder the schoolboys had pricked with a pin. He took his horse from the stable and prodded him grumpily back into town.

The day dawned drizzle-grey, the mist from the sea almost palpable over the land. By the time he arrived he felt sodden and dreary, quarrelling with the stabler over the cost of leaving the horse. Nor did his mood lift in the north street, for the doctor had gone out, locking all his doors. There was no sign of Paul.

Giles was in church, kneeling on the earthen floor of St Salvator's chapel, mouthing out the words of private prayer. He would have liked to make confession, and afterwards to light a candle. In their place, he opened his soul before God. He asked God what to do with Nicholas. Upstairs, he had locked the door and sent Paul on an errand out of town. He trusted no one else to see the patient. Nicholas lay white-lipped and cold, without trace of a pulse. In the flame of a candle the pupils of his eyes did not dilate. Giles had been about to call the proctors to remove him. Yet after several hours the corpse was lying limp, and shallow breath fell misty on the glass. And so Giles knew he was not dead, but lying in some secret place that was neither death nor life. Meg's poisons had bewitched him. The doctor set the bones and bound the broken face in strips of linen cloth to hold it firm. He stripped and cleansed the wound, yet still the patient did not stir. And so he prayed.

God sent him Hew, which was not what he had hoped for. He was sitting outside in the dust of the street, damp and bedraggled. Reluctantly Giles let him in.

'Your friend's asleep.' The doctor closed the door. 'We'll not disturb him now. Come dry yourself off by the fire.'

Meg's absence had alarmed him further. He needed her to bring the patient back to consciousness. Without food or water, Nicholas would die.

Hew stared at him. 'Is something wrong?'

'Aye, tis Nicholas. The illness is reaching its crisis. He suffered seizures in the night, and his jawbone has cracked. I fear he's on the brink of death.' It was literally true: *suspended*, Giles thought, neither living nor dead. He could not have explained it.

'I'm sorry,' Hew said wretchedly. 'Meg will be upset. Is there nothing she can do?'

'No, no. I don't say that. I should be glad if she could come tomorrow. The hours ahead are critical. His life lies in the balance, but the cleansing of the wound has cleared the corruption. The putrefaction and the fever both are gone. Even the lockjaw recedes.'

'And yet you say he's close to death? I don't understand.'

No more did Giles. He shook his head. 'He's weak and must have nourishment. But with a broken jaw . . . it may not heal. It will be hard for him to eat.'

'I don't know what you're saying. Will he live or die?' demanded Hew. 'If I'm going to make a case I'll have to talk to him, Giles. Do you tell me I'm wasting my time?'

'I'm sorry, Hew, I can't say more. You must put your questions elsewhere. But at least you have time on your side, for if he lives it will be weeks before he's fit to answer any charge. Ask your sister here to nurse him. We'll feed him through straws. Hew – you'll think this odd – I know she's your sister, but tell me, how well do you know her?'

'In truth, not well at all. She was a child when I last saw her. But why do you ask? Does she seem strange to you?' Hew pursued anxiously. 'Is she unwell?'

'I expect she has her monthly courses,' the doctor reassured him. 'It would explain the reticence and shifting, don't you think? There's many a gentle lass brought to her bed when it comes.'

'Truly? How vexing,' Hew said, perplexed.

His confusion must have flickered in his face, for Giles explained kindly: 'She is not to be pitied the pain, for it's a natural process. In fact we ought to envy her, for nature's her phlebotomist. We men must bleed ourselves, you know. When you know a woman well, even your own sister, you will observe how as the month draws on she grows out of sorts, and is ever more tearful, shrill and discordant. But when the menstrual flux follows its course and the balance of her humours is restored, she returns to her sweet loving self.'

'Think you, truly?' Hew looked sceptical. 'I must ask her.'

'Well, perhaps not,' Giles put in hurriedly. 'They don't always see it that way.'

Hew decided to return to St Leonard's. There was nothing to be learned from Giles. With the rest of his profession he excelled in the equivocal, trained in prevarication in the best of schools. What was clear was that his friend was hiding something. If Nicholas was close to death, then why had he left him alone? Nor did he in the least believe that what ailed Meg were her courses. Giles had hoped their mention would embarrass and deflect him. But whatever was the matter, it could wait.

Gilchrist was surprised to see him back so soon: 'Master Cullan! Have you come to join us? Term does not begin until October.'

'I know it, sir. In truth, I'm anxious to begin. My father took the news of my appointment badly. I've come to see about a room. I wondered if perhaps you knew of someone who might share? I find that cost becomes a factor, as things stand.'

'Ah. There may be. Well there may.' But he seemed rather doubtful. 'There's one man, Robert Black, about to take the first-year class. His father is a goldsmith in the capital. He shared a room with the regent who left, so he may have a place. The other regents still share a bed.'

'That sounds grand. When may I meet him?'

'I don't say he'll agree. He has been content enough since Master Colp left. He claims that the solitude suits him. And then, of course, he has no need of funds.'

Master Colp. He was testing the waters, trying out the name to see if Hew remarked upon it, watching him with narrowed eyes.

'But if expense is such a grave consideration, then you might be better bedding with your students. That's always good for discipline. Why not find your board at someone else's cost?'

'Perhaps. But I'd prefer to be among the regents. I'm not a pauper scholar. Master Colp, did you say?' Hew echoed carefully. 'I know him, sir. We lodged together once when we were boys.' It was pointless to deny it. 'And is he the one who's sick? I'm grieved to hear it. You know, I do wonder whether I should make my peace with my father and return to the law. It's been a long time since I had to lie with undergraduates.'

'No, no, not at all,' Gilchrist protested, 'I will take you now to Master Black. I think you'll like him, Hew, and he will find you very different from Colp.'

Robert Black sat hunched at his desk. His objections had been swept aside, and Gilchrist had left him confronting the stranger. It was clear to Hew that he did not want to share.

'I knew him, you know,' Hew was saying softly.

'I know. He spoke of you sometimes.'

Hew began to walk round the room, looking out at the view from the window, picking up inkhorns and books. 'Those are my things,' he knew Robert Black wanted to say to him, 'this is my room,' but the words did not come. Hew leafed through a quarto. 'I recognise this grammar. Was it his?'

'I haven't packed up his things yet,' Robert said defensively.

'I can take them if you like. He's in St Salvator's, did you know? Listen, if you'd rather sleep here on your own I'd understand. But can you tell me what has happened? We were friends.'

Robert shook his head. 'Then you wouldn't want to know.' He looked earnestly at Hew.

'I have no quarrel with you, Master Cullan, and I've none with Nicholas. I also once thought him a friend. I am glad to have you as a regent in the college, and I'm content to dine with you. But I'd prefer it nonetheless if you'd look for other rooms.'

'Principal Gilchrist has promised me this one.'

Robert flushed. 'Then I shall look elsewhere myself.'

'You don't have to do that. Listen, may I call you Robert? I took my licence here six years ago. Nicholas Colp was my room-mate. We were the same in age, but he was paid for by the burgh, a foundation boy. He was supposed to light the fire and make the bed, that sort of thing, you know. But in the event we were friends. I remember my father sent me a coverlet embroidered in orange and blue. We huddled under it at night, arguing our themes long after dark. I gave it to him when I left.'

'He has it still,' whispered Robert. 'I have put it in the chest.'

'Truly? Then I'll take it to him. He'll be glad to have it, for the evenings grow chill. But you understand what I am saying? I lived for four years with Nicholas Colp. It hasn't put me off sharing as much as it seems to have you. But, of course,' he added thoughtfully, 'he hadn't been accused of sodomie or murder at the time.'

The regent looked stricken. 'Who told you?'

'Professor Giles Locke, the provost of St Salvator's. Another good friend. He has the care of Nicholas there. Though I prefer Giles as friend to physician. He has what I call the blustering flux. It's a common affliction in men of his class. Equivocates – you know the sort of thing: "if he fart or piss clear divers times by the wax of the moon on a Thursday and *if* (but not also) he should happen to down a pint of crushed lettuce without it runs out, then he surely shall live; or else not.'"

In spite of himself, Robert smiled. 'You think it a jest then?'

'By God, I do not,' Hew said fiercely. 'I would like to be told what to think, for thus far I know nothing. I'm a lawyer, or intend to be.' For the first time he acknowledged it. 'I have not come to chart the movements of the spheres but to find out the truth about Nicholas Colp. I hoped to make a case in his defence. And yet the case is lost before it starts, for Nicholas is sick, and no one else will talk to me. I can discover nothing, nor even if he's likely yet to live to face the charge.'

Robert stared down at the floor. 'It would be better if he died.'

'So everyone tells me. Tell me why *you* think so, Robert. Do I take it you heard him confess?'

'To murder? No. And not to sodomie, it's true. But still . . .'

'But still you think him guilty? You have lived with him here in these rooms and you know in your heart he committed these crimes?'

'I'm sorry, but I have to think it. Though I swear he was out of his mind.'

'Then we have a beginning, for that's a defence.' Hew told him earnestly. 'I would like you to tell me what you know. Begin with Nicholas, how you came to be friends, if you were, or what your relationship was. If it changed, tell me how. Leave nothing out. Then tell me all you can recall about the weeks before the deaths.'

Robert proved a willing witness after all. He made his speech as though he had rehearsed it, like a student called from class to make his last responsion in the hall.

'I have known him for almost two years, since first I came here to St Leonard's to replace a Master Gray, who died of a cankerous blot. Before that I was working in Glasgow. Nicholas had shared with Angus Gray. He was looking for someone else to help him meet the cost. I had enough money to rent rooms of my own, but he seemed honest, and I liked him. He helped me prepare for the term. My students were about to begin their third year, then shortly to proceed to their examination. His were in their second year, but he'd taught the texts before. He was a conscientious teacher, working tirelessly on behalf of anyone who struggled, reading over the principles time after time. Last year he helped me take the magistrand class through their final disputations, though he had bachelors then of his own. You'll find them ahead of their year, if you really mean to take them. We got on well enough, though he was often quiet and reflective, somewhat serious and sad. He had very little money, save what the students brought. He might have expected,' he added ruefully, 'to have reaped a little more at the end of this year, when his crops come to fruition. The parents are generally grateful. But I don't think he cares for money. He thinks we favour rich men's sons, and has complained against it. It isn't true, of course; they still have to make their mark. But though he did not make distinctions when he taught, he has always believed St Leonard's should remain at heart the home of the "poor scholar clerks". That's all but gone now. Well, so we went on, until about two months ago the principal Gilchrist asked him to tutor a boy whose father wished him to matriculate this term. His name was Alexander Strachan, the son of a merchant from Perth, lodged here with his uncle in the town. The father Gilbert's a great friend – if that's the word – of our man Gilchrist. He deals in all manner of spices and wines as well as fine cloths. I believe he furnished Gilchrist's cellars both in college and at home.'

'Did Nicholas know?'

'Suspected it, I think. He knew that Gilchrist in effect had sold the boy a place, and sold it cheap. In the weeks before the deaths he had become convinced that the principal was hawking places out to boys without the wit to last the course. Some were underage. Alexander Strachan was himself a little off fourteen.'

'And he put this to Gilchrist?'

'Not directly. He became increasingly bitter and outspoken, making it known more obliquely – abstention from meetings, recalcitrant questions. Gilchrist had asked him to write a masque for his students to perform before the king and the royal commissioners next year. He has a talent, quite surprising, for that sort of thing.'

Hew nodded. 'I remember.'

'But Nicholas threw out so many squibs and wry remarks the principal had started to have doubts, fearing he would find himself exposed before the court. He asked,' his voice began to falter, 'he asked me to look at the play.'

Hew had noted his discomfort. He would return there later, probe the spot, like Giles Locke with his lancet, but for now he would set it aside. He wanted Robert's confidence. He stood by the window, his back turned away, looking outside, and listened intently. 'Yet Nicholas accepted the post as tutor.'

'Yes, naively, at first. Or perhaps for the money; he still had to eat. Later I think he grew fond of the boy. But it was clear he did not want him to matriculate. We discussed it, because I should have had him in my class.'

'Was there something in their closeness you thought odd?'

'No, not then. But he did once say . . . he thought the boy had seemed distressed and he himself was troubled. He felt the family asked too much. Though he said the child worked hard. The uncle was a bully. Nicholas disliked him.'

Hew nodded. 'Aye, I met him. Do you know the Strachans?'

'I confess, not well. My father knows them slightly, Gilbert more than Archie. Though Archie is the master of the gild of weavers, and likes to think himself a figure in the town. The daughter Tibbie, now,' unexpectedly, he grinned, 'is something of a strumpet. Worth going down to kirk upon the Sabbath just to see her toss her curls. Her mother Agnes Ford is a steady, sober woman, and a blacksmith's daughter, I believe.'

'You draw their likeness well,' encouraged Hew. 'Now tell me what you know about Alexander's death. Where was Nicholas?

How did he seem to you? What happened in the hours and days before he died?'

'On the Saturday, Nicholas went to the house to hear the boy's lesson. He did not return to college until much later that night. I was already in bed when I heard him come in. When I got up for chapel on Sunday he was still asleep. Sometime in the afternoon, Mistress Ford came to college to report the boy had gone, but Nicholas could not be found. He turned up for the evening service, dirty and dishevelled. There was blood on his shirt. It looked as though he had slept in his clothes.'

'Did you ask about the blood?'

'He said he'd done it with his pocket knife. He'd been whittling driftwood, I think that's what he said. Apparently the blade had slipped and gone in very deep. It did not seem plausible. But he was wounded, certainly.'

As Robert seemed to falter, Hew encouraged him. 'Go on. What happened next?'

'He must have had the message, for he went on to the Strachans'. I did not see him leave. I came back to the room and read until dark. Then I fell asleep. It was almost daybreak when he returned. He was shivering, seeming distracted, and drenched to the bone. He had walked for hours on the shore through the rain. His shirt was stiff with blood. He told me that they'd found the boy dead, but said nothing more. He crept between the sheets and shivered through the dawn, sometimes laughing, sometimes crying. He didn't speak of it for days. But later I discovered it was Nicholas who found the boy. He was wrapped in some sort of cloth. He lifted out the body and held it in his arms. So the blood was Alexander's. They found the weapon lying in the bed beside him, a shuttle from the loom. There were fragments of bone and of thread in his hair. Nicholas carried him upstairs into the house, still very calm, and helped the weaver's wife to lay him out upon the bed. Then he walked on his own through the night. I'd like to stop now, if I may, and take a drink.'

Hew nodded gently. 'Please. I'll ask the college servant for some wine.'

The Lye

'Tell me about the letters.'

Robert was caught by surprise. Hew had sent out to the cook-shop for pottage and pie, and with a little bread and wine they made their dinner on a board beside the window, talking of desultory things in the afternoon light. The drizzle fell softly. The clouds were beginning to clear. Aristotle's *De Caelo* lay open before them, and as they touched upon the motions of the meteors and the spheres his fears had begun to recede. In a dull voice he answered, cupping his hands round the broth as though to draw strength from the warmth of the bowl.

'I found them in the chest.' Robert paused to look at Hew, who did not comment, then went on. 'I was looking for . . . I found . . . I did not read them all, but there were letters and poems from the boy. I gave then to the coroner the day that the dyer was killed.'

'Why?'

'They were evidence.'

'Of what?'

'Of unnaturalness between them. They were letters of affection. And the poems . . . were of a nature most corrupt and intimate.'

'*Unnatural and filthie converse.*' Hew spoke almost to himself, as if reciting from a script.

'Well . . . I believed so,' Robert confessed. 'Indeed they could be read that way. In the mind of the boy . . . I have the sense that he felt overwhelmed. I don't say Nicholas encouraged it. I truly think he did not know, until he had the letters, how Alexander felt. But they were many hours together, quite alone. I think the boy felt homesick and friendless. It was natural perhaps he should be drawn to Nicholas, who was always the most patient of teachers. But from the letters it would seem that there was more than that. The boy seemed increasingly anxious and bold. My sense is that he struggled with his feelings until he found he must express them. He felt very deeply, it seems.'

'And do you think the feelings were returned?'

There was a long pause before Robert replied. 'I have asked myself the question many times, and yet I have not found the answer. That Nicholas might hold him in affection, yes; perhaps even love. It is harder to imagine carnal lust. For if he has a fault it lies in his detachment, almost as if he does not feel the frailties of the flesh. He goes for days without eating or sleeping, sometimes without drinking; he seems indifferent to sickness or cold.'

'Has it occurred to you that he may use these deprivations as a way of self-control?' suggested Hew. 'Excuse me if I play the devil's advocate. Go on. You found the letters, and were shocked to learn their content. I allow they suggest an unnatural bond with the boy. But what gave you to think they had a part to play in Alexander's death? Was there blackmail implied?'

'Not that I saw. In a way it was clearer than that, for they were speckled with blood, and wrapped in a blood-crusted gown. I last saw Nicholas wearing that gown the day before the boy died, when he left here to give him his lesson. He had not worn it since. I remarked particularly that he did not have it on in church on Sunday evening. It was a cool night, and he was already ill. And as I said before, he seemed on the edge of his wits. I believe that he had read the letters and the poems, or else the boy confessed his feelings. Perhaps Nicholas repulsed him, and there was a fight. Perhaps even,' Robert brightened slightly, 'the boy came at him with his pocket knife, inflicting the wound he sustained in the thigh, and Nicholas took up the shuttle to defend himself, but hit out too hard. Might that be it, do you think? Could it be self-defence?'

Hew did not reply.

'In any case,' Robert went on miserably, 'he suffered so deeply from guilt and remorse it drove him further to the brink of madness when he learned the wrong man was to be hanged for his crime. I spoke with him before he left the college, on the day that he took ill. He was determined to speak to Tom Begbie, though he would not say why.'

'You think that was remorse?' Hew asked uneasily.

'Aye, what else then?' Robert looked surprised. 'When I found the letters and the provost told me Nicholas had died, I realised he had meant to make confession, and I set the letters out before the court. But,' he dropped his head to his hands, 'it has all gone awry, because Nicholas still lives, and the coroner has put him to the horn and holds him in the Auld College to be charged with the foulest and filthiest of crimes.'

'And Tom was freed?' Hew concluded.

'He already was free. A young lass from the country came to speak for him. She claimed he'd been with her all night.'

They sat together awhile without words, Hew going through in his mind what Robert had told him, turning it over, looking for flaws, swilling and sipping the wine. The dregs in his stomach ran cold. Eventually he spoke. 'You give a motive for the murder of the boy, but what about the dyer? Why should he kill him, and why did he go there that day? It makes no sense.'

Robert sighed. 'The coroner suggested that the dyer knew about his closeness to the boy. It was like him, he was always prying. Dyer was an elder of the kirk, and he pursued his offices most fiercely. He was well known to the college, for he often made complaint about the students' conduct. Nothing pleased him more than punishing transgression, or sniffing out some secret shame or lewd and filthie crime.'

A man like that would have to have had enemies,' observed Hew.

'No doubt. It hardly matters, for the fact is that Nicholas was in both places and as good as caught red-hand. Do you think the crown will trouble to investigate? They do not know, or care, how

Nicholas could kill the dyer when he was all but dead himself. What matters is that he was there, he did it, there's an end to it. And I gave them the proof,' Robert ended wretchedly.

Hew was uncertain how to proceed. 'I confess, it looks bad,' he acknowledged. 'But there may be something else that we have not considered. A feud between the Dyers and the Strachans, or someone with a grudge against the gilds. As long as Nicholas has not confessed, there must be hope. I'll go looking at the dyer's house this very afternoon.'

For the dyer, he believed an answer might be found. But did it matter after all? The evidence about the boy had chilled him to the bone.

The road to the dyer's house was quiet. Few people seemed to pass this way. Hew left his horse at the west port stables and walked the muddy path along the Kinness Burn. At length he saw a smoking cottage chimney, then a little house set back within a ragged garden overgrown with weeds, a row of sodden sheep-skins curling by the door. A small sallow girl sat among them combing out the fleece. In a wooden box beside her someone squalled.

Jennie Dyer was bored. The little ones grubbed round her in the dirt and burrowed like insects, fractious and squabbling, spoiling the wool while the youngest one bawled. She felt like bawling herself. She had wanted to go to the town to the market today, but Will had said no, she must stay at home with the weans, for her mother was sick. She stuck out her lip in disgust. They hardly needed minding now that Nan was almost eight, and big enough to stop the weans from falling in the burn, or big enough at least to fetch the boys to hoik them out. It was worse than when her father was alive, for the boys had to do what he told them; he'd never favour Will or Jem and she was his pet: 'Och, Janet, let the lass have her bit play!' And there might be sucket candie then. And when he was cross – which was often – she would drop her lip low and call up the tears, soundlessly and soft, not letting them fall. And he'd pull her down onto his knees, reeling her in like a slippery fish and spin her and tickle her roughly, kissing the curls of her hair. Only he had understood how wrong it was for her to live among the stink of dyes, to go into the town to be sneered at by the country folk. When she was grown she meant to be a lady, and live in a grand house on the south street with braw painted ceilings and embroidered pictures on the walls, everything smelling of flowers.

There would, of course, be a price, but she knew how to pay it. She would have to pay it anyway. For her mother lived here in this stew and worked hard all her days and still she paid the price; now she was with child again. They took her for a fool if they thought she did not know. She remembered all too well the last time when the baby came, and father had said words that even Will was shocked to hear, godly as he was. And then he had wept and prayed and prayed and wept to God and had them crying, praying half the night while Mother almost died. 'Why did they not *learn*?' she heard Jem whisper tearfully to Will, and Will had said when Father died, 'At least this one's the last.'

There was a stranger coming. She pulled the baby to her hip in a gesture of protection, but the baby struggled crossly and continued to bawl.

'What's wrong with it?' Hew asked her mildly.

'Don't know. Perhaps it wants a penny for candie.' She was ever hopeful.

'It looks a bit little for candie. Has it any teeth?'

'Three. And it likes to suck on comfits. Piece of rag soaked in honey, it likes that. So do Geordie and Susan and Nan.' Three small faces turned towards him.

'And my name is Jennie. And it isn't an *it*, it's a girl. Name of Bess. It likely wants its mother. She has,' she searched to find the word, 'she has the lying-in. She's very sick of it.'

'I expect she is.' Hew squatted down on the grass and gingerly tickled the baby. 'Hallo, little Bess. There may be a penny for you when I've finished my business with your father.' In an instant the other children dropped their game and crowded expectantly round him.

Jennie played her best card: 'Faither's deid.' The trembling of the lip was only partly feigned. 'We put him in the ground not two days since. He fell into the dye pot and was boiled.'

'I'm truly sorry to hear it. I'll leave something for your mother then.' She could have howled her disappointment. 'And for Bess,' he gave a solemn wink, 'we'll have to see. Who does the dyeing now? For I see there's fleeces still laid out.'

'My brothers. James is at the burn, but Will's out the back with the pots.' She gestured to the house. 'You can go through there if you like, or round by the side. And if you wanted to make water,' she suddenly brightened, 'we'll all turn our backs for a penny. Else the little ones say things and stare.'

'I'll bear it in mind if I'm ever caught short.'

Hew went by the side, turning his face from the barrel of lye which caught at his breath, scalding his throat as he passed. His eyes watered still as he came to the green at the back of the house.

'Good day to you, sir.' Will Dyer stepped aside from the pot and looked at Hew suspiciously. He held a crumbled block of purple litmus in his hands. Since his father's death he had found himself wary of strangers, though this one wheezed and spluttered too conspicuously to pose a serious threat. 'Can I help?'

'I hope so.' Hew had recovered his breath. He fingered strands of wool in variegated shades of violet drying on their frames. 'What extraordinary depth of colour! Will it last?'

'It's likely to fade a bit,' Will admitted. 'But it's a foreign dyestuff I'm improving, litmus mixed with woad and cochineal. We're working on the set. It's the mordant makes you splutter. It catches in the throat. Was it purples you were wanting?'

'Saffron. I've a dozen old shirts I'd like to have dipped. I've just returned home from abroad, and I find the French fashions too fine for my current employment. My name is Hew Cullan. I'm about to start as regent in the college of St Leonard, but the townsfolk seem to take me for some foreign merchant and charge me to fit. I find I can't afford to keep the colour of my cloth.'

Will laughed. 'We're a bit behind on the leines. I've been busy with this. But I'll have a pot of saffron ready by the middle of next week if you would like to bring them then. How long were you in France, sir? I'd like to go myself to see the dyes. There's merchants come to market but you cannot trust their wares.'

'Five or six years, more or less. They've very fine silks. Ice greens and blues. There's a salmon-pink shot watered silk in fashion with the gentry now. I've seen nothing like it here.'

'Indeed? I don't suppose you know how they make it?'

'I fear not. But I never saw purples as vibrant as this.'

'Think you not?' Will was pleased. 'It doesn't go well in the town. It's no Alexander Blue.'

'I'm sorry?'

'It's a sick enough jest, Master Cullan, forgive me. The wound's a bit raw. You may know my father was recently drowned in a vat of dark purple; it wasn't this one, but more of a puce. We won't make it again. But folk prefer the blue.' He waved at the pot. 'It's named for a poor murdered lad who died in a shop in the town. His body was wrapped in some cloth of a similar shade. Since then we cannot make enough of it, for dresses, drapes and shawls.'

'How singular. But my condolences for your loss. The little lass told me her father had drowned.'

'She thinks it was an accident.' Will looked at him shrewdly. 'But if you're from the college you'll have heard of the charge against Master Colp.'

'Forgive me, I had heard that he was indicted for murder, but I didn't know of the connection or I might never have come. I hope it doesn't cause offence? Please accept our deep regret and sadness for your loss.'

'I thank you, but there's no offence. I'll gladly dye your shirts. And in truth, I do not believe that Colp did it. In fact I'm sure he did not.'

'Truly? I thought they had caught him red-hand?'

'Quite the reverse. It was I who found him. Colp was lying sick and insensible by the front step. I thought he was dead. He could not have finished a mouse in a trap, the state he was in.'

'They say that madmen have great strength,' suggested Hew, 'even in adversity. Supposing he was mad?'

'Even allowing for that, he still could not have done it. I don't believe he even saw my father.' Will held out his hands. They were crusted with lichen and livid with dye. 'Call this red-hand, if you will. My father was struck on the back of the head, and then tipped, *while he lived*, into the great pot of dye. The grass is still spattered with purple. The killer must be marked on his hands and his clothes. Look at these nails, sir. It never comes off. But when I turned over Nicholas Colp, I found not a mark or a spot.'

Hew returned through the house in search of the children, reflecting on what Will had said. He found them still outside, building walls of mud and stone to make a babies' castle in the yard. Stooping to admire it, he felt into his pockets for a pile of shiny pennies which he laid out on the ramparts one by one. 'There's a penny for you all, and there'll be sixpence for your sister who looks after you. It's Jennie, is it not? You're a good girl to mind them, and the littlest so fretful. You might fetch her some milk. It will be better for her teeth than sucket candie don't you think? But I expect you'd like some ribbons or a gingerbread horse from the fair?'

She nodded and solemnly stretched out her hand. He held back a moment. 'There's a thing I would like you to help me with. Do you always play here?'

'Aye, or down by the burn.'

'Can you remember, Jennie, if you played here on the day your father died? Did anyone come by the house?'

She shook her head. 'We were down at the stream with Mother, all of us, helping. Except for the boys. They'd gone into town to do work for the weaver. Only Father was here. That's why no one came to help him when he fell. There was no one but the man.'

'What man?'

'The one that was ill. Will said he must have come after. He found him close to where you're standing, by the door. But I never saw him come. You can't see to the house, where we were.'

'And no one passed by on the road?'

'I think I saw a lass, coming up from the fields to the town. She didn't want us. She's not from the kirk, so I don't know her name. But maybe it wasn't that day.'

She thought she might tell him the truth, but of course she could not. For there had been a man, a fine one at that, dressed in a long dark-green cloak, like the pelt of a mole and muffling his face, and gloves and a matching green hat.

She had left her mother and the bairns at the burn and come back to the house to make use of the pot. For so they were always supposed to, every last drop to be saved for the lye. She had hung on as always as long as she could, hoping to cheat necessity, knowing always that necessity would beat her in the end. But as she ran clutching her skirts towards the house and its familiar smells, something inside her gave way. She had lifted her dress as high as her head and crouching down by the wall in the lavender bed, had voided her stream wet and warm into the spiky sweetness of the earth. Instead of the stoor and the stench she smelled flowers. She was free. Then she had heard a discreet little cough, a snort of laughter right behind her. And pulling down her skirts in her confusion, dabbing at the dampness that appeared to spot her dress, she had seen him smiling at her, stroking the hairs of a darkened-red beard.

'A thousand pardons, little lass. It seems you and I had similar intentions, though I'd thought to use your father's barrel in a more conventional mode. But perhaps there's no one home, that you disport yourself in front of it?'

She whispered, blushing, 'Father's out the back; there's no one in the house.'

'Indeed? Well unlike you I prefer to be private. It's a place I'm ashamed to be seen. Here's a shilling. If you run off now as fast as you can and let me loosen off in peace, child, and don't tell your friends and family I came by, I'll make up your father's losses in the bucket and I won't tell your mother I saw you bare-arsed.'

He laughed aloud as she fled, not even peeping backwards through the trees to watch him fetch his thing out by the pot. She had the shilling still, sewn in a little pocket in her dress, close and warming next to her heart.

Hew was looking at her. 'And the little ones saw nothing? No? I thank you. Here's sixpence for the lye.'

'What lie? I have not lied to you, sir, you have no cause to say it. I'll tell my da . . . my brothers!' To her dismay she could not stop the tears. He knelt by her side in concern.

'Hush, child, there, I don't mean to doubt you. I meant instead the lye for the cloth . . . a bawbee for the jakes. I find I have no call at present to make water. Here, take a shilling, don't cry.'

Why indeed should she lie, he was wondering. What might she know? And who was the lass she had spied on the road?

Jennie dried her eyes. Maybe she would run away, and make a better life. She knew ways to make a shilling now, and more than one. This man had paid as much for tears as the other had for silence. Or had that been for showing off her arse? She wasn't sure. She knew it did not matter. She could give it all, her secrets, silence, tears and lies, to please a man who dandled her. Who else would love her now her da was gone?

Hamesucken

Hew returned to Kenly Water as the mists began to fall, reining his horse through the haar to the track. He felt Dun Scottis tense beneath him, quivering hot, picking reluctantly over the stones. The rubble path dissolved into the landscape, flowing loose as water from the shoreline to the sky. At last they saw the yellow smudge of lamplight bleeding through the edges of the fog. The windows of the tower house flared with candles, row upon row, spiking the mist with the scent of their smoke. Hew dismounted gratefully and walked the last yards to the gate, where Meg ran up to greet him, crying out, unshod with streaming hair and wanton as a wean expecting toys. He held her at arm's length, perplexed at this wildness, chilled and remote in the lap of the fog. But Meg was ablaze, aflame in the candlelight, kissing him, prattling off questions, pulling him in to the warmth of the fire.

'The haar came so thick we were feart you were lost, Hew. You're late! Come then, your cloak! Leave the horse for the groom. What's the news? I've physic prepared for your friend.'

In response he felt heavy and dull, having little to tell but the bare scraps and rags of the day. At length the bright flush of her chatter fell away. She fetched them slabs of beef and sippet wine. They ate and drank in quietness, curled by the edge of the fire. Matthew too was dour and silent. He frowned a little, looking at the pages of a book, until his daughter stretched out on the hearthrug like a cat, declaring that she was worn to a shade and was off to her bed. Hew downed his cup and followed her, his footsteps trailing hers upon the stairs.

In the dark folds of his father's house he slept like a child, in a blue Flanders coverlet patterned with leaves. Still he felt cold, even here, the dense feather mattress drawn closed from the draughts, thick pleats of yellow velvet sewn with white and scarlet flowers. Against the pitter of the moths he dreamt of violet-puddled shrouds. He saw Nicholas lying, a flower in his mouth, a dark fragrant bloom of bright blood. He knelt down to touch it. It burst like a poppyhead spilling its seed, streaming black blood to his hands. Nicholas screamed. Hew dreamt the sound had woken him, but still the dream went on. He heard the voice again and woke at last to find himself still cloaked within the choking drapes and fabrics of the bed. Agape in the blackness, he wrenched at the air. The drapes fell apart and the shadows reformed, shaping the windows, the closet, the door, the pallor and the coolness of the stone. For a while he lay watchful, allowing the fear to subside. Sleep did not come. He rose and lit a candle, feeling for the floor. In the depths of the hallway the lamplight still burned. He opened the door to find Matthew awake, stirring a pot by the fire. The old man turned to smile at him, ghostly in the flame.

'Come away with you, Hew. I heard you cry out. I've a posset on the boil. You'll sit here awhile, will you not?'

Hew pulled up a gossip-chair, shaking his head. He felt raw to the bone.

'A little wine. I thank you, no. I confess to you, sir, I'm sick to the stomach tonight.'

'As you will then, some wine. A little talk perhaps, as physic for the soul. I'll set the pot here on the hearthstone. See, it thickens nicely. In an hour or so we'll sup it, for you'll likely change your mind.'

They sat in silence while he stirred, Hew thinking, 'If he sups it through his beard without a spoon I'm like to spew into the flames, God help us both.' It looked like vomit, freshly brewed. He took the goblet of wine in his hands and cradled it close. His father was watching him keenly, nurturing the fire.

'You're shivering, child. Won't you go back to your bed?'

Hew smiled, for he felt like a child, frightened from sleep by his dreams.

'It isn't the cold, only thoughts. And wild dreams that woke me.

I'll drink a cup to chase the ghosts before I go. Do you remember, Father, how we used to beat them from the bed?'

'Your mother's face when once we brought the drapes down was enough to fright them all. I doubt they ever dared come back again.'

There was silence, a crack of sharp flame, and then Matthew said gently, 'Have you come to the truth of it then?'

Briefly, Hew recounted the events of the day. His father stirred and listened all the while. At length he left the posset on the hearth.

'Not Colp who killed the dyer. Nor the son, who does the dyeing now the dyer's dead. A pretty pun. Then could it be the wife perhaps? She does well enough without the man.'

'The woman's with child. It could scarcely be her.'

'She would not be the first. Consider it hamesucken then . . .'

'I had not considered it.'

'To come like a friend, but with evil intent,' Matthew glanced around, 'even here, to the home, where a man is most unguarded and lax.' He glowered into the posset pot suspiciously. Hew felt the dampness of the fog beneath his shirt. 'Hamesucken,' he objected, 'is a worse charge still.'

'True, a little worse,' Matthew acknowledged. 'But I believe we may acquit your friend of it. Now, let's suppose that someone with a grudge despatched the dyer. Meanwhile Nicholas comes by to beg a pinch of saffron for his shirts, when falling faint with fever, and the *smell* . . .'

Hew smiled and shook his head. 'You were lost to the law. You plead the case so plausibly I almost could believe it – aye, I do believe it – if it wasn't for the letters and the poem. It is the *boy*. The dyer counts nothing in this. But for the boy, I cannot find a plea, another explanation, but that Nicholas was guilty of his death. I'm not sure I can speak for him. The penalties are cruel. Perhaps it would be better if he died.' His voice had dropped low. Matthew leant close.

'Look, though, Hew,' he urged, 'the case is not proved. There is a wildness in the letters, but it's coming from the child. How can we know how Nicholas responded? Perhaps he corrected or counselled the boy, and kept the letters safely for his own defence. They do not prove he was complicit in the boy's affections. He received them, but he did not write them.'

'The evidence is plain enough. He wrapped them in a blood-soaked gown.'

'Aye, there's that,' conceded Matthew. 'You must ask him to explain it.'

Hew shook his head hopelessly. 'Ask him? If only I could!'

'I had forgotten. Meg explained he could not speak.'

'Then I wish she would explain to me. She keeps her counsel close. As you do, sir,' retorted Hew.

'What counsel can you mean? The broken jaw? You spoke of it yourself.'

'It came as no surprise to her. And here's another puzzle. Giles refused to let me see him. He claims he's close to death yet leaves him unattended half the day. And as for Meg, he spun some tale about a woman's courses – now then, sir, I see you start; I knew it for a lie. She's bright and wild as any child tonight. Do you suppose I don't detect the change in her?'

Matthew rubbed his beard. 'Her courses, you say? Well, in truth, boy, you do make me start. For what should I know of such things? I wonder you allude to them. Your doctor knows nothing. He probes in the dark. Don't you know that physicians are fools? And yet I do know why he's anxious to conceal your friend, and I thank God for it. For it involves Meg, as you say. Be quiet and I'll tell you. Don't interrupt awhile. You really must acquire the skill of letting people talk if you would practise playing advocate. I'll lose my place with your forever butting in.'

Hew, who had not said a word, swilled down his reply with a deep draught of wine and stared into the fire. Satisfied, Matthew began. 'I have my own ghosts which keep me from my bed these darkening nights, and most concern your sister. I am afraid I was wrong to allow her to be drawn into this. She is in danger, and what I am about to tell you must be kept secret, even from your friend the doctor. You will recall your mother died when Meg was born, and for a while it seemed unlikely that the lass would live. She was a scabbed, unholy creature, born before her time, still covered with the hairs that wrapped her in the womb. You'll understand I thought she was the devil's child, a matricide, livid-black and squalling. I wanted to cast her aside. But the midwife looked after her. The wife was Annie Law, who stayed with us until she died four years ago. She took Meg to her home and gave her suck – I know not how for Annie Law was ancient even then. And in a month or so the infant seemed to thrive. The coarse hair had rubbed off and she grew quite a mane of black curls, and she smiled with her mother's green eyes. She was beautiful, Hew. She came home to us.

'And for the next few years we stayed there in the High Street. I took you into town to see the courts, and by and by you joined the grammar school. Meg was ay a dreamer; she used to gaze out of the casement up at nothing sometimes. When we spoke to her, she scarcely seemed to hear. Annie said she saw her mother, that she had the gift; I bade her hold her tongue. But the child became ever more distant. She slept very deep, as if nothing would wake her. At last when she was six years old upon a bright June day she went out with Annie to play on the green. The sky was cloudless fair. I was at the sessions. I can still recall the case. You were in the schoolhouse at your books, and Annie, she came running into court to tell me Meg had had a great seizure there on the green, frothing and foaming. She couldn't be waked. The men were feart to lift her. They called her possessed. And Annie Law carried her home. I knew at last what I had always feared; she had the falling sickness. It was in your mother's blood.'

At last Hew broke his silence. 'She has the falling sickness, and for all these years . . . I took her into town. The noise and dust disturbed her . . . You should have *told* me, sir!'

'She would not have it,' Matthew answered sadly. 'She did not want it so.'

'But I have *never* known. And all those years ago . . .'

'You were just a child. For pity, Hew, how could I have told you? Your sister suffered cruelly, I'm ashamed to say. Blistered and purged, bloodied and blessed, she howled at the doctors and spat at the priest. I left the town and courts, and put you to school, to bring her here, where she could live in safety and in quietness. Annie told us she was blessed, not cursed by God. She planted the gardens with herbs. She showed Meg prophylactics, how she might protect herself and so deflect the fits. And so we have lived here in quietness since, Meg learning how to grow the plants that keep her well, away from the stoor of the town.'

They sat silent for a while, until Hew remarked thoughtfully. 'Some would say, of course, that Annie was a witch.'

Matthew whispered, 'There were some that did. And so you understand why I have kept this quiet. I did not know myself if Annie was a witch. I do not know it now.'

His son looked up at him and smiled. 'I don't believe in them,' he answered simply.

Matthew was taken aback. 'You don't believe in witchcraft, Hew? Is that your education? It's a dangerous position.'

'Aye, I am aware of it. I do not make the claim too loud. But the truth is I give thought to many things, and you may call it education if you will. I have not believed in witches since I was a child. Tell me, though, do you?'

His father sighed. 'I have seen them drowned and burned and strangled at the stake, and they have wrung my heart. I have heard them confess in fear for their families, hearing their children distracted by tortures. I have seen brave women hang, wise and skilled like Annie in the healing arts, because their neighbours cried them for a witch. And there were others, too, spiteful, twisted crones who wished their neighbours ill but scarcely had the wits to make them so. Whether they were witches or were not, I was powerless to defend them. I don't know if witches exist, but I know that where they are suspected, good people, brave people, die.'

'And so you could not trust me,' Hew concluded quietly.

'You forget we have not seen you since you were eighteen. Meg felt she did not know you. And she was half ashamed. We should have known you, Hew.'

'What has happened since to change her mind?'

'The matter's this. You left her there with Nicholas. Hush, I don't reproach you, it was unforeseen. But Nicholas relapsed. She found him racked with lockjaw, taut and jerking. And because she has the sickness, and is skilled in natural arts, she did her best to help him, and she gave him hemlock. She sent him to a sleep as deep as death.'

'What then, she poisoned him!'

Matthew shook his head. 'She had medicines and she used them. The little that remained she took herself. The doctor found her faint from her exertions. He does not know about her sickness, but he understood at once what she had done to Nicholas. And so he is afraid.'

'I know Giles. He's a good man. And he will not think it witchcraft,' Hew assured him. 'He will understand.'

'His fear is more pragmatic, that the patient will be given up for dead. I have seen it in the hills, where shepherds have told tales of sheep that grazed on hemlock, seeming dead and flayed, coming bleating back to life. But in a day or two your friend will wake. The hemlock, by the by, is growing in the garden by the carrot tops. It's not unlike sweet cicely to look at. If you've a mind to make a pottage, have a care.' Matthew forced a smile.

'God love us and save us!'

'*Amen.* But come now, a cup!' He turned to the pot, where the posset was bubbling and crusted, and ladled it carefully into a bowl. 'Sup slowly now, to ease your sleep. Here's cinnamon wafers and nutmeg besides.'

Reluctantly, Hew drank his share, sipping the spray through the spout of the pot. The mess of froth foamed sweet and hot. He swallowed gingerly, allowing the sweetness to swill to his bowel, warming the cup to his hand. Matthew neither drank nor turned to look at him, absorbed in dampening down the fire. Presently Hew spoke, his voice a little thickened by the brew, polite across the awkwardness. 'A pretty thing.'

'The silver cup? Your mother's piece. She ay liked pretty things.'

'Aye? I never saw a caudal pot so delicate. The channel here is so fine it scarcely allows for the sup of the whey.'

'She never cared for custards much.'

'The spout seems better purposed for the weaning of a child.'

'Indeed? I believe it may have served that purpose once or twice.'

'Or for the sick perhaps. For one who might not eat, the stream of liquid flowing here just so.'

'I think it very like,' the older man agreed. 'You are decided then?'

Hew shook his head. 'To take the case? I see no other way. We all of us are drawn too deep in this. Besides, it is my fault.'

'Have courage. Meg will bring him back to life. I believe in her, Hew.' His face belied the lack of passion in his voice.

'Aye, I think you do. But tell me this, how can she do it? She has not the strength to be taken back and forth. Now I must take up lodgings in the college. She cannot stay there, nor with Giles Locke.'

'There is somewhere else, a place where she might stay. I've long been thinking of it, for she cannot live alone when I am gone. With her sickness I despair of a husband for her. Then consider this. A cousin of your mother living in the town has taken a young wife. She's nervous and frail, now newly with child. Her man's a merchant on the south street, often gone from home. The lassie frets and pines for want of gentle company. This man has offered Meg a place with them, if she will bring some comfort to his wife while he's abroad. Indeed, he's asked for her now several times. Our Meg's a stubborn wench, and will not go. But now, as suits your present purpose, we are likely to persuade her. Once she's there . . . I am an old man, Hew, we may convince her she will come home when the child is born and Nicholas is well. You and I knowing, it is not to be so.'

'What do they want with her?' Hew sounded sceptical. 'Is she to be a serving girl until she has a seizure and they turn her out of doors?'

Matthew did not meet his gaze. 'They know about her affliction and are prepared to overlook it,' he answered wearily. Your mother's family have always been close. At heart Robin Flett is a good enough man. And his wife may be kind to Meg.'

'*Kind* is not enough. She shall not be a servant while I live.' But as Hew spoke he saw his father's face. The old man's eyes were bright with tears. 'And yet it cannot hurt her for a while. We'll speak of it tomorrow, when we both have slept.'

'Aye, goodnight, my son.' His father wiped his eye. 'The fire begins to smoke. Take up the lamp. There's little light enough upon the stair.' He added quietly, 'Nor yet below.'

Matthew sat motionless, watching Hew go. Presently he rose, a little slow and stiff. He did not follow his son, but walked towards the windows shuttered from the night. He fumbled with the catch, unfastened it, and peered outside into the rasping dampness of the fog. The dawn brought neither light nor sound, the baffled seabirds mute as clouds, his farmlands unfamiliar, fused and indistinct. He drew the plaid a little closer round his shoulders, momentarily confused, as though uncertain of the place. The room was almost dark. He stood awhile, then stooped to light a candle, now a second, shying from the frankness of their glare. From pockets deep obscured within the darkness of his robes he drew a strand of beads, and kneeling down, he prayed for both his children in the gloom, whispered on and on until his eyes began to close.

Anatomies

The physician wiped his hands. He could hear the servant in the other room, lifting the shutters and pouring out water. He longed to rinse his teeth. Below him on the little cot Nicholas lay still, his purple mouth split open like a plum. Giles had spent the night by his side, swilling the mouth with salt water and scooping the slush from the folds of his cheeks. He had woken quite by chance to find his patient dying, drowning in blood. Bound skull to craw, Nicholas had bitten his tongue. He lay there unable to swallow, blood beading soundlessly from nostril and lip. Giles had saved his life, stripping off the bandages to clear the blackened carcass of his throat. Now the airways were open, the patient breathed as faint and dreamless as before, sinking back into that strange unconsciousness. But Giles, as he began to set the jaw, had reconsidered. He fetched down his anatomies and spread them on the board beside the bed, squinting through the smoky stub of candle-light at Vesalius, his skeleton: the joints and sinews, skull and jaw, the brittle disc of cartilage that held the bone in place. Presently, he ran thoughtful fingers the length of his patient's face, feeling for the bone in swollen flesh. The jaw shifted, loose and compliant. At last, as the end of the candle gave out, he made his experiment, a little pressure from the thumbs behind the teeth, coaxing the face into shape. He closed his eyes as he felt it snap into place, lips like a flower in the darkness, curling in close. The mouth was still too swollen to meet true, but the teeth were aligned and the tongue safely nestled within. Carefully he retied the cloths and with the cleanest sheet he tucked the body tightly to the bed. He bundled up the soiled strips, balanced on top the basin of mud-coloured water and joined Paul in the outer chamber, closing the door with his foot.

He was wearily dishevelled. The servant looked startled to see him. There was blood on his cheek, on the sleeve and the hem of his shirt. He set down his burden and gestured. 'These rags are for the fire, Paul. Take out the slops.'

Paul did not move. He looked at the blood. 'Had you the surgeon?'

Giles locked the door. He was fretful: 'A fresh shirt, I'll thank you. Some water. The surgeon? No. Mark you, you must burn the rags. Master Colp does very ill, but he is settled now. You'll not disturb him.'

'Is it blood in the basin? What will I do with it then?'

'Do with it?' Giles appeared puzzled. 'Do what you do with the slops. But keep it from the drinking vessels. Have we any bread?'

'I've set out the last of it.' He watched as Giles Locke swilled his mouth and changed his shirt, scrubbing very hard at his gums with a sage leaf.

'Professor Herbert had the surgeon, sir, to his wife,' Paul said carefully. 'He bled her last night. But she does very ill, and Professor Herbert begs you call on her this morning. When you've broken your fast, sir, and dressed.'

Giles peered through the window into the half-light. The haar was beginning to lift, and thin streaks of sunshine forced through the fog. The air tasted stale. And before him a hard little bread-loaf sat on the board like a stone. There must be compensations, after all, for the exertions of the night. Perhaps an egg. He brightened. 'No, I'll be gone. I'll have something from the bakehouse on my way.'

Paul sluiced the bloodied water down the ease pipe, whistling softly. The liquid puddled gloomily upon the street outside. With luck the rain would wash it clear before his master stepped in it, and he had saved himself the trouble of the journey to Foul Waste. He spat on the edge of the bowl and wiped it with his handkerchief. Locke's weakness was comfits and sweet coffin-crusts.

He would linger awhile in the cookshop. There was time for Paul to take a look at the books. He smiled to himself and hugged close his secret. He would come to her soon. Whistling through his handkerchief, he bundled the soiled clump of rags on the fire and used the tongs to pack up a parcel of shirts for the laundress. Privately, Paul thought it better to have burned the shirts as well, for they would fester till the laundress lumbered down to scour them in the Kinness Burn and lumbered back to college, with the laundry just as black as when it went. But the shirts were French linen, finely stitched and perfumed with lavender under the stoor. He tied back the curtains and straightened the counterpane, nibbled the loaf with a mouthful of ale and swept clear the crumbs on the floor. At last, when all else was ordered and neat, he turned to the books on the shelves round the wall, his pulse already quickening at the thought.

Paul could not read, but his master kept picture books: puppets and sly-looking mannequins, coy blushing lassies and proud-standing men. Once the doctor had caught him admiring them, and laughing had peeled back the pages, frailer than garlic skins, layer upon layer of them, sinews and muscle and bone and blood traffic, rivers of blood coursing deep. Paul could not comprehend. It disgusted him. There were so many leaves there could scarcely be a place for the soul in this repellent flaying bare of flesh and blood. But there among it all a picture of a lass had caught his eye. He was affronted to the core when Giles Locke turned the page and stripped the lass beyond the bounds of decency, but to the very bone. Paul had liked her clothed in all the modest contours of the flesh, beautifully, decently naked. He remembered her sad little face – sad and no wonder – wistful and fair in the swell of her belly and breast, right hand resting coyly on her sex. The left arm lay open, quietly gesturing, modestly calling him, 'Come to me.' He would answer the call.

But to his frustration, even as he ran his fingers through the shelves, he realised that the book could not be found. His master had taken the anatomies – not that Paul knew what to call them

– back into the little chamber where his patient lay. All that remained here were words. For a moment he allowed the disappointment to defeat him, and then almost unthinking, he drew back the curtain that hung by the door, took down the key from its rusted iron hoop, and unlocked it, passing quietly through to the darkness beyond. The doctor was doubtless still deep in his sweetmeats; these promised sweeter, and Paul retreated only once, to take up the lamp from the wall. A quiver of defiance stirred agreeably inside him as he cast its glare about the room.

The chamber was fragrant with garlic and sickness, the air scented sooty and hot. Paul moved quickly. He could see the pile of books by the bedside. The patient lay quite still and soundless. He lifted the lamp where the first book lay open, and the top of a skull appeared cracked like an egg. He turned through the leaves. A mandible grinned at him, wrenched from its face. There were horrors here, but he would not allow them to distract him. And in a moment she was waiting for him shyly on the page. He set down the lantern and smiled, and looking up a little in the cast of its shadow he took in unthinking the lie of the room, books and bed and quiet fire, the clean and decent silence of the corpse.

It was clear to Paul, as the lamp cast its glow on his cheek, that Nicholas was dead, as lifeless and drab as his grey winding clothes. The man was dead beyond a doubt, and Giles Locke had known he was dead, locked with his instruments close with the corpse, for whatever dark purpose Paul was afraid to suppose. The body was bound to the bed, lapped in a winding sheet, soberly, properly dead, but the face was a paper-frail picture, more macabre than any in Doctor Locke's books. The cloths about the head were tied so tight the eyes protruded blankly from their sockets. The lashes were fringed with dry blood.

'What are you doing?' Paul had not heard the steps. His master was watching him, full in the doorway. He thought he saw another figure moving in the room beyond. There was no menace in the voice, but a simple, urgent quietness. He swallowed, afraid.

'I thought . . . I thought I heard a cry.'

'You did not hear it.'

'No.' It was dangerous perhaps, but he said recklessly, 'I did not, sir, because he is dead.'

The doctor was upon him now, taking the lamp in his hands. He glanced at the book by the bed. 'Ah, I see the way of it. Comely, is she not? Do not adjust your dress on my account. If you *asked*, I would show you the pictures.'

Paul burned with shame.

'But for the rest, trust the doctor,' Giles said softly. 'He is not dead. He may however be infectious, so do come away from the cot. Will you take back the book? You don't care to? Then come, there's a risk of lying broken there beside him, if you persist in breathing in his air. The bands have been tied to restrain him. He is indeed very ill, and he sleeps, but you must know he is not dead.'

Their visitor was watching curiously. It was Master Cullan, looking tired and worn, shifting about the room.

Frightened, Paul appealed to him, 'Yon master's dead, sir. There is no breath, no light in the face; he's been gone these last few hours, sir, I would swear it. And I must call the bearers to take him away from here, else . . .'

Hew grasped him by the shoulders. 'Don't you hear your master, Paul; *he is not dead*!'

'Hush, Hew, you're frightening him; come, let him go.' The servant was trembling. Giles Locke took a purse from his pocket. 'Swill out your bowels with strong ale. I recommend it. We do not lie to you, and in a day or two, God willing, we may prove he is not dead. Go with you now.'

Hew cried as Paul fled, 'Are you mad? But think what he'll say to the alewife! He'll have the town here in his wake!'

'He'll have to think twice on it, Hew. We discovered him at his most private pleasures, dampened no doubt by the sight of our friend. I don't think his tastes run so rare. He'll drink to drown his blushes before he dares speak. And if, when he's done, he blurts out the tale, we'll say he's a drunkard and imagined it.

It were easier to reassure him, if you had not put the fear of God in him. For pity, Hew, but need you seem so wild? Have you not slept?'

'No,' Hew replied shortly.

'Nor have I. Your coming cut short all my hopes of my bed or a breakfast. But since you are come, you may see him. Bear witness after all that he lives on.'

Hew followed him reluctantly. He understood Paul's apprehension. In the lamplight he could see no sign of life, though Giles Locke fussed about the bed, paring back the sheets to strip the bandage from the thigh.

'You see the wound? Quite clean. Feel for the heartbeat.'

Hew shook his head. Only the face remained bandaged, pitted and sightless, lips cracked with blood. The mouth appeared to work a little, bubbling as Giles dabbed it with a sponge. Hew hoped he had imagined it, the workings of the hanged man's lips still mouthing their last protests in surprise. But Giles was saying something, '. . . barley to strengthen the bone, garlic and hops and the wild onion flower, which being herbs under Mars and the sign of Aries may strengthen and nurture the head and the face and mend those parts by sympathy, the bones too by antipathy. But the best news is the mandible, which I believe was merely dislocated. And after all, your sister, impressive though she is, has scarcely enough strength to break his jaw. The spasm itself could unsettle the joint. It may go again, but we must remain hopeful. You see, Hew, the bone fits together like this.'

He thumbed through the leaves of a book.

Hew shrugged impatiently, turning away, 'Well then, he'll live?'

'We may have every hope of it. And if you can find me the hour of his birth, I'll draw him a horoscope.'

'What use would that be?'

Giles looked pained. 'Well now, his weakness or strength as controlled by the stars. Let us say that – for argument's sake – I had given him hemlock . . .'

'For argument's sake?' Hew echoed wryly.

'Aye, as I say. Now hemlock is said to hold sway of the skeleton, which is good, but it's governed by Saturn, and so if your friend . . .'

But Hew interrupted, 'Could you cast one for Meg? A horoscope, I mean. She was born in the sign of the twins.'

'Your sister?' The doctor looked grave. 'Does she ail?'

His friend answered cryptically, 'I know not. I'm afraid for her.'

'Ah. Then it's not quite the same. I'm afraid I can't help you. If she were to ask for herself . . .'

'She'll not do that. But would you not consider, if you thought that we might save her?'

'Save her from what? Aye, if she comes, and she's sick, I will do it for nothing. I cannot cure by proxy, and in truth I doubt she needs it. For the present patient, what he lacks is her good care. After all, she saved his life.'

Giles paused, then ever circumspect conceded, 'If he lives, of course. Now, I have a notion that will cheer you. Have you brought that horse of yours?'

Hew grimaced ruefully. 'He's stabled at the west port, costing me a fortune. He's eating twice as much as any other horse, and drinking twice the drink, and he is twice the trouble, voiding twice as much. Besides, he needs a boy to keep him to his stall.'

'Now there's a horse that needs a horoscope,' beamed Giles. 'Bring him to the east sands when I've had my dinner. Let's say one o'clock.'

'Whatever for?' objected Hew.

'Fresh air and sunshine. We'll put him to school!'

The ale cooled the shame from Paul's cheeks. After several more drinks he swaggered a little, bolder in his cups. He had chosen a small tavern shuttered from the street, which overhung the little lane between the marketplace and south street, almost empty at this hour. The inn was a good place to hide. The nether rooms were open through the hours of church and darkness, and the place had secret exits for the college boys who broke the rules of term. One other customer stood by the bar, debating the cost of the wine. He glanced across at Paul, but did not speak. Paul thought he looked familiar, and a little out of place. A merchant perhaps, buying in bulk, for presently the landlord led him to the cellar to inspect the wares. Emboldened by his holiday, Paul ordered yet another jug of ale, leering at the serving girl as she scooped up his coin. He imagined her bare as the lass in the picture book, and took courage to try her, for all she was pimpled and plain.

'Aye, you may look while you drink, but you haven't the money for *that*!'

She'd go ready enough with the college lads, purses or no. His cheeks were aflame once again. It was a small humiliation, one of many, but compounded by the landlord coming with a tray. He supposed that the girl had complained. But the tapster said merely, 'The gentleman there would like to speak with you, once we are done in the cellars. You'll be staying awhile? He'll be up by and by.'

He set down the tray on the board. The flagon was filled with a dark brackish wine, thick as syrup. Paul rose to his feet in alarm. Did the man know him, then? Could he somehow have detected his most secret shame? The landlord stood blocking the way to the door. Whatever exits were provided for the student boys were closed to Paul. He felt the landlord's hand upon his arm. 'Ah, though, stay. But what's your haste? You'll hae another draught.'

The ale was fetched and persuasively poured, and within a few moments the gentleman arrived, drawing his stool next to Paul's.

'You don't mind if I join you? Landlord, fresh cups.'

Paul recognised him now, soberly dressed but with soft polished fingernails, painfully neat in the curl of his beard. An equal to his master right enough, but scarcely a friend. He gulped.

'I was about to go back to my work.'

'Indeed?' the man said pleasantly. 'Then you may take a message to your master. I know you, don't I? You are Giles Locke's man. If he can spare you to the tavern quite so early in the day, he no doubt will excuse you a little while longer. Though I confess I am surprised to see you in this place and at this time, you are certainly well met. Pray you, have some wine. I'm buying for the college, and I like to taste the wares. Sadly, though, I cannot drink the bottle. Oblige me then, and share it. I can see you like a drink.'

The servant flinched. 'My master sent me out here for physic. I was taken bad. A little ale, he says will set the stomach. But I'm quite recovered now.'

'Indeed?' His companion drew close. 'Are you sure? You are a trifle pale. Some brandy wine perhaps would better serve your purpose. Try this, do. My habitual supplier, a man of great integrity, is indisposed of late. We must take our choices as they come, though they be bitter ones. Drink it, man. Not over sweet? A little more will bear the proof. Here, but try a cupful, and I'll not detain you long.'

The wine settled warm on the ale in Paul's belly. He slumped on the stool, defeated, and finished the draught.

'That's better now,' the man was saying, 'well then, you must know me. For you are Giles Locke's man.'

'Aye, the doctor's,' Paul replied thickly. 'You're a professor from the college are ye not, sir? From the south street.'

'I am the principal professor of St Leonard's and your master, of course, is new appointed to the same position at the Auld College, the first mediciner we've had here. He is much admired. So tell me then, how does he do?' Gilchrist answered genially.

'He does well enough,' the servant sniggered.

'No doubt. And his patient, Nicholas Colp? He was one of my regents you know, but no one has seen him these past several days. How does Master Colp in your good doctor's care?'

It was perhaps the wine that began to make Paul feel reckless, the warmth of the tavern, or Gilchrist's soft voice. He had drunk after all far more than he realised of the dense, sweetened drink. Gilchrist's share was hardly touched. At once it seemed to him a grand play, and he snorted, 'How does he do, sir? Well and I'll tell you. He does somewhat ill, for he's dead.'

And he laughed very loud at the jest, so that the tavern girl looked startled to their table. Gilchrist frowned and gestured her away.

'How so, dead? He died this morning? I had word that he was still alive.'

'Aye, that's the *word*. But I'd wager he's been dead, stone dead, these past few days.'

Paul giggled. Tempted to slap him, Gilchrist filled the cup instead with the last dregs of wine and called for a thimble of brandy. 'My friend is unwell.' The brandy wine swallowed, he persisted, 'Well then. What do you mean? Is it a jest?'

'No jest.' Paul leaned forward. Gilchrist shuddered at the hot breath on his cheek as he answered with the drunkard's earnest slur, 'I found him this morning, dead as is dead, sir, long dead. Twas a shock, you understand, and the reason that my master prescribed me drink strong liquor. Which you see,' he was helpless once more, 'I have done, sir.' He belched.

'Aye, aye, but you found him dead you say,' Gilchrist said impatiently. 'Master Locke will have made the arrangements?'

'Nay, sir, not he. All night he was closeted dark with the patient, then this morning he comes out with a *look* to his eye and quite disarranged, in his shirt, and his *shirt*, sir, now mark you, was covered in blood.' Paul paused for effect.

'He was bloodied? That's strange.'

'Aye, sir, so says I.' The servant admired his own cunning. 'So I said to him as innocent as you may please, "Had ye the surgeon?" though I knew no surgeon had passed through the house, for I know my brave master will not call the surgeon. He claims he can't afford one, and must bleed the wretch himself. But you know, sir, my family and I have been bled here at the kirk door every winter time and summer these last twenty years, for fending off the plague, and Mr Parker, sir, has never spilled a *drop*. My master's clothes and hands were red, and there were bandages besides and sheets, and the water pot so black I shrank to touch it. Well then, "No surgeon," says he, "but the patient does ill, very ill, though the crisis has passed.

You must leave the man to rest, Paul. He wants for nothing now."'
Paul gave a hollow laugh. 'That's true enough.'

'But you had not seen a body?'

'Whisht, for I come to it. My master washed and dressed and presently said he would have to go out. He left me behind at my work.'

'Whereupon you disobeyed your master and peeked into the room.'

Paul was convinced enough by his own tale to feel genuinely hurt. 'Peeked, sir? Not I. But the doctor was gone such a very long time, that I was set to thinking of the poor man left alone, without a drop to drink. No nourishment had gone into the place for two or three days. He is a man for all his sins, and I'd not let my dog die of thirst.'

'Truly? How commendable. Have you a dog, do you say?' Gilchrist asked dryly.

'Well, no, sir, no dog, tis a figure of speech. But I thought to offer him drink, sir. As I believed my master had not meant to have been gone so many hours.'

'An act of great charity. Were you not feart of the blood?'

'I had put it behind me. But when I unlocked the door and went into that room with no other purpose than to bring a drink to ease a dying man, I found . . .'

He leant a little closer for the climax. Gilchrist took out his handkerchief.

'Aye, man, well, you found him dead,' he pressed impatiently behind it. 'How can you be sure?'

'I can be sure of it, because my master's books were flat open all round the room, with their pictures of innards and entrails, and his instruments lay wet beside the bed, and the corpse in the sheet, sir . . . my master had *cut off its head.*'

'Good God, the thing was headless?'

'Aye, sir . . . well, no . . . . the head was on him right enough, but tied with ribands, bound together, eyes bulging blinder than a villain on the gibbet. You see, it was an awfu' shock, and so my master chancing in upon the moment sent me here for liquor for a cure.'

'You were discovered with the corpse? Then how did he explain it?'

'He says, sir, bold as you will, "Tush, Paul, tis not as it seems, the man isn't dead, but only seems so." As if without a head he might return to life again, by force of his experiments. And he's quite calm and quiet, only his friend there was angry and feart enough, God knows, to give up the game there and then. Anyway, he persists, "He's not dead, he's not dead," but I know what I saw. So what do you think, sir? Is it witchcraft?'

'I think not,' Gilchrist said softly. His mind had worked quickly. 'Down your voice a little, I will tell you what I think. Doctor Locke is an uncommonly clever man. He has trained among anatomists who believe the physician must dirty his hands if he is properly to comprehend his art. What these men do for instruction is to take apart the frame which God has put together limb by limb, as if in the parts they might make sense of God's whole living mystery of man. In short, they dissect, *anatomise*, Paul. Now, Master Locke's books are filled with drawings of dissections made by other men, and these are most instructive, but there is none so instructive as a fresh corpse to work on. You see,' he went on smoothly, 'the law allows men like Locke perhaps two or three dead men a year, the perpetrators of the most heinous forms of crime, to practise their anatomies within the schools. But there are very strict limits on these, and the doctors, who are good men, mark you, are often frustrated in their yearning to know more about the workings of the flesh. What I think has happened here is this, and in part I blame myself for it, because I gave the man into his hands. Your doctor finds his patient – a murderer, recall – has fortuitously died. The doctor ought at once to give the corpse up for burial. But instead he sees a chance and takes it. Within a day or two, his practice done, he'll sew the whole together, wrap him up and market him again as freshly dead. There's none alive would look upon his face. It is a crime perhaps, yet does no hurt. Consider this: by *dying*, Colp denied the law the right and proper justice of his death. Is there not some justice therefore in this fitting desecration of his corpse?'

'It's horrible,' protested Paul.

'But just. You may let go your burden, for in a day or two your master will give up the last of him for burial. Be aware, if the word were to spread you might yourself be tainted with the crime, and you would hang.'

'I? But I knew nothing of it. You know that.'

'You will realise of course that I could not admit to any part or knowledge of the case. But I'll keep your secret safe. God be with you, Paul, be easy, and I'll pray for you.'

Gilchrist could scarcely have hoped for a more satisfactory outcome to his questioning. It was Providence indeed that he had met Paul in the tavern. That Colp was dead was grand enough, but the stain upon Giles Locke had been an unexpected gift. Aye, it would out before long, whenever the time appeared ripe. He distrusted, nay *feared* was not too strong a word, the recent appointments, the hateful interference and prescriptions of the Crown. As for physicians, damn them all. 'They are a godless lot,' he observed fondly to the tavern lass pouring out his wine. He patted her behind.

Colp was dead, the physician ripe for his disgrace, and the wine, though not to Gilbert Strachan's standards, was drinkable enough. Indeed his sun shone fair. It was only later, much later in the afternoon when he awoke from napping with a furred and aching head that he remembered Paul had said – but how had he forgotten? – 'Only his friend there was angry and feart'. Too late he remembered to wonder, what friend? Paul had long since fled, his confidence shattered. And waking, his pleasures ran cold.

The Merchant's House

Hew had walked down to the harbour where the brisk sea wind and bare expanse of water helped to put the world back in perspective. The visit to the tower room had unsettled him. He half believed, with Paul, that Nicholas was dead. He felt as he had once done as a child when he had come upon a hanging in the street. This was not a commonplace for Hew, for his family did not jeer and jostle with the crowd, and the image of that swinging bulbous face had stayed with him for days.

The harbour also was a place of execution, picked clean by the scavenger gulls. The slabstones were smeared dark and wet. And though the fishermen were gone, their pickle-fingered women casting entrails to the waves, the reek of the herrings remained. A cat on the wall considered the gulls, feigning indifference. It was coloured like marmalade, a gingerbread tom.

In the cool September sunshine Hew watched the little boats sail out, unsteadily buoyant with oilcloths and sea-kists, returning from the ships moored on the horizon. Someone – the harbourmaster, was it? – asked him rather brusquely whether he had business here, and he felt conscious of his strangeness, answering, 'No business, sir, no, none at all.'

He had not slept. At the clearing of the mists he had been ready for the town, while his father stood out in his nightcap, dispensing advice. 'Your cousin Robin Flett . . . his wife is young. He minds her charms, and keeps her close confined. Now, of course, she *is* confined, he keeps her closer still. Don't vex him, I would counsel you, with inward looks or gestures. He is a proper man.'

'Then *properly*, I'll deal with him.' Hew had answered grimly. 'You cannot think my sister will requite him quite so well. For when was *she* inclined to keep her place?'

'Hush, we'll hold her to it. When you find a better, I'll be glad to see her there. Now, take the letters, child.'

The *child* made small the parent, not the son. Hew had looked at him, diminished in his shirt, and bitten back the words. He tucked the letters in his belt and took his leave.

The voice reminded him that he had business still. He shook himself. The gingerbread cat took a gamble, and leapt on the trail of a one-legged bird. It missed its quarry by a claw and, nonchalantly furious, began to wash its fur.

His cousin's house, among the finest in the street, still lacked the leafy warmth that marked the south-side colleges. The windows, cased and glazed, appeared to squint upon the close, allowing neither light nor air. Hew knocked once or twice on the heavy oak door, before turning through a gate to the side of the house onto the backlands closed from the sun. The door to the nether-hall stood open, permitting the daylight its passage. Cautiously, he stepped inside, and called out, 'Robin Flett?'

The house had a strange, medicinal smell, like green wood newly oiled. He felt his way into the central hall, and in the pricking of the light began to make sense of what he saw. It was like looking in a glass, his fears illuminate, the rafters grim and lurching like a gallows in the fog. He saw sullen purples lolling, slack and swollen blues. The hanged man's face became a bowl of fruits.

'Look out for the palettes, there! Who, pray, are *you*?'

Robin Flett was watching him behind the open door. And Hew was looking not into a glass but up to ceilings bright with pictures, florid birds and trailing foliage, varnished apples, bulbous pears. Painted serpents coiled the timbers. Rags and palettes strewed the floor. Hurriedly, he stepped aside.

'Coming from the sunshine to the darkness, these images unnerved me,' he excused himself. 'I see them now for what they are, only artist's daubs. I am Hew Cullan, son of Matthew, here with letters from my father.'

Robin said, 'Hew Cullan, is it?' somewhat doubtfully, and rubbed his beard. For Hew was a queer enough picture, with his pale mottled features and paint-puddled clothes. 'You come through by the vennel like a thief.'

It was a bare statement, and Hew in the darkness could not see enough of the other man's face to be sure of the tone.

'Forgive me, sir. I knocked.'

Flett studied him a moment, as he might inspect a painting, and appeared to let him pass.

'We are disordered here and do not use these chambers,' he confirmed at length. For, as you see, we have the painter. Which is to say,' he smiled a little sourly, 'that we do not have the painter, since he does not come.' He turned abruptly to the stairwell, calling out, 'It wasn't yet the painter, Linnet. Here's my cousin, Master Cullan! Don't come down.'

'My wife is with child,' he explained. 'And the stench of the pigments is foul. Lucy has set her poor heart on ceilings – cherubim, trees and the like. I brought the artist here from Antwerp, but it turns out he's a drunkard. As much as he paints,' and he snorted, 'he drinks. No matter, though. How fares your father? I do hope he isn't dead?' He seemed to dwell on Hew's pale looks, then suddenly exclaimed, 'God damn it, Lucy Linnet, I told you not to come!'

She was standing on the stair, pale pink and almost spherical, her small hands resting shrewishly upon her swollen hip. Her lips and cheeks were bright and fresh. Beneath her curtsey, mischief flounced. Solemnly, Hew held out his hand. But Robin interceded, scolding. 'Cover your head!'

She kissed him on the cheek, her eyes on Hew. 'Don't fuss so, Robin, please, the colours are long dry. I come to greet our cousin, as is proper in a wife, and since we're kin, he will forgive my lack of dress. But are you not to introduce us?'

Without waiting for his answer, she threw open the shutters, allowing the sunlight to scatter the dust.

'Are not the pictures pretty, Master Cullan? All the bonny beasts and flowers, And look, upon the pippin tree, the linnet and the robin, *us*, you see. And here's the lark and Katie wren. Oh Robin, do you think,' like a child she clapped her hands, 'that we might name her Katherine, if the babe's a girl?'

Her husband smiled and kissed her full on the belly. 'Katherine Flett. It is a good name, Lucy Linn.'

Hew turned to examine the paintings. They were, in the light, unexceptional sketches: bright-coloured flora, animals and birds. Perhaps the painter shared his own ambivalence towards the merchant and his wife, for he thought he spied a sparrowhawk, shadowing the little birds below. For sure, the robin redbreast was puffed up to inordinate size, and the linnet curled below its wing had eyes upon a brighter bird astride a bigger tree.

'The pictures are remarkable,' he answered tactfully. 'I thank you, sir, my father is still well enough. However he grows old, and is concerned for my sister. You were kind enough to offer her a home and he had hoped to see her settled here. But I fear in your present confusion, it may not be opportune.'

'On the contrary,' said Robin unexpectedly. He dropped his voice. 'It will be most convenient. My linnet, I pray you, go ask the girl to fetch wine. You'll drink a cup of claret. Hew? We'll sit among the paintings. Here are stools.

'Believe me, you are welcome,' he acknowledged privately. 'I'm glad to have your sister at this time. I have been at my wits' end to know how to comfort Lucy while I'm gone. You see, she bears her frail condition ill . . .'

'Frail!' thought Hew.

'. . . And I have put off sailing several times. Now the winds are strong, I can delay no longer. I shall speak plain. Margret has the falland evil – no, sir, do not frown, my youngest sister died with it; I see no shame. But nonetheless, you will allow, it is a *private* sickness, and in this it serves us well. My wife has want of friends. In truth, she has made friendships I wish to discourage, and I would not have her go among the world when I'm abroad. Well then, Meg shall be her company. Now, do not mind the works, for she shall share her bed with Linnet, where the air is pure and clean. It's providential her affliction keeps them both confined.'

Confinement, thought Hew, was appropriate enough for this jewel-encrusted coffin of a house. Its freshness masked a dark sense of enclosure. He thought of Meg, and of the long-dead sister, nameless, kept indoors.

'You understand?' persisted Robin.

Hew murmured recklessly, 'Like birds.'

His answer seemed to satisfy, for Robin gave a small tight smile. 'I have had horoscopes drawn,' he confided suddenly, 'and am assured, no trace of this unhappy stain shall taint my child.'

'The girl has gone to market.' Lucy had returned, a banquet balanced on a tray, with all of the pride of an infant who bakes her first bannock. 'Look what I found for us. Marmalades! Robin brings ships full of suckets and sugarplums, Hew, and I shall grow fat, you must help me. Here, these are cherries.'

She offered a sticky red sweetmeat, close enough almost to touching his lips. Hew felt a wave of nausea. He shook his head. He took solace in the sharpness of the wine, gulping deep to clear his thoughts. Robin, for his part, allowed his wife to sweeten him by sips, with the pressing of a nectarine, a pippin and a plum.

'So Meg will come?' said Lucy, and she clapped her hands again. 'How soon?'

'Tomorrow, if you will,' Hew promised. 'I can ride with her. I will be living at St Leonard's, where I have taken employment as a regent, beginning next week. I think I may arrive a little early, for the man I am to share with is already in possession.'

Lucy nodded eagerly. 'I have heard that the last regent there was taken for the murder of the Strachan boy, though the Strachans do not talk of it, and there is indeed a great mystery shrouds the affair.'

She sensed her husband moving to protest, and popped another candied plum into his mouth.

'But I've heard very little of late,' she pouted, 'for Robin forbids me the town. I may not see my friends. He's told the minister that I'm too frail for kirk, which as you see, is a wicked lie. Is aught spoken in the college of the crime?'

'I have not had much converse there,' Hew answered carefully, 'as yet. But I believe I heard the rumour in the town. Forgive me, sir, for you must know the family. I do not mean to gossip on their grief.'

'Tis no good thing. But aye,' the man conceded, 'I know Gilbert Strachan well, indeed we both have a part share in the *Angel*, which sets sail tomorrow. His loss affects him cruelly. Tis a pitiful sight, to see a brave man brought so low. So I confess I am uneasy to hear the matter talked of lightly.'

'I have no wish to make light of it,' Hew replied earnestly, 'and I applaud your proper feeling. The truth is, I knew the last regent. As boys we shared rooms in the college. So I confess, I am uneasy to have heard him indicted for murder.'

Lucy's eyes grew very wide. 'You shared a bed?'

'Whisht, Lucy, pray!' It was as close as Robin came to irritation with his wife, and then at once he softened it, saying, 'Shush, forgive me. I'm weary, my love, with so much to be done. And you mustn't tell our cousin I have kept you from your friends, for you know how it pains me. You are indeed too ill for kirk. You seldom find the strength to dress before noon. I have spoken with the minister, and have asked him here to pray with you.'

Lucy sighed. 'But might I not go once or twice to kirk, and Meg and Hew come with me, and put the seat nicely, and blankets and all?'

'Well then . . . we shall see.'

Hew sensed him weaken, then revive. 'As for the Strachans, I fear you must no longer count them as your friends.'

Lucy said appealingly, 'But *Agnes*, Robin, and *Tibbie*, am I not to see them?'

He took both of her hands in his and said gravely, 'come, Linnet, no. The lass is pert and loose. I would not have you there, nor yet our child, among such viciousness. For you are both of you too good,' he brushed her cheek, 'to suffer such corruption.'

'Then we shall not be corrupted,' she said sweetly.

'Please me, Linnet; do not go,' he countered in a sharper tone. And you, sir,' directed at Hew, 'would do well indeed to warn your sister from that place.' He cleared his throat. 'Master Cullan, please excuse me, but I was on my way out to the harbour when you came. I must oversee the loading of my ship. If the weather holds fair, we shall set sail at dawn. Walk with me, will you? We will talk a little more.'

'No, Robin,' Lucy cried pettishly, 'our cousin has not finished his wine.'

Her husband scowled. 'I cannot stay longer, my love.'

'Then Hew shall keep me company until the girl returns.'

Hew glanced in mild entreaty from the husband to the wife. He had risen to his feet, the better to accommodate whichever won the clash of wills. It was of course Lucy, without another strand to her defence. Robin merely shrugged, 'Then drink your wine. I shall see you, sir, at the harbour when you leave. Within the quarter hour,' he added pointedly.

'Well then,' Lucy patted the stool beside her, 'now he's gone, I long to hear your news. All about that *villain* and his crimes. Why did he do it?' She settled back complacently among the painted trees.

'I've heard very little gossip, as I said,' Hew said apologetically.

'But you hear *some*?'

He conceded, 'I did speak with the regent, Robert Black, who shared the villain's room and his confidence . . .'

'Aye?' she pressed, 'his confidence?'

'He told me . . . though he would not have it spread . . .'

He made a brave show of reluctance, until Lucy begged him, '*Say*! Whoever should I tell it to?'

'Aye, who indeed?' Hew wondered. He relented. 'Well, he did say that the villain thought we should be teaching Ramus' logic now, in place of Aristotle's. Which, according to our principal, must *prove* the man a scoundrel, or at least of dubious worth.'

She flushed. 'I think you tease me, sir.'

'A little,' he confessed. 'Forgive me, but I fear your questions might offend your husband.'

'I care little,' she said sulkily, 'as long as they please me. Know that my husband, come tomorrow, will be far across the seas. Ah well then, if you won't tell, I must forgive the cruelty. I think, sir, you are less severe than you pretend. But peace, we'll talk about your sister. Will she like it here?'

'Well,' considered Hew, 'for all the house is fine—'

'You will not find a finer.'

'—Meg's love is her garden. She prefers to be outdoors. And living out of town, she has been free to wander where she will. I think to be confined may prove a problem. She has a need, at times, to be solitary. It may not fit well with your own expectations.'

Lucy looked thoughtful. 'Meg has the falling sickness?' she asked seriously.

'Aye. You're not afraid of it?'

'It does not show to look upon her. Does she slaver and spew?'

He felt his face grow hot. 'She takes physic, and controls the fits. I hope it won't alarm you.'

'She's not violent?'

'Not at all.'

'Then it won't alarm me. But if she likes to be solitary, and I like to have company, then we shan't be friends. And our garden you know is a dry little drab of a thing that scarcely sees the sun. Meg will be unhappy here.'

'I fear it,' Hew said simply.

'And yet . . . I see a way,' she mused. 'Meg could take her walks upon the shore. It's quiet when the boats are out, and she might have her solitude.'

'Then you would be alone,' he pointed out.

''Tis true. I do not like to be alone.' Her sighs seemed almost artless. 'Oh! *Unless* of course . . . *unless* I called upon my friends.'

Silently, Hew gave applause to Lucy's cunning. The flight from the birdcage was prettily done.

'I notice that you do not share your husband's scruples,' he observed.

Lucy sighed impatiently, 'I allow them pertinent, yet cannot feel them sharp. Do you?'

'In conscience, I confess,' he said in seriousness, 'that they do prick. Perhaps you might tell me a little more about these friends of yours, the weavers and the dyers, just to help to put my mind at ease?'

She gave a full radiant smile and, with alacrity, deprived of gossips as she had been for the space of several days, helped him to another glass of wine.

'It is so unreasonable of Robin,' she complained, 'who fostered the friendship, to forbid it when it blossoms, and when Agnes has the need of all her friends. For in truth, Gilbert Strachan has soured to his brother, and Archie as a consequence is bear-headed and cruel to her. Why at the lykewake, I would swear it, I saw bruises to her arms, as if he had used her roughly, though she hid them with her sleeve. As to the dyers,' she wrinkled her nose, 'I know nothing of them, save that the dead one made himself most noisome in the kirk. Oh Hew, you must persuade my husband to allow me to the kirk! I hear no news without it. Tell him you will take us!'

'Meg may wish to go,' he said judiciously. 'Then Agnes was your friend?'

'Aye, and her daughter Tibbie. Robin introduced us, when first he brought me here upon our marriage, that Agnes might be as a mother to me, who have none. And in truth, she was kindness itself. Tibbie too, a bright and lively lass, is full of the lore of the town. The Strachans of course have converse with the dyers; they can hardly help it, for they must do business there. Archie was ay thick with them. Tis true enough, he is not gentle like his brother.'

'Because he works with his hands, and has dealings with dyers?'

'Aye,' she answered, guileless as a child. Hew smiled to himself. 'When did the brothers fall out?'

'After Alexander died. Gilbert felt his brother was to blame.

A mite unfair, I grant, for *Gilbert* chose the tutor, yet because it happened in his brother's house, he held him responsible. Archie did not care much for the boy.'

'In what sense?' Hew asked her, interested. 'Did not care for him, or failed to give him care?'

'Robin says, both. He said we might have better lodged him *here*. Which I cannot count it sense, for it would *not* have been convenient to have had him here, and besides, the boy would still have had the tutor, and the tutor still have killed him, don't you think? How horrible!' Her eyes had opened wide, 'to have found him dead here in our bed! I wonder Robin could have wished it!'

'I'm sure,' Hew interrupted hastily, 'that he did not. He must be close to Gilbert to have thought of it.'

'He's close to Gilbert, aye. Which is why he takes his part against his brother.' Lucy heaved a sigh. 'It was the selling of the cloth they took amiss. The boy was found inside a bolt of wool, and Archie traded off the colour. It was *quite* the vogue,' she added wistfully. 'Though I suppose, it was not kind.'

'It was not kind,' Hew said severely.

'No. But the colour was rare. Archie keeps sheep and deals in their wools, which Gilbert takes, both fleece and cloth, to market overseas. And in return, he brings him back finer cloths, ribbons and lace, that can be bought from Strachan's booth here in the marketplace.'

'Then he cannot have a licence for their sale,' observed Hew.

'I know nought of that.' She sounded bored. 'He does not sell to strangers. But for those who want them, there are pretty trinkets to be had. If Meg would like a lace or pair of ribbons while she's here, I'll introduce her.'

'So you might. I am sure that would please her. In truth, she ought to have a gown, for at home she has nothing but country things.'

Lucy nodded slyly. 'I'll take her there myself. Because for Meg to make a purchase in the shop is not to offer friendship, in my husband's sense. We need not go into the house.'

'Indeed, you need not,' he agreed.

'And if I were to feel a little faint, on account of my con-dition, and required a cup of something and to sit upon the bed, that too could scarcely count as converse.'

'Scarcely at all.'

'Well then, we may go. For myself, I have not seen the Strachans since the lykewake. They won't presume on our affections if we do our shopping there.'

Hew rose to his feet. 'Well, if it will please you, Meg shall come tomorrow, and to kirk on Sunday. And at the risk of dismaying your husband, my sister must have some new clothes.'

'So she shall,' winked Lucy. 'What my husband does not know may not disquiet him. And I knew you were not cruel, as you pretend. But hurry, he will wonder what has kept you. Whatever he advises, thank him sagely. Present to him your scholar's face, most proper and severe.'

Hew bowed and left her preening, fluffing out her skirts. He thought her petted, squat and spoiled inside her painted house. For a moment, irresistibly, he pictured her squab linnet plumes in the maw of the gingerbread cat.

The Angel

'I confess,' said Robin Flett, 'I took you for a stranger when you came into my house so pale and wild of countenance. I fear your education has impaired your wits, taking you so far from the world, or else the cruel affliction we have spoken of affects you too. From a child, you are much changed.'

They were walking in the harbour by the sea gate. On their left, the high walls of the priory rose to the cathedral; on the right, the fishing boats lay bleaching in the silt, the fishermen mending their nets. Hew bowed ironically.

'You are blunt, sir. It is true my sister's condition has affected me, though not in the sense you imply. I have been away from home these past ten years. In truth, I left a child. Last night my father told me of my sister's illness. It was news to me. In consequence, I have not slept, being much disturbed in my mind as to what should now become of her. If I alarmed you or your wife then I am sorry for it.'

''Tis no matter,' Flett said graciously. 'Let the news itself excuse the manner of its coming. I have read your father's letter. You may tell him I accept his terms. But you were talking to my wife. What did she say to you?'

'She asked about my sister, and whether she might go with her to kirk.'

'Ah, did she? We shall speak on that. I do not wish my wife to have acquaintance with her former friends, the Strachans. I expect you to assure it. Do you understand?'

'I understand you, sir. But, may I ask you why?'

Robin sighed impatiently. They had come upon a group of sailors, making fast their craft. He paused to let them pass.

'Walk with me to the pier.'

He led the way beyond the inner harbour, high upon the rocks
hewn from the old cathedral, looking out to sea.

'Do you see that ship? It is the *Angel*.'

Hew gazed across the water. The boat was moored out of the
shallows, quietly sketched upon the horizon. The small boats had
ceased their traffic back and forth, and were beached upon the
sands. The sea was still.

'She's a beauty,' he said cautiously.

'Aye, is she not? She's small and light enough to take the slightest
rivers, yet she carries eighty tonnes. Ye would not think it, though,
to look at her.'

'What does she carry?'

'Fleeces, hides and wools from the Michaelmas markets. Our
first port is Campvere, our staple in the Low Countries. With a
following wind, it should take us four or five days. From Campvere,
if the winds hold, I hope to make the journey down the Rhine
to purchase apples, onions, spices, wines – fodder for the winter
months, when luxuries are scarce. My main lines are hardware,
timbers and iron; I rarely deal in trinkets. Then back here by St
Andrew's Day in time for the birth of my child. You see how I
am pressed, and how relieved I am to have your sister come to
help us at this time. But – in answer to your question – a third
share in the ship belongs to Gilbert Strachan. He is my partner
and friend.'

'Does he sail with you tomorrow?'

Robin shook his head. 'He is, you understand, a most prodigious man. His elder sons are based in Campvere, and will take
care of his particular cargo when we land. For the moment, it is
under the watch of the shipmaster, who owns the final share. It's
evident that Gilbert speculates in something, and has cut the man
a part of it. He paid him richly to take care of it, and he guards
it well. There was a time when I myself should have been privy
to this fortune. I regret that the death of his son has left him
mistrustful and uncertain of his friends. In particular, he has turned
against his brother.'

'And you in turn reflect this turning?' Hew said shrewdly.

'Aye, I do. I want Gilbert to know that I am his friend.'

'And partner in his fortunes. What's his usual trade?'

'Before the boy's death, he exported wool. His imports are luxury goods, laces and silks, suckets and soaps, colours and candies, perfumes and wines. Archie's cloths are of poor quality, and Gilbert makes little from their sale. He has been generous to his brother; trading with him for silks of far higher value. Now relations have turned sour. For what went on in that house, Gilbert cannot forgive him. That he turned it to his profit was more shameful still.'

'More shameful than what?'

Robin dropped his voice, as though the foreign sailors might interpret as he spoke. 'The weaver has been privy to most loose and scandalous conducts. I know my wife well, Master Cullan, and I know she will beguile you with her tricks and wiles to suffer her acquaintance with her friends. On no account permit this. I cannot tell to Lucy the true nature of the evil in that house, but I must counsel you, the place is vile.'

'It may be counted as evil enough that Gilbert Strachan's son was murdered there,' Hew reasoned. 'That she knows already. Is there worse?'

'Aye, there is worse.' Robin scowled. 'As if it were not bad enough that Archie Strachan's prentice kept a whore, aye, beneath his nose, he left his nephew prey to most unnatural friendships. That friend of yours, the tutor, sodomised the boy. I see by your face, sir, you did not know *that*.'

'I did not,' Hew lied gravely, 'but how do *you* know it?'

'Because Gilbert Strachan told me so, here by the shore and in his own words, come fresh from the justiciary to swear the change against him.'

'It is a serious charge. Can there be proof of it?'

'Aye, there are proofs. Agnes Ford, the weaver's wife, has sworn it to the Crown. She witnessed him removing letters, which afterwards were brought before the justice clerk and proved the tutor's guilt. She was with him also when he found the body, for it was he who led them there. And she bears witness also, that the dyer had suspected them. He warned the tutor, who killed him for his pains.'

'How did the dyer know?' Hew asked uneasily.

'He was the sort of man who sniffed out secrets. Though how Agnes came to hear, I cannot say. But since all this was under Strachan's roof, I do not wish my wife to grace his house.'

'I understand,' said Hew. 'Then it was Agnes who swore the disposition?'

'Aye. She is a good woman, and the soundness of her testimony, as Gilbert said to me, must be his only comfort. What's your interest, Hew?'

Hew shrugged. 'It is the law that holds my interest, little else.'

Flett nodded. 'You are your father's son. You say you know the man. You cannot hope to make defence of him?'

'On this account,' his cousin answered quietly, 'it would appear that I cannot. Now, sir, you will excuse me; I must exercise my horse.'

When Hew arrived with Dun Scottis at the east sands Giles was already waiting, pacing back and forth the sunlit bay. He wore his doctor's gown and cap, spilling out his full black beard, and underneath, incongruous, a pair of riding boots, great billowing waders that rose to his thigh, above which his breeches were pillowed and taut. Under his arm swung a stout stick, less riding crop than cudgel, and in his hands he held a clutch of books beneath a pair of spectacles. To Hew's alarm, he was also wearing spurs. 'Ah, there you are,' he beamed. 'You brought the horse. Now, ordinarily, of course, it were better to begin his lessons in the early morning, before he has his provender . . .'

'There is no "before" his provender,' interrupted Hew. 'He has it all the time.'

Giles cleared his throat. 'Quite so. And for that reason, you know, we have brought him to the shore, away from temptation of pasture. So, to begin . . .'

'May I observe,' Hew said pleasantly, 'that if you mean to use that cudgel on my horse, then I shall have to wrap it round your neck. Which would prejudice our friendship, don't you think?'

Giles looked startled, then a little hurt. 'It's only for effect. You need not take that tone. No, listen, this will please you.'

'Forgive me for asking, but do you know anything at all about horses?' Hew retorted.

Giles brandished the books. 'It's all here: cavalry, chivalry, surgery, husbandry . . .'

Hew laughed ironically. 'It was a book that got me into this.' He remembered Duns Scotus.

'Aye, and books will get you out. Why, if every man who had a horse would only buy a book . . .' Giles seemed slightly flustered at the prospect. 'No matter. Horses are like medicine, just the same. You see, your dun-coloured horse is of the element of earth, that makes him dull and slothful. It's a melancholic horse. And as with humans we can let his blood in order to redress . . .'

Hew shook his head. 'I'll have none of it. If I did believe his disposition rose from his complexion and that my sad-coloured horse is a sad-*natured* horse – and I *don't* believe it – then still I vow I would not have him bled. I would cure his melancholia with tenderness and cherishing.'

Giles stared at him a moment. At length he said, 'God knows, I love you, Hew, but you have strange ideas. Now, listen, here are instructions for correcting faults in horses, just like yours.'

He thumbed through the leaves of a book. 'Here's one: "To remedy a horse that rears up its head when corrected for faults with a blow to the head with a stick."'

'Aye, here's one,' interjected Hew. 'Don't hit its head with a stick.'

'Aye, that would serve,' allowed Giles. 'Now, *this* is your horse: "To remedy a horse that stops short when tired, and will not walk on in spite of correction . . ." oh, this is no good!' He frowned as he read, 'For even if it were not cruel, I should hardly call it practical.'

'What is it?' Hew looked up in interest.

'"Have a man put a flame to its posteriors." No, that won't do at all,' Giles declared judiciously. 'For first, as I admit it does seem somewhat cruel . . .'

'If a flame were put to your posteriors, I dare say even you would run fair like the wind,' Hew put in unkindly. Giles chose to ignore him.

'. . . and for second, it would not be thought expedient to have a man beside you all the way to Kenly Green, his torch forever blowing out. I see that you are right. We must move on to the practice. Hold his head still, Hew, for I intend to mount him.'

'Mount him?' Hew echoed faintly.

'Aye. You have made him too soft. We must show him who's in charge. Though I confess, it is a while since I was on a horse. Should I run and vault him, do you think?'

'Ah, perhaps not,' Hew answered hastily. Let me lead him to the rocks where you may find a vantage point.'

He held the horse steady, shielding its eyes from the onslaught about to descend on its back. At the third or fourth heave Giles arrived in the saddle. To Dun Scottis' credit he did not buckle or sag. Giles straightened up, looking pleased. He motioned to Hew to pass him the books, and held them open in his lap, balancing the spectacles on his bridge of his nose. He had to screw up his face somewhat to keep them in place. With his left hand he took up the rein, and in the sternest of tones instructed the horse to walk on. Dun Scottis embarked on a delicate trot. Then, without warning, he slid to the ground and lay on his belly, his head sinking low to the sand. For a moment, Hew thought Giles had broken him, quite literally. His friend did not dismount, but seeming perplexed, freed his boots from the stirrups and planted his feet on the ground.

'Get off him!' Hew hissed. But Giles did not heed. He lifted his heels and drove them full hard into the flank on either side of the horse. Perhaps he had forgotten the spurs. Dun Scottis roared. He reared not his head but the whole of his self, with effortless strength tipping Giles from his back and over the roll of the saddle, boots flailing deep in the sand. The horn-rimmed spectacles flew in a graceful arc into a clump of seaweed. And Dun Scottis kicked up a billow of dust and fled down the beach with the wind in his hair, as though someone had set a white flame on his tail.

Giles sat up cautiously, spitting out sand.

'It's a fine enough day still,' he ventured, 'Perhaps a short walk by the shore?'

They followed the trail as far as the pier, where the hoofprints disappeared into the sea. 'Do you think he could have swum across the water?' Giles asked, perplexed.

'Anything is possible. Let us walk back as far as the cliffs and come up to the harbour from the south, for then we cannot miss him. There is nowhere else to go.'

They traced their steps back to the edge of the bay and the coarse clumps of seagrass known as the bents, but there was no sign of Dun Scottis nuzzling in the reeds. Giles was crestfallen.

'I fear he has been stolen.'

'Well and good, if he has,' muttered Hew. 'But rest assured, if he is stolen, he will likely be returned. Come, we will walk up the Kirk Heugh and look down from there, where we are sure to see him. He cannot be far away.'

They climbed the stone steps that led from the harbour towards the cathedral, to the old kirk of St Mary that stood on the rock, and from that vantage point looked back down to the bay. Beyond the tall masts of the ships and wide flanks of the fishing boats the beach was empty. Only the foaming white waves reared and bucked, as if they had swallowed him whole. Giles lowered himself gingerly onto the grass and shook the sand out of his boots. Hew felt a little sorry for him. He suspected he was bruised. 'Well, it can't be helped,' Hew told him philosophically. 'We should be going home.' He helped

Giles to his feet, for he was moving stiffly now, and further up the hill towards the Castlegait. At the entrance to the castle was a dewy clump of grass, and there they found the dun horse Scottis, like an old and faithful soldier, standing sleek and salty from the sea.

'However did he get there?' Giles cried in astonishment. He rubbed himself reproachfully. 'Surely he could not have climbed the cliff!'

Hew returned home in the late afternoon, Dun Scottis trotting meekly as a lamb. He found Meg in the garden, gathering armfuls of white-rooted flowers. He watched her as she carried them, back and forth, into a small stone outhouse, where presently he followed her inside, and leant against the door. She paid him little notice, binding tight the bundles on the stone and slicing through the roots. The walls were lined with jars and the air savoured earthy and dry.

At last she whispered, 'Father told you?'

'Aye. It does not matter, Meg,' he reassured her.

'How is Nicholas?'

'He's still alive, at least. Giles is looking after him.'

'You did not tell Giles about the falling ill?' Meg answered anxiously.

'I did not, for you did not wish it. But,' he hesitated, 'if you chose to tell him, he would understand.'

She shook her head. 'Aye, I know. But all the same, I will not tell him. I cannot explain.'

'Then you need not,' he said gently.

'Can you pass the pocket knife?' She changed the subject quickly. 'It has fallen off the wall.'

She sliced into the seedheads, shaking loose the grain, and cupped a shallow palmful in her hand. 'Carrot seed,' she answered him before he spoke. 'The flowers and leaves distilled into a water cure the dropsy and the gout, which may prove beneficial to our father. This has flowered late. The seeds are most effective. This central flower,' she plucked it out, 'is said to fend away the falling sickness. It's pretty, don't you think?'

'I thought it might be hemlock,' he observed.

'Side by side, they are not easily mistakable. The root is similar, and both taste sharp and pungent, which is fortunate, perhaps. Hemlock has a purple spotted stem, and its leaves and stem are smooth, unlike the feathers on these.' She touched her fingers to the plant. 'Look, these are almost like hairs.'

'What of the seed?' he questioned.

'One seed is very like another. I have use for both, and so I keep them well apart. This,' she took down a small jar from the shelf and spilled out the seed in her palm, 'is spotted hemlock. And it has to last until the spring.'

'Won't it grow in winter?'

'Aye, but it becomes more deadly as the year goes on. In the young plant the poison distils in the leaf and the seed, and does not reach the root, but as the year goes on the strength intensifies until the whole plant becomes deadly and the leaves and seed are most poisonous of all. Once it has seeded I cut down the foliage and burn off the root. The rabbits forage here in wintertime. It is a quiet death, but death nonetheless. The dried parts are less potent. Is Nicholas awake?' she asked.

'Not yet. He has a coldness and a pallor, and his face is swollen and discoloured like a drowned man's. Giles says he bit through his tongue.'

'Then the paralysis is passed, which is a good thing. But the spasms may return. And still he has not woken?'

'I have seen no sign of it.'

'Then the sickness must be grave.'

'I fear it, but Giles appears sanguine still. It is unlike him,' Hew remarked.

'He's a good man,' Meg said simply.

'Aye, he is.' He grinned suddenly. 'And I confess I have misused him. If you have liniments, spare him a pot, and he may return your regard.'

'Why, is he hurt?' Meg looked alarmed.

'He has a bruising to his pride, and a stiffness in the fundament,' he smiled.

He watched her strip the stalks and hang the herbs to dry. At length he said more seriously, 'I had thought hemlock an incontrovertible poison.'

'Aye, if it's fresh.'

'There is something . . .' he hesitated, 'something come into my mind when I was looking down at Nicholas, and I cannot quite assuage it. It is what Plato said of Socrates. That when he had drunk of the hemlock a stiffness and coldness passed gradually over his body, but that at the last he was able to speak, being quite sensible and quiet in his thoughts.'

Meg nodded. 'It might well be so. Who are Socrates and Plato?'

'Ancients, tis no matter, Meg. But when I was looking at Nicholas, it struck me, suppose that he were sensible still in his mind, though his body should not be responsive, and he heard, and saw and felt, but could not speak and move, what horror would that be, Meg, such a Hell.'

Meg was silent a moment. Then she said, 'it would be.'

'You have eaten of the herb,' persisted Hew, 'can you not know?'

She shook her head. 'It calms and stops the spasms in my limbs, but when I am awake I don't remember. If I am sensible sleeping, I am senseless of it waking. And as for Nicholas, I cannot think him sensible. Do not imagine it.'

'I have tried not to. But he is sensible still in my mind.' He smiled foolishly. 'Well then, you should know I have made arrangement for your lodging with our cousins. They were glad of it, for Robin's ship is about to sail.'

'Father told me,' she said flatly. 'I have said goodbye to him. The carrot now,' she changed the subject, 'there is goodness in the root, though it's too sharp to eat.'

'Not quite goodbye,' insisted Hew. 'It's an hour's walk, scarcely that, from Father's door to Flett's. Or two hours,' he tried coaxing her to smile, 'if you take my horse.'

She shook her head. 'My father does not mean me to come home again.'

'He has not said so,' he objected.

'No.' She gave a watery smile, 'I know him, Hew. He means to die. He would not send me else.'

Meg packed a few possessions while her father fussed relentlessly. For Lucy, she prepared a sour-milk cheese, a poke of pippins and a dish of hedgerow jellies dark as blood.

'She is pretty, and spoilt,' Hew had replied to her question, 'and I fear will be a trial to you.'

'Meg will bear it bravely,' Matthew countered, 'will you not?'

'You did not tell me,' Hew went on, 'my cousin Flett had business shares with Gilbert Strachan.'

'Truly? For I did not know it. We keep ourselves close from the world. Yet it does not surprise me. As I understand it, the shipmen and merchants are most intimate together, and share their lives and business very close. Theirs is not a world that I am well acquainted with. Then it may serve your purpose well for Meg to lodge there.'

'I think it may be more convenient than I'd thought.' Hew glanced at Meg. 'Robin Flett desires to sever the connection between his family and the weaver's, but his wife is keener to advance it. Meg can work on that while he's away.'

'Why does Robin wish to drop them?' wondered Meg.

'If he is to be believed, in deference to his friend and partner Gilbert, who no longer favours his brother, and to protect his wife from immoralities in Archie Strachan's house.'

Matthew Cullan frowned.

'But I believe,' his son continued smoothly, 'it's the twist in Archie's fortunes that provokes his change of feeling. Robin Flett is most conscious of person and place.'

'You do not persuade me to like him,' said Meg.

'Indeed, I am persuaded that you will not like him,' answered Hew, 'brought up as you have been,' he shot a dry look at his father, 'without a sense of the most proper improprieties.'

Matthew feigned offence. 'Your sister is most moral in her judgements.'

'Aye. She does not prejudge, which I allow will serve her here. But put simply, I need her to make friends with Strachan's wife and daughter, on whatever count she can. For according to Robin Flett, it is Agnes Ford the weaver's wife, who is the witness for the Crown and upon whom rests the case. She has sworn, one, that to her knowledge Nicholas and Alexander were unnaturally enamoured of each other; two, that she was witness to the letters Alexander sent him; three that Nicholas knew where to find his body; and four, most singular, that the dyer intimated to her his suspicions of the crime. Her evidence has sealed his fate.'

'Truly, it would seem so,' Matthew said. 'I can see but three alternatives.'

'What are they?' questioned Meg. But it was Hew who answered.

'There are four. The first, she is telling the truth. The second, she tells partly the truth. The third, she is mistaken, but believes she tells the truth. The fourth and most contentious, that she lies.'

It proved an uncomfortable ride into town. Meg wanted to walk, and since Hew had been warned that she must not be tired, he had no choice but to lift her onto the mat of hair behind him on the horse, where she raged and glowered at him, 'you do not need to treat me like a pot. I will not break.' Dun Scottis, for his part, was stubborn and recalcitrant.

Also, Hew had argued with his father over Robin Flett. 'My cousin has agreed the terms,' he reported stiffly.

Matthew grinned. 'I thought he might.'

'Aye?' The lawyer in Hew spoke. 'What terms were those?'

'The terms need not concern you.'

'You have sold her, have you not?'

The old man sighed. At length he answered wearily. 'The contrary, my child. You have talked with Robin Flett. You do not think he takes her, with her cruel affliction, out of simple charity? He came to me some time ago with a proposal: he wants another ship, something for his children. Meg requires a home. If she were married, she should have a dowry. But with none to wed her . . .

well, it's done. Robin Flett shall have the money for his ship. It is her settlement.'

'Then you have deceived me,' Hew accused him. 'I would not have gone to him so willingly if I had known. Her settlement! What's left to her?'

'Protection, Hew. She cannot live alone when I have gone.'

'But there are servants, surely.'

'Servants talk. And with her herbs and potions, with the fall and ill, she would be suspected. A sheep or a cow, perhaps a child, would happen to fall sick. And then the day would come when they would come for her. The world is cruel. I have influence and money still, and I may pay for her protection, yet I cannot leave that influence to her when I am gone.'

'I could have protected her,' his son protested.

Matthew shook his head. 'I cannot see you well content to stay here all your days. She must have peace and constancy. It would not suit you.'

'I would have found a way,' Hew answered stubbornly.

'Whisht, I know your heart. You must know mine. She shall be settled there.'

Holy Trinity

At the second bell, the minister set down his bible and yawned. He had an hour to learn his sermon by heart, not that he needed it. He had read the same lesson for more than six weeks. All that remained was to review the minutes of the last kirk session and put its recommendations into practice. This involved inserting a fresh string of names into the weekly schedule of rebukes. The transgressors bowed their heads before him in monotonous succession, unruly bairns, the lot of them. There was little variation in their sins.

He unfolded the paper and consulted it thoughtfully. It had been a particularly acrimonious meeting. To begin with, they had had to elect a new elder to replace the poor dead dyer, and against his better instincts he had appointed Thomas Brooke the baxter, who was equally assiduous. The minister was a kindly man at heart. He disliked the starker cruelties of his church.

'The session met,' he read aloud, 'to discuss the scandalous carriage of the weaver's apprentice Tom Begbie with Katrin Fyffe, the drover's daughter. Tom Begbie was called and confessed to antenuptial fornication. He found caution to submit to discipline, as it might please the kirk. He was disposed to marry her.'

But the matter had proved harder to resolve. The weaver Archie Strachan had given evidence that his apprentice was precontracted, (chastely, he assured them) to Isabel his daughter and therefore was not free to marry Katrin. Moreover, he stated that if Tom married Katrin it would break the terms of his apprenticeship. Archie would dismiss him and the couple would be destitute. This had left the kirk session with a vexing dilemma. If the pair were married, as their sin demanded, then they would have no means of support. And if a child were born, it would fall upon the parish to look after it, at considerable expense. The court had then turned its attention to Katrin. It was discovered that the drover's cottage fell between two parishes, the ministry of each of which assumed them faithful to the other. There was a strong argument, forcefully put by Tam Brooke the baxter, to give up the lass and focus their wrath upon Tom. The minister could not assent. He felt it fell to him, no matter what the cost, to recall the lost sheep to his fold. So he had proposed a more radical solution. Both Katrin and her father should be brought before the session to explain themselves. Katrin would do penance for her antenuptial fornication and would be forced to marry Tom. The sheep would be shorn, atoning for their sins, and would share in the Lord's supper once again, assured of their salvation. If the parish had to raise a child, then it was worth the cost. But his plans had been thwarted, for someone forewarned them. When the kirk officers arrived at the hovel to make their arrest they found it deserted. Of the drover and his daughter, and their few fragments of possessions, there was nothing to be found.

The last person to see them was Strachan's wife Agnes, who had gone to the house with parcels of clothing and food. She was in the habit of bestowing such acts of charity upon the drover and his daughter, who lived without mother or wife, and were very poor. She had said, a little tartly, as the minister recalled, that she had not been aware that people were judged and condemned before they were called to the session, or that an act of charity might be held amiss. It was coincidence indeed, and an unhappy one, if through her kindness she had supported their flight. The elders had been forced to take her at her word, for she was a woman of good character whose father had been master of the gild of hammermen. The birds were proclaimed to have flown, and the session contented themselves with sending letters to the parish clerks of Aberdeen, Dundee and Perth, and even as far as Edinburgh, warning against strangers. They cautioned them to give to such no residence or work without the proper counsel of the kirk.

This done, there remained the question of Tom. Unless he was married, as the baxter pointed out, his crime became the greater one of simple fornication, and Brooke was all for nailing the lad by the lug to the tron. He would do it himself as a warning, quite gladly. But the minister had intervened again, arguing that Tom had expressed his willingness to marry, and if the lass could not be found to marry him, then he could not be blamed. That was on the first account, and on the second, the boy had already spent some nights imprisoned, not in the comfort of their own kirk steeple – where the beadle as they knew exercised his kind attentions on the prisoners – but in the tolbooth gaol, by all accounts a hellhole. All this for a crime that he had not committed, but of which he was suspected as the direct result of his unhappy fornications. And on the third account, his master, Archie Strachan the weaver, had imposed the most severe and lasting penalties upon the youth, both spiritual and corporal, and having brought him to a proper and most abject state of repentance, might vouch for his future behaviour, with five or more pounds for the poorbox. The fourth account, the loss of his lass, they discounted as nothing to Tom.

So it was concluded that he must 'stand for three Sundays barefoot in sackcloth inside and out of the kirk; make true confession and repentance in the face of the whole congregation, and be fined forty shillings.' His master paid the fine for him, on whatever private terms it was not the session's business to inquire. Of his three weeks of penance today was the first. The minister had seen the boy positioned by the door at half past five, long before the bairns were come to snigger and throw stones at him. Cowed and trembling in his shirt, he set a pitiful example to them all.

At the third bell, Meg and Hew Cullan began their struggle down the street, lugging their cousin's oak settle between them. It was a heavy compromise, but Robin Flett's parting demand of a seat for his wife had held firm: 'She cannot sit without a back in her condition, man! If she insists on going to kirk, then you must take a chair for her.'

The chair, the only one in the house, was inordinately burden-some, and as the lady in question was too delicate to help, she walked a pace or two behind, daintily distancing herself from the foolishness of the spectacle. Fortunately, the kirk was no more than a matter of yards and having staggered in and placed the chair in the selected spot, all three of them were able to sit down on it, to face a blaze of envy, ridicule and scorn. Lucy professed herself faint from the walk. Indeed, she coloured slightly and intimated that perhaps she might be better to go home again. But Hew ignored her, stretching out his legs to stake their claim, and glow-ered at anyone who looked likely to attempt to filch their seat.

Holy Trinity was far greater and noisier than the chapel of St Leonard, and now that the reader was finishing his lecture and the minister stepped forth, it was filling with townspeople, chil-dren and dogs, all fighting over stools and for a place within the shadows near the door. There were no seats installed, the sermons were long, and the damp floor smelt of a sinister, sweet rotting foulness below.

'Now that we're come, we'll stay for the sermon,' Hew told Lucy firmly. 'Look at the penitent, Meg! It's Tom Begbie!'

Tom had come into the kirk as prescribed, to face the congre-gation. He stood stark and shivering up by the pulpit, lost as to the part he had to play. The minister concluded his discussions with his elders, which appeared somewhat heated, and mounted the stand without glancing at Tom. He appeared about to speak when he caught sight of something, and instead he gave a full, exasperated sigh. In a broad fruity accent Hew swore was assumed, he thundered, 'Wha's taken yon cutty stool noo?'

The congregation shuffled into silence. Even the dogs looked up expectantly. Tom began to stammer, as if compelled to answer, but the minister ignored him, speaking to the crowd.

'Which of ye has taken the stool of repentance to comfort his ain idle arse?'

Hew thought he cast a contemptuous glance at that point to the three of them sat on the settle.

'Whichever of ye has it, put it back to its rightful purpose, or ye shall discover that true rightful purpose yersel'. The cutty stool is no fer sittin' on.'

No one moved.

With another great sigh, the minister spoke in a voice loud and slow as if to the wee'st of weans. 'Very well. I will turn ma back.' He did so quite emphatically. 'And I will coont ter ten. And whan I turn roond again, yon cutty stool will be back in its place, and yon sad transgressor,' he gestured at Tom, 'will be standing on it as is proper in the face of all ye guid and honest folk. And if it is not as I say, then Maister Blair the beadle will be roond with his staff and will hoik up the skirts of all of the lassies and laddies forby till he *finds* the thing, and ye would do well to remember the eighth commandment, wad ye no', and the *tenth*.'

A woman seated not so far from Hew flushed red and reluctantly lifted her dress, revealing the stool, which passed from hand to hand until it reached the front. Someone helped the boy ascend it. Blind to the commotion, the minister turned round on the count of ten and gave a saintly smile.

'Weel now, you maun ask your man to buy you a stool for to sit on, or else ye'll sit doon in the stoor,' he advised the culprit. 'Now that's said and understood, we'll mak a start. And when our sermon's done, we'll let the young lad here set forth his sad confessions, his most filthie fornications, and a' that. Face the congregation, son,' he exhorted kindly, 'for I've nae desire to look on you mysel'.'

There followed a mutter and rustling as the service settled down, as best it could, into the psalm. The minister set out the hourglass and beamed at them.

'Weel noo, I've a treat for ye all, who canna but help yersels snoring awa' through the sermon, for I've a mind to change the ordinar today – aye, and ye may glower and ye will at me, Tam Brooke the baxter, but for seven weeks we've heard the second verse of Samuel and the bairns are awfy sick of it, so this morning we'll hae a wee change for oorsels and stir oorsels up fae oor slump. We'll take as oor lesson the seventh commandment. And for all we come fresh to it noo, it may furnish twa turns o' the glass; which is to say, Tom Begbie, you being so conveniently placed here this morning, ye may turn her over when the sand's run through; we'll treat oorsels and hae the second hour.'

His words were undermined a little by an infant's cry. It had started with a grizzle, a low undertone that echoed but did not obscure his voice, but now, as he began the sermon proper with an ominous slow turning of the glass, the wailing had increased in its intensity, until he struggled to be heard.

'Silence that bairn! What do you there, child? Where are your parents?' The beadle could stand the yowl no longer, and thundered through the church, prodding his staff at a small scowling girl. Hew turned towards the source of the commotion. The child was Jennie Dyer, crouched on the dirt floor with Geordie, Nan and Susan, and the discontented baby bawling at their feet. Jennie had run out of candies, or tiring of the lesson, had pinched the infant's bottom to ensure an early close. Struggling to her feet, she rearranged her plaid with dignity, pulling the fat baby up into its folds.

'Ah, tis you, Jennie Dyer,' the beadle backtracked.

'Aye.' She played to the crowd. 'And my *faither* lies cold in the kirkyard. And my *mither* lies abed. Her time has come. My brother Will has gone to fetch the midwife, who's after a baby at one of the farms. And my brother James,' she shot him a savage dark look, 'sits up there with the Strachans, for he disna care to bide with us. And the bairn *won't* be still. It's yon great booming voice,' she pointed at the pulpit, 'that maks her greet.'

'If ye cannot keep them quiet, lassie,' the beadle roared back, 'ye will have to go out.'

'Aye, and we shall.' And with that she bundled out her little brood before her, with as close to a flounce as her heavy burden of the baby would allow, Geordie and Susan and Nan trotting silent and submissive by her side. Their older brother seemed to shrink between the Strachans, perhaps at his prayers still, hands to his face.

'Tsk,' observed a wifie, 'bold baggage.'

The preacher cleared his throat and carried on. After these initial distractions, he was able to warm to his theme, and gradually the congregation settled, with only a cough and occasional snore, the slight smothered cry as the beadle hoiked up a plaid with his creek or prodded some sly sleeper from his dreams. So it fell comfortably still, and for almost an hour the voice had rumbled on, when suddenly the door flung open and the napping dogs startled and scattered, resuming their yapping once more. And here was Jennie Dyer come again, but with a fresh demeanour, no longer defiant but tearful and hoarse.

'Please, you must come help our mother. She's bad with the bairn, for she can't push it out, and Will's not come back with the midwife. I'm feart she will die.'

'For shame, lass, in the *kirk*!' There was a general tutting.

Rank hypocrisy, thought Hew, given their delight in Tom's misfortunes, from the ladies in the crowd. The girl began to cry.

'Will no one come?'

There fell an awkward silence, while the minister himself had paused, perplexed, until Agnes Ford the wife of Archie Strachan rose up from her stool and resolutely said, 'I'll go to her.'

Hew was intrigued by the violence of her husband's response. For Strachan pulled her down with unexpected force. 'Nay, you will not go! You'll bide where you are now and hear out the preacher his text!'

She replied with great meekness, covered her head, and sank to her knees out of sight. As Hew wondered what occasioned this charade, his sister stood beside him, tying fast her cloak.

'I will go,' Meg said quietly. 'Stay here, Hew, and see Lucy home.'

In conscience he could not dissuade her, though Lucy made her protests clear enough.

'God speed you,' he whispered, 'I'll come when I can.'

*　　*　　*

149

The sermon seemed interminable, for the minister fulfilled his promise of a full two heavy hours, and Hew could swear the glass was stopped for ever halfway through the second one. At last it was concluded, the banns and blessings were proclaimed, and finally, Tom stammered his confession, a most colourless account of his woes. Lucy was tying her strings when the minister came bearing down upon them and held out his hand.

'I am glad indeed to see you well enough to come today, Mistress Linn. And provided for in safety. Who's your friend?'

Lucy blushed and simpered, pleased with the attention. 'This is my cousin Hew Cullan, who is a graduate of the university here and recently returned from France to take up a post at the college. His sister Margret, who has gone to help the dyer's wife, is to live as my companion while my man's abroad.'

'That must be a comfort.' The minister turned then to Hew, and spoke, as he had suspected, in clear scholar's tones without trace of the vernacular. 'Good day to you, sir, and you're welcome. We don't see many scholars in the town kirk. I'll be glad to sit and talk with you one day. It is a fine thing your sister has done in helping those poor children. I fear our wives want charity, at least where that sad family is concerned. But tell me, is it the regent's place you take here at St Leonard's?'

'I'm afraid so. Nicholas Colp is a friend of mine. Do you know him, sir?'

'Only by name. He's another lost soul, so I've heard. But let us not cast stones.' He changed the subject tactfully. 'The public examinations for university bursaries are about to take place. I wonder, have you influence in their result?'

Hew shook his head. 'I shouldn't think so. I shall of course be present, but I believe the principal will have the final say. Why do you ask?'

'I have a boy in the parish I would like to propose as a bursar. But I doubt there's much hope.'

'You don't think him a strong enough candidate?'

The minister gave him an odd look. 'I think him exceptional.

But I have put young men forward for scholarships before, boys of great promise, yet none has proved successful. The fact is, sir, that your college of St Leonard has not admitted a single poor scholar in the past three years. The master puts out that none met the standard.'

'Truly? You amaze me. I thought the statutes made provision for twelve bursars in all. There are only two among the magistrands.'

'As I believe. Well, you will observe the examinations, as shall I. Perhaps you will honour me with your opinion of my charge, whatever the outcome?'

'Gladly. But I cannot think that if the boy shows promise as you say he would be turned away. Moreover, I have a friend appointed to the chair of St Salvator's, whose word will have weight, and who will not take part in wrong practice.'

'Ah, the mediciner. I've heard something of him. Well, I will let you get on. That's an impressive piece of furniture you have there with you. I wonder how you mean to take it home?'

'It belongs to Lucy's husband,' Hew said wryly, 'and is the price I paid for coming with her to your most pungent sermon. I had wondered whether I might leave it in the kirk?'

'Well, you might,' he sounded dubious, 'if Robin Flett did not care much to have it back. But to my eyes, who have nothing so grand in my own house, it looks to be of value in proportion to its ugliness, and I do not rate your chances of still finding it in half an hour, let alone next week. I have a better idea. You see, I have forgotten to dismiss Tom from the cutty stool. Come, Tom. This gentleman requires some help home with his settle. You may take the other end.'

Tom came, remarkably truculent. 'My master expects me at home.'

'Well then, he has no business to, upon the Sabbath. You may count it in your penance. Go then, take the bulk of it, you're strong. I shall see you, sir,' he added to Hew, 'if not before, then at the examinations. Pray convey to your sister my kindest regards.'

The Crying

Lucy Linn moved surprisingly quickly. Before Hew and Tom had struggled more than a step with their burden she had turned down the alleyway into her house. By the time they arrived, she was nowhere to be seen, no doubt already resting in the upper rooms, recoiling from or sulking at the morning's rude excitements. Tom dropped the settle by the door and was about to leave when Hew placed a restraining hand on his shoulder. Through the rough cloth he felt the boy tense. He seized the opportunity.

'At last we have the chance to speak in private. I have questions I would put to you.'

'What questions?' Tom was defiant. 'I don't know you, sir.' His voice was low enough, but Hew saw twin spots of anger colour his cheeks. The boy had not been softened by his morning on the cutty stool. It was bravado, perhaps, but Hew sensed he would not be bullied.

'But I know *you*. I was in your master's shop when Alexander's corpse was found, and again on the day that you were arrested. I am a man of law, and I have been watching you. You were witness to a crime and must give evidence in court. I am here to take your statement.'

'I was cleared of the crime,' Tom said stubbornly. 'None can say otherwise.'

'Nonetheless, you are a witness. If you are cited and will not compear, the penalties are most severe; the least of which may see you put to the horn. For bearing false witness in so grave a case you will forfeit your hand or your tongue.' He spoke in a light tone, almost offhand, as if he saw this happen all the time. From the corner of his eye he saw it met its mark.

'I swear to you, sir, I have nothing to tell.'

'Then you have nothing to fear. Nonetheless,' Hew feigned a yawn, 'it is my job to read your answers to the court. Now we can do this several ways. You can answer now, and willingly submit to question, or I can come back to your master's house, and hold the inquisition there, or I can report that you refuse my questions. In that case you will be summoned in person to give your account, on pain of the aforementioned penalties. Perhaps you would prefer that? Then you may go home. And thank you for your trouble with the chair.'

'Wait!' Tom cried, bewildered. 'You might ask your questions, if they won't take too much time.'

'Indeed?' Hew glanced carelessly out at the sun. 'I've little time myself. So let's be done. Sit on the bench there. I'll fetch ink and paper. I'll write what you say, and you may find a friend to read it to you later if you will, when you have made your mark. Comfortable? What shall we say?' He chewed the quill. 'You are Tom Degbie, prenticed to the weaver Archie Strachan, taken up in error for the murder of his nephew, and present when the body was discovered in your bed.' Tom nodded cautiously.

'So far so good. Now tell me what happened that day.'

'We were in Crail for the market,' the boy remembered. 'Alexander was meant to come too, but he didn't appear. We thought he was asleep in bed.'

'And no one went to wake him?'

'The master said to leave him. Not for pity, but to spite him. He cared little for the boy.'

'Did you like Alexander?' Hew enquired.

Tom's reply was guarded. 'I had little to do with him, sir, but had no cause to wish him ill . . . in truth . . . in truth, is this private, sir? I mean from my master.'

Hew nodded. 'If you give a full account, then he need not know it.'

'I had reason to like him, sir, for he drew off the attentions of Tibbie – she's my master's daughter – which were troublesome to me, for I had . . .' The sentence trailed away.

Hew smiled sympathetically. 'You had attachments of your own, which brought you to a sorry state, as I infer. Well, it's atoned for. The courts will not trouble with that. Did Alexander return the girl's affections?'

'No, I don't think so. Not that that stopped her. You must not think . . . she's a flirt, sir, a sport. Her passions have no depth.'

'I understand.' He made a note. 'Who was the last person to see Alexander?'

'My master, his uncle, spoke to him on Saturday, and told him to be sure to be ready at dawn. They quarrelled about something. It was his work, I think. He had been taking lessons with his tutor, and I don't think they were going all that well. In the morning he cursed him and called out his name. But he didn't go up to his room.'

'Could your master have killed him?'

Tom looked confused. 'Was it not Master Colp?'

'*That*, Tom, is slander,' Hew said severely. 'The writ is not served.'

'It's what my master said,' Tom stammered. 'But I hoped it was a lie. I saw him in the gaol.'

'Aye, so you did. What did he want there?'

'Like you, sir, the truth. And he went to tell Katrin. In truth, though he meant well, I wish he had not. But my master . . . why would he kill him? For he could not profit from it. He was reliant on his brother for a good share of his income, which he has lost since Alexander's death. We've all felt the loss, in more ways than one.'

'Suppose it was an accident?' Hew put to him. 'Suppose he struck the boy, so hard it killed him, and then placed the body in your closet, hoping to incriminate you?'

'It's possible . . . but no, my master did not come into the shop. And besides, he would not have put him in the closet. He expected me to be asleep there.'

'He did not know you had gone out?'

'I cannot think he did. I should have felt it,' Tom said meaningfully. 'I do not think that he dissembled, when he *did* discover it.'

He winced. 'Truly, sir, when I look back, I cannot think that he killed Alexander, even in the foulest temper. You will not write I thought it possible?' he added anxiously.

'Since you retract it, no.' Hew pretended to have made a mark upon the paper. Mentally, he made a different note.

'Was there anyone else who knew you left the shop unlocked at night? Apart from Katrin?' he continued.

'No one. Only Alexander.'

'*Alexander* knew?'

'Aye.' The boy looked up at him. 'He liked to walk about at night. Sometimes he came home to find the house was locked and then he slept below the counter. In summer months, I lie there myself. It's far less warm and choking than the bed. I kept his secret. He kept mine.'

'Then is it possible he slept there on the night that he was murdered?'

'It's possible. I know that he felt hot and closed up in the loft. But he would not have climbed into the bed. He disliked the walls around him and could never bear to be enclosed.'

'And all the night, you left the place unlocked?'

'Until just before the dawn. If he was there, I did not see him. Though it's possible he kept beneath the counter. He had the knack to lie there very small and silent when his uncle was around. I left my *wife*,' he spoke the word defiantly, 'a little before the dawn, loaded up the cart with cloths for the market, and made fast the doors. I left the keys with Agnes. My mistress must have come into the shop while we were gone, for when we returned from Crail I found the doors unlocked.'

'You're sure of this? And certain that you locked them?'

'Certain, sir.' He flushed unhappily. 'My master has gone into this most rigorously. He no longer allows me the use of the keys.'

'I thank you,' Hew said thoughtfully. 'You have been most helpful.'

'Then there need not be a summons, sir?' the boy asked anxiously.

'In all probability, not. There may be further questions. I shall have to speak to Katrin. Can you tell me where she lives?'

The boy shook his head, so hopelessly that Hew could scarcely doubt he told the truth, and whispered, 'I went to the cottage to look for her, to look after her and make her my wife. The hearth had blown cold and the chimney pot was empty, sir. She and her father are gone.'

As Tom returned home, Hew arrived at the Kinness Burn. Jennie Dyer sat on the grass a little way from the house, up wind from the lye pot, hugging her knees in her dress. He could not read her expression.

'Ma's done with her crying,' she said, 'but ye canna go in.'

He dropped down beside her. 'How does she now?'

She rolled her eyes upwards. 'She's cast out the bairn. Wee crabbit scrap of a thing, skin boiling red, an' it roars.' Hew felt for her, remembering her struggles with the fat untrammelled infant in the kirk. He looked through his pockets and offered a sticky sweet plum, stolen from the merchant's house. She nibbled it cautiously.

'Candies. You came here before.'

'Aye. I remembered you like to eat sweetmeats.'

She feigned indifference. 'That's for the babies. They're down at the burn with my brother Jem. The lassie says, "Go wash the sheets," for she wants to be rid of them. Gurning and greeting they were, my brother the worst of them. Not any help to her.'

'I expect *you* were, though.' He had taken out a little box of fruits, and she reached out a greedy thin arm.

'Mebbe I was. Will I sit on your lap?'

He was startled. 'Aren't you a little old for that?'

'I'm twelve. I'm not too young.'

Hew decided to ignore this. 'Twelve's too old for sitting on a stranger's lap, don't you think?'

'I thought that you might like it,' she seemed chastened for a moment, and then quickly recovered, 'in return for the candies. My dada liked me to.'

'But that's a different matter, as I think you know. Here, you may have the whole box. I've no taste for sweetmeats. My cousin is a merchant, and he brings these by the shipload for his lady wife, peaches and damsons and pippins and pears. She fears she grows so fat and foul of tooth he will take his sweets elsewhere, and so she palms them off on me.'

This forced a grudging smile. 'Does he live in a grand house with pictures and paint on the ceilings?'

'He does indeed. I think you must have met him.'

'No. But one day I will live in a house like that.' She had crammed her mouth with sticky marmalades.

'I wouldn't eat them all at once,' Hew winked, 'they might be useful in the kirk come Sunday next.'

Jennie scowled. 'I won't go back.'

'I don't blame you. Won't you have to, though? I thought you were very brave, to stand up there and tell them all.'

'My brother didna think so.' She pulled back her sleeve and revealed a new bruise, shiny and blue as the plum.

'I'm sorry. Are your brothers not kind to you?'

She considered it, sucking the sweets. 'Will's alright. But he only cares about the dyes. He went for the midwife, and never came back. James is after being prenticed to the Strachans. He thinks that if he sits by them in kirk and makes eyes at Strachan's daughter he will take him for his son, but they'll not take him. No one wants to know the dyers, Dada says . . .' She frowned. 'Yon lassie,' she turned quickly to the house, 'says the bairn will want a wet nurse, for my mother has no milk. Do you think that we will find one in the town?'

'It's not a thing I know about. But I suppose they may be had.'

'When there's a *hoor* with child.'

'You ought not to speak so,' he chided.

'Why not?' She seemed puzzled. 'If there's a hoor in milk, she may give suck to pay off her penance. It's in the kirk I heard it. How can it be wrong? You heard the confession. Yon went with hoors. Twas his lass, did I tell you, came by here the day that my father died.'

157

'Katrin? Are you sure?'

'I saw her at the Strachans' house, on Thursday last. Mammie sent me to buy threads. And she was standing by the door. I recognised her face. Archie Strachan came out bawling, called her hoor, and strumpet. She was crying. Agnes came and whispered to her. Then she went away.'

'On Thursday last? And since she's fled,' Hew muttered thoughtfully.

'Aye, so she has. And if *I* had to marry, I'd make off myself. Who will we have, if there aren't any whores? You saw how it was. None come to help but a stranger, who'd not smelt the stink.'

'She's my sister, and strong in the lung. I hope you don't call her a whore,' he teased her.

She stuck out her lip, unrepentant. 'You know that I don't. I did not know she was your sister, though. She says my mother needs some herbs, and she'll come back with them tomorrow. Do you think that she will?'

'If she says it.'

'She's kind to us, then.' She fell silent. Hew felt once more in his pocket and brought out a purse.

'How many children are there now?'

'Eight living, and three in the kirkyard with Da.'

You'll no doubt want some money with another mouth to feed.'

Jennie Dyer coloured. 'I'm not to take your money. We don't need it.'

'I'm not saying you need it, but perhaps you deserve it? You like pretty things. And you took it before.'

'Aye. And my brothers did not like it. I was not to tell you things.'

'You don't always do what they tell you, I think. How did they know what you had said?'

'The weans told the boys 'bout the pennies, and Jem said not to go talking to strangers, nor taking their money.' She had closed in a corner, nursing her arm. Hew sighed and put the purse away.

'Well, do what you will. For I think you've a mind enough to do that anyway. I will ask you a question and you can answer or ignore it as you please, and since you won't accept a penny then you can't be said to break your brothers' rule. You remember me asking about the day your father died. You told me a lie, and I'm not sure what the lie was, or why you told it to me, but I do know you told me a lie about something. Now, you and I do not have many friends here in the town. A friend of mine, who was taken ill the day your father died, has been accused of killing him. I don't believe that he did so, and nor, for that matter, does your brother Will. You were here on that day. If you know anything to help me help my friend, then please remember it and tell me. We both need all our friends now, don't you think?'

The child's eyes had grown very wide. 'My father was drowned, though,' she whimpered. 'He slipped in the pots. It was an accident.'

'Is that what they told you? Come now, you're a clever girl, you can't believe that. Why do you think there are whispers and gossiping still in the church? You've seen the size of the dye pots. How could your dada fall in? Was he drunk? Of course he was not. He was struck from behind, and mercifully dead before he hit the water. I am sorry. You loved him. But someone did not.'

'There was a man here,' she said softly, biting back the tears, 'there was a man, with a beard and green cloak, who wanted the piss pot. He's not from our kirk, and his voice was quite fine.'

'A gentleman, think you? A merchant? A scholar?'

'I don't know. I'd not seen him before.'

'Would you know him again?'

'No, I don't know, I was turning my back. I might know the cloak, though.'

If the cloak existed still, it would be steeped in dye. Hew sighed. 'I do not think he will have kept the cloak. Would you know the voice?'

'He was a stranger. Not from here.'

'An Englishman? A Frenchman? Dutch?'

'Of course not,' she said scornfully, 'he spoke perfect Scots.'

'How old was he?'

She shrugged, 'A man.'

'Alright.' Another thought occurred to him. 'Did Katrin see him too?'

'She might have done.'

Hew gave a sigh. 'Well, we've sat out here awhile. It must be safe to go indoors now, don't you think? Will you not show me the way?'

The child shook her head. She had pulled her plaid tight round her arms. Hew awkwardly patted her shoulder, impossibly thin, and said gently, 'Let me give you something. If not the money, then another box of candies. You could come up to the house sometime to see my cousin's pictures.'

'No, I'll not. It's not because of you,' she added seriously, 'but because your sister helped us. I'll take nothing from you.'

He nodded. 'Jennie, I will find him for you.'

Jennie whispered, 'Aye.'

She scraped at the ground with a stick, as though intent on finding some small answer in the dust. He saw her set her lip against the tears.

Hew knocked lightly on the doorframe and called out. Inside all was quiet. Meg stood by the fireside warming towels. She looked relieved to see him.

'Hush, they're asleep. I don't know how she'll do, for she's lost a lot of blood. There are one or two herbs I could give to her – mistletoe, yarrow – but I haven't my things. When the boy comes, I'll send him to town. Where have you been, Hew? I looked for you.'

'Outside, talking to Jennie. She told me she saw a man in a green cloak, a stranger, use the piss pot on the day her father died.'

'You think it signifies?'

'Perhaps. Katrin saw him too, and now she's gone. Forgive me, Meg.' He had forgotten her exertions. 'Sit here a while.' He took the linens from her. 'Is the danger past?'

Meg shook her head. 'The babe seems so small, it cannot be full of its time. Thank God it came safe, for I had no idea how I could help her.'

'Did you not, though? I thought . . .'

She smiled a little ruefully, and pushed a strand of hair out from her eyes.

'On the farm, Hew, with the horses and the lambs, is not the same.'

'I did not realise.' He stared at her. 'Yet you still came.'

'It was for Jennie, in that kirk, despised and crying so. I thought the midwife would be here, and I should wash the sheets and fuss the children, boiling water on the fire. I little thought I'd have to help deliver her. She's lost so much blood, Hew! I've used all their linen. Do you think Giles would come? Whisht!' The baby was crying. Meg drew back the curtain and Hew saw its angry red face, no more than a mouth in a blanket, tiny red fists pulling free. The red face mewled a little and resumed the angry yowl. The mother stirred on the pillow. Meg helped her shift the infant to her breast, where it restlessly foraged, spluttered and gasped. 'If she gives suck, then the milk may come through. I fear she is too weak.'

The dyer's wife opened her eyes and smiled at them.

'This is my brother come to fetch me,' Meg explained, 'he will not stay.'

But the woman merely nodded, too exhausted for surprise. She tried to clamp the bundle closer to her breast.

Meg was pouring water. 'If you drink, you'll help the flow. There, look, he's quieter now.'

'It's a boy,' remarked Hew, 'then what will you call him?'

'Call . . .' her voice was very faint, 'call him George, think you, after my husband?'

'George?' Hew was taken aback. 'Forgive me, but haven't you a son called George already? Geordie?'

'I suppose I have.' She giggled unexpectedly. 'You must ask my husband, he calls all the names. Oh, but he's dead. Did you know?'

'It is the loss of blood,' Meg whispered, 'that has left her light-headed. Don't encourage her to talk. I'll take the child.'

But the mother murmured restlessly, 'Aye, what name . . . what is your name? I'll call the wean that name.'

'*My* name?' said Hew startled, but her eyes had closed before she heard his answer, head falling back on the bed. Meg slipped a finger in the baby's mouth to break its suck, and it drew fiercely on the bone then slackened off and sighed, the little mouth relaxing into sleep. Meg swaddled it tight and tucked it to the bottom of the bed.

'Well, little Hew,' she teased, 'what think you to your name-sake?'

'It can scarce be as little as I think to mine, ugly red ball of a thing,' replied her brother wryly, 'pray God that she forgets.' But nonetheless, he stood for a long while and looked at the baby, hands on the bed. At last he spoke. 'You brought him forth, Meg, and he wasn't here before.'

She whispered, 'Aye, I know.'

Presently the children came back from the burn with the sopping wet sheets to admire their new brother, though Jennie was nowhere to be seen. At last, as Meg and Hew were making their good-byes, Will Dyer came home. He had searched for the midwife at farm after farm, and had found her at last at a baby's updrinking, soused to the bowels of her, dead to the world. He had scolded and bribed, bullied and comforted, all without purpose; the woman was drunk. He came home then fearing the worst, to find his mother stirring from her sleep to fasten on her bairn.

'George,' she offered, smiling up at Will.

'I'm not my father, Ma,' he muttered gently. Then he understood. 'That isn't George. He's Henry. You remember what we said.'

'A likely name for one so livid,' Hew whispered to Meg.

'She's thinking about the lost bairns,' explained Will. 'There were three died in crying, and all were named George, born between James and Geordie. It was the same when Bess was born. But this,' he gestured to the child, 'his name is Henry, for my father chose it. God knows why. I suppose he had drunk to the dregs of the names. You'll have a drink with me, won't you, to welcome him into the world?'

'I'll not stay, Hew,' Meg whispered, 'I'm tired.' And indeed she seemed uneasy on her feet.

Hew hesitated. 'You are kind,' he demurred, 'we shall drink a brief health, but my cousin awaits us; we must hurry home. Good day to you, mistress. God bless your child.' The mother had rallied a little, and rose from the pillows to thank them.

'Tis good of you, lass, to come out to help us. Look, and there's blood on your fine Sunday clothes.' She picked at the sleeve of Meg's dress, and as she did so her eyes momentarily darkened.

Meg was alarmed. 'Has the bleeding begun again? Are you unwell?'

Janet sounded far away. She closed her eyes and whispered, 'Aye, quite well, I had forgotten, and remembered. Ah, tis nothing now, perhaps a dream.'

'It's you who look to be unwell, if we do not take you home,' protested Hew. He took Meg by the arm, and felt her rest upon him. 'You shall come again tomorrow, if you will.'

Henry Dyer lived for three days. And on the fourth, his brother Will compeared before the kirk and bargained long and hard to find a place for him below the cold earth of the kirkyard, nameless though the child remained in sight of God. And his mother Janet, closed within her bed, fell back without a tear upon the fresh-laid whiteness of the sheets.

Coming to Light

On the day Henry Dyer was born, Nicholas Colp regained consciousness. It was unwilling at first, dredging from dream into dream, but eventually he began to make sense of his feelings. He sensed he had been there a while, though he did not remember the place. The shape of the cot appeared welcome and comfortable, hugging him tight to its sides. The scents of the place, as sharp as turned milk, were familiar. He felt loose in the belly and heavy in limb, neither too hot nor too cold. In his throat he felt a thousand fissures filled with sand, cracked to the core, as if even the last drops of blood had drained to the surface and dried. There was no voice to cry out for water; no tongue to make the sound. He found it massed and spongelike in his mouth, but could not make it shape the words. Surely this was Hell.

But then Nicholas felt a hand upon his face. He felt it far away, as if his face was swathed in fleece. Someone tilted back his head to trickle a warm bitter fluid in drops down his throat. And the drops he felt evaporate like spittle on a griddle pan. They sizzled for a second and were gone. He wanted to sit up and seize the cruel wrist and its cup, to pour in a flood of cold water, and saturate and slake all the cracks of his throat and his thirst and its chasms and channels cut deep to the churn of his belly, but he knew he could not do those things. He could not lift his head from the grip; he could not hold his hands still, hold open his lips to pour in the drink, nor close his throat to swallow it. He did all that he could, and that was an effort; crusted and gritty, he opened his eyes.

'I know you want more.' The devil had set down the cup. 'And trust me, you shall have it, but I cannot give it now. You see, until you are stronger, and able to swallow, we must take it drop by drop. If you can keep awake, you may gradually absorb a little more, and little by little, you will find yourself restored. Let me look at you.'

He moved a lantern closer to the head of the cot, and tucked a small piece of wadding round his thumb. Then he dipped the thumb into the bitter dark liquid and forced open the mouth once again, carefully wiping the root of the tongue. It brought a little relief to Nicholas, who was in any case still powerless to object. The doctor cupped his hands around his face.

'I see you have no pain, which is promising,' he said. 'That is, of course, in part the power of the medicine, which has not worn off, and in part a result of the swelling, which deadens the feeling there to a degree. But nonetheless, if the jaw had been broken, I would expect you to notice considerable pain, which in your eyes and body set is not apparent. Therefore, I think we can safely conclude that the jaw was dislocated, and will return to normal sometime soon. Which, you see,' he added cheerfully, 'is the happiest of news for you, since a broken jawbone requires setting by the surgeon, a man of great enthusiasm unparalleled by skill, and frequently leads to decay of the part, and then death. We must take a look at the rest of you now, and feel for any lasting stiffness in the limbs. If we do not find it, we may indeed say that you are on your way, God willing, to the first stage of recovery. In short,' he whispered, confident that no one else could hear, 'you may be *cured.*'

On that rare note of triumph, Doctor Giles Locke stripped back the bedclothes from the cot and subjected his patient to the most chill and thorough scrutiny of those bodily parts to which, as Nicholas discovered, the feelings were more readily restored.

Nicholas tried hard to sleep, to regain the lost world of oblivion. Each time he closed his eyes, his tormentor appeared at his elbow to prod him awake, promising water, incessantly chattering, delivering dry little dribbles, snatching back the cup. Nicholas wondered what it was that he had done. It must be something bad, he thought, to merit his own private demon, score upon score of subtle indignities, torture so delicately cruel. But gradually, reluctantly, he found he did become more comfortable. And he began, if not to listen, to ease into the voice that droned around him. There was talk of a friend. What friend could he have? There was a girl would come tomorrow, which was grand, because the speaker lacked the time to play the nurse and to nourish and bathe him. Nicholas flinched. Could there be women in Hell? But for him, aye. He learned that he had been taken ill outside a dyer's house – *what did he there*? – and he had a fever from a suppurating abscess in the thigh. The fever had raged for days, turning into lockjaw. Many times, he'd all but died. In the clutch of convulsions, he had damaged his face.

For days he had been there. What did he remember?

He remembered nothing. There was the sense of something dead, numb as the mass on his face, like probing his tongue in the raw mouth of memory, finding it toothless and vacant. Still it returned there, still there was nothing, but depth after depth of vacancy, loss.

'Tomorrow you'll be stronger, and each day you grow stronger will give us less time. You must tell him everything you know. I warn you, trust him as your friend. Hold nothing back. It is your only hope.'

And then at last he understood that Hell was yet to come. The forgotten place, freshly drawn, splintered and sheared into pain, and with it he found his voice.

Giles Locke was torn between fascination and frustration. For days, he had studied the patient, keeping all the while his own account, meticulously noted, in his careful hand. He charted the return to life and the restoration of the vital signs for three days in abeyance: first the quickening of the pulse and then the breath upon the glass and last the slight expansion in the lamplight of the fixed and glassy stare. One by one, and almost imperceptibly, the life signs had returned and Giles Locke had recorded them. He saw the flicker of the eyes below the lids return to dream.

Return from where? Giles ached to question him. But Nicholas, of course, could not reply. He lay there helpless as a child. Come from the womb of death, he could not speak of that unknowing place. As medic, as philosopher, as man of God and sceptic, simply as a *man*, Giles yearned with all his soul to have a moment's converse on the secrets of the grave. He knew it was hopeless. When Nicholas began to speak, he would already have forgotten it. There was everything, and nothing, to be learned.

Giles was an honest scholar, and he made the case notes full, though he knew they would never be read:

Colona conium maculatum in hortulo domestico coluit et radice equum convulsum pavit. Equus superavit.
    A farm girl grew poison hemlock in the garden of her father's house and fed the root to a horse suffering from convulsions. The horse survived.

Colona, a country lass. It was the wrong word, he knew, but he had not known how else to phrase it. He could not use her name. *Pagana*? *Sanatrix*? *Magus* perhaps? None of them seemed to describe her. She was something apart.

The horse survived a little lame, and had not succumbed to madness. A horse was not a man. But horses were highly strung creatures, sensitive to memory and ghosts. They had a sense, for certain, of the evil in a place. That the horse remained sane was a positive sign. He looked at Nicholas, who might never become whole again. Frustration gave place to pity. 'Ah,' he said quietly, 'what could you tell us of death, when even that one comfort, at the last, has been denied to you? Drink a little more.'

He kept the patient alive by touching and talking, insistent he should not relapse into that dark unconsciousness. For his physical recovery, these hours were critical. Giles had seldom seen a patient in so weak a state from lack of food and water. It was like a wasting sickness, where the body gave in gladly at the last and closed itself to sleep. And Nicholas was frail. The muscles in his legs were growing weak and withered. It would be many days, if not weeks, before the man would be able to stand. He might be crippled then. He might be mad. And mad as he was, they might carry him too broken to resist towards his final fate. Could God be so cruel as to insist upon the last, most vengeful manner of his death? He suspected it. Nonetheless, he talked to the patient with a bright and cheerful urgency, forcing him awake. At times he saw the spark of understanding in the eyes, as the buzz of his converse was shaped into words. And then he saw the painful stricture of the neck, the tremor of his lips, and heard him cry. It came dry and sorrowful, scarcely a sound, a pitiful rasp from the back of the throat.

The term began in three days' time, and until then, Hew counted himself free to go where he would in the town. No one raised objection to his going. On one of several visits to inquire about his friend, he discovered the physician was prepared at last to countenance a little gentle questioning. Nicholas, Giles warned, must try to speak gradually, holding the jaw still for fear of further dislocations, and avoiding sudden movements, that would push it out of joint. With this advice, he tactfully withdrew. He regretted the absence of Meg. The constant supervision of the patient had begun to tell on him, and in term would prove impossible. God willing, she would come and come alone. He had devised a system of manoeuvres for the limbs, to stimulate the worn and wasted parts, which he was hoping Meg might implement, and which he sensed her brother might impede.

Hew sat by the bedside, talking quietly. He touched upon their boyhood years. He retold his recent travels and adventures overseas. Once or twice, he almost raised a smile.

'And now I have taken your place, until you are recovered, and walk the self-same halls where once we played as boys. Again, I will sleep in your blankets and read from your books. I'm sharing with your friend Robert Black.'

Nicholas stirred a little. 'Has the term begun?'

'Not yet. It starts on Thursday. Nicholas,' Hew went on seriously, 'Robert found some papers in your room. Do you know what they were?'

He did not blanch but answered simply, 'Yes.'

'He took the papers to the coroner. After you were taken from the dyer's house. He thought you were dead.'

There was a long pause, during which Nicholas stared straight ahead. At last he gave a small sigh, which Hew could not read. Resignation, perhaps? He thought almost relief. 'He did right,' Nicholas said quietly.

Hew swallowed. 'You know that these papers, in the light of the boy's death, incriminate you?'

'I understand.'

'Did you kill him?'

'No.'

'Did you kill the dyer?'

There was a catch to the quietness, almost a sob.

Hew said, 'Why did you go to his house?'

'To plead for Tom. He thought the dyer would denounce him in the kirk, for his relationship with Katrin. So I went to talk to him. He was not there.'

'You did not, I suppose, see someone else there? Katrin?'

'Katrin? Why? What would she be doing there? I saw her at the drover's house.'

'Then did you see a man there, wearing green?'

'I have no recollection. I am told that I was found there. I do not remember it.'

Hew changed his track. 'But you remember how we found the boy? How did you know where to look?'

Giles had returned to the room with a basin of water. He set down the bowl quietly and waited by the door. Nicholas half closed his eyes and whispered. 'I did not know. But we were searching for some cloth. He was limp inside the cloth. I saw the blue wool trapped inside the closet, and I thought it was the cloth. He fell into my arms. You saw him. He was dead.'

'Were you aware that Alexander sometimes slept in the shop?'

'It was never mentioned.'

'Under the counter, according to Tom. You visited the dyer to make a case for Tom.' He returned to the same questions, hoping to discover truths in his confusion. 'Tom was not the murderer. How did you know?'

Nicholas appeared surprised. 'In truth, I did not know it. In my heart, I felt it, when I spoke to him.'

'A poor enough defence. Who killed him, then?' continued Hew.

'I suppose it was his uncle, in a fit of temper. I cannot think that he intended it.'

'No,' Hew accepted. 'Suppose he came into the shop that night, perhaps to make some final preparations for the market, and found Alexander there, asleep below the counter. They had words, and then the uncle struck and killed him, with the shuttle of the loom. But where was Tom? His master thought him fast asleep inside the closet bed. If he had killed his nephew, the bed was the last place he would hide the body.'

'Tom was with his lass.'

'Tom swears that Strachan did not know that. It will be hard to prove. Did he wear a green cloak?'

'No. Perhaps. I do not know. Alexander wore a green cloak,' Nicholas said dreamily.

Giles begin to frown upon them both as Hew persisted. 'A moment more, one question still. When was the last time you saw Alexander?'

'The *last* time,' his friend replied simply.

'Yes, as you say. But the last time you saw him alive?'

'I saw him at his lesson the day before he died. I looked over his work. He was not well prepared.'

'Did you reprimand him?'

'No, in truth not. Or not then.'

'But that was the last time you saw him?'

Nicholas sighed. 'His uncle spoke with me before I left. He was his brother's instrument, a brutal and unhappy one. I told him his expectations could not be met, and we parted on less than good terms. I had set Alexander his task and left him to finish it. However he appeared at college after dark, and begged to speak with me. I was sharp with him, and told him to go home. But there was something in his look that made me call him back. I thought perhaps that he had deeper troubles than I'd realised, or perhaps it was his uncle. The man is loathsome. And so I agreed to walk to the shore, intending to offer him counsel. Whereupon he came very meekly, thanked me for my time, and did not speak again until we reached the sands. I recall, the night was clear. We walked for a while, and I spoke to him about the university. I said I would explain to his father that I thought him too young, which was no fault of his, and that he might attend the grammar school a term or two and then matriculate next year. And as I was explaining this, I glanced at his face and realised that he had not heard a word of it, but he was staring out to sea, his cheeks aflame. I was vexed, and thought to remonstrate, when suddenly he burst out with a wild impassioned crying. He said that he loved me, all his thoughts and hopes and prayers were placed in me, that the thought of me coloured his studies, his daylight, his dreams, that I was by turns both gentle and cold to him, *cruel*, he suggested. He could no longer bear it; I toyed with his heart.'

Hew felt a growing uneasiness. 'Had you not known?'

Nicholas had given it thought. He said carefully. 'I don't think I had known, not then. But looking back, the signs were there.'

'And so you were forced to repel him.' He was leading his witness, he knew. He wanted to discount the alternative quickly. 'You cast him aside from you, sent him away.'

There was a long pause before Nicholas answered. 'I sent him home, yes. I dealt with him gently. I told him I was moved by his affections, I cared for him, and wanted what was right for him. That it was not proper that he should express himself in this way to me, but I could see his loneliness, and excused him. I said that we would speak of it again, in calmer tones, he should not be distressed. And because . . .' his voice had dropped low, 'he was so very desolate. I sought to comfort him. I saw it had begun to rain, darkening the sand. The drops on his hair were like dew. And I kissed him lightly on the hair. I kissed him on the head, and told him not to fret, and sent him home. And when I next saw him, the place I had kissed was splintered and cracked, and all of his dampened bright hair was made heavy with blood.'

He closed his eyes. Giles took Hew by the arm. 'Enough. He's exhausted.' For a moment more, he fussed around the bed and made his patient comfortable. Nicholas appeared to be asleep. 'Come into the other room,' Giles said. 'We're finished here.'

At first they did not speak of it. Giles asked politely, 'How do you find your room in the college? You're settled, I hope?'

'It feels strange to be back there,' said Hew. 'The place has changed. And for the worse, I think. Shall I see you at the examinations on Thursday?'

'That is a pertinent question. I had this morning a most cordial communication from your principal, who has assured me that my presence, contrary to statute, is not required on that occasion. It is, he writes, a mere formality, which need not prey upon my conscience or my time, preoccupied as I must be with preparation for the term. Now is that not considerate?'

'Uncommonly.'

'As I thought. Therefore rest assured that you will see me there. It shows promise of diversion.'

'I fear it. Giles, do you think that Nicholas will live? Ah, do not answer that!'

'Did you imagine I might?' Giles asked, amused. Then he was serious. 'Not many men survive the lockjaw. The wrack of limbs and lungs is not so easily recovered. The truth is, I believe that he will live a year or five or ten, but that he will not be restored to what he was. His breaths are painful and spittled with blood. His legs are weak; he cannot stand. And what is worse, his will has been broken. Well then, that's enough. I have been wondering, Hew, about the finding of the corpse. I heard Nicholas say in there that he was limp inside the cloth. He spoke it quite distinctly.'

'Aye, it's true. He was.'

'Because if the corpse was limp you know, it could not have been dead above a few hours. On a warm day, and wrapped in a blanket, in a warm place and dry, perhaps five or six hours at the outset. If the corpse was not yet stiffened, Alexander must have died that day.'

'We found him in the evening, after kirk.'

'He died then in the afternoon, no sooner.'

'Then it could not have been Strachan or Tom,' exclaimed Hew. 'They were in Crail the whole of that day. They declared him missing at the moment they returned. It could have been Agnes, his aunt, for she held the keys to the shop. And Tom has sworn they found the place unlocked when they returned. But still,' he cursed, 'this does not help. It could still be Nicholas. Robert Black declared him missing in the afternoon.'

'Could it be Robert Black?' suggested Giles unhelpfully.

'Aye, and the porter, the baxter, the principal too. Don't muddy the waters. But where was Nicholas? Has he offered, by the by, a proper explanation for the wound in his thigh?'

'I have an idea about that,' Giles answered thoughtfully. 'I doubt he will confide it.'

'I will put it to him that he must. For tis most poignant.'

'I suspect he counts it poignant to himself and to his God. If I can gain his confidence, perhaps he will divulge it. For the present, he resents me deeply for my forced attentions to his person.'

'You think he made the cut himself?' Hew inquired astutely.

'It's possible. I will say only this: there are other, older marks upon his body.'

'Then their purpose may itself arouse suspicion.'

'I pray, for pity, do not ask him yet, but know he is a most devout, unhappy man. Find what you can to bear out his statement.

In the meantime, let him rest. There is another possibility that has occurred to me. I hardly like to mention it.'

'But you feel that you must.'

'Well then, I must. The boy died from a blow to the head?'

'Without question. His skull was smashed in.'

'I have known men with head wounds behave in improbable ways. Soldiers left with half a brain have battled on to win the field, or with most savage injuries have strolled around for hours. Is it possible he could have climbed into the closet bed himself?'

'Aye, if the blow had cured him of his horror of small spaces,' snorted Hew. 'And did he also wrap himself up in a parcel of cloth and place the weapon of destruction neatly by his side?'

'I grant it unlikely. Alright, he was placed in the closet by the killer, to conceal the crime. But we don't know when he died. Perhaps he was alive when he was put there, and did not die for several hours.'

'Which puts the crime as possible again the night before. I thank you, Giles. This does not help. Is there no way out of it?'

Giles shook his head. 'If I had the body, and the cloth it was wrapped in, from the pattern of effusion, it might be possible to tell. Without the corpse, or even the cloth, which I imagine is long gone, I can tell you nothing.'

'I'm lost here, Giles. You have widened the scope. Explain to me quite how this helps us.'

Giles appeared hurt. 'I merely mark the possibilities. Let me reiterate, I think it most likely that the boy was dead when he found his way into the closet, and that he died at some point in the afternoon. Unless you find out to the contrary, I should accept that as the starting point. But where you go from there, I cannot say. You seem ill-tempered, Hew. I cannot think college life suits you.'

'Remind me, Giles, why we are friends.'

'You for the sake of my wit, and I for the sake of your sister.'

'What?' said Hew, startled. But Giles had dismissed him: 'Now, my good friend, I bid you good day. I must prepare to face the rigours of the term.'

Loose Women

In her cousins' house on the south street Meg was suffering. She had returned from Janet's labour to find Lucy Linn in tears on her bed. She sobbed so profusely that Meg was in fear for the child. When at last she fell still, Meg crept out to the moonlight, crouching on the barren scrub of ground. She searched among the shadows for familiar shapes, the longed-for gardens, herbs and trees. But Lucy woke and called out from the window, and the ground remained stony and bare. Lucy's moods were fuelled as much by terror as by petulance. Alone with the thought of her child, a monster distilling inside her, she gave way to her fears. And all her bright chatter of gossips and furniture, all the trivial comforts of her pretty painted house, were lamps against night terrors, lit in the darkness to fend off the fiend. That morning in the kirk had confirmed her worst suspicions. It was the spectre of the dyer's child, who pled so wild and tearful for her mother's life, that had brought the horror home to her. The dyer's wife was low and coarse, yet still she had come close to dying. Lucy Linn was soft and fair.

Worn though she was, Meg soothed the sick fancies, lay by her mattress and smoothed out her hair. She told her over and over how Henry Dyer had appeared into the world, how Janet's labour had been brave and safe at last, until her cousin like a bairn appeared to sink exhausted, only to begin again. In despair, she made up a draught that would lull them both to sleep. They slept through the night and half the next day, rising vexed and languid in the early afternoon. Meg felt she could no longer bear the air of torpor in the house. Lucy sat and sighed, sighed and sat, staring at her pattern sheets, the scraps of infant linen left untouched. Meg placed a hand on her shoulder.

'Lucy, perhaps we will not stitch the frocks today. I have promised to return to see the dyer's wife. She has need of herbs.'

Lucy recoiled. 'You won't leave me again?'

'I thought we might go to the market,' Meg pursued gently, 'and visit the apothecary. And I should like some linen for a gown. It will lift your spirits to go out in the air. And you might see your friends.'

'Aye,' conceded Lucy weakly, 'I should like to see Tibbie and Agnes. And Archie may have trimmings for the shawls.'

Meg felt drunk in the sunlight, light in the head from the lack of good rest. On the corner of the Mercatgait she found her shop beneath the symbol of the rose. The counters were well stocked with herbs both dried and fresh, and with a little guile Meg was able to induce the man to make his medicines to her own prescriptions, disguising her knowledge as innocent inquiry. By describing one or two imaginary ailments she was able to procure some medicines for herself and a calming draught for Lucy. An apprentice was despatched with herbs for Janet's bleeding. Meg wished she could have gone herself. But Lucy pressed her on.

'The air smells bad here, like a sick room. *Shall* we go? The weaver will have shut his shop. Why so long among the pills and potions, Meg?'

'I have had the man make up a draught to calm your spirits, Lucy, and to cool you in the night,' her cousin soothed. 'It will help you sleep.'

A single lamp burned in Strachan's shop and the booth seemed drab and crowded, dingier than Meg remembered it. Although the shutters were open, they allowed for little light and the brighter of the plaids were buried at the back, protected from the light that filtered through. Row upon row of black wool and hardens, coarse woven stemming and beggar-grey blanket gave the place a gloomy feel, with an unpleasant aftertaste of rancid grease and sweat.

At the sound of the door the weaver came gushing, unpleasantly rubbing his hands. His welcome hid reproach beneath the flattery. 'Mistress Linn! But can this be business or pleasure? We have missed you, as I do believe, on both accounts. We have not seen your husband since the wake. Tibbie, go tell your mother her good friend Lucy Linn is come at last. Agnes will be glad of it. For these are troubled times for us. Still, I hope you are well. And Robin Flett also . . . and this,' he turned shrewdly to Meg, 'but who is your friend?'

Lucy waved away his hand, carelessly dropping her glove.

'I thank you. My husband is well. For myself, I am in thrall to my condition as you see, and may not come among my friends as I would please. This is Margret Cullan, my cousin.'

'Indeed.' He looked at Meg suspiciously. 'You know the dyer's wife, I think.'

'Indeed, I did not know her until yesterday.'

'Truly? A rare act of charity,' he sneered.

'Meg is very charitable,' interrupted Lucy, sounding bored. 'She is come until my lying in, and since she is come from the country, she has need of new clothes. *I* require some lace.'

'But certainly. Tom here will show you the dress-stuffs.' He motioned to a rack of cloths, 'and here, Mistress Linn, are the laces. Which do you prefer?'

The prentice showed Meg to a rack of wools. 'What colour did you want?' he asked indifferently.

'Grey, perhaps, or blue. I don't know.'

'Popinjay, partridge, watchett, plunkett,' he catalogued patiently, 'clodie, crane, clay-colour . . .'

'So many?' Meg said helplessly. She looked across at Lucy, who was talking to the weaver and fingering some lace.

'Alexander, milk-and-water, sad-colour, rat-colour, gentleman, ash . . .'

'Rat?' Meg asked, startled.

'Rat-colour, aye.' He pulled a bolt of grey-black fabric from the shelf and dropped it with a thud upon the counter. Rat. How much do you want of it?'

Meg stroked the heavy cloth with sinking heart. 'Something a little lighter. Mouse perhaps?' She smiled appealingly.

He stared at her. 'There's no such shade.'

To Meg's relief, her cousin rescued her, for there was nothing new in Strachan's shop that could be found to please her. She dismissed the proffered ribbons. 'These are plain and dull. They are not silk, I think. Where were they made?'

The weaver bridled. 'For sure, they are the finest . . .'

Lucy shook her head. 'I wanted something for my baby's shawl. I would not have this for a pillow for my lapdog, it's so coarse and rough. Where is your Flemish lace?'

Strachan's face darkened. 'We have none in stock. Perhaps when my brother comes . . .'

'Tsk, then I'll have Robin fetch it. Well then, I like nothing here. Are you coming, Meg?' She pulled her cousin away from the counter, insisting, 'You do not want *that*, such a dirty colour, not fit for a beggar. Do I see Tibbie there?'

'What are you thinking of?' Strachan raged at Tom. He hurried over to the counter. 'Is *rat* a proper colour for a lady? Show the Alexander, or the crystalline, you fool.' He gave a look that promised ill when once the shop was empty.

The boy said sullenly, with sudden reckless spirit, 'Lady asked for greys.'

Archie turned towards the shelves. Heavily, he pulled out a bolt of soft greenish-blue and slammed it down on the counter. 'This is our most special shade, most popular among the more discerning,' he glanced meaningfully at Lucy, 'in the town. As fate has it, this is our very last length.'

'There's more in the back,' Tom put in truculently. Strachan ignored him.

'Don't you think it suits your friend's complexion, Mistress Linn? Feel how fine the weave is, and how soft.' He touched a corner of the wool against Meg's cheek, and she suppressed a shudder. Thankfully, Lucy snatched it away.

'How can you, sir? For was this not the cloth that wrapped your nephew?'

'Well,' Archie answered, a little nonplussed. 'Tis not the *self-same* cloth.'

She squealed. 'It disgusts me. And I'm feeling quite faint. Tibbie must take us through to her mother. Leave the cloths, Meg, and help me up the stair.'

Oblivious to her father's glower, the girl led them willingly up through the back of the shop. Meg glanced surreptitiously around her, suppressing a slight swell of nausea, at the place where Alexander had died. The scent of oil and dust felt stronger here, and there were wools at every stage from pelt to plaid, in all the drabs and dyes from plum to puce. And yet there was no sign of industry. The two large looms stood still and vacant, and the floors were clean of threads. At the back built into the wall she saw the closet bed. But there nothing in the room to indicate what had happened there. All was quiet, still and neat.

Tibbie opened a small door upon a narrow twisting staircase, leading to the upper floor. Above, a corridor ran the length of the house, with a ladder to the loft at the back. The tiny gabled room was now reserved for Tom, and through this narrow passage he could come and go between it and the shop without encroaching on the family in the hall below. The main part of the house was a large and well-set family room, with a small pantry and a closet bed offset on either side. The standen bed of oak was over-stuffed and furnished; the walls, though unpainted, were heavily hung with new tapestries. The board was set with plate and clean green cloths. A gallery, part glazed, overhung the street, and in what remained of the daylight there Agnes sat sewing. She looked pale and tired. But when she saw her guests she set her work aside and forced a smile. 'Lucy, come at last! You are most welcome, and your friend. We saw you at the kirk,' she glanced at Meg approvingly. 'Tibbie, help your father in the shop.'

Tibbie pulled a face 'My father has no work for me. I only try his temper, which God knows, is sharp enough. And then he will vent it on Tom, which *you* say disquiets you.' Meg feared he had already done so. She thought she heard him cursing as they turned upon the stair.

'What nonsense, lass, go to your spinning!' Agnes snapped.

'Minnie, the fleeces are done,' Tibbie told her patiently. 'And Tom has stopped the looms. We have wools and threads enough. Since my uncle will not take it on his ships, we shall not sell what we have already spun. My father is falling over it, and the sight of the bales makes him angry. If I spin, then I make even more of it; Tom will have to weave it and my father has to pay for dyeing of the cloth. And if I am idle, it enrages him further, since it proves the point we have no purpose to our work and no orders to fulfil.'

'You must not speak so,' Agnes scolded. 'The wools will sell at the Andermas market, and we must be prepared. It's not so far away.'

'Will they, though?' the girl protested, '*Where* then will we sell them? Unless my uncle comes, we shall not have a stall.'

'For shame, Tibbie, what would your father say?'

'He would say I was wrong, and know differently. Minnie, he cannot find the work for Tom, he has him sweeping up the threads a hundred times a day. There are no threads. Without my uncle, we cannot find the market for our leines, and the good wives who come to the shop here are looking for ribbons and laces and silks – uncle's things,' she shot a caustic glance at Lucy, 'not coarse woollen shirtstuffs and plaids. Ask my father, has he sold a shirt today.'

'You are wrong,' said Agnes, stricken. 'He will sell them on St Andrew's Day. You must not say these things.' She fumbled in her pocket. 'Well, if you won't spin,' she recovered bravely, 'you may go to market. Buy some flour and oatmeal. We shall have some cakes.'

Tibbie heaved a heavy sigh, shook her head, and took the coin. She clattered down the stairs and slammed the door.

'Young quenes,' sighed Agnes helplessly, 'are every one the same.'

'Is it true?' Lucy asked her, 'Your brother has left? He does not do business for you?'

Agnes flushed a little. '*Archie's* brother sailed some time since for the Flemish markets. It's true he did not take our wools.

But he is sore distracted by the murder of his son. You know this from your husband. He has interests in the ship.'

'He has an equal share,' corrected Lucy. 'They are partners. Robin will be back before the fair.' She cupped her hands upon her womb to force the point. 'He *must* be back. Perhaps Gilbert will come too, and he will bring the ribbons and the lace. He's certain to return.'

'Perhaps.' Agnes changed the subject. 'Come, I forget myself, for you look worn. Lie on the bed awhile, Lucy, I'll warm up some milk. And if Tibbie comes with the flour, and is not waylaid by her gossips, which we cannot count upon, I'll make us all some cakes.'

'I wonder you have no flour in the house.'

Meg blushed at Lucy's tactlessness. But Agnes answered patiently. 'I like to buy it fresh. When Tibbie does return, you'll taste the difference. Meanwhile, won't you rest?'

'It's true, I have a headache. I will rest a little.' Lucy lay back on the bolsters of the oak standing bed, and sighed theatrically.

'Will you sit, Margret, here by the window?' Agnes drew up a stool. 'We'll speak softly, so as not to disturb her. I saw you at the kirk. I'm glad you helped the dyer's wife. In fact I felt ashamed of it. I wished I might have gone myself. Tell me, though, how does she now?'

'I have not returned to see her.' Meg glanced warily at Lucy. 'I regret it.'

Agnes understood. ''Tis difficult, I know. I doubt you have done what you could.'

'It is my hope.' Meg dropped her voice. 'Yet I fear she bleeds profusely and has need of herbs to stem the flood. We are come from the apothecary. His prentice goes to see her now.'

'Which do you use?' Agnes asked in interest. 'My husband does not rate him in the marketplace.'

'Ah,' called Lucy keenly from the bed, listening all the while. 'Meg knows all the secrets. You should have seen how she tricked the man. She wrote the script herself. And she devises it so cleverly, that the man thinks it was his idea. With flattery, you know.

How silly these men are. She is a cunning creature, Agnes. I am greatly out of spirits with the waxing of my child, which the physician says must be borne,' she chuckled at the pun, 'and tis perverse it does not please me, but Meg knows the secrets to settle and soothe me. She is wise indeed.'

'Lucy was fevered and fretful,' Meg corrected quickly, 'I gave her a water of lettuce to calm her heat. It will not harm the child.'

'Where did you learn this?' wondered Agnes. 'Are you a midwife, Meg?'

Meg shook her head. 'It is a family receipt. My country nurse taught me.'

Agnes nodded thoughtfully. She glanced at Lucy, who lying on the bed quite like a dying actor, closed her eyes. Meg thought her buttock and belly swell spoiled the effect, plump as the pillows she slumped on. Agnes gave a snort. For a moment she said nothing, but briskly attended the fire. 'My father was a blacksmith,' she resumed. 'He sometimes dealt with horses that were lame, or had the colic. He was said to have the touch. But his lore was not passed on. I never learnt it.'

'Tis the pity,' Meg said simply.

'Aye.' They talked on a little, politely, while Lucy closed her eyes and appeared to fall asleep. Agnes looked at Meg and murmured, 'What herbs do you prescribe for Janet?'

'Shepherd's purse, yarrow, and mistletoe to slow the effusion of blood. And then a purgative to cleanse. Physicians think that spilling blood restores the humours. I have never found it so.'

'Well then, there are limits, I suppose,' suggested Agnes. 'What you say intrigues me. What do you prescribe for Lucy, who grows out of her humours and sick in the carrying of her child? I swear she was not quite so petulant before. The same medicines, then, that close off the terms?'

'No, no, that would not do for her. For Lucy, we must lift her spirits without danger to her babe. I confess, she is too easily aroused. I recommend her rest, and more diversion, air and exercise.

Nettle broth, rose syrup, camomile and lettuce waters; not so many sugarplums.'

Agnes laughed. 'She may not thank you, then. It's sound enough advice. I wonder . . . .' She had come quite close to Meg, passing her a cup of frothing milk, 'if I might ask you your opinion on a private matter?'

'If I can give it, then I should be glad to,' Meg said cautiously, 'though an apothecar, perhaps . . . ?'

Agnes shook her head. 'I have consulted one. He did not help.'

'Are you melancholy?'

'Melancholy, aye, but tis a matter of the womb. Since Tibbie, I have not been blessed with child. It is a great trial to Archie, who for many years has sought a son. Lately,' she paused, 'this failing has become the more bitter, with the death of our nephew and the disgrace of our prentice, Tom Begbie. Now, more than ever, Archie feels his disappointment. I would like to give him the son he deserves to inherit the business. Some years back, Archie consulted his physician, who explained that the lack of a child was the result of blackened vapours in my womb. The womb had unseated itself and, restless, had stopped its course. He gave me a receipt to help provoke the menses. I don't know what it was. It tasted foul.'

'But did it work?'

'It seemed to, for a while. The courses were restored but they were still irregular. Yet I did not fall with child. Archie took me back to the physician, but he so misliked that man's conclusion, he would not allow me to consult with him again. I never did discover what made up the remedy.'

'What were his conclusions?' wondered Meg.

Agnes flushed. 'He hinted it was lack of carnal conversation that most often caused the stopping of a healthy women's terms. He proved it with the horoscope, wherein he showed my husband cold and dry.'

'He said as much?'

'As much as Archie understood he had maligned his manhood.

My husband was enraged, and he said, twas my black vapours did pollute his seed, denying him his right and proper heir.'

'And still you want his child?' Meg asked her doubtfully.

'Exceedingly.' She looked at Meg. 'Can you tell me the herbs I might use, to restore my monthly courses?'

'Well,' Meg said gently, 'Have you considered, after all these years, they may have *run* their course?'

'I have considered it,' admitted Agnes, But in spite of what you say, if bloods are gathered there, and blackened in the womb, then it were curative, surely, to unloose them?'

'You may be right, I do not know,' said Meg, uncertain. 'After all those years?'

'They have not *altogether* stopped,' Agnes explained. 'Occasionally, they do recur. I know that I grow old. This may be our last chance to have a child.'

'You might consult another man of physic.'

'Archie would not have it. And I cannot pay.'

'Well,' conceded Meg at last, 'there are herbs effective in bringing on the courses, but they may be prejudicial to the planting of a child. For the three or four months that you take them, you should not conceive.'

'At present,' answered Agnes eagerly, 'a month or three or four may prove of scarce account.'

'I understand. Well then, when the pattern of the courses has come regular for several months, you must stop taking the herbs, and try for the child.'

'I pray you, *what* do you prescribe?'

Meg considered. 'There is pennyroyal, but that is not native to these parts, and unless you buy it from the apothecary, I know not where you may find it. You can boil up the leaves of sage and saxifrage and drink the liquor, but the usefulness is limited. If it were myself, I should try wild carrot seed.'

'Carrot?' Agnes looked sceptical.

'Wild carrot, which grows here in abundance. The roots are too pungent to eat, but the seeds are fragrant in a broth or stew.

Boiled in wine, you may drink them to bring down your menses. And afterwards, when your terms run true and you are potent to conceive, you can use the same to salt your husband's meat. It will strengthen his seed and provoke his lusts, and so the seed shall serve you twice in your design.'

'I know the plant, and where it grows. It does not seed,' said Agnes, hopelessly. 'I cannot buy it from the shop, without my husband's ken.'

'Well . . .' Meg hesitated, 'If you like, I can give you some.' She produced a small pocket from inside her sleeve. 'I carry a little for my own use *in extremis*. It has several applications. Here, there is not much. You make take it all.'

'I thank you, can you spare it?' Agnes took it eagerly. 'Shall I take it now?'

'If you like. I have more at home.'

Agnes set a cup of wine to warm upon the fire. 'When will it work?'

'If the courses are ready to flow, perhaps in a day or two. But be prepared, the time may not yet be propitious for the taking it.'

'The better to begin at once. Forgive me, I have waited so long, I must seem impatient. I hardly can believe that we have come to this at last.'

She swallowed down the draught and pulled a face.

''Tis a remedy only,' cautioned Meg. 'It may not effect a cure.'

'It will cure me, I'm assured of it. I thank you, Meg. Your cousin stirs, I doubt.' Her tone had changed abruptly.

'Aye, she does, and I must take her home.'

Without her prophylactic settling in her pocket, Meg felt vulnerable. An inauspicious cloud was falling, and she did not see clearly. As quickly as was possible, they made polite farewells. Lucy Linn, restored from sleep, professed an appetite.

'You'll want to have your supper, then,' concluded Agnes, firmly. She made no further mention of the cakes.

Bursaries

On the first Thursday of the Martinmas term, a clutch of impoverished supplicants aged between fourteen and twenty gathered in the long hall of St Leonard's to compete for places at the university. The college was quiet, for most of the scholars had not yet returned. The boys clustered anxiously, thinking in Latin, praying in Scots, and made their way forward in silence. Hew watched them from the window of the regents' room. Behind him, Robert Black sat reading at the desk. When the last boy turned the corner and the courtyard gates were closed, and the last of the fallen leaves caught in the wind of their footsteps had settled again, Hew turned to him: 'Are you not coming?'

Robert yawned, stretching his legs. 'I rather thought not. I have a little work I'd like to finish here before the class convenes.'

'But you are responsible for the first-year class. How can you ignore the elections?'

'If there was an election, I should be glad to take my part in it. But I'm afraid you are ignorant still of the way things are done here. There will be no bursaries awarded in the hall today.'

'The auld and new colleges have filled up their quotas,' argued Hew, 'but I have seen our statutes. We allow for twelve, of which only two are taken. By my reckoning, that leaves another ten.'

Robert smiled gravely. He closed his book, drawing out the piece of parchment he had used to mark the page. 'Do you see this paper? It is the first-year class list. The principal gave it to me yesterday, the thirty-six intrants already subscribed. There will be no bursars, because the class is full.'

'How can the class be filled before the examinations have taken place?' objected Hew.

'I see you have not fully understood our master's method. Look, *this* is the boy,' Robert pointed to the name, 'who takes the place of Alexander Strachan. The principal has taken pains to welcome him.'

Hew looked at the paper. 'The name meaning nothing to me.'

'Ah. It does to me. He is the son of an earl, about sixteen years of age. He was lately a student of Glasgow University where a friend of mine is regent. The lad enrolled last year, when it pleased him not to linger in the kirk or lecture hall, but rather while his time away with whores. He spent and drank heavily, brawled in the taverns and flourished his sword in the street. He was finally called to account for forcing a lass from the town. My friend wrote that the girl had been cut on the breast and the face. The lad's excuse was that she liked it so. His father bought her off. The university was not so easily appeased and the boy was required to submit to college discipline by his regent, whom he violently misliked. To show his remorse, he broke the man's nose. Whereupon the regent referred the matter to his principal, who required the offender to fall upon his knees and beg forgiveness in the presence of the full assembly of the college hall.'

'And did he?' Hew inquired.

'Reluctantly, on pain of public flogging and of excommunication from the college and the kirk. He also offered, under similar caution, a purse of gold coin, which the regent refused. However he forgave the hurt, absolving him of sin, on the promise of confession, and a proper true remorse. And this wilful proud boy made the promise, as black as he was in his heart. On the following Sunday as the regent came from kirk he was intercepted by his lordship and his friends, and attacked with knives and clubs. It was only through the passing of some soldiers, who happened to be quartered in the town, that the regent escaped with his life.'

'Then were no charges brought?'

'It was settled by the father, who paid bloodwite to the college and the Crown, and promised a pension to the regent for his life-time. Unhappily, at least for us, the boy was dismissed from the faculty.'

'An unhappy end indeed,' reflected Hew. 'Can Gilchrist be aware of this?'

'Assuredly. Which is why he has no places for those poor but worthy striplings in the hall. But to look on the bright side, have you not noticed that our college has a brand new set of plate?'

Hew shook his head in disbelief. 'I cannot think you are content to collude in this, Robert. Come, in your conscience, you cannot make light of it.'

Robert Black sighed. 'I am here for a lifetime, and the jest has long gone cold. Peace, I will come to the show. I bid you, though, don't ask for courage too.'

Giles Locke was already in the lecture room, looking through the list of candidates. He was sitting in the large oak chair that belonged to the principal. This was inauspicious, and Robert Black began to wish he had not come. Hew looked over at the huddle of boys waiting by the door. He saw few witnesses. There were one or two schoolmasterly types, the minister from Holy Trinity, to whom Hew raised his cap, and between eighteen and twenty-four scholars in varying degrees of abject misery. He had begun to count them when the doors opened to admit James Gilchrist, followed by a young man with an armful of papers and books. Gilchrist scraped his feet furiously, sniffing the air. 'A horse has got loose, polluting the courtyard. Pray someone see to it.' Hew stifled a groan. Politely, and shrewdly perhaps, the physician stood up from the chair. The principal frowned.

'I had not thought to see you here, Doctor Locke. Perhaps you have not had my letter?'

Giles replied pleasantly, 'I did receive your letter, thank you, but I disregarded it. As I understand, it is incumbent on me to be present on occasions such as this, and to cast my vote. I'm anxious, you know, to play my full part.'

'That is your prerogative, of course,' the principal said stiffly. 'My concern was to allow you more time to complete your dissections before the rigours of the term had taken hold.'

'You are kind. But I'm afraid you have a misconception of my work here. I'm not licensed to perform dissections in my college rooms, though I confess I find the inference diverting. My anatomies, sadly, are bound to the page.'

'Indeed,' said Gilchrist enigmatically, 'then I am misinformed. I can't insist upon your going . . . .'

'Quite,' inserted Giles.

'. . . but since you stay, I must insist upon the chair. This is my college. Master Cullan,' he had turned to Hew, 'have you met Duncan Stewart? He is one of your magistrands, you know, and we expect great things of him at the end of the year, do we not, Duncan? Master Cullan is your regent, who replaces Master Colp.'

The young man set down his papers and extended a cool hand. 'I'm glad to meet you, Master Cullan. I hope we may be friends.'

Taken aback at the ease of his manner, Hew nonetheless accepted his hand. 'I fear I may prove a poor enough second for Nicholas Colp.'

Duncan laughed rudely. 'Then it's clear you don't know him.'

'What do you mean by that?' He kept his voice light, and Duncan failed to catch the menace in his tone.

'You can have little in common. For he was a whelp, sir, a low and ungentle man.'

'No, no,' Gilchrist intervened. He did not like the way the conversation was turning, nor the look he saw upon Hew's face. 'Come, Duncan, you forget yourself. You will not begin on good terms with Master Cullan here if you malign your last regent. He cannot know your purpose, nor the cause.'

'I'm sorry, sir,' the student said. 'The truth is that Master Colp misliked me intensely, and I him. He made bad report of my work to my father.'

'To be fair,' Robert Black observed mildly, 'You did no work.'

Duncan Stewart ignored him. 'He disliked me on account of my breeding and birth. He was a bursar, and his favours he kept for the bursars. They had the best of him, and I will own he did not spare them his attentions. When they were lax, he overlooked their faults, while for myself, when I had overslept or mistaken my task, his reproaches were most stringent and severe. And when I first came, as a boy, and childishly played in his class, he answered me so cruelly that I thought to leave the college, but for the respect I felt owed to my father and friends here.'

Hew looked at him thoughtfully. 'Then you accuse him of prejudice?'

'As I recall,' mused Robert, 'your sport consisted in the threatening of the bursars with your pocket knife, if they would not fulfil the task for you, and Nicholas did remonstrate, and took away the knife. Tis a good knife, mark you, I still have it in my room, and if you will not puncture scholars, you may sometime have it back.'

'Well, well, enough,' said the principal. '*Nil nisi bonum*, what say you, Doctor Locke?' He gave a look of great meaning, which Giles received, baffled. 'No more of this, gentlemen. Shall we begin?'

'We may not proceed,' the doctor protested, 'without the New College principal, and without your other regents. Where are they?'

'Professor Lamb,' explained Gilchrist patiently, 'a man of eighty-three, has not left his college rooms for twenty years.'

'Well then, his depute?'

'*That* man is an out-and-out papist, under present caution to the Crown. I assure you, his opinion counts as nought. For my regent James Guthrie, he has had a tooth drawn and is sorely afflicted. Poor man, I have sent him back to bed.'

'That leaves one more.'

'The regent, Samuel Ross.' Gilchrist furrowed his brow. 'Now he has gone to find a haircut. I believe to Perth,' he concluded in triumph. 'It's the fashion, I am told. Enough, now. This meeting is quorate.' Firmly, he called out a name.

A tall pimpled youth approached nervously. Gilchrist frowned at him

You were a candidate last year, I think?'

'I was, sir.'

'Have your circumstances changed?'

'I have worked very hard at my grammar, sir.'

'I see. Well, we need not trouble you, I think. We have the reports here. Thank you for coming. Failed to meet the standard,' he said in an audible whisper. 'Next boy: William Collins.'

The boy looked very pale. Hew hoped he would not spew. The principal began with him pleasantly enough.

'Who is your father, William Collins?'

'He's a fisherman, sir. We live in St Monans.'

Gilchrist nodded sagely. 'That's a very fine pair of boots you're wearing. New, I think. Were they made in St Monans, I wonder? You must have grand shoemakers there. What do you think, Master Black, shall we go down to St Monans for our shoes? What I am wondering, William Collins, is how a poor fisherman can afford to buy his son so fine a pair of boots?'

'The shoemaker said he could pay off a herring a catch, sir.'

'Indeed?' Gilchrist raised his eyebrows. 'That is uncommonly kind.'

'Because, sir,' the boy had begun to hesitate, 'I walked here from St Monans, and I had no boots. The shoemaker said it was a fine thing for a fisher boy to go to the university, and if he had a son, sir, he would wish to send him too. I think, really, he gave us the shoes out of kindness.'

'Did he indeed? Now tell me, who has taught you Latin grammar? Is there a school is St Monans?'

'Yes, sir. At the minister's house.'

'And who pays the minister to school you? Does he do it for kindness? Or does he take fish?'

Hew could hear Duncan Stewart sniggering behind him. He turned round to glare. The boy appeared confused. Then he brightened. 'But I have testimonials from the minister.'

Sighing heavily, Gilchrist consulted the paper. 'Yes. He makes good report of your morals and character. You're well versed in grammar. But you see, William Collins,' and he wagged a playful finger, 'we can't give bursaries to boys whose fathers have the means for schools and shoes. You must explain to your father that if he cares to work a little harder, and will meet the terms, you may enrol here as a scholar. I should warn, though, we do not take fish.' He gave a genial smile.

'But . . . am I not to take the examination?'

'No point.' His tone changed abruptly and leaning forward, he said sternly, 'let not the bursars' places be diverted to the rich, for would you take provision from a poor but worthy man?' To the others he said in explanation, 'Not eligible,' and bid Duncan Stewart make note of the same. Hew stared, incredulous, at Giles, who began to frown as Gilchrist called, 'Next boy.'

The third and youngest applicant, after an intervention by Giles Locke, was allowed to proceed to the examination. This was conducted by Robert Black, and consisted of the reading of a random text, here chosen from the Georgics, for analysis of grammar, shape and sense. The boy began well, and was into his flow when Gilchrist said suddenly, 'Do I not know you?'

'No, sir.'

'I know you, I think. Were you not with some boys who threw stones at myself and the magistrands once on the links? Don't you know the boy, Duncan? Was it not he?'

'I believe that it was, sir,' answered Duncan.

Giles muttered something in Latin, beyond the boy's sphere. The boy began to feel panic, but tried for recovery. 'You are mistaken, sir. I do not play on the golf links.' He remembered the boy with the shoes, and said cunningly, 'For I have not the wherewithal to buy the ball and clubs.'

'Then I have seen you somewhere else, and up to no good, for I never forget a bad face, and I never,' the master leaned over him, raising his voice, 'forgive an ill deed.'

'I don't understand, sir.'

'It's nothing,' said Robert Black grimly. 'Read on.'

The boy sensed that the masters were angry. Two were talking, too quickly, in Latin. Their voices were raised. The regent with the book turned round to glare at them, and they fell silent. Now all of them were looking at him. He tried to go on. He had continued for a line or two, and had begun to gain confidence when the principal slammed his fist on the table and thundered out, 'In truth, I have discovered you.'

The other man roared out *intolerantia*, as like a bairn he blurted, 'Ye canna hae though for I wisna there,' and to his great shame, he dissolved into tears.

'I can see, after all, that I may be mistaken,' Gilchrist allowed, very gently. 'But you know, at the university, we expect our scholars to be able to argue the case. Think, boy, how would it be if men of law wept in the courts? It would never do. Also, though I scarcely like to mention it, we cannot permit of the tongue that you speak. I fear these young scholars,' he confided to his colleagues, 'so far have shown no aptitude in disputation.'

There followed an adjournment, brusquely demanded by Giles, while the masters retired to a corner and whispered together, after which Doctor Locke himself came to the boy and inquired of him kindly, whether he would like to take the test again. He answered, he would not.

The fourth supplicant, following this interlude, was the boy from Holy Trinity, and the minister stepped up with him to the bench. He was, he said, Thomas, named Burns, for on Kinness Burn braes he was discovered a foundling, brought up by the parish since his infancy, fed and schooled and clothed at their expense. He was a pupil at the grammar school, where he had shown exceptional ability. In the hope of sating the boy's hunger for learning, the minister had taught him the rudiments also of Hebrew and Greek. This was impressive, for the Hebrew tongue was not then taught within the university. Robert had opened his Vergil when Gilchrist stayed his hand.

'Perhaps we might try young Thomas with Homer, since he is proficient in the Greek. Have you *The Iliad* here?'

The minister protested, 'He has the basic grammar, scarcely more.'

The boy himself lifted his eyes and said bravely, 'I am only a beginner, but I should like to try it.'

Robert gave an encouraging smile. 'Read us a little, and if you can turn it into Latin, we shall be pleased to hear it.'

The boy took the book, and bravely enough he read out the Greek, before turning the verse into Latin.

'Well then, enough,' broke in Gilchrist. 'You are not here to give a lesson, Master Black.

Thank you for your patience, sir,' he nodded to the minister. 'You may have our answer by and by.'

'Are we not to have it now?' the churchman asked him bluntly, 'As you can see, there are still other scholars in line.'

'Then am I to infer that some of them will presently be bursars?'

'You may infer what you will, but no decisions will be made until we hear the rest. Good day to you.'

Hew Cullan smiled at the boy, 'That was prettily done. I thought you read well. If you came into my class, I should be glad to have you.'

'Thank you, sir.' He blushed a little. 'I should be glad to come.'

'Why did you say that?' Gilchrist protested to Hew as the boy turned away. 'I may remind you, Master Cullan, yours is not the class in question. You needlessly raise the boy's hopes.'

'How so, needlessly?' inquired Hew. 'You cannot intend to deny him. He far exceeds the standard.'

'I agree. Tis a consideration. He may overshadow the other men, put them off their stroke. I do not say no, understand me, but we must give a careful notice to his character. I fear he lacks humility, which is essential in a bursar. I suspect the influence there of the schoolmaster, a most forward sort of man.'

Giles had come dangerously close to him. 'I have witnessed these proceedings, sir, with increasing abhorrence, and I may say that I intend to make report of them before the chancellor. This is not, as you must be aware, a true interpretation of the bursars' charter. That boy, and no doubt several others here, are worthy of election. I suspect you of prejudice, sir, that you fill up their places with sons of the rich.'

'That is a serious charge.'

'Then let it be proved. We shall examine all the intrants like for like, both scholars and bursars, and if we find ten bursars who surpass ten of your scholars, then according to the statutes, let them take their place.'

'No, no,' said Gilchrist easily, 'they shall never submit to it. *Pax*, we must put it to vote. What say you to the foundling Thomas Burns? Shall we offer him a place, Master Cullan?'

'I say aye.'

'Doctor Locke?'

'Aye.'

'Master Black?'

'Abstention'

'How droll you are, Robert. Do you wish the boy as bursar in your class or no?'

'In truth, I should like to include him. In conscience I feel I must not.'

'Don't play the fool now,' hissed Hew, but Robert stood stubborn.

'Well, we may go by your conscience,' Gilchrist said smoothly.

'You may go by my answer, sir. I have abstained.'

'As you will.' Gilchrist shrugged. He called to the magistrand. 'We have a difficulty here. I find I cannot do without the other regents. Hurry to their room, pray, and explain the situation. Bid them come and join us. While we're waiting, gentlemen, we may perhaps inspect the other candidates.'

No one had quite the heart for it. Hew glowered at Robert, who did not meet his eye. Giles Locke took to reading a book. Eventually, the interviews concluded and the magistrand returned. He had found no trace of Samuel Ross, while Guthrie, in his nightshirt, begged to be excused. His gumboil had tripled in size. If it pleased them, he would place his vote by proxy, as against the foundling boy from Kinness Braes. Giles offered, somewhat viciously, to seek the fellow out and lance his boil. But Gilchrist gave a smile. 'Two for, one against, and one abstention. We may I reckon Samuel Ross, being *in absentia*, to have cast his vote upon my side. As principal . . .'

'And you force this,' Giles Locke cautioned, 'I must take it to the chancellor.'

Gilchrist studied him with grave indifference. 'Since you mention the archbishop, I must warn you, he has spent the last few years abroad, and has had no concern with our affairs. I wonder you are so belligerent. For did I say I had decided to refuse the boy? On the contrary, I propose to award him the bursary. As for the charge of prejudice, I can assure you, nothing could be further from my mind. To prove it, I shall place him in the care of a young friend of mine, who may have much to learn from him. He is newly arrived, and the son of an earl.'

Hew glanced at Robert, who shook his head hopelessly.

'You hurt me, Doctor Locke,' their principal went on, 'and you have caused offence here in my college, where I count you as a guest. I must warn you I hold it amiss. I am, as Master Black will testify, a reasonable man, but be assured you will not like me as an enemy. Good day to you.'

'I am assured,' Giles countered testily to Hew, 'I do not like him as a friend.'

Controversies

Outside the college, Hew gave voice to a stream of expletives, evenly distributed between the ancient and vernacular. He kicked at the scattering leaves. A small group of students gazed at him curiously. One ventured, '*Salve*, magister.'

'*Salve, salvete*,' Hew muttered savagely, '*damn*.' Giles suppressed a smile and took his arm.

'Let us vent our spleen a little further from the gate. Walk with me a while. We'll find a cookshop.'

They bought spiced pastries from the baker in the marketplace and ate them on the sands like truant schoolboys, sucking beads of sugar from their sleeves.

'Come and see Nicholas,' suggested Giles. 'I left him with Paul.'

'I wonder, was that wise?'

The doctor laughed. 'Your sister came to nurse him yesterday, and Paul and I were wranglers for the place of best relieved. Poor Paul! If he had glimpsed the devil, he could not be more afeared. We neither of us speak of it, and I, for my part, have made no mention of his rude transgressions. I notice he avoids my books. I bid him, all the while with most sweet and gentle courtesies, to do me this and that, and this and that he does without demur, always providing that I do not ask him to be left alone with Nicholas. The answer then is no; I may not count it wise, and yet I know of no alternative unless your sister stays.'

He unlocked the door, and Hew knew at once by the fragrance that Meg was there, the melting dark falling of flesh from the bone.

'Beef and oyster stew,' she called, in explanation, 'and a spinach tart with plums. Forgive me, Doctor Locke. Paul let me in.'

'Thank God,' said Giles with feeling. 'But how have you escaped from Lucy Linn?'

'Syrup of red poppy. She will sleep for several hours.'

'God save us, Meg! What have you done?' cried Hew.

'It does her good.' She had closed the door upon the room where Nicholas lay resting. Standing on the threshold like the mistress of the house, she glared at them defensively. 'Lucy is distracted with the bearing of her child, beset with wild thoughts and sick fancies. She imagines the babe is a demon inside her. It discolours her dreams and darkens to despair her waking hours. The poppy juice allows her some respite, and the rest she requires to balance her humours. Tis not for my sake, nor for yours, I give it her.'

'An unnatural case,' Giles observed. 'In general, falling with a child will serve to anchor down the womb, its restlessness the source of such afflictions; *graviditas* the cure, and not the cause.'

'Ah, you think so, do you?' Meg rounded on him angrily, 'Tis *unnatural* to fear the throes of childbirth? *Anchored* by the terror, and the sickness, and the pain? You think all our ills may be cured by a man in the bed and a bairn in the womb? That what does not kill us must cure us?'

'That,' he said mildly, 'is what I think.'

Hew said, shocked, 'For shame, Meg! How can you speak to him so?'

'The dyer's child is dead,' she answered, turning to the fire.

There was a moment's silence, then Giles said very quietly, 'Then I am sorry for it.'

Meg affected to be busy with the pot. Hew swallowed. 'When did you hear?'

'The minister. He called to see us after he left you this morning. He said to thank you,' she looked at Hew, 'for your part in the examinations.'

Her brother shook his head, 'It was a poor one.'

'He spoke well of you. He mentioned the death. Will had come to him to ask permission to inter the baby in its father's grave, but the session had opposed it.'

'Why would they do that?'

'The infant died without the sacrament. But the minister said – he is a good man, Hew – he said that there was nothing marked the case apart but idle superstition, and that Henry in the eyes of God was a chrisom child. He would see to it himself that Henry would be buried with his father, as was proper and most practical.'

Hew nodded. 'That is a blessing.'

'So we thought. But the minister said that when he said the same to Janet, she refused. She would not place the baby in her husband's grave.'

'She may not have accepted that the child is dead,' suggested Giles. Meg shook her head.

'She swore that if they took him there, she'd tear him from the ground. He is to lie instead outside the city gates, I know not where, in this world or the next. The minister felt vexed for it, but for all his good prayers he could not dissuade her from the force of her despair.'

'This is a sad and strange story,' said Hew. 'Yet I do wonder what has moved her quite so violently against her husband, that she would deny her child a proper burial. He was, I'm told, a godly man, and lies well placed in death before the kirk.'

'What say you, Doctor Locke?' Meg rounded sharply, 'is it the widow's helplessness – the absence of her man – that makes her so unreasonable?'

Giles cleared his throat. 'I wonder how our present patient does?' he ventured.

'I left him sleeping, or at least, pretending to. He does not like me here. I followed your instructions and began with the manipulations, and I fear he liked them less, though was too polite to say. Our attentions are sorely a trial to him, but still in spite of them, and of himself, he makes a slow recovery,' Meg answered seriously.

'You begin to sound like Giles,' said Hew, 'except for that word *recovery*, which I swear, I never heard him say.'

'Tsk, tis bad luck,' Giles insisted sternly, 'like milking the cow before market, or cutting your toenails at sea. Or stirring your oyster stew backwards.'

'I have not heard that one.' Meg laughed, in spite of herself.

'That is the very worst of them. For it does not exist.'

'What manipulations?' Hew asked suddenly.

Giles and Meg exchanged a glance.

'Doctor Locke's instructions for the workings of the limbs,' Meg explained carefully, 'which are weakened by the illness. They prove difficult to implement.'

'I beg to ask, what limbs?'

Giles interrupted hurriedly, 'Have you met the Strachans yet, Meg? Did you not say you had gone to the shop?'

'Aye, and they were strange,' said Meg. She frowned. 'The weaver is a bully. I might think him capable enough of having killed the boy, were the death not so plainly to his disadvantage.'

'How so?' Hew was momentarily distracted, as the doctor had intended. 'How has it affected him?'

'His business fails without his brother's patronage. There is the hint of a quarrel between them. Gilbert left for the Low Countries without their wools as export, and has left none of the lace and silks they have come to expect of him.'

'I had heard the same. Still, we may suspect him capable of killing in a passion, even to his disadvantage,' Hew reflected. 'But it is harder to suppose he had the opportunity, if Alexander died on Sunday afternoon.' He looked reproachfully at Giles. 'It's Agnes, Strachan's wife, who holds my interest now. She was alone that afternoon. She swore a statement for the Crown. Could you make a friend of her?'

'Perhaps,' Meg faltered, 'but I liked her, Hew.'

'I do not ask you to deceive her. Since you like her, be her friend. She may confide in you.'

'She did ask me for advice upon a personal matter. She looked for a receipt to bring on her courses.'

Hew raised an eyebrow at Giles, who said nothing.

'She hinted,' Meg went on, 'that all has not been well between

200

her and her husband now for years. He blamed her for all their misfortunes, and most, for the lack of a son, claiming the bloods that blackened and congealed in her womb had somehow polluted his seed. She wished for a son to put right the harm, but was hindered by the stopping of her menstrual courses, that had thickened in her womb and would not flow.'

'Forgive me,' interrupted Giles, 'for this rude intrusion, a novice though I am in these affairs. But do I understand her to request a potion to provoke the menses that she might procure a child?'

'Yes. For the disease of the womb that stopped her courses after Tibbie was born, on and off for thirteen years. I told her pennyroyal, wild carrot seed, or saxifrage and sage leaves in a broth might serve her well.'

'Indeed they might. But consider, for I do like to consider, as you know, for sake of argument, suppose that she required a potion to provoke the menses that she *not* procure a child?'

'I . . . had not considered it.' Meg coloured. 'She has a husband.'

'So she has,' Giles agreed gently. ''Tis curious, you know. But if she does not want a child, the herbs you recommend will serve her just as well.'

Meg was silent. Then she said, in a small voice, 'I have been foolish.'

'No. But it's a possibility. Indeed, it does surprise me it has not occurred to *you*, since you consider childbed such a cruel encumbrance.'

'You mean,' it dawned on Hew, 'that Agnes wanted medicines for *loosening* a child?'

'Probably not,' said the doctor. 'Most probably, she is afflicted with a blackened vaporous womb that is − forgive me, Meg − the cause of all her sorrows and her husband's too and has left them both without a son. I merely make the other case, as possible, that Agnes finds herself unhappily with child, and looks to be relieved of it. Either may be true.'

'Why do you do this?' Hew cried, exasperated, '*Either* this, or *yet* the other; either *yes* or *no!*'

'Because they are alternatives,' Giles answered in astonishment. 'Did they teach you nothing at the university?'

Nicholas was woken by the voices. He tried to lift himself from the cot, but the exertion overwhelmed him. There was stiffness in his limbs and thick fog in his lungs, as though they were not his, as though he tried to move and breathe within a heavy cloud of sand. His illness left him faint and short of breath, but unexpectedly detached. For months he had fought to take possession of his limbs, for self-control, and now command was lost, the cause was lost, he found the loss purgative. All that was done, in sickness and in cure, he now accepted quietly, and lay submissive, broken by his peace. The corpse did not belong to him. And though he knew the time would come when they would force it home, that he must take possession once again before he died, that men would come to do him hurt, he did not care. He could not imagine that it could belong to him again. It belonged to someone else.

'How do I know I am alive?' he asked aloud, 'I think, but do not feel.'

''Tis a question of some pertinence,' replied a voice. Nicholas opened his eyes, which cost him effort.

'Hew. I did not hear you come. How long have you been there?'

'I was talking with my good friend Doctor Locke, when the discourse turned a touch sophistical, so I resolved to come to you. You were dreaming, I think.'

'You have more questions,' Nicholas sighed.

'For the moment, no. There will be questions, though.' His friend looked grave. 'And it were well to be prepared for them.'

'What shall I say?'

'The truth.'

'I have considered it. Why do *you* ask it?'

'I am resolved to make a defence for you.'

'Perhaps I do not want one.'

'Perhaps I do not want to make one. Yet I am resolved.' Hew changed his tone, 'I met one of your magistrands today.'

'Which one?' His friend stirred a little, lifting his head.

'A man called Duncan Stewart. He assisted at the examinations.'

'He is not the best of them.'

Hew helped him to sit forward on the pillow.

'I am relieved to hear it,' he confessed. 'I have to take the class next week, and find myself in awe of them. So I have come here for advice.'

Nicholas smiled. 'I do not think that is why you are come,' he whispered.

'No, but it's a start. I see you are comfortable here. Shall I bring you some books to read?'

'Perhaps. What happened at the examinations? Was anyone elected?'

Hew told him what had happened. 'What vexed me almost more,' he concluded, 'was Black's prevarication, "for myself I should elect the boy, in conscience I cannot". Too weak to speak against the principal, yet he pretends he sees some greater end. What the devil did he mean about his conscience?'

Nicholas was interested. 'Do not blame Robert, though I grant he may be weak. He does not care for complication in his life. But he has a conscience. He has reservations, as to what awaits the boy.'

'Then he must protect him.'

'And he had the power. You overestimate his standing with the principal. I can tell you this: there is no doubt that this boy will suffer cruel misuse within the college. If he is fortunate, he may retain his life; God willing, he may even take the wreath. His days will not be happy ones.'

'If he is bullied by the earl's son, and his regent turns his back to it, then I will take his part myself.'

'You may try.' Nicholas sighed. 'I had the same problem with young Duncan Stewart, but to a lesser degree. The principal took exception to my interference, even when he threatened fellow students with his knife. There are two bursars in the magistrand class, where once there were twelve. They are devout, hard-working men, and worthy of the laurel wreath. At the end of this year they will graduate. There will be no feasting, no gifts of gloves, but their honours nonetheless will be deserved. They may well go on to be regents. One of them may take *my* place. Assuming,' he said wryly, 'that you do not mean to hold the post for life.'

'You will return to it,' Hew interjected firmly.

'I think not. *One* will take my place, where he will have no sway upon his students, but will himself be helpless, bullied and enthralled. And when he complains to the principal of violent misbehaviour and of truants from his lectures, he will be told, most graciously, that he may charge them sixpence and be glad, for each additional reading of the text. Your friend Stewart was perplexed,' he smiled a little ruefully, 'I would not take his sixpence to review the text, when he preferred to spend the lecture hour in bed.'

'You do not ease my qualms about the teaching.'

'The magistrands are well prepared. Theirs is a solid year, apart from one or two. But you see, without the bursars the balance tips towards the sons of men who buy their way. The bursars now are left exhausted. They share the work of twelve, and college servants too, for Gilchrist makes economies wherever he can misdirect their ends. The bursars, as you know, must sweep the floors and fetch the coals and light the fires. Aye, and they empty the waters and slops. And fetch the meal and air the beds. And being prepared in their texts, they are expected to assist their betters form their feeble grasp on learning. If I do not read over to the likes of Duncan Stewart, it will fall to them. And they are the last in their beds, the soonest to rise.'

'You do not seem to care for rich men's sons.' Hew felt uncomfortable. As a boy at college, he had counted Nicholas his friend, and yet he was aware it had been Nicholas who turned their bed, who rose before the dawn to bring the light, who, when Hew came to wash, had brought the water for the jug. And he had accepted it. Had it been resented then?

'For some of them,' his friend said softly, 'I have cared. For others, no.' He fell silent, and then smiled a little. 'Do you count it irony at all, that your sister is performing those most gentle offices which once I undertook for you?'

'What offices?' Hew asked suspiciously.

'She reads to me. She trims my beard and combs my hair. But do not fret. I have no feeling for your sister.'

'Not gratitude, I see,' said Hew abruptly.

'Not even that.'

'I understood her to perform some strange experiment. To help you walk.'

'She does so. It's a trial.'

Hew's temper flared. 'She is come here to help you, at what personal cost and risk you cannot know. Whatever debt is owed to you from boyhood I will swear she has repaid a thousandfold.'

'There is no debt. You claim me as your friend. I do not want your help, Hew, nor your sister's. Why are you come, playing advocate? Have I engaged you? Leave me alone.'

'Hang you, then!'

'They probably will,' he conceded, quietly closing his eyes.

Hew let the door slam behind him. Meg and the doctor had apparently resolved their differences, and were talking together over a dish of beef broth. Hew begin to wonder whether he was not the alchemist of savage turns of temper, but then Giles was reconcilable to anything through food.

'He is a difficult man to help,' he interrupted crossly.

'Ah. You've discovered that,' Giles answered thickly, his mouth full of meat. 'Take him some stew.'

'We are not all so easily appeased.' But nonetheless, Hew accepted the bowl that Meg prepared for him, and reluctantly returned to Nicholas.

'I did not think that you would come again.'

'Since you do not seem to care for my sister, I am resolved to feed you myself. You may pretend to like it, if you will, or not. It's all the same to me. I see that she at least has left you clean and neat and your linen fairly fresh. Your company is now more pleasant than it was a week ago, for though you could not speak then, yet you stank.'

'Forgive me.'

'Why? Could you have helped the stink?'

'My rudeness to your sister. I am sorry, Hew.'

'Aye, it's a trial. Take the spoon. You will be sorry indeed to have slighted her, once you have tasted her stew.'

He waited until Nicholas had finished eating. It was a slow and painful process. The muscles of his throat were tight and sore, and once or twice he gagged and could not swallow, though the veal dropped off the bone. The effort of eating exhausted him. At last he fell back and whispered, unselfconscious, 'Can you call the servant? I need to make water.'

'I'll help you. Where's the vessel?'

'In the corner by the door. I cannot stand.'

Hew helped him up upon the bed, and held the pot. He watched as Nicholas arranged his clothes and sank back on the mattress. Then he asked bluntly, 'Why do you draw your own blood? Is it some form of mortification?'

'Phlebotomists do so to balance the humours.'

'Aye, but not like that. Why would you not go to the surgeon?'

'It is a private matter.'

'To do with Alexander?'

Nicholas whispered, 'Not in the way that you think. I find the effusion of blood brings release from disordered affections. When Alexander laid bare his feelings to me, I thought that he had been able to detect it, that somehow he sensed my weakness.'

'Which weakness was . . . disordered affections?'

He said simply, 'Lust.'

'But Nicholas, we all have lusts for women. If we do not act upon them, it can scarcely count as sin.'

'I have never lusted after women,' Nicholas said sadly.

'We never came upon them in the college,' Hew retorted. 'Since we were boys, you have known nothing but men. Effie the laundress may once have been young but has not stirred the loincloth of the loosest lad in college now for nigh on twenty years. That's why we use her.'

Nicholas gave a faint smile. 'Your sister has been kind to me. I know that Doctor Locke thinks well of her attractions, and for myself, I see them, but I cannot *feel* them, for my passions lie elsewhere.'

'Doctor Locke? Does he . . . ?' Hew was distracted a moment. 'No matter, tell me if you will then, where your feelings lie.'

'With one of your magistrands,' Nicholas confessed. 'I swear to you, he does not know. I have behaved to him as I behaved to all the others, through the last four years. You would not pick him out among the crowd. He is a cheerful, quite ordinary lad. I cannot explain it to you. My comfort is that he does not suspect it. He is a trifle wayward in his habits, but they do not lean that way.'

'You've had no hint of converse?' Hew insisted.

'Never.'

'Then it's not to be reproached. However we control our actions, we may not control our thoughts.'

'This is how I have controlled them.'

Hew looked upon the scar. 'Giles Locke tells me if you had gouged a little deeper, you would have spilled the artery.'

'And washed the trespass clean. I have tried prayer and fasting. Still the thoughts come. I find that the blade brings release of a kind. There is a purging of the spirit in the flowing of the blood. This alone offers some peace from the turmoil. So yes, if you will, it is a form of mortification. It scarcely atones. But the pain is a reminder; I shall never act upon the will.'

'Alexander's revelation must have brought you great disquiet.'

'I thought he saw through me.'

'Yet you had never desired him?'

'Why should I?' he asked quietly. 'Because I love one boy, must I therefore love all boys? Do you lust after every woman in the street?'

'Most of them. In passing.'

'Ah. I see you smile. I do not think you do. But understand how I have fought this.'

'I begin to understand. But when you knew how Alexander felt, for all you protest, then you kissed him.'

'Yes. For pity, for I did know how he felt. I know not how we should have resolved it. And for that kiss, I did the violence to myself which brought me here. Had I caught the vein, I could have washed the sin away. But there are many depths to Hell. The irony is, it was a chaste kiss.'

'He left you letters,' Hew persisted. 'I saw you take the letters.'

'Aye. I could not read them, though the drift was plain. You would think, would you not, I might have done him that last courtesy? I had not meant to keep them.'

'And I suppose he gave no word of blackmail when he spoke to you?'

Nicholas was startled. 'Blackmail? How? For he was artless, Hew. He was a child. He spoke wildly, from the heart. He could not threaten or conceal. How should I have killed him then? For passion, for love, for anger or fear? For *pity*, Hew! I kissed his head and sent him home. I promised him he should not fear, and when I saw him next, the child was dead.'

208

Seeds

Agnes had repented her deceit. The lass had come as guileless as a child. It was providential, surely, and simplicity itself to trick Meg into giving up the remedy. It was only part a lie. 'I did no wrong,' she whispered. God had disagreed, for what was done was not so easily resolved. She felt it now, the flutter in her ribs, the pittering of moths against a flame.

'Where are you taking the sheets? It is too late to wash them.'

Tibbie was watching her. Wearily, she forced a smile. 'It's fair, and there's a good brisk wind. I thought I'd rinse these out before the winter comes.'

'But Minnie, it's so cold!'

'They're Alexander's sheets. I would not have them lie until the spring.'

'Oh. Then I'll help you,' the girl said reluctantly.

'No, lass, bide at home. I'll call upon the dyer's wife. The house is a low and foul place, but Janet has kept there since she lost her child. In pity, I should call on her. Don't tell your dad.'

Her daughter nodded, understanding. 'Aye. I'll keep him sweet.'

'I'll not be long.'

This she must do on her own. And in the wind and water after all, with bloodied feet and breaking back, she might be rid at last.

The sheets had wanted washing, Agnes thought bitterly, shaking out the creases in the burn. The water was achingly cold. She had taken off her dress, and knelt down in her smock upon the stone. She pushed her skirts high, and pummelled with her bare arms on the rocks. When her arms became to ache, and she could not feel her fingers, still she did not stop. She looked at her wrists. The marks were faded now, the colour on her breasts become a film of grime. The other thing she could not cleanse. She stooped and scrubbed and bent into the freezing flow. The heavy load, the dragging of the damp sheets through the mud, the scrubbing with the soap of ash and lye, the dredging through the icy stream, the wringing out and stretching on the bank, were purgative, surely. Again and again she dragged and scrubbed and sluiced, until her spine ached hot and heavy to her belly and her thighs, and the sheets flopped sullen on the green. Agnes rubbed her arms and legs and rinsed off the trailing weeds, drying her feet on the gorse. She fastened her shoes and straightened her skirts, tucking the loose hairs into her cap. Hugging close her plaid, she made her way to the dyer's house through the long grass.

She had not wanted to come. Not for the squalor, and the pity of the place, but for the fear.

She was afraid of Janet, frightened of her little house, perfumed like the sink with its smoke trails high and bluing, frightened of the dyer who lay dead. Dead, aye, and his bairn was dead, there was the rub. God knew, you could not clear the air around the house. It hung oppressively heavy, an indigo cloud. She swallowed, deliberately breathed in, a long choking draught of it, blinding her. She drank as though she hoped to drown in it, rattling at the door. And then Will came. He put out a hand to steady her, made bold by his concern. 'Mistress, you breathe in too deep.' And it was like drowning; she took in a great gulp of air, drinking in poison. He put out his hand to steady her. 'Gentle, now mistress, breathe low.' She felt his fingers stained with dye, and flinching, saw him colour at the hurt of it. He dropped his hands. 'I cannot help you, mistress,' he said abruptly, 'if you are unwell, ye maun go home. My mother's sick. My sister's gone. There's nothing for you here.'

He was a good man, and she had not meant to offend him. It was only the blue of his hands. There were tears in her eyes then, and not just from coughing.

Shivering, she recovered herself. 'Ah, forgive me, Will,' she pleaded, 'I forgot the lye. It was for your mother, in her sickness, that I came. I fetched her some sugar.'

She had scraped an ounce or two from the sugar loaf Gilbert had brought, crusted, almost black within the centre, and wrapped it in a paper, close inside her bodice from the water and the wind.

'I'm cold, Will. Won't you ask me in?'

Uncertain, he stepped from the door. 'This is no place for you. And my mother is not well.'

'I came to bring her sugar,' she grew a little more confident. 'I heard of her loss.'

'I thank you for your kindness, but my mother will not see you.' He wondered why she had not come earlier; nor had she come when his father died. 'She's distracted, barely speaks.' He softened unexpectedly, 'The bairns will like the sugar, though. I'll tell her that you called.'

'Well then, where's your sister?' she said desperately.

'She's run wild. I know not where she goes, without her dad to hold her here. Sometimes she'll be gone for days. My mother does not care.'

'Wee Jennie? She's a good girl.'

A wilful child. She remembered the disturbance in the kirk, the stubborn features streaked with tears.

'She used to be. Now when the weans come greetin, she's nowhere to be found.'

'She wants a mother,' Agnes thought, and felt a prick of pity. 'I might help,' she pleaded.

'Well,' he shrugged, 'I've work to do. But you may try my mother if you will. And if you mak her mind her bairns, I'll be obliged to you.'

Agnes could not stop the shivering. It was cold from the water, she knew, and a dark and giddy sickness that had crept upon her. It was fear. She did not want to see the dyer's wife. Yet she made herself go on. She stepped into the house and called out brightly, gulping down the bile, 'Why Janet, it is Agnes, Agnes Ford has come to call on you. You'll get up from your bed and sit with me?'

A child was crying listlessly. Agnes found the infant, Jennie's smallest sister, sitting in a box beside the fire. She scooped her up into her arms and felt her scrabble damply at her breast. Resolutely, she pulled up a stool and settled herself upon it, with the infant on her lap. She opened the paper of sugar, and scraped off a piece with her fingertips. The child sucked greedily.

'Janet,' Agnes called again, 'you maun nurse your bairn, she's wet and famished. Here, it's Agnes, brought you sugar loaf. Come, see.'

'My bairn is dead.' The curtains parted slowly.

Agnes saw the thin face streaked with dirt, for all its cares still curious. She felt a coldness grip her bowel. But brightly she said, 'Aye, and I am sorry for it. But you have other bairns. Wee Bessie, is it, damp, she wants her mammie too.'

'Why have you come?' Janet stared at her. She pulled herself up to her knees to peer through the curtain. The drapes framed her face like a shroud.

'I have heard you are unwell, and you do not come to kirk. You have no husband now, and as your friend, I come to help you.'

'He died a while back,' Janet said reasonably, 'and I had his bairn, and that too has died. What of it, though? Why would you come?'

Agnes shifted in her chair. Why would she? It was easy, after all, to stay away. She swallowed nervously. 'To comfort your loss. I hear your daughter's gone.'

'Jennie? She'll be back. For all the use she is.'

'Well,' Agnes pointed out, 'she might mind the weans.'

'Aye, once she would. She's like her brother James and thinks herself too grand. For all they're dyer's bairns. They'll die like their da, with his filth on their hands.'

Agnes shivered. 'Janet, I am sorry for your loss. But I need to talk to you about your man.'

The child became restless again, paddling like a cat against her breast. She twisted her face towards Agnes and attempted a wail. Janet repeated, 'My husband is dead.'

Agnes set the infant down and gave her the sugar-loaf paper.

She clutched it with fat fists and tried to cram the whole into her mouth. Her eyes upon the bairn, Agnes said carefully, 'He was not a good man. He did hurt to me before he died.'

Janet stiffened. 'What hurt?'

'He defiled me,' said Agnes, barely audible. Janet gave a sigh, and for a moment Agnes thought she almost smiled. When at last she spoke, she seemed resigned to the point of indifference.

'You say it. It cannot be proved.'

It was as if she had expected something else. Some deeper, some more penetrating hurt. As if the hurt to Agnes irked her, or was of little consequence. 'What could be deeper?', Agnes wondered. She persisted, trembling.

'He had the dyes grained in his hands, that when he took me, left a stain upon my throat and on my breast, and round my wrists a bracelet, bruised in ink. Those are proofs.'

Janet pulled back the curtains completely and looked at her close. She looked at her wrist.

'I see no such stain,' she said scornfully.

''Tis long since rubbed away. I scrubbed it raw. And yet I think you recognise the mark, and here, on my shift, it has not washed clean.'

Janet considered this in silence. Presently she said, 'A smudge on a smock. A blot on a sleeve. Who would believe this?'

Agnes kept her eyes upon the child, intent in cramming in the loaf and paper lengthways in its mouth. Its cheeks were blotched and sticky.

She said softly, '*You* would, I think.'

'Believe your slanders? Why?'

Agnes looked at her now. 'Because you know what sort of man your husband was.'

Janet had turned very pale, 'And if I do,' she whispered, 'why should you ask it? My husband is dead.'

'He left me with child.'

'Ah,' laughed Janet mirthlessly. 'I lost my child.'

'And I would lose mine. Forgive me, I have no wish to hurt

you. But your husband has done me great wrong. He has forced himself upon me and I bear his child. I have tried to be rid of it. The woman Meg Cullan, who helped you with Henry, gave me seed to bring forth the courses, yet the courses do not flow. I dare not ask for more. In despair, I have tried to shift it with rough work and starving.'

'That must come hard,' said Janet, without irony. She showed a little interest. 'But you have a husband. Might the child be his?'

'There is the horror of it, for my husband will not deal with me. The child cannot be his.'

'Well, tis plain enough, if you can't shift the bairn then pass it as your husband's. Make him lie with you.'

'How, when he cannot?'

'How should I know? Deal with him then as you dealt with my husband,' Janet said tartly.

'He dealt with me, as you must know, most cruelly. You cannot think I had encouraged it!'

'Well,' Janet softened, 'I know him well enough to know he would not need encouragement. God knows, I know you well enough, mistress, to know you would not soil yourself to be a dyer's whore. Aye, you were defylit right enough. And what has it cost you to come here, and sit among the foulness of the hearth, to ruin a dead man's sons?'

'Janet, don't. I have not come to quarrel with you. I want nothing from your sons.'

'Aye? But you want to spread scandals about their dead father?'

'Believe me, I do not. I'd die for shame if it were known.'

'For *shame*?' Janet laughed aloud. 'What *do* you want?'

Agnes looked down, evading the question. 'Did he not tell you?' she whispered.

Janet snorted. 'What, that he *had* you?' Then she sensed a real distress and softened. 'Whisht, lassie, tell me what happened.'

The tale was still raw, and Agnes had not meant to tell it. Somehow, it spilled out. The infant turned her solemn face towards her as she spoke.

'He came on a Sunday, after kirk. He said he was employed by the session to inspect illicit working on the Sabbath day. He had gone round all the taverns while the readers read the lecture and had turned the drinkers out of doors. Now, he said, he was to go to all the booths and workshops and make sure that none were doing business on the Sabbath. He knew my man had gone to market, yet he made no exceptions, he must see the looms.'

'Aye, tis very like him to do that,' Janet commented.

'I protested that the shop was locked and empty. Yet he would not be deflected till I fetched the keys and let him in. Well, he looked around. And then, he professed himself satisfied. And then he professed himself *not* satisfied. He said that I had sinned and he must take my penance; he called me whore, and filthie names, he said, he *knew* things.'

'Aye,' said Janet bitterly, 'I know the things he said.'

Agnes stopped dead. 'You know them?'

'I know the names,' conceded Janet. 'Aye, tis true, he knew things, dug them out, and he imagined others. He groped around in filth; his mind was like the mire; he saw filth everywhere.'

'Did he say things about me?'

'The things were in his mind. Imagined sins. He saw them everywhere. You and your husband, you thought you were better than we were. Nay, do not deny it. He wanted to prove you were worse.'

'He made no accusations,' Agnes had recovered her composure, 'because he had no proofs. Aye, well, you must know that he took me by force. I did not encourage him. It was the day that Alexander died.'

She had returned the conversation to the place where she had wanted it, and Janet frowned a little. 'Aye? Then what of that?'

'And in the face of that, it did not seem important. Then your husband drowned.'

Janet said cautiously. 'What is it that you say?'

'That the deaths are linked.'

'How, linked?' Now Janet listened intently.

Agnes said clearly. 'It was the tutor killed the boy, and then your husband. I have sworn a statement to the first, and am witness to the second. Yet I dare not speak it at the court. It is for that, that I have come.'

'How were you a witness to the second?' Janet wondered. 'Were you at my house?'

Agnes shook her head. 'I know why your man was killed. Your husband told me, in his taunts, I kept a filthie house, and that my nephew had been used badly by his tutor. He meant to blackmail Master Colp. Did he not tell you?'

'He told me nothing,' Janet answered.

'Then I am undone. For I hoped you might swear to it. I do not want to give this evidence in court. I swore the statement for our brother Gilbert's sake, who lost his son. But if I am examined in the court, then I must tell about my converse with your husband, and I would not speak my shame for all the world.'

Janet whispered hoarsely, 'Aye, I understand.'

'I had hoped that your husband might have confided these suspicions to you.'

'And if he had?'

'And if he had, then you might swear to them in court. Your swearing would complete the case, and prove the murders without question, and I should not need to speak. Your children would not know their father's shame. You might say, perhaps, that George suspected Colp his lewdness with the boy, and was minded to denounce him to the kirk. You need not speak of blackmail.'

Janet considered this awhile. At length she answered carefully. 'I have suffered the loss of a husband and child.'

'And I am sorry for it.'

'Aye. And in my loss, I have forgotten things I now remember. I remember, for instance, that my husband did confide to me his knowledge of your tutor's inward yearnings, on the very night before he died. His meaning was concealed. I did not understand it. Now I understand, I see the meaning clearly. He did hint at such depravity. And I can swear to it.'

'God be thanked,' cried Agnes, 'then my shame shall not be made public.'

Janet asked her practically, 'But what about the child?'

'Surely you were right,' said Agnes absently, 'I'll bind Archie to it, bewitch him and bed him. He will have his son.'

'George's son,' Janet reminded her stiffly.

'Hush, now. Don't say so. You'll swear to it, Janet? George suspected the tutor?'

'Aye, for my children, I'll swear.'

It was a small enough lie, Agnes reasoned. And a small lie where the truths amassed so pitiless and dark might hardly matter after all, a grain of sand remaining on the spotless sheets. In her belly she felt grumbling, like a thankless child.

Jennie came home singing. She had combed her hair and washed her face, and rubbed her cheeks with chalk to make them white like the fine lasses did. Among the painters' colours she had found a pot of red. She put it to her lips like blood, and pinched her cheeks. And there were other colours too, blues and yellow ochres, and a little pot of gold. She longed for them. She wore them to the harbour where the sailors were. At first she was afraid of them, with their loose flowing shirts and tall pointed hats. They brought a sour-like smell of rope and sweat, oil and liquor on the breath. And they had laughed at her. And some had called things after her, in crude and foreign tongues, and she had pretended to cry. At first, she thought it had not worked, then one had called her back. And he had made a lap for her, inside his sailor's sark. She would not mind the smell, for it was like the lye, and she grew used to it. She had buried her head in his shoulder to dampen it. And he had stroked her hair. He soothed and petted her, and chased away the men who called her names. He smiled a broken smile, and bade her not to cry, in his strange broken tongue. He had given her a ring. It had a jewel in it, round and red like a sugarplum. She tied it on a ribbon round her neck. It was too big to wear upon her finger. And she sang for him. As she washed her face clean in the burn she felt it glint against her throat. It was almost dark when she returned. And then her mother wrenched the ruby from her throat, and stole her song.

'Where did you get this? Thief!'

'I did not steal it, though!' she cried indignantly.

'Whore!'

She would not cry. Not when her mother pulled her hair and slapped her face, and called her wicked names; and when she told the filthie things about her da she did not cry, but put her fingers in her ears and would not hear.

'Your belovit father! Shall I tell you what he was? What it was he did? You think you're better than the rest! You're just as bad. Your father had a stain upon his conscience, deeper ay than any on his hand. You think you can be free of that? For he was a whoremonger and you are a whore. Go where'er you will, you'll always be the dyer's child!'

She began to understand, confronted by the angry figure huddled on the hearth, that she had never had a mother, dropping as she did into the line of infants born and swaddled, given suck and pushed away. She would not listen to the words. And the last wicked lie that her mother had told had proved it beyond doubt. She had no mother now. She was alone.

The Dyer's Child

Dipping his quill in his inkwell, Giles Locke paused and looked around the room. The scene was touchingly domestic. In a low voice, Meg was explaining to Paul how to make a wash of myrrh and comfrey crushed in claret wine. Nicholas sat reading by the fire, a blanket round his knees, and in the pot a mutton rack bubbled with rosemary, garlic and prune. He felt, for a moment, as if he had family, and smiled at himself. Meg caught his eye. 'Do we disturb you?'

'Not at all. Though I confess, I find the savour of the pot a touch distracting. What is it that you put with it?'

'A little fruit and herbs. It will be ready soon. If you can encourage him to take some meat,' she looked hopefully at Nicholas, 'it may restore his strength. Whatever is that?'

They were disturbed by a knocking, loud enough to shake the shutters down below. Giles cursed. 'Go to the window, Paul. If it's Robert Black's boys again, tell them you have all their names, and will make them known to him. Have they nothing else to do?'

'It is their play hour,' Nicholas said softly. Since he seldom spoke, the others turned towards him in surprise. But Paul was agitated. 'It's the master of St Leonard's, with the coroner. Should I let them in?'

'Ah. So soon?' Giles set down his pen. I hoped we might have had a little longer. Well, we may do what we can. You must of course admit them, Paul. I wonder, Meg, if you could help Nicholas into his bed, and keep him quiet there. I will try to put them off their purpose for a while. If I cannot . . .'

'I understand.'

'Gentlemen,' Giles rose to greet them, 'I fear you have had a wasted journey. Master Colp is not yet well enough to leave.'

Gilchrist smiled unpleasantly, nudging the coroner. 'So I do believe.'

'Then I am at a loss as to the purpose of your visit. I beg you, keep your voices low.'

The coroner looked uncomfortable. He stepped forward unhappily, prompted by Gilchrist, clearing his throat. 'You are Doctor Giles Locke of the Auld College?'

'Certainly, yes.'

'There are complaints against you, for the mutilation of a corpus, and for its desecration, and concealment of that corpus from those who have the right to its disposal, and the keeping of a body from the grave.'

'I see,' Giles said, astonished. 'Where then, may I ask, is this desecrated corpus you suppose me to have kept?'

'I am authorised to search your rooms until we find it.'

'That may take some time. May I ask whose corpse it is?'

'It is the corpus of Nicholas Colp, who falling ill became entrusted to your care a month ago, and was reported dead by Master Gilchrist.'

'Then all becomes clear. Paul?' The servant turned a little pale. 'Enlighten us. Is Master Colp deceased?'

'No, sir.' Paul was solemn. 'Yon's his blanket, there. When the gentlemen came knocking, he was sitting by the fire. He left his book.'

'*Lego ergo sum*,' concluded Giles facetiously. 'The logic is skewed, but nonetheless accurate. He was sitting there, and here is his book, and now he has gone to his bed.'

'This is an outrage!' cried Gilchrist. '*This* is the man,' he pointed to Paul, 'who gave the report of the death and dissections.'

'Did you, Paul?' Giles inquired calmly. 'That was careless of you. I am afraid my servant has been suffering from delusions,' he explained to the coroner. 'He came upon the patient in a very weak and debilitated condition, bound and bloodied from the lockjaw, which twists a man's carcass more cruelly than the rack. Faced with such horrors, he convinced himself that evil had been done. However, I have taken him for bleeding, and in consequence, he finds his addled humours much restored. He now understands his mistake.'

'Is this true?' the coroner questioned Paul.

'Yes, sir,' the servant grinned. 'I did think him dead, until the doctor had explained it and the patient recovered. Tis a very cruel illness. The man was a wreck.' Paul carefully avoided Gilchrist's eye.

'But you told me the doctor had cut off his head!' the master spluttered.

'I was mistaken, sir.'

'How could you mistake a thing like that! Know you not, there are forfeits for bearing false witness?'

'There are indeed,' said Giles smoothly, 'but Paul has not done so. He has told the truth.' He fixed his gaze upon Gilchrist.

'Do you wish to pursue your complaint?' the coroner asked.

'I . . .' The meaning dawned on him. 'I made it in good faith.'

'Yes, sir,' he countered patiently, 'then will you now withdraw it?'

'On account of a book and a blanket, man? Can you be mad? I will withdraw it when you find the man alive and prove to me he has no marks of mutilation on his throat.'

Giles sighed. 'I was afraid you would insist upon it. Bear in mind, he is not well. But if you must intrude, you will find him at his rest.'

The coroner hesitated, but already the principal pushed through the door. Giles followed him, frowning. Meg was sitting on a stool besides the bed. She rose to greet them, obscuring the view.

'This is a sick room, sir,' she protested, 'what can you want here?'

'A word with the patient,' Gilchrist snarled.

Nicholas stirred painfully. Attempting to speak, he gave way to a paroxysm of coughing, spitting helplessly into a cloth. Giles shook his head. 'The lockjaw has left a black scab on the lung. This bloody phlegm and tremor he may not shake off.'

Warily, the coroner approached the patient. 'You are Nicholas Colp?' he ventured.

Nicholas whispered, 'Yes.'

'Is this the man?' he asked Gilchrist humorously. 'He seems to be alive.'

Gilchrist reached out, pulling the blanket from Nicholas' shoulders. Incredulously, he tipped back his head, looking into his eyes, mouth and throat. Nicholas submitted quietly while Giles looked on detached. Presently he said, 'Do you find him alive, sir?'

James Gilchrist scowled. 'And if he is,' he demanded abruptly, 'then let him be taken. As he lives and breathes, he'll answer for his crimes.'

The coroner scratched his head. 'I thought we were come to prove the question of his being killed?'

'Aye,' retorted Gilchrist, 'and having proved him not, you may repair to your original design, to take him as a killer to his trial. He is indicted, is he not? And the October sessions are upon us, are they not? Then take him, sir.'

'Is he fit to stand trial?' the coroner asked Giles doubtfully.

'Fit to stand trial? You see how he fares. He's not fit to stand.'

'For pity,' Meg protested. 'Sir, he would not last the hour.'

'What is she doing here?' Gilchrist rounded nastily, 'Who is she? I doubt you keep a woman in your rooms but to compound your magic, Locke. You know it is forbidden?'

Giles ignored him. 'You must mark his frailty,' he advised the coroner. 'At present, he can barely speak. He is, as my servant well observed, quite racked and broken by the illness. Only God's good grace has spared him.'

'Well and good,' observed the coroner. 'Since he is alive, he must stand trial. But I cannot think, by this report and by the evidence of my own eyes, he might make the journey now and live to take the oath. Therefore one or other of you must make surety for him to appear at the justice ayres next year. The circuit court is due to sit again in spring. If you will nurse him here and pay his bail, you shall have the keeping of him until then, when I promise *you*, sir,' he turned to Gilchrist, 'he shall stand his trial, unless he has been called to face a higher court than this. I thank you, Doctor Locke. You may bring the monies to the tolbooth in the morning. And I would counsel you,' he added rather quickly as the principal began to speak, 'not to raise reports against your friends which may construe as slanders, unless you wish to answer in the courts. Master Colp, I'll see you in the spring. God willing,' he allowed.

Gilchrist stared at Nicholas.

'Will you leave, sir?' Giles urged him pleasantly, 'I fear your precipitate haste to see him hanged may vex the patient more, and discourage his recovery. Tis a slow process, you see, and a difficult one. I wonder you do not think to congratulate me on it?'

'I will see *you* hanged,' spat Gilchrist. 'How have you done this, mediciner? I will swear, your servant thought him dead.'

'I doubt he did,' Giles answered easily. 'He was mistaken. Paul is not a learned man.'

'No. And he was not mistaken.' The master leaned over the bed, and once again lifted Nicholas' face to his. He looked into his eyes. 'What *are* you, Colp? Twice killed? I saw you dead myself, and heard you dead again, and you live still. What devil are you, then?'

Nicholas gave an odd smile. 'Perhaps I am your Nemesis, principal,' he answered quietly.

'I assure you,' smiled the doctor, 'there is no cause to pull so on his head. You'll find it quite secure.'

Gilchrist countered, 'No one has the lockjaw and survives. This is witchcraft, mediciner. I shall expose it.'

'It is a little physic and the grace of God.'

'Aye,' whispered Nicholas, rubbing his jaw. 'God's grace I should survive to see you shamed.'

'I shall see you damned.' Gilchrist leered close again. 'If you survive, it is to answer for your inwardness, your sodomies, your murders and your lies.'

'I find your humours somewhat thick,' frowned Giles. 'Come, you are heavy and hot, sir, and sweating. I recommend phlebotomy. My friend Mr Parker is an excellent man.'

'I shall not be deflected, sir. I know your tricks.' The principal did not look well. An angry vein throbbed purple in his neck.

'What is it, Meg?' It was Nicholas who noticed her, as she began to fall. It came upon her at once, and she was powerless to prevent it, insidiously brewing through her dark fatigue. The strain and weariness of the last hours allowed it to take hold and it possessed her. She felt it coming with the light. It stopped the light and all her thoughts, and all her powers were useless then. It threw her to the ground.

'What is it?' he asked again.

She could not hear. She was returned among the demons of her dreams.

'Lord,' the coroner said unhelpfully, 'she is possessed.'

It was Giles who recovered first and came to her, dropping down upon the ground to hold her head. He glared at the others. 'Can you not see it, fools, she has the falland ill? 'Tis you have brought this on, with your intrusions. Don't you know that this is a sick room? That these are my patients? I swear to you, you shall be made responsible for this. Leave us! I'll attend to her.'

The coroner stared down in horror at the flailing girl. 'Come. Master Gilchrist,' he said hurriedly, 'we'll leave the brave physician to his task. There's nothing for us here.'

Gilchrist looked disgusted. 'It is a show. The matter will not rest here. Can't you see the man's a charlatan? This is done by art, to deflect our purpose.'

'For pity's sake, her lips are blue. But come away. I see no trick, and I would rather not be here. It turns my stomach. You have wasted my time, sir.' The coroner left abruptly, without turning back.

'Go now, Gilchrist,' Giles said coldly, 'before I have my servant throw you out of doors. Preserve some scrap of proper feeling, I implore.'

Gilchrist was trembling, 'I do not believe this,' he said menacing to Meg, 'I know not who you are, nor what you do here. Doubt not, I shall discover it. I will return.'

'That was cleverly done,' the servant said admiringly as Gilchrist slammed the door. 'I did not see the signal. How did you arrange it?'

'Fool,' said Giles, 'this is no trick. This is your fault, Paul.'

Nicholas had pulled himself up from the bed. Gingerly, he lowered himself upon Meg's other side.

'Tell me how to help her,' he pleaded.

'Sit with her while I go for medicines. No, do not restrain her. Make safe the path of her head. Dear God, I should have guessed it,' answered Giles.

'She has the falling sickness?'

'Aye, for certain. Send for Hew.'

Hew was gone from college, for it was the play hour. The regents had led their slow straggle of boys along the castle cliffs and down to the west sands. Those with bow and arrows practised at the butts, while a ragged game of football broke out on the shore. The rest continued to the links, ostensibly to play at golf, or rather to chase rabbits through the dunes. Robert Black asked pleasantly, 'Will you play a round with me?'

'Aye, then,' Hew agreed.

'Clubs, if you please!' Robert called across into a group of students, and the smallest boy hurried towards them.

'That's your bursar, Thomas, is it not?' Hew looked at him.

'The same. I thank you, Thomas.' Robert took a pair of clubs and handed one to Hew.

'Has he carried all the clubs himself? That is a burden, surely, for so slight a boy?'

'He is the bursar,' Robert answered simply, 'and, as I recall, you were the one who wanted to elect him.'

'Aye, but not to that. Is no one else to help him?'

Robert shook his head. 'I did advise you of it. Your own two bursars brought the bows, and went with Master Guthrie to the butts. One of them, the black-haired lad, shows promise as a bowman. He is our hope for June, when we have our competition.

The Auld College archers are weaker this year. Thomas here is too small for the longbow and is made guardian of the clubs. It is an honour, is it not?' he asked ironically, 'though he may not play himself.'

'*May* not?'

'Aye, he cannot. For he does not have the clubs. Run now, Thomas, for the magistrands are calling!'

The small boy disappeared behind the dunes.

Hew played several strokes without success, and finally declared his ball lost in the rough. Robert peered into a rabbit hole. 'Aye, tis gone. I have another. You can play from here. If I may say so, you do not play well today.'

'I'm sorry, Robert, I have something on my mind.'

'I thought you had.' Robert straightened gloomily. 'Oblige me, pray, by not divulging it. Well, we shan't play on. For I can see you have no heart for it, and if you will not try, then I do not care to trounce you. Which I should, of course.'

'For certain,' Hew said solemnly. 'May I ask a favour? Can you mind the magistrands?'

His colleague looked alarmed. 'Why, where are you going? You are too often absent, Hew. Gilchrist has been asking questions. I fear he will suspect you, and you know I cannot lie.'

'Tell him I went looking for lost balls,' Hew smiled at him. 'I'll not be long.'

Robert sighed. He waited for his friend to disappear across the links, resting on the handle of his club. When Hew was out of sight, he called out to the bursar. 'Thomas! I am weary of the game,' he told him as the boy approached, 'and since I do not care to play today, then I shall help you caddy. Come, we'll share the load.'

Hew hurried southward through the town to the west port and down past the Kinness Burn, into the farmland beyond. It was Katrin he was looking for. Her disappearance troubled him. Once he thought he saw a wisp of blue smoke curling in the distance where the drover's cottage stood. He looked again to find it disappeared. It was a phantom, after all, a trick of wind.

When he arrived he found the place deserted. He folded back the hide that framed the door, tucking the folds into a rusted hook, and allowed a little air into the room. From the hole above the hearth a smoky daylight filtered down. He fingered the ashes, and found them still warm. The earthen floor was clean. There were blankets neatly folded on a fleece beside the fire. But most striking were the walls. From ceiling to floor they were painted, a shrill wash of colour on compacted earth; yellows and crimsons, emeralds, blues, all sticky-bright as marzipans. Hew smiled in recognition as he heard the sound of footsteps; turning round, he felt too late the trickle of the knife-edge on his skin.

A voice said, 'If you touch them, I'll kill you.'

'Why would you do that?' he answered evenly. 'I thought that we were friends.'

She sketched a light line round his throat, a trailing, deepening necklace of dark beads. He caught his breath as he felt the blade shiver.

'Will you put down the knife, Jennie? I mean you no harm.'

'Sit over there on the bed.' She motioned to the fleece.

'*Pax!*' He held forth his hands as she prodded him. Meekly, he dropped to the floor. 'Tis a pretty toy you have. A little sharp.'

She had drawn back to study him, the dagger still poised, allowing his fingers to feel for the blood. He licked them ruefully.

'How did you know I was here?' she demanded.

'I didn't. Not until I saw the pictures. I expected Katrin.'

'Don't you listen? Katrin's gone. I live here instead. What do you think of them?' she retorted unexpectedly.

'They are as grand as the ones in my cousin's house. Grander, I think,' he assured her solemnly, shrinking from the knife. 'Must you prick me so?'

The child was satisfied. 'I took the colours from the shop. Twas not stealing, you see, for they were Dada's dyes, not Will's, and Dada would have wanted me to have them.'

'I am sure that he would. How long have you been living here?'

She shrugged. 'Tis mine now. You won't take me back.'

Hew wiped his face with the back of his hand.

'I *could* kill you, I think,' she said thoughtfully.

'My friends would come after me.'

'Would they, though? No one comes here.'

It was absurd. Held at the beck of a twelve-year-old girl. And yet, he thought, he could not risk disarming her of quite so sharp a blade. Instead he said mildly, 'I am in your hands. Why would you kill me? I thought we were friends.'

'We were, weren't we? Did you bring sweets?'

'I'm afraid not.'

'No matter now.' She pulled out a ribbon from under her dress, and unhooked a small silver key. 'Look under the bed.'

Hew lifted the mattress to find a wooden box within a hollow in the floor. 'Open it,' she pointed with the knife. He considered reaching out to grasp the thin arm, thought better of it, turned the lock, and opened the lid on a treasure of candies and gems, silvercraft, laces and trinkets. The child leant forward to spear up a plum, and dangled it, teasing, in front of him.

'Take it. It's my turn to treat you.'

Warily, he plucked it, with an eye upon her wrist, marking the quivering blade.

'Are they not fine?' Jennie demanded.

'Precious indeed. Where did you get them?' He let the plum fall to the floor and wiped his fingers on the bed. She saw the slight and flushed.

'I did not steal them.'

'I had not thought you did,' he answered gravely.

'I *earned* them,' she persisted.

'So I feared.'

'If you tell my brothers, I *will* kill you,' she said earnestly. 'Why will you not eat it? It's honestly bought.'

'I never cared for sugarplums.'

She stared at the blanket. 'You think I'm a whore.'

'Aren't you?'

'I never did *that*.'

'Then I thank God for it. How did you come by your treasures, though? How do you live?'

'There are men at the harbour less pernickety than you,' she said defensively, 'who pay well to dandle me, shipmen and merchants far from home, who miss their own wee lass and would have a wean to spoil. I bring them comforts.'

'*Comforts*, Jennie?' he mocked her, 'And you do not play the whore?'

'No,' she countered stubbornly, 'I will not have them *do* it so.'

'You go among sailors, child. Someone will force you.'

'Someone has tried,' she said softly. 'I carry the blade in the sleeve of my blouse. I cut him, down *there.*'

'*Jesu*,' whispered Hew. She gazed at him reproachfully.

'That's a bad word, from a kirk man. The sailor said the same.'

'Nonsense. Tis a prayer. For thanks that you're not killed.' He did not take her seriously. She frowned.

'He would have to catch me, and he wasna after running, at the time. His friends made merry sport of it. But I made sure to lie low till the ship was sailed. There's a tavern by the harbour where the sailors go. And there's a place in the rocks where I can hide. But here's my proper home.'

She gestured proudly with the knife. 'Tis brave enough, until I have another. I do not mean to stay here, though. When I have sufficient saved, I will pay for my passage on one of the ships, to England, perhaps, maybe France. And I will become a fine lady.'

'I wish you good fortune!' Hew shifted slightly. She spun at him, flexing the blade.

'If you move from there, I will cut you where I cut the sailor. Libbit like a lamb. I swear to God, you will not give me chase.'

He winced. 'I could wish you a little less bloody,' he grumbled. 'May I have a towel to wipe my neck? This is a new shirt.'

'Aren't you afraid?' she asked him, disappointed.

'I probably should be. But then, I was ever a fool. I had some hapless notion I might catch your father's killer. Misbegotten, I can see.'

'I had forgotten,' she conceded, 'as to that. But I know who he is.'

'You know him?' He stared at her, startled at last.

'Well then, not his name,' she qualified, 'but what sort of a man he must be. I did not know so much about men, about *sorts* of men, when you asked me before. But I have learned things since. There are rough men, the mariners, stinking of ale; and there are the kirkmen, dour, and from the university, they like me well enough; and the bravest are the merchants, with their velvet cloaks and strange caressing voices, and their trinkets fine and rare. He was one of those.'

'A foreigner? From overseas?'

She pouted. 'No, I *told* you. Don't you ever listen? He was Scots. Not local, though. He came here on one of the ships.'

'But you've not seen him since?'

'No. But when he comes I shall be waiting. I will let him dandle me. And when he does, I'll carve him to the bone.'

Hew groaned. 'You are the most bloodthirsty baggage I ever clapped eyes upon. Were it not sufficient to declare him to the coroner, and see the blaggard swing?'

'You think they would believe me against a rich man?' she said scornfully, 'No, I swear, I'll slit his throat.'

'Suppose he will not come? You'll have a better chance of finding him if you leave me whole.' He looked pointedly up at the knife.

'Well then, I doubt I shall.' She tossed him a napkin, and gingerly he dabbed at his throat.

'What would you do,' she asked, 'if I should let you go?'

'I'd go and be damned, and to Hell with your father and his killer. I am bloodied and sore and heartily sick of it all.'

'And what about me?'

'What about you? You cannot think that I care for *you*, Jennie? A cut-throat, a cheap little whore?'

She ignored this. 'You do though,' she said shrewdly.

He conceded, smiling, 'Aye, perhaps. Why did you run away?'

She fell silent a moment. 'My mother said things,' she answered at last.

'What did she say?'

Jennie set her lip. 'She said that my father was black in his heart, and I was like him and a whore. That I will always been the dyer's child, polluted with his stain. Well then, I will show her, for I am my father's child, and he did want a better life, and I will make one too, and will not live like she does, in the stink and stew.'

There were tears in her eyes. Hew had not seen her cry before. She no longer noticed him. He was able to stand up, and take the knife. Gently, he set it down. He held out his hand to her, almost touched her, and withdrew. 'I must be gone. I'll come again.'

She made no objection. Only as he left she said, 'I won't be here.'

It was days before he came again, days spent in college and with Meg, where in the fright of Meg's attack, and the fear of what succeeded it, he forgot the dyer's child. And when he came at last it was as if he had imagined her. The trinkets and the plums, the little chest and bed had disappeared. The pictures on the wall had been scrubbed away.

A Coffin Crust

Lucy Linn had not known what to do. As Meg lay frothing in her bed she tried to recall the doctor's instructions. Doctor Locke had been terse and Lucy was afraid of him. Now the convulsions had returned she could not remember what he had told her. The maid was no help. She had taken one look and fled the room in terror. Lucy could not manage it alone. In despair, she risked her husband's wrath and did the one thing she could think of: she sent for Agnes Ford. It was Agnes who undressed Meg and gave her the medicines that the doctor had prescribed, Agnes who nursed her and soothed her to sleep. And it had worked out well, for as Agnes had folded and hung up her clothes she found what she was looking for, the little leather pocket filled with carrot seed. And Agnes knew that it was providential after all. She had the means to make her husband lie with her. She left Meg sleeping soundly and went home to make a pie.

Tibbie stared out of the window at the rain. It seeped through the casement, spotting the wall. '*Why* has my father gone to Cupar?' she demanded, pushing down the latch.

Her mother sighed. A strand of pale hair had escaped from her bonnet, softening her frown. Impatiently, she tucked it back. She was making pastry with the last of the white wheaten flour. They would have to bake their bread with oats and barley, or at worst, with stony peas. Archie would not suffer it. He would return from Cupar out of sorts, and if the trip had shown no profit, nothing would be right. She made the pie to mellow him, the remnants of a hare dismembered in the dish with parsley and sweet cicely in a sauce of wine and blood. There was not enough pastry to shape a full coffin.

'He hopes to win the markets there, since business here is slow.'

'His cloths will all be sodden. He'll scuttle homewards crosser than a crab,' her daughter said relentlessly. She ran her finger down the windowpane, chasing the drops. 'Could you not have dissuaded him, Mother? You know he will vent it on Tom.'

'He'll not be driven from his purpose. But you're keen to take Tom Begbie's part. I thought you despised him?'

'Aye, mebbe. *Perhaps*,' she gave a subtle smile, 'the tide will turn, now that his lass has gone.'

'You father will not countenance the match. No more will Tom,' her mother warned. 'He has no eyes for you.'

'We'll see, then.' Tibbie came towards her. 'What is that you're making? Coffin-crusts?'

'It is your father's pie. You shall have a pudding.'

'You know I hate blood pudding,' Tibbie pouted. 'Anyhow, what about Tom?'

'Whisht will you, harping on Tom! There's bread enough, and cheese.'

'Minnie, are we poor?' the girl asked seriously. She rolled a piece of paste between her fingers. Agnes snatched it back.

'Of course not. Do you want for meat?'

'Yet we do not have the dainties we were wont to have,' the girl persisted. 'The little cakes with currants, and the raisins of the sun. Our ale is weak like water, and the bread is hard and coarse. I almost broke a tooth today.'

'Ungrateful wench!' Her mother scolded, yet her tone was fond. 'We wait upon your uncle to return with these good things. Your father will not waste his coin to buy them in the marketplace, when Gilbert can fetch them for nothing.'

'Except he does not fetch them. So we're poor.'

'You must not think it, for your uncle will come soon. There! I've shaped the crust to pattern like the hare. It's bonny, don't you think?'

Tibbie looked critical, wrinkling her nose. 'There's not enough paste for the ears. It looks like a cat. It *smells* like gib-cat too!'

Agnes laughed. 'Strong-seasoned, aye. To tempt your daddie. Meat to please a man.'

'He's welcome to it then. What is it that you tempt him to? What would you have him do?' the daughter teased.

'Nothing, hussy! Tis a sweet to coat his humour when he comes home from the fair.'

'Ah, then you confess it, that his humour will be sour!'

'I do *not* confess it, but indeed the rain . . . if he does not prosper . . .'

'Then, for sure, we *are* poor.' Tibbie stamped her foot.

'Pray, do not sulk. It spoils your looks. You may take this pie to the pastry-cook, and ask him to bake it in his oven till the crust be good and brown, and send it with his boy. And if you *see* the boy, you need not flirt.'

Tibbie ignored this last. But she objected, 'In the *rain*? It will prove a damp pie, for all that.'

Agnes was exasperated. 'Take it in a cloth, it is not far. Here's a penny for to pay for it. And here,' she felt a little deeper in the pocket, 'buy some comfits, if you will.'

Tibbie reaching out her hand to grasp the coin had caught her look of hopelessness. She paused, and shook her head. 'I'll wrap it in my cloak to keep it dry. I will not stay for comfits. Not today.'

They could tell from the rattling of the shutters to the shop, that the trip had not gone well. Presently they heard him on the stair, and Tibbie, sinking back into the shadows, sat as though intent upon her needlework, quiet and hidden until she was called. Agnes stood nervously, close by the fire. The pie had returned from the pastry-cook, and kept warm, pungent, on the hearth. In places the coffin had split, and hot pools of gravy spilled from the crust. Agnes set out bread and butter on the board. It needed nothing more.

Archie Strachan was drunk. He swayed a little as he walked towards the bench and sat down heavily. Agnes smelled the whisky on his breath. She did not meet his eyes. She could feel them hot upon her, belligerent within the fat red face. Without a word, she cut into the pie and began to ladle liquor on his plate. The weaver sniffed suspiciously. 'What's that?'

'It is the last hindquarter of the hare. I put him in a pie-crust with the leavings of the wine.'

'Tis pungent.'

'It is the liquor of his blood. You like him so.'

He did not comment further, but began to eat the pie. The crust was crisp and melting and the hare flesh black and cloying, dripping from the bone. Dribble glistened on his chin. At length he broke a piece of bread and mopped the liquor from the plate. He licked his fingers carefully.

'A piquant hare.'

'Aye,' she said. 'Will you not finish him?'

'No more tonight.' He patted his great belly, satisfied. 'Some ale, though. Where's our daughter?'

Tibbie slipped out from the shadows, pouring the ale. Boldly she enquired of him, 'Father, did you like the pie?'

'The pie?' He belched contentedly. 'I liked it well enough.'

'My mother was most curious to make it well for you.'

Agnes shook her head in warning.

Archie frowned. 'Curious? And she might well take pains with it, when I am up at dawn to tout my wares. And what have you done this day, I ask you, save watch your mother bake indifferent pies?'

''Twas a good pie, Father, I am assured of it.' She stood her ground. 'And I have sewn new seams on all the linens, and have finished off the sheets. My mother says I stitch as neat as any semster.'

'Does she? Tis well, for you may yet have to sit and sew linens, to make us our bread.'

But he did not seem angry now, as though the hot pie in his stomach had perversely cooled his heat. Tibbie stroked his hair. 'I shall do it, if it comes to it,' she soothed him, 'yet I cannot think it will.'

Her father closed his eyes. He did not seem to hear her. 'Ale!'

'May I have the leavings of the pie to take to Tom?' she pressed him.

'Tom?' He stirred. 'Why, let him starve. He has sold nothing today.'

'Leave it,' murmured Agnes, tugging Tibbie's sleeve. 'We'll feed Tom later. Pour the ale.'

The weaver complained of a thirst, drinking deep. He trembled. 'Wife, tis cold in here.'

'I'll put a log upon the fire.'

'My toes are cold. Like ice within my boots. Undo the laces, Tibbie. Rub my feet.'

'Minnie, it's not cold,' his daughter frowned.

'Like as not the rain has soaked him. Do what he asks.'

She pulled off the boots. 'His feet are quite dry.'

'Rub them, child,' her father whispered, 'for I cannot feel them.'

'I'm doing it, Father. Minnie, look, his feet are blue. I cannot warm them.'

'You must come towards the fire,' urged Agnes.

Archie struggled to stand. 'Where is the place? The world is spinning.'

'It is the whisky,' she told Tibbie. 'Go and fetch Tom!'

Archie took a sudden lurch, flailing with his hands. He staggered, and his legs fell under him. Agnes caught his head before it struck the board. His eyes were fixed. 'I cannot move my legs,' he whispered, 'tis a heaviness, a creeping over all, that drags me down. I cannot move them. *Help* me, Agnes.'

'Hush, it is the drink. You're dull through lack of sleep. Here's Tom. He will help you to your bed.' The three of them lifted him, legs trailing useless behind him, onto the bed. '*Minnie*,' said Tibbie, and pointed. Dark waters spread over the quilt.

'Shh, tis nothing. Tom shall fetch a pothecar. Archie, do you hear?'

'Aye,' he answered faintly, 'I can hear you far away. I do not want the pothecar.'

'Are you content?'

'Quite peaceful, aye. It's strange, I cannot find my hands.'

'I must change your hose.'

'Ah, let me rest. For why would you change them?'

'Archie, you have pissed yourself,' she answered boldly. Her daughter blinked. 'You're lying in the stew. But surely you must feel it, wet and cold.'

'You lie,' he said uncertainly, 'why would you lie? I tell you, I feel nothing.'

He did not stir as she began to strip his clothes.

Tom said, 'Mistress, tis not right. I will fetch the apothecary.'

Agnes looked upon the bare legs, draped unfeeling on the bed. She frowned a little. 'Aye.'

Archie lay three hours upon the bed. He felt no pain. Even his choler had evaporated, leaving him a sombre quietness, his sanguine looks at last drawn sad and pale. He answered all the questions put to him, in a distant, lucid voice, as though he found some place of relaxation far away, where everything was clear to him. The apothecary was fascinated. He pricked his soles with pins, moved boldly to the calves and thigh and pinched the inner surface of the groin. He pressed the palms and fingertips, the nailbed to the quick, and at the last was satisfied there was no feeling there. When finally the pulse grew slow, he shook his head, and with complacent sorrow said, 'He's poisoned, then. There is no hope.'

'Poisoned?' Archie Strachan's unfixed muscles jerked their last response. His eyelids and his brows flew open in astonishment, and locked. '*Poisoned*, Agnes? How?'

He spoke no more. The paralysis that crept upon his body reached his heart and stopped it dead, with that last look of hurt surprise, indignant, frozen there forever on his face.

'Poisoned,' said the pothecar, and closed his patient's eyes.

'What did you put with it?' The coroner prodded the remains of the pie, and sniffed the liquor dubiously. Agnes sat very still.

'The quarter of a hare.'

'No roots or mushrooms? Parsnip? Grass?'

'None of those,' she whispered. 'Twas a plain roasted hare, with a pudding in his belly, and we ate him yesterday. The remains I put in the pie, with onions and sweet herbs in a blood wine sauce.'

'Twas good meat, and not tainted?'

'Aye, for sure.'

'And no one else did eat of it today?'

'My daughter ate the pudding, which had roasted in his belly.'

'And yet no one ate the pie?' he repeated patiently.

She shook her head.

'Well then, it seems clear to me, the poison that he took was in the pie.'

Agnes shrank. 'It was a good pie.'

'As you say,' he answered pleasantly, 'then you shall prove the point, by tasting it.' He pushed the dish towards her.

'Sir,' she faltered, turning pale. 'I cannot, sir.'

'Why not? If it were a good pie, as you say, why would you shrink from tasting it? And you will not then it would seem to prove you know it for a *bad* pie.'

'Sir,' Tibbie spoke out tearfully, 'consider that the pie my mother made . . .'

'You saw it made, I'll warrant?' he enquired of her.

'I did so, I swear. It was a good pie. But we did not have it by us all the time. It went for baking at the pastry shop.'

'I see.' He said good-humouredly, 'You think your pie was poisoned there?'

'Well, sir, no . . . we do not know it *was* the pie.'

'Then would you care to taste it?'

'No!' cried Agnes fearfully. Tibbie looked at her. 'But Mother, why?'

'I fear it.'

'Be ware,' cautioned the coroner, 'that your refusal proves your guilt.'

'It does not prove,' Agnes answered with a sudden flare of spirit, 'that I know the pie is poisoned, only that I fear it *might* be so.'

'I observe the difference,' he remarked. 'Then *why* might it be so?'

'Because my husband ate it.'

'Aye, and no one else. Which brings us back to this. Why did you make the pie for him alone?'

'For there was little meat. My husband had the choice of it. And what remained, we might have shared, when he was taken ill.'

'*Might* have, aye.'

'I think that you suspect me, sir.'

'I do suspect the pie. Come, lass, Tibbie is it, will you take a bite?'

'I beg you, no,' cried Agnes. 'Sir, my husband died. I fear it for a bad pie.'

'Then confess it. Spare your daughter,' he said clear and kindly. 'Come now, tell us, what was it that you put with it?'

She stammered, 'It must have been the seeds.'

'Good lass,' he coaxed her gently, 'aye, the seed. And what was that?'

'I had them from a herbalist. She was a witch, I doubt. I was deceived in her. I swear to you, I meant no ill. They were carrot seeds, promised to provoke my husband's lusts.'

He raised an eyebrow, glancing at the body, 'Did it work?'

Agnes flushed unhappily. 'You see that it did not.'

'Well,' he scratched his head, 'and I may put this to the justice clerk, I do not think that it will help your case. Witchcraft will compound the crime. I must tell you, things look grave for you. The pothecar has sworn he heard your husband speak your name before he died. Few indictments are more damning than the accusation of a dying man. Unless you eat the pie, and prove him wrong, I must take you into ward to face your trial.'

'Shall my mistress not be bailed, sir?' Tom asked bravely.

'Tomorrow we shall look to it, when I make my report. Mistress Ford, I have ever found you honest, and am loath to take you hence. It must be done.'

'You should know,' whispered Agnes, 'I am with child.'

'*Mamma*!' Tibbie cried.

There was a long pause while the coroner tried to make sense of this. At length he said sceptically. 'You are with child?'

'I am.'

'And yet your plea is that you fed your husband seeds to stir his lust?'

'That's what I said.'

'A pregnant wife solicit husband's lusts! Forgive me, mistress, this is new to me.'

'It is quite simple, sir. The child is not my husband's.'

'Not your husband's? Ah.'

'It is not what you think. I was raped.'

'Enough of this. Come, mistress, you must see this does not help,' he coaxed. 'Come quiet now. This is what we'll do. I'll take you to the kirk tonight and put you in the steeple. You can think upon your story there.'

'I will come there if I have to, sir. My story will not change.'

'Hush. If it does not, we'll have the midwife try you. Come now, quietly.'

It was a form of words, no more, for she did not resist. She paused only to appeal to Tibbie, holding out her arms. Her daughter shrank away.

'Did you cheat my father?'

Agnes answered quietly, 'It's true I am with child. The child is not your father's. I wanted him to lie with me, so that he might accept it as his own. I meant no more than that.'

She touched her daughter's cheek. 'You must write at once to your uncle, and explain what has happened here. God bless you. Tom, take care of her.'

The kirk session had already met that week, and on the afternoon of Agnes' arrest dispensed its justice in the marketplace, from which fleshly entertainment came the baxter, somewhat flushed. He was surprised to find another prisoner in the tower.

'Wha's that ye brocht?' The Strachan wife?' he demanded of the coroner. 'The minister is out of town. We are no' due to sit.'

'Ah, she's not for you. She'll come before the circuit judge. She's taken for the slaughter of her man.'

'Archie Strachan, deid?' The baxter gave a whistle. 'Who'd have thought it, though?'

'Poisoned,' the coroner grinned. He knew that in committing Agnes to the kirk he had ensured her full confession when she came before the magistrate.

'She has confessed, I doubt?' the baxter went on greedily. He felt a frisson of excitement, stirred by his exertions in the market-place, a mingled sense of pleasure and disgust.

'There's witchcraft involved. A convolute case.'

'Witchcraft?' The baxter's eyes were open wide. 'Tsk! You'd have her watched and waked?'

'Aye, that I would. Twere better that she did confess before the session court.'

'I see. That I do see. Come, then, tell me all!'

At dusk he took the gaoler's key and let himself into the steeple where Agnes was locked for the night. 'Mistress Ford,' he told her pleasantly, 'I have the candle. Here now, let me look into your face. A terrible thing, is this not?'

'Master Brooke,' she knew him; he was like the dyer, and she did not trust his kindness, 'It is a mistake, and will be put right.'

The baxter had the softest hands, made white by the kneading of bread, the barley stone pumice of oatmeal and peas. Blank as a child's and milk-clean, they harboured a sinuous strength. His fingertips had long since lost all feeling, numbed and scorched by force and fire. Only memory preserved their subtlety of touch, prodding and probing resistance, knocking and shaping the bread. He looked from these hands up at Agnes, pale in the candlelight, flexing his fingertips, plying the joints. 'Ah, Agnes Ford,' he said softly, ''tis a sad, sad thing that has befallen you. Perhaps it was the demons drove you to it?'

'What demons?' she whispered. 'I have done nothing.'

He considered this, inspecting his fingernails. Presently he said, 'Did you hear the brangling at the cross?'

Agnes shook her head.

'Ah, did ye no'? A woman was lashed for a whore, the mouth on her foul as you like! She's to compear for blasphemy next week. The world's a wicked place, what say you, Agnes Ford?'

'I cannot think her much improved,' she answered hoarsely.

'By whipping? Ah, you'd be surprised.' He smiled a little, dropping the words into the darkness. 'Did you bewitch your husband?'

'I swear it, I did not.'

'Tell it to the minister, at the session court. Goodnight now, Mistress Ford.'

Without another word, he closed the door.

'That woman is a witch,' he informed the beadle. 'There can be no doubt. Did you look upon her mark?'

'I did not lift her dress,' allowed the beadle sheepishly. 'Did you?'

'Forget the mark.' The baxter changed the subject. 'Guard her close. She will confess. She'll come before the session when we meet. Meanwhile, we must wake and watch, observe her, mark the signs. You may take the first shift, and a shilling extra for your pains.'

'Two shillings,' said the beadle narrowly. 'If she is a witch, there is a risk.'

The baxter tutted, 'Tsk, there is no risk, because, you see, you will restrain her, that she may not use her artifice or conjure you with tricks. Neither heed nor talk with her, but place her bread and water only just in reach. Better, keep her chained. And keep her dark and waking, and I'll warrant you may hear her devils yet. Peace, man, they won't harm you! Two shillings, then. So be it. You shall have another when she hangs.'

'You must pay me to release her, even if she hangs,' the beadle pointed out. 'Two shillings now, and two for her release, and two for her confession, and another when she hangs.' He counted on his fingers. 'Seven shillings in all. We'll call it eight.'

The baxter raised an eyebrow 'Would you rob the parish to despatch a witch?'

'Witches are expensive. There's the pyre or scaffold, and the lockman's fee, a quantity of rope and kindling for the fire . . .'

'Aye,' the elder chuckled, 'there's ay a price to pay. Well then, Jock, I cannot promise, but the parish is likely to meet you. If ye'll mind her while the lockman comes, I'll put it to the minister to approve your fee. I can't see he'll dispute it. As ye ken yourself, he does not care to know the details of these things.'

'He's a guid man,' posed the beadle doubtfully.

'Aye, that he is, the better to be clear of this. He's weak in heart and stomach, and he will not like this news. Therefore we'll not disturb him till the time is ripe. Meanwhile, guard her well.' The baxter winked at him. 'Ye widna want her devils makin' eyes at you.'

Watching and Waking

The beadle had set the lamp behind him low on the ground where the prick of the light did not show his face. Still she seemed to know him for as he approached she cried hoarsely, 'For pity, Jock, I am with child!' He blanched a little at the calling of his name, cupping her face in his hand, and placed his necklace tenderly, like a lover's trinket, at her throat. The wall supplied a collar and a chain, the partner of the jougs that rattled at the mercat cross, and this the beadle used to encircle her, beading her neck with twin bracelets, buckling its manacles close. He restrained the witch so that she might not sit or lie, the better to arouse and wake her. If she fainted it would wirry her or strangle her, and jerk her back into life. He forced the rusted padlock fast against her breast, where it hung grinding and pendulous. Agnes could taste it, metallic like blood. The beadle retreated as soundless as he came and taking up the light, he closed the door. He left the witch alone and in the dark.

Depriving her of light and speech, the beadle felt less afraid of the witch. He set the lamp upon the table by the psalter, and the tremor within him began to subside. He was a candlemaker by trade. Now, to calm his nerves and while away the hours of night watch, he wove strips of hemp into candlewicks, laying them carefully out on the board. And when the witch's pleas came loud enough to unnerve him, he whispered his catechism under his breath, and sang to himself.

He would have liked to use the branks to still her tongue, but the baxter had forbidden it; 'Allow her loose her voice, and your silence shall shape her confession.' So he sat quiet, methodically fashioning his wicks, until he heard her falter and fall still. Only then did he take up a splinter of light to peek through the grating, undo the locks and feel for her face in the darkness, prodding and pricking her awake again. It thrilled him to go to in to her, a cudgel by his side to keep him safe. Once she pawed his sleeves and clung there close. He had to shake her off. When she could stand no longer, he roused her choking from the irons with water to her lips, and sat her squarely on a stool below the chain. In doing so he saved her life. That done, he flashed the splinter flame before her eyes to reassure himself that she was conscious, locked the door and left her till the hangman came to make the second shift. This lockman, more accomplished in the arts of torment, was less fearful than the beadle of approaching her. Cheerfully, he kept her waking. It was he who forged the plan to ring the hand-bells night and day, that starting from her sleep, she might not know the passing of the hours. And so the two of them did watch and wake her, hour by hour and turn by turn. And neither of them spoke to her, but pricked and teased and stung her, buzzing round her dreams like flies, until the baxter, when he came by for his third watch, was pleasantly astonished to remark the change in her.

As Agnes lay waking, Meg Cullan slept. Through long nights of sickness, Giles Locke had attended her, calming the demons that kept her in thrall. When he was content at last the seizures were discharged, he was reluctant still to leave her side. He wrote out stern commandments for her rest. His prescriptions vexed and baffled Lucy Linn. Yet, as she could, she did comply, and with the promise of a nurse, both Giles and Hew returned to college life. And so they went on quietly, until one afternoon, some three days after Agnes' arrest, Hew called in at the merchant's house to find his cousin weeping in the hall. This in itself did not alarm him. He was used to Lucy's fancies, and resigned himself to comfort her. He had fetched her salts and cushions, herbs and wines and comfits, enquired upon her health and bairn and husband, all to no avail, before the floods had settled and the tale began to spill. It came out in blurts, like a blocked water fountain, blunted with spouting salt tears.

'That girl! I did not think she would be bold enough to come here! God forgive me! What will Robin think!'

Quick-witted as he was, Hew could not untangle this.

'There is nothing that cannot be managed,' he assured her patiently. 'Tell me, who has come? Has someone threatened you?'

She shook her head. 'The Strachan girl,' she whispered, 'came here to beg for help. My God! If Robin knew!'

'Tibbie Strachan? Why?'

'Have you not heard? It is her mother Agnes, taken for a witch. And she has killed her husband and is in the tower. And Tibbie says that they torment her there, and force her from her rest. My God, Hew, Agnes is a witch, and she was *here*!'

Hew's mind had begun to make sense of this parcel of words. He felt chilled to the pit of his belly. He spoke very calmly, clasping Lucy's hands.

'I had not heard this. Our college walls are thick. Agnes killed her husband? How?'

'With poisoned seeds. She had them from a witch. And she is taken to the kirk, till she confess, and name the witch, and both shall surely hang. If Robin knew I had her in the house!'

Hew pressed on urgently, 'Was it *Tibbie*, then, you had here in the house?'

'Tibbie? Twas *Agnes*. Pity, Hew, don't blame me!'

She flinched from him, and fleetingly he almost pitied her.

'You will not tell Robin,' she whimpered. 'Pray, don't let him know. Professor Locke insisted on a nurse, and Meg was wild and frothing and the maid afraid to sit with her.'

'And so Agnes nursed her,' Hew concluded desperately.

'Aye, do not blame me,' she clutched at him. 'For I doubt she did no harm. But Agnes is a witch!'

He shook his head. 'It was not your fault. I should have found a nurse for her. Though I think it very likely that the matter is mistaken. Agnes Ford is not a witch. In any case, she cannot come here now, so put her from your mind.'

'You think not?' Lucy blew her nose. Unburdening had brightened her.

'It matters not, though, if she is a witch,' she remarked with unexpected shrewdness. 'Come the session court, she will confess. And to think, I had her here!'

Hew forced himself to smile at her. 'Well then, you see, there's no harm done. We'll keep this quiet, Lucy. You have not told Meg?'

She shook her head regretfully. 'I do not speak to Meg. Tis only these last days she has been sensible. It is an *uncouth* ailment, and I do not fault the maid. That's why I was so glad to have had Agnes. No, I have not told her. The physician is insistent, she must not be vexed.'

'It's proper that we keep it so. Poor Lucy,' he expressed a sympathy he did not hold at heart, 'this is hard for you.'

'It has been,' she simpered, clutching his sleeve. 'But I can bear it now.'

It was harder to conceal his true concerns from Meg. He did not like to lie to her. Sleepy as she was, she sensed something amiss. 'What has happened to you, Hew? You have a cut upon your throat.' She traced the scratches with her finger.

'A close shave from a drunken barber.' Gently, he removed her hand. 'You were gone for days. I'm glad to find you waking. I have been afraid for you.'

'I am recovered,' she replied a little sourly. 'Only Giles enforces rest. And he is most officious. Pray advise him, I am well.'

'You must listen to him, Meg. The seizures were severe. You remember little, I suppose?'

'Nothing, till I woke up yesterday. Lucy says you brought me here with Giles, and that Giles has since attended me. It's good of him, though he has been boasting how well he has cured me.'

Hew was too preoccupied to smile at this. 'You don't remember your nurse?'

'What nurse?'

'Someone undressed you.'

'Was it not the maid?' She flushed a little. 'Hew, you don't mean Giles!'

'No, no,' he reassured her hastily. 'Look, here are your clothes on the stool. But I do not see the pocket where you keep your hemlock seeds.'

'It's there inside the dress. There is a little ribbon ties it to the sleeve.'

'I see it now. It's empty.'

Meg sat up in bed. 'The scoundrel, Hew! Doctor Locke has taken it, and dosed me with the seed. He who has the nerve to boast he cured my fits without resort to *poisons*, as he calls them! Well! The quacksalve! We have found him out! He will not grant my arts superior to his.'

'It seems that you have solved it,' her brother answered grimly. 'Well then, let us humour him. It will not do us good to wound his pride. What matter, though? You're well. And if you rest a little longer, you'll be quite restored to us.'

He tucked the empty pocket in his shirt and left her with a heavy heart.

When Hew had been a student in his first year at St Andrews, two men were taken from the town as witches to the scaffold. One was hanged, and one was burned. In the college the reporting of their trial was met with lewd excitement as the young men feasted on the details of their crimes. When the regents' backs were turned they spoke of little else. Some had begged for leave to watch the executions, which was granted with good grace. Hew had felt the revulsion, squeamish and soft, that threatened him still to this day. The necromancers preyed upon his mind, both in the crude accounts of their confessing, sniggered in the hall from boy to boy, and in the heady whispers of their discourse with the dead. At length he almost had believed himself bewitched, haunted by these nightmare tales of demons and the engines that had moved the men's confessions. Only Nicholas had sensed his friend's disquiet, and had whispered to him on the night before the hanging that he doubted whether witches did exist. Hew was startled from his fears. 'Twere heresy, for sure, to say they don't *exist*.'

'Aye, heresy, for sure,' his bedfellow had smiled at him.

This cheerful confidence had brought Hew comfort. He confessed he would prefer a whipping to the watching of an execution, witch or no. And so amidst the clamour they had slipped away to spend the afternoon upon the links, chasing conies through the dunes, where truant, they had forged their friendship far beyond the crowd. As the term progressed, Hew became acclimatised to torment and the ruthless casual cruelties of the kirk. He saw vagrants and whore-mongers scourged through the streets, branded and bloodied like parcels of meat. Yet though their disfigurement moved and disgusted him, the cruelty had inured him to their suffering, for it turned their human faces to grotesques. Three years later, when he heard John Knox pour scalding words upon a witch before the pulpit, he watched her trudging forth towards the pyre with little sense of horror or regret. The flames found her shrivelled, dehumanised.

Once a witch was named, there was little could be done to stop the turning of the screw, the long and slow trudging through darkness to death. Agnes was already in the shaft of sleepless dream, whose only light and end was her confession. To urge her not to confess, he was aware, was like urging her to walk alone across an open precipice, closing off from her the last glimpse of the light. Yet Agnes Ford must not confess. She must not denounce his sister as a witch. If Agnes once gave name to her, Meg Cullan would be wracked and bowed to the most intricate of cruelties, turned to human torchlight, rope around her neck. Therefore Agnes Ford must be released, and he must be her advocate.

He ran to the Mercatgait and hammered on the door of Archie's shop.

Tibbie Strachan had changed remarkably since he had seen her last. The girl who looked out on the street bore no resemblance to the strumpet who had tossed her curls in kirk. She gave a bare glance at the stranger, and the apprehension in her voice did not quicken into curiosity.

'We're closed, sir. For bereavement.'

'You're Tibbie Strachan?'

'Isabel, aye.' She stared at him, grey with mistrust, her pet name discarded. 'What would you want with me, sir?'

'I come from the house of my cousin, Robin Flett, from Lucy Linn his wife, who has lately been a friend to you.'

A little colour pricked her cheeks as she said stiffly, 'Lately, aye. You need not take the trouble, sir, to warn me from your family. Lucy made it clear.' She began to close the door.

'You misunderstand me. I came to speak about your mother. I'm a man of law.'

'Aye, lass, tis true, he is a man of law, and you maun speak with him,' urged an agitated voice. Hew saw the figure of Tom Begbie, shifting in the room behind her, peering through the crack.

The girl appeared to hesitate. 'I know this man,' persisted Tom. 'He's privy to the courts, and you must give him heed. Ye *must*.'

He shot Hew a look of appeal, as though only terror had halted his flight, and Hew had a sense of how little he or Tibbie could begin to comprehend the horrors that enfolded them. Masking pity in a frown, he played the part. 'Aye, that's right. And I must look into the case, and talk in private with you, Tibbie . . . *Isabel*.'

Without a word in answer, Tibbie led the way into the house. Hew held the door just long enough for Tom to flee this present threat before he followed her. She settled on a stool, arms in her lap, like a penitent in kirk, cowed into submissiveness. She had kept the chamber tidy since her mother left, the work folded neat in its basket, the pots scrubbed and clean. And Hew, who had come here intent upon helping Meg, felt with a prick the true depth of Tibbie's tragedy, closed in the dark of her quiet neat house. Softly, he said, 'Are you left here alone? With Tom Begbie?'

The kirk had soiled her conscience, for she rallied in alarm.

'Tom lies in the shop. He does not sleep here . . . and besides . . .' she spoke the words reluctantly, as if they were foreign objects in her mouth, rolled about her tongue like pebblestones, 'he stays upon the trial, for he is wanted there.'

Hew inclined his head and answered gently, 'For sure, I meant no impropriety. I only thought to ask, you have no friend? To see you through this time?'

Tibbie shook her head. 'When my father was alive we were something in the town. Now all doors are closed to us. I hoped that Lucy Linn . . .'

'Understand, it's hard for Lucy, with her husband gone from home,' Hew excused his cousin. 'Yet she sends me in her place. I can help you. What was it that you wanted from her?'

'Her husband Robin Flett does business with my uncle overseas. If I could send the tidings . . . but I know not where to – how to – send the news to him.'

'Ah, is that all?' he interrupted earnestly. 'Then it is the simplest thing. I will write the letters and send them to the Scots house in Campvere. You will reach him there, you may be sure of it. Your uncle then will vouch for her, and Agnes may go free.'

'You don't understand. It is too late for that. My mother has been taken for a witch and imprisoned in the kirk. They will not let me see her there. Her friends – the people who were once her friends – will not intercede for her. And Tom . . .' her voice was thick with tears, 'Tom says they torment her, and that, witch or not, she will confess. I came into the kirk and heard her cries. I could not bear to stay. And yet the elders say that if I shun the kirk I am a witch as well, so I dare not shun the kirk, or stop my ears to block the sound. It is a torment, sir,' she told him simply.

He shook his head, moved at this horror. He told her truthfully, 'Aye, I understand you. Still, there may be hope. Tell me what has happened here. I'll help you if I can.'

'I know only that my father died.' And she told her tale. Hew allowed her to spill out the whole, resisting the urge to question her, until the tears began to prick, and his suspicions were confirmed.

'She did not say,' he echoed softly, 'where she had obtained the poisons?' It was the question he had come to ask, yet he felt ashamed for asking it.

'Only that a witch had sold them to her, and she was deceived.'

'Aye, she was deceived,' he answered bitterly. 'And may be damned for saying it. Forgive me, but there was no witch. Your mother took the medicines from my sister's pocket, while my sister lay insensible. My sister is Meg Cullan. You have met, I think?'

She nodded doubtfully.

'You said yourself, she claimed to be with child.'

'Aye, she did . . . you say there was no witch?' she faltered.

'*That* is her defence, and with it we may face her trial. Only understand, if she does confess to witchcraft, there will be no trial, and I may not defend her. I will put it to the kirk there is no case for witchcraft, and your mother must be free to face the Crown.'

Tibbie shook her head. The tears were flowing now. 'It's hopeless, then. For she is warded in the kirk. No man may see her until she has confessed. Tom Begbie says no creature could resist the torments they contrive for her. It were better to forget her, and to sell the looms and go from here, he says. But, sir, I cannot; though she killed my father I cannot forget her.'

'Nor should you,' he retorted fiercely. 'She's your mother still. They cannot keep you from her. How can they torment her when she is with child? She must be freed. If you were not a fatherless lass, and had someone else to speak for you, she would be freed.'

'The minister himself would not appeal for her. He says the law must take its course. There's nothing he can do against the kirk.'

Hew snorted. 'I will write the letters. With your uncle's word behind us we will make our case before the justice clerk. Meanwhile, Agnes must be freed. The kirk shall clear its conscience of this crime.'

Confessing

Hew found the Reverend Geoffrey Traill, incumbent of the Kirk of Holy Trinity, surrounded by that group of bairns he called his grammar school. He led his little pupils with the same cajoling vigour he delivered from the pulpit, redirecting his attentions to delinquent Latin verbs. Behind him came a straggle of reluctant infant voices piping ineffectually beneath his baritones. Hew was intrigued to find a small girl among them, her hair severely scraped beneath her cap. The master kept the tune, booming broad his welcome in a brave show of delight.

'Children, hush your chanting, look, see who has come to us! Here's a grand treat and an honour! Master Cullan, scholar, from the *uni-vers-it-ie*! Welcome, Master Cullan, to our little school! Shall you now decline for us, to show these imps and striplings how it's done?'

Hew bowed. 'Another day, I should be glad to. My business here is pressing. I beg leave to speak with you.'

'Do you hear him, children? He's *declining* to decline.'

Hew smiled politely but did not respond, and the master looked perplexed.

'Ah, so grave. It's urgent, then? If you would come this evening, we might talk awhile and sup. I should appreciate your company,' he ventured hopefully.

'I am obliged to you, sir, but I'm afraid this cannot wait. Tis urgent, aye, and *private*.'

The master sighed. 'Aye, very well. I see that you are troubled. Well then, wait within. There is a closet where I have my books. I'll join you there directly. Allow me a moment to settle the boys. Elizabeth,' he beckoned to the girl, 'run and help your mammie in the house.'

A moment or two later he bustled into the chamber where Hew stood waiting, and explained a touch defensively, 'Elizabeth's my daughter. I am teaching her the Latin, for she has a scholar's wit.'

'I do not doubt it,' Hew assured him. 'It was grand to see her there.'

'Well, well.' The minister seemed pleased at this endorsement. 'That is the proper view. And yet I fear the lads are apt to tease her when my back is turned. She will not complain of it, wherefore I might amend it, understand, but oftentimes, I find her brought to tears. In consequence I do not like to leave her in their company.'

'It is a sad sin that the lass should be tormented so,' Hew answered thoughtfully. 'A case, indeed, not far removed from that which brings me here.'

'You speak very soberly, sir. Has something happened to the bursar, Thomas Burns? I must confess, I felt uneasy there.'

'I doubt you may have cause. However, it's not Thomas that concerns me. And the last I heard, the boy was well. I speak of Agnes Ford, who presently lies warded in the kirk.'

'Agnes?' The minister stared at him. 'This is unexpected, man. Why would you concern yourself with that unhappy soul? You have no connection, I think?'

'I concede, no natural one. Though I would count it unnatural indeed not to feel disquiet at the ills that have befallen her. Agnes is locked in your steeple, apart from her family and friends. For three days and nights she is kept subject to torments. Her crying is heard in the kirk.'

'*Whisht*, there are no torments. Agnes Ford is watched and warded while she waits her trial. She is a little vexed.' The minister himself looked vexed, and anxious to be done with an unhappy conversation. He turned towards the door. 'I doubt I hear the boys. If that was all . . .'

'She is denied the comfort of her friends, who may not bring her hope,' persisted Hew. 'Day and night she cries. We may surmise she does not sleep. Guards torment her, wake and watch.'

'Aye, that is to say,' Traill rallied brightly, 'they are wakeful and watchful, diligent as they watch over her.'

'We both of us know what it means. Tell me, sir, have you spoken with her there? Have you been to see her in her gaol?'

The minister shifted uneasily. 'Agnes comes before our court on Tuesday. I will hear her then.'

'You are content to let her lie until her wits are left her? If Agnes were your daughter, left among the boys, you would not turn your back so willingly. Yet you have left Agnes at the mercy of your elders. Her shrieks carry to the pulpit. You cannot be deaf to them.'

There was a long silence, after which the minister replied, in measured tones, 'If you compared my daughter to a witch, I'd wonder at your manners, sir. I know you for an honest man, else I should scorn to answer you. There is nothing I can do for Mistress Ford. She is indicted for witchcraft, which is the business of the kirk and none of yours. Presently she will compear before the session and confess; thereafter to the magistrate, or to the privy council, for the slaughter of her husband using charms. The wretched woman will be strangled at the stake. You are a young man. I applaud your compassion. But with a little more experience, you might have understood your pity is misplaced. You should know I am lately come from Archie Strachan's grave, and have delivered him cold to the ground. An apothecar within this town, whose word I trust, told me Archie named her as he died. But, stay, I will not answer this. Her consequence is no concern of yours.'

'It does concern me,' argued Hew, 'for I am her man of law.'

'Her man of law?' The minister softened, shaking his head. 'Ah no, my young friend, you make a mistake. Do not, I pray, allow your name to sound with witchcraft or it will resonate against you. Understand, that cause is lost!'

'In conscience,' Hew returned quietly, 'I wonder you can say so. You spoke of compassion. I took you for another man.'

'You don't know what you deal with here. For pity, let it rest.'

'For pity, I cannot.'

'What cause have you to meddle thus? What's Agnes Ford to you?'

'The daughter has engaged me as her mother's counsel. Therefore, I must speak with her.'

'The daughter! Good God! That poor child! How has she *engaged* you? You are not, as I recall, an advocate?' he countered shrewdly.

'As good as, and I know the law. She has no other friend.'

'No, no,' the clergyman protested. 'When all is done, and Agnes gone, the kirk will be a friend to her. Be assured we will not leave her destitute. For Agnes, though, you plead a hopeless case. Or do you defend witchcraft, sir?' he rounded nastily.

'Witchcraft, no. Do I defend the charge that Agnes is a witch, I do, and I deny it. Something else has happened here. Or tell me truthfully, sir, do you believe the woman is a witch?'

The minister fell silent.

'Do you, sir?'

'Agnes as a witch must answer to the kirk and Crown,' the other answered wearily. 'Twere madness to defend her, when the kirk concludes her guilt.'

'What say you, her guilt is concluded? Has she confessed?'

'I understand, not yet.'

'And what if she does not confess?'

'Well then,' he struggled helplessly, 'if she does not confess, and the court can find no proofs of witchcraft, she is free to face the magistrate, for slaughter of her man. It's one and the same, don't you think?'

'They are not the same. For as to the slaughter, we may make a defence. But will you not allow that Agnes, even though she is no witch, is likely to confess it from compulsion, from the tortures she has suffered in your care?'

The minister protested, 'I do not allow that. And if it is true that most in her position do confess, then I think it likely most are witches, and our discipline does comfort them in setting free their fault. They make confession freely and most willing, when they understand the nature of their sin. It is the duty of the kirk to teach that understanding where they have been blind to it.'

'Aye, and I have read such, in the transcripts of the trials,' Hew replied sardonically, 'and their tortures underwritten there as the "most safe and gentle."'

'I will not have this. What torments have been brought to Agnes Ford, I do protest *are* safe and gentle, such as leave no long impressions on her flesh. Whatever has been done to her, it cannot match the torment of her soul, the devil's twisting of her heart, which only her confession can relieve.'

'You do concede that she is tortured?' Hew replied coldly.

'You have had my answer. I will say no more.'

'I see I may not move you. Tell me, therefore, what will become of the child?'

'We will not see Tibbie starve. I have been patient, Master Cullan, in my regard for you. Now you must understand, you have no business here. If you spread these rumours you will cause offence; at worst you may invite the charge of heresy.'

'I understand. But I did not mean Tibbie. Were you not aware that Agnes is with child?'

The minister looked startled. 'Is she? Do you know this for sure?'

'It is not proved, but Agnes has protested it, and don't you think the matter should be tried before you instigate your safe and gentle tortures? Are they harmless to the bairn? Or do you think the devil draws so deep into the womb, her bairn itself must undergo your purge? Does it square your conscience, sir, to sacrifice her child? I believe that you have not looked at all into the detail of this case, but have allowed your elders to proceed with it, for the matter is distasteful, and you would not soil your hands with Agnes' blood. It will appease the bishop and the magistrate, if Agnes comes compliant and confesses.'

The man was visibly distressed. He shook his head. 'The kirk is resolute in its reproach of witchcraft. Tis a rampant evil we must lift out by the root. I cannot seem to let it flourish undeterred. I knew nothing of a child. I do not know it now.'

'But you do, sir, in your conscience. I ask only this: the matter should be tried. Allow a midwife to examine Agnes Ford, and if the midwife says there is no danger to her child, then you may keep her in your tower until the trial. But as her man of law, I must satisfy myself she does not suffer torments that endanger her.'

'Very well,' the minister agreed reluctantly. 'But I will have to put it to the elders, for there must be funds. The midwife must be known and trusted. I know a wife who will do it, who has done for us before, when wanton women giving birth will not declare the father. She is most assiduous in questioning. She'd serve us well. 'Twill not come cheap, a *witch* and all . . .'

'Let her name her price, and I will pay it,' Hew concluded in disgust. 'Come, we'll fetch her now. Take her to the tower and we shall try her, and if Agnes proves with child, have her released.'

'Well, it may be possible. Now, you say? There are the boys . . .'

'Come, declare a holiday. I'll send them home myself. If you resolve this matter, you may look your little daughter in the face with lighter heart and conscience when your school convenes again. Or what would you tell her? You murdered a child?'

Agnes had begun to know the men by scent: the beadle, rank with candlefat; the baxter scuffed with flour, the odour of the hangman, like a nosegay in a sickroom, faintly sweet and foul. She could not know their voices, for they did not speak to her. And somehow in that way they took away her name. She did not understand what had become of it. She sensed them moving round the room like vapours. Clutching at their clothes, she found them flesh and blood, yet still they would not answer her; gradually their scents were fused as one. Like ghosts they flitted through and disappeared. The darkness enhanced her sense of the physical. She could feel but not see the jougs around her neck, the manacles confining her. She tasted flakes of rust upon her fingertips, scraps of blood and metal mingling with her bread. She ran her hands along the chain to stroke the coolness of the wall, or slipped a finger's width beneath the iron to shift the shafting collar from her throat. The chain did not allow her fully to the ground, but she might lean her back on the wall, shaking out her limbs to ease the strain.

These things brought her reassurance, made an anchor in the shadows where she knew the space she filled. But as the hours passed, Agnes felt less certain where her space began and ended, where the outside was. She was puzzled by the rapping in her womb, the deep drum and thud of her heartbeat, improbably loud. She lost her sense of balance to the dizzy peal of bells. Sounds were discordant, no longer distinct. She heard the cries she made as something they contrived within that place to frighten her, her own voice stolen from her and transformed. She could no longer eat or drink. The crumbs began to choke her, for she could not swallow them. She spewed into the darkness, turning inside out. Gradually, she forgot herself. Hunger, thirst and fear, her belly and her limbs, became externals, voiding in the dark air that hung outside her. All were displaced by the yearning for sleep. When she could stand no more, they propped her on the stool, which cruel support exhausted her, and forced her throat to close in terror, constricted by the iron. And all her voice and soul did cry for sleep; she yearned for it, and would give all she had for it; she wanted nothing else. Only death did seem so sweet, and yet it was withheld from her, while she wept and begged for it. By their tricks they waked her and would not allow it in.

In this waking gulf of darkness, Agnes felt herself disintegrate. Her terrors danced around the room. Archie wagged a playful finger, shook his head at her, dragged the purpled dyer's hose about his feet. Once, she saw Alexander, sweetest of children, sticky-sweet with blood. She did not remember his name. The ghosts brought her comfort, and she talked to Archie, scolding him for dying, and to the red-haired boy. She told them both about the bairn that fluttered in her womb, and Archie held his tongue for once. 'I wish

I could have told you,' she explained to him. He rolled his eyes and clucked her chin, saying not a word; and then she saw it was not Archie but her father come to kiss goodnight to her, not her father but the hangman, and the apparitions fled, and would not return.

There came a tap-tap-tapping, like the iron of her father's anvil, ringing the steel outside the door, and a slow prick-pricking, creeping of her skin, until her flesh squirmed around her like a living thing. Then she knew that there were fiends and devils come to haunt her, that she really was a witch.

When they brought the light she reared up, spitting like a tomcat, and it took the beadle and the lockman both to loosen and restrain her, pinning her down upon the straw. The lockman struck Agnes hard upon the face to quiet her, and pulled her filthy shift above her head. This shielding from the sudden light subdued her, like a kitten in a poke. She submitted passively while the midwife pumped the swollen nipples and the blue veins of her breasts, ranged her restless womb and answered shortly.

'There is no question that this woman is with child, I would hazard some four or five months. Aye, no less, for I feel the bairn quicken.'

'You're sure?'

Perhaps it was the candlelight; the minister had turned a sickly shade. He pressed a handkerchief against his face, perspiring in the chill damp air, and mopped his brow.

'There can be no doubt,' the woman answered.

'Then you must release her,' the minister said thickly to the beadle, 'pending trial.'

When the man looked likely to protest, he countered, 'Witch or no, it is not right that ye should treat her so.'

'We have tret her well,' the man objected, 'and ye will not find a mark upon her, I will swear to it, save the hangman had to slap her, which you witnessed for yourself. And she has vexed us sorely with her crying and her cursing and her spit and scratching. Then there is the fee for her release and for her warding, which was long and arduous.'

'Aye, it was,' said Hew abruptly. 'Here's your money.' And he threw the man a purse. He pitied her, but did not blush to see her mauled and stripped. Their cruelties had reduced her to a wild, inhuman creature, and in her fear and filth she scarcely seemed herself.

'Agnes, you are free to go.' Hew gave her back her name, and covered up her nakedness. He lifted down her dress.

Agnes did not stir but, blinded by her darkness, blinked bewildered at the light.

'Agnes,' said the minister, in his booming kindly voice. 'You may go home to your Tibbie. And we'll summon you next week to compear before the session. Do you understand? To answer,' he began to look uncomfortable, 'are you a witch, and all. I'm sure you'll make an answer, when you put your mind to it. That you understand the charge, and are under no compulsion, and so on. Sleep now, change your clothes. Go home and prepare yourself.'

He cleared his throat and rounded on the beadle.

'Clean this place. There's a stench cannot be fit to breathe. It may spread sickness to the kirk.'

''Tis sickness, sir,' the beadle answered brightly, fingering his purse. 'I'll change the straw.'

He gestured to the lockman, and together they lifted Agnes by the arms and bundled her downstairs.

Hew followed Agnes into the street, where he found her shrinking, baffled by the day. He could not persuade her to walk with him. Her limbs refused to carry her and in the end he had to lift her in his arms. She clutched and murmured vaguely but did not resist as they stumbled the few yards to Strachan's shop. Tibbie laid fresh linen on the bed and Hew set Agnes down on the counterpane, on the white embroidered pillow that was Archie's final resting place. In the absence of all other friends it fell to Hew to fetch the water and to heat it on the fire while Tibbie washed her tenderly, sombre as a mother laying out her child. She coaxed the tangles from her hair, wiped the dribble from her lips and burned the filthy clothes upon the fire. As Agnes was made clean, Hew felt a little shy of her. He turned his eyes away, embarrassed at her nakedness, though he had seen her stripped and foetid in her prison cell.

When all was clean and fresh, and the room restored to its accustomed neatness, Tibbie bowed her head and wept. Hew came close to comfort her. He took the candle from her hands and drew the curtains round the bed, leaving Agnes to her rest. As he closed the drapes she stirred and smiled at him. 'Gilbert, is it you?' she murmured. 'Do not leave me now. For I have told them nothing.'

And so it was it was Hew Cullan, gentlest of inquisitors, who heard her name the father of her child.

The Reckoning

On Tuesday, Hew represented Agnes at the session court. Giles came with him as a witness. Agnes was surprisingly recalcitrant. 'Physician, what physician?' she whimpered in bewilderment. 'I do not know him, sir.'

Hew hissed at her. 'Listen, and be silent. He has evidence to help you.' He informed the court, 'This case is not in your juris-diction. It is an accidental death.'

Thomas Brooke the baxter sneered. 'What are you, an advo-cate?' He appealed to the minister, 'By what authority has this man had her freed? She was arraigned for witchcraft.'

'That I shall contend. I am her counsel. And this man is a witness to the case. He is a physician, Doctor Locke.'

'I've heard the name.' The minister looked closely at Giles. But before he could explain himself, Agnes cried out wildly, 'He cannot be a witness, sir. I do not know him.'

'He is a mediciner and a scholar and has information crucial to this case that he will put before you,' Hew answered patiently. 'I pray you, hear him out.'

Thomas Brooke began to rant. 'The woman has confessed she baked the pie and fed it to her husband. She confessed the pie was poisoned. She was caught red-hand.'

'Therefore she must be arraigned for slaughter, not for witchcraft,' Hew proceeded smoothly. 'This is not a matter for the kirk.'

'There,' roared the baxter, poking his finger, 'is where ye go wrong, for she admitted to the coroner that she had the poison from a witch. *Therefore*,' he concluded triumphantly, 'she is indicted for witchcraft, and for conjuring with charms, and etcetera, and etcetera, which she must confess.'

'No, sir, I did not,' protested Agnes. 'For I am no witch. The *lassie* is the witch. She said the herbs were harmless, knowing they were poison. I bought them in good faith.'

'That is a lie,' observed Hew.

'A lie?' The baxter sniggered. 'I thought you were her counsel!'

'I counsel her to tell the truth. Come, madam,' Hew prompted her gently, 'for you know you stole the seeds.'

'You promised to defend me,' Agnes cried.

'If you tell the truth. The truth is,' he addressed the minister directly, 'that Agnes stole the seeds. She had no knowledge what they were.'

'And what were they?' the baxter asked snidely.

'Hemlock,' interjected Giles. 'They were prescribed to a patient of mine who suffers from convulsions, wherein their sparing use is proven beneficial. This woman stole them from my patient's bedside in mistake for carrot seeds.'

'Confession of this theft,' Hew whispered to Agnes, 'is essential to your cause. Or you will burn for witchcraft and be wirrit at the stake.'

Agnes nodded fearfully. 'Aye, it's true. I took them.'

'Then there was no witch?' the minister asked sceptically.

Agnes hesitated, looking from one man to the other, and conceded, 'No.'

'Agnes is with child,' explained Hew smoothly, 'by a man who is not her husband. You will hear her claim that she was raped. That you may look into as and when you will. Her husband has not dealt with her for years. She had met Doctor Locke's patient, and knew her to keep carrot seeds as prophylactic for her fits in a pocket in her dress. The seed has a reputation as an aphrodisiac and is harmless. She resolved to ask for some. Unhappily, when she came into the house, she found her friend insensible, in the grip of a convulsion. What then should she do? It was clear to her. She found the pocket by the bed and took the seeds inside. Only now, the seeds were hemlock.'

'Is this her defence?' The minister frowned.

'It is, sir. She confesses to the theft. And she confesses to the pie. She does not confess to murder or to witchcraft. You must let her go to trial.'

The minister sighed wearily. 'I doubt you speak true, sir, when you say this is not in my remit. No, Thomas,' he assured the baxter, 'I will not be swayed.' He turned to Giles. 'Your practices are strange. Is it your habit to prescribe your patients poisons?'

Giles assented. 'In minute amounts, when all else fails. I deal with some desperate cases.'

'Then was it from your own house that the seeds were stolen?'

'No, sir, it was not. Agnes took them from the patient's bedchamber. I keep my medicines locked away.'

'And yet you did not think to warn your patient to do likewise? Agnes Ford could simply walk in from the street?'

'I confess, it was a dereliction, and my fault. I was careless with the herbs, and it is my negligence that brings about this tragedy.' Hew motioned to protest, but Giles continued quietly, 'But that the physic was unnatural, I cannot allow. There were no charms, no witchcraft here. Medicines can be fatal when they fall in careless hands, for which this tragic case is surely the exemplar.'

'Aye,' the minister conceded. 'I understand your plea. Well then, look here, counsel, I will set the case before the magistrate. Agnes Ford,' he put to her, 'do you confess to witchcraft?'

'No, sir, I do not.'

'Did you consort with witches, seeking charms to cure your husband?'

'I did not.'

'Then I must conclude. At present, I can find no case for witchcraft. As more evidence is found, we'll deal with it. I will report my findings to the justice and appeal for a commission. Meanwhile she is free to go.' He spoke in a low voice to the baxter. 'Let the law untangle it. Firstly, Agnes is with child; second, she has not confessed. But in a month or two, we shall return to this.'

It was a grim little party that left the session house. Agnes turned on Hew. 'I thought you were my friend, sir. Yet you accused me of lying and theft.'

'You did lie,' Hew said reasonably, 'and you did steal. And I am your friend. For that you stole and lied must make up your defence. Believe me, if you plead that you consort with witches it can only be the worse for you.'

'I am grateful that you freed me. But it will not come to trial.'

'I fear you are mistaken there. Our work is just begun.'

'When Gilbert comes, then all will be resolved,' she answered boldly. 'I thank you, sirs. I have no further need of your defence.'

''Tis strange she puts her faith in him,' Giles pondered as she left. 'When she has killed his brother, accident or no.'

'They were lovers,' Hew said softly.

Giles whistled. 'Truly? Then did she mean to kill him after all?'

'I know not. Time will tell. For us, what matters is the present danger. Though it is diverted, yet it will return.'

'Well, your sister's name is spared. I thank the Lord.'

'But what of yours?' Hew countered. 'You expose yourself to censure, knowing this is not your fault. You did not prescribe her physic. It were perjury, if you were asked in court.'

'Is it? I know nought of that,' his friend considered carelessly. 'I have not read the law. Perjury, you say? Well, my back is broad. Listen, though, you shall not mention this to Meg? I would not have her hear I took the credit for her medicines. She thinks me vain enough already.'

'Took the credit?' Hew smiled wryly. 'What a wit you are!'

They walked in silence down the south street to the priory gates, and parted at the entrance to St Leonard's. Hew shivered in a breeze blown off the sea. He watched his friend tug close his coat and hurry past the glower of the cathedral, where he turned the corner into the north street, and was gone.

Gilbert Strachan did not repay the trust that Agnes placed in him. The letters that Hew had sent to the Scots house were returned unread. From Lucy they received the news that Gilbert had moved on. To prove the point he sold his third share in the *Angel* to his partner Robin Flett. Robin had a good deal more to say about the matter. But the crux of it was that the Angel was his, and the partnership with Strachan was effectively dissolved. Neither Archie's death nor Agnes' despair would bring Gilbert Strachan home from foreign shores.

Within a week or two, the writ was served, and Agnes indicted to appear before the justice ayres for the slaughter of her husband Archie Strachan, that she had fed him poisons in a pie. There was no citation of Giles Locke, though he was named as witness. Hew remained uneasy on his friend's behalf. He read the paper pinned up in the marketplace, and noted that the charge did not expressly state that Agnes knew the pie was poisoned. Nor was she charged with murder, out and out. This provided hope, for it allowed the way to her defence. It was a peculiarity of law that the defendant might not contradict the terms of the indictment. The prosecution might well prove the pie was poisoned, and that Agnes made the pie. That was understood. It would be harder to prove that Agnes had *intended* it to poison him. Encouraged by this, Hew went to see her.

It was Tibbie who came to the door. The house stood in darkness, closed to the street, and he was about to turn away when he heard the bolts draw back. She was thinner than he had remembered her. Behind her the lamps were unlit. 'Forgive the dark. We're quiet here. My mother sits below stairs in the shop.'

'I did not know that you were open.'

Tibbie sighed. 'She makes a show of winding wools, she says for when my uncle comes. But the shop is closed. Boys throw stones at the windows. Yesterday, a man came offering to buy the looms. My mother turned him out of doors. This morning, the coroner came.'

'I read the libel in the marketplace,' he told her gently. 'That is why I'm here.'

She nodded. 'It has happened, then.'

'The trial will not take place until the spring, at the next circuit court. But I must talk with her.'

'You can go down the backstair. Tom has gone. I don't know where.'

'Thank you. Are you hungry? Would you like to buy some bread?' Hew felt for his purse.

Tibbie hesitated, shaking her head. 'Is it not we who are meant to pay you? No thank you, sir. I do not care to go to market, with my mother's scandal blazoned on the cross. It is not only those that read, that can throw stones.'

He was touched by her dignity. But there was something else he had to ask of her. 'Tibbie, when your cousin died, what happened to his clothes?'

'I expect my mother gave them to the poor. It's what she did with our old things.' She smiled a little at the irony. 'Now we are poor ourselves. I remember there were some things that my uncle wanted kept. He could not bear to part with them.'

'There was a green cloak. It was lying on the floor by Alexander's bed,' he prompted her.

'Aye, that's right. I think that that was one of them. He said that he would have it for himself. I never saw him wear it, though. Perhaps he changed his mind. Sir, when you have finished with my mother call up and I'll open the door. We have to keep it locked now. Times have changed.' She turned her back to him and knelt before the fire.

He found her mother in the shadow of a single candle, in the bare hull of the back of the shop. It was where they found the boy. Yet there was nothing to remark it, no pervasive sense of violence. As if she read his mind, she said, 'It is an ordinary place.'

Unconsciously, she smoothed her belly with her hand. He saw the swell.

'I did not think it would come to this,' she faltered, 'for I did not mean to kill him.'

'It has come to it,' he told her. 'We must work on our defence. You wanted to provoke your husband's lusts.'

'He would not lie with me.'

'And yet you were with child.'

'For I was raped,' she answered simply.

'Tell me about the rape.'

'It happened here.'

Perhaps he had looked sceptical. She read his mind again, for she went on. 'You wonder how it is that I can sit here, winding wool? People imagine that ghosts inhabit places, engraved in walls or blood-drenched beds. Ghosts do not haunt places. They haunt souls.'

'Whose ghost? Alexander's?'

'*Alexander*? Ah, poor boy. I almost had forgotten him. And the day we found him – aye though, you remember – I forgot the rape. It hardly mattered then.'

Hew was startled. 'That day? You were raped the day that Alexander died?'

'Aye.' She looked at him curiously. 'Did I not say so?'

'I must ask you what happened.'

Agnes sighed. 'The men had gone to market. It was after kirk.'

'What time did they leave?'

'Before the bells, at daybreak. I remember Archie grumbling, and I waited in the house. Tom was loading up the cart. Afterwards, he locked the doors and brought the keys to me. We keep them on a chain behind the curtain in the hall. And at the second bell I went to kirk.'

'You did not see your nephew?' Hew demanded.

'No. How should I, though?' Agnes seemed surprised. 'I thought that he had gone to Crail with Archie. When they left, the house was still. I did not know he was the cause of all the fuss. Well then, I went to the kirk, and after the psalms and the sermon I came back here to the house and sat before the fire. I may have dozed a little, for the day was warm. I was awoken, I know not when, perhaps at twelve, by a knocking on the door. It was George Dyer. He had come, he said, upon the order of the session, to inspect the shop and see no work was done there on the Sabbath day. I protested my man had gone to Crail, which has statutes still for Sunday markets, which he knew, detesting it. But he insisted he was required to go to all the booths and workshops in the town and make report. There could be no exceptions. He was an elder in the kirk, and most assiduous. And so to appease him I took the key from the chain and unlocked the shop.'

'Did you come here, through the house?'

She shook her head. 'No, I took him into the front of the shop, where the shutters were drawn and the counters closed up, lighting the lamps to let him see that no one was there.'

'You are certain that no one was there?'

She looked at him curiously. 'For certain. The place was in darkness. Then he examined the back of the shop, where the looms were kept, idle on that day as they are now, and then he came here and looked at the spinning wheels, fingering the threads. And of course he found no sign of industry . . .'

'And then?' Hew pressed.

'Then he turned his back to go. And then . . . and then he turned again. He called my name, he called me names. He said . . . most filthie things. He pushed me to the floor and raped me.' She fell silent, staring at the ground.

But Hew persisted urgently, 'What happened next?'

The words came very softly. 'The rage had left him. He was gentle, coaxing. To hear him, you would not have thought . . . He was standing in his shirt, his britches on the floor. And I ran into the house, by the backstair, locking the door behind me. I took off my clothes and scrubbed my skin raw, and where his vile hands had defiled me were blue spots of dye. He had stained me. Yet the next day, when our boy was dead, he came with his condolences, lifting off his cap, as if the rape had never happened. And when we found the boy, I thought it had not happened, that I had imagined it. In that deeper horror, it seemed like a dream.'

'You accuse a dead man,' Hew observed, 'who may not speak his answer. Some will say that is convenient; others, that it is no mere coincidence.'

'I know it,' Agnes answered. 'Yet I speak the truth.'

He nodded. 'Well, what happened then? When your husband came from market?'

'Archie had done well that day. But he had had a drink or two. He called for Alexander, spoiling for a fight. When we found him missing we sent for Master Colp. You know that, you were there. And the cloth was gone. We were looking in the shop. The master found the body in the closet bed. The horror is, the poor boy must have lain there all the while. And while . . .'

She paused a moment; closed her eyes. Hew prodded gently, 'While the dyer raped you? Aye, perhaps. Go on.'

'We were looking for the cloth,' she whispered, 'and Master Colp had opened out the bed, and there the cloth came falling, and he opened up the cloth, and in it was the boy.'

'Agnes, do you recall Doctor Locke, who is to give evidence for you at your trial?'

'I remember,' she acknowledged, 'though I do not understand him.'

'He is a learned man. He swears that since the corpse was limp when we discovered it, Alexander must have died that afternoon. He was not long dead. Therefore he could not have lain within the closet all the night.'

'But then . . . but he was not at home.' She looked perplexed. 'Where was he, then?'

'Perhaps he was alive, and hiding in the room.'

'He would not hide there,' she objected. 'He was feart of closed-up spaces. It was what tormented Gilbert, when they nailed him in the kist. Archie used to threaten him; he'd shut him in the press.'

'He was quite a man, your husband,' Hew said dryly. 'May I look about the shop?'

'Aye, if you will.'

The place, once so neat, had begun to accumulate dust. Hew looked beneath the counter where the floor was bare.

'Once there were blankets,' commented Agnes. 'No one sleeps there now.'

He felt into the corner.

'What is it? Have you found something?'

'It's nothing. Only dust.' And he withdrew his fingers, scraps of fabric, threads and fluff, and a scattering of sand.

'Do I have a defence?' she asked him at the door.

'I know not. You have lied to me.'

'Lied? I have not lied!' she objected. 'Everything that I have told to you has been the truth.'

'I almost could believe it. Yet you lied about the father of your child.'

'I was raped. I swear it.'

'I believe that you were raped. The conundrum, though, is this: it is not three months since the day that Alexander died, since you say you were raped, and yet your child has quickened in the womb. I saw the midwife with you in the kirk. She said that you were four or five months gone. Therefore you have lied to me.'

'The midwife was mistaken,' she said stubbornly. 'I carry low and large. Tibbie was a big child for her time.'

'I do not think so,' he said softly. 'Tell me, Agnes, who is the father of your child? Is it Gilbert Strachan?'

'My brother?' Agnes started 'Why would you think that?'

'He is not your brother, but your husband's. And I heard you in your sleep. You spoke his name.'

'In my sleep?' she challenged. 'When my wits were gone? You know that I meant nothing.'

'I did not mistake the meaning. You have pinned your hopes on him. And yet his brother's death was at your hands. How can you be sure of him?'

'What you suggest,' she protested, 'though he is not my brother, the law would count as incest. If it were proved, we should hang.'

'I am aware of it. You do know he has abandoned you?'

'He would not.' She stared at him.

'Madam,' he said gently, 'have you heard from him?'

'I think my letters have not reached him. When they do, he will return.'

'He received your letters. Did you know that he has sold his share in the *Angel* to my cousin Robin Flett?'

'Why would he do that?'

'Because he does not mean to return. He told my cousin there was nothing for him here.'

'You lie,' she said uncertainly.

'Do I? Well, perhaps you know. Perhaps you've heard from him.'

Her eyes were bright with tears. 'I did not lie,' she said, 'about the dyer. Only I did not tell all the truth. He said he had observed me with my husband's brother, and he knew I was adulterous, a whore. And he would denounce me to the kirk unless I lay with him.'

'He blackmailed you?'

'I know not how he had discovered it. We were so careful.'

'Aye, perhaps you were. Yet somehow he had guessed it and your face confirmed the guess. Forgive me, you do not dissemble well. How long have you had converse with your husband's brother?'

'You do not understand,' protested Agnes weakly. 'Gilbert was not like his brother. He's a gentle, loving man. And when his wife died young . . . Archie was coarse, and has always been cold to me. It was Gilbert I loved.'

'It was for your sake that he brought Alexander here?'

'It was.'

'And for your sake that he sold his brother's wool.'

'Aye. But understand, though Archie was unkind, we did not wish him dead.'

'You might have wished the dyer dead, I think.'

She flushed a little. 'Well, we might have done. And when the tutor killed him, it seemed providential.'

'I'm sure it did. But then you knew the tutor had not killed him.'

'I don't know what you mean.'

'I think you do,' he chided quietly. 'You swore a statement to the Crown that Nicholas Colp had murdered George Dyer. You condemned a man to die for it, knowing he did not commit the crime.'

'I thought it made no difference,' Agnes whimpered. 'He killed Alexander. He had murdered Gilbert's son.'

'Suppose that I could prove to you that he did not kill the boy. Would you still condemn him?'

'But I saw him take the letters. And I saw him find the corpse. You saw it too.'

'And you believed you owed this debt to Gilbert, to relieve him of the burden of his crime. I ask again, if I can show he did not kill your nephew, will you still let him die?'

'Can you prove it?' challenged Agnes.

'I wish I could,' he sighed. 'The truth is that the law forbids my answer. I may not, in defence of him, accuse another man.'

'Then you may not say,' she answered cunningly, 'that Gilbert killed the dyer.'

'Yet we both know that he did.'

She whispered, 'It was an accident. You must not think that Gilbert meant to kill him. He is not a violent man. He was provoked.'

'You told him that the dyer raped you?'

'I did not, at first. He was distraught at Alexander's death. The dyer scarcely seemed to matter then. But when he turned up at the lykewake, he insinuated he would make report of our affair. He'd tell Archie everything. Gilbert would be ruined.'

'So Gilbert went to see him.'

'Aye, but not to kill him!' she protested. 'We had hoped to buy him off.'

'Men like that are not bought off,' he told her sharply. 'Doubtless, Gilbert knew.'

'He did not mean to kill him. He charged him with the rape. The dyer mocked him. He vilified his son. Gilbert lost his wits, and pushed him in his rage. He fell into the dye, and Gilbert could not save him, though he tried.'

'Was that how he told it?' Hew snorted.

'That is how it *was*,' she answered stubbornly. 'He fell into his pot. It was an accident.'

'Then Gilbert must have walked home dripping dye.'

'He was spotted, aye, though less than you'd suppose. There was a blot upon his cheek, blue like a bruise. We scrubbed it till it bled. He was wearing gloves, and his long green cloak that covered all his clothes was violet-stained. He wrapped it round a stone and dropped it in the Kinness Burn.'

'Convenient, then.'

'I do not understand you,' she insisted. 'He was vexed about the cloak, for it was Alexander's.'

He nodded. 'Then the cloak would not be missed. Katrin saw him, did she not?'

'Poor lass, aye. She was wearing one of Tibbie's cast-off plaids, and Gilbert called to her. He recognised the cloth. At first he took her for his niece, and after, felt afeared that she might know him. She came here to the house in search of Tom.'

'Katrin posed a threat,' he iterated slowly, 'so he saw to her.'

'Ah, but not like that!' cried Agnes. 'Sir, you must not think it. Katrin was to be denounced before the kirk, and her father too, for his delinquencies. She could not marry Tom. My husband would not loose him from his bonds.'

'The kirk would force the marriage,' argued Hew.

'There were moves against her father. He foresaw the future, and was glad to leave. Gilbert gave them passage on his ship. We offered them a new life overseas, for they had nothing here.'

'The *Angel*'s secret cargo!' Hew exclaimed.

'I do not understand you.'

'Where is Katrin now?'

'That is the worst part. She was distraught at the parting from Tom. We did not count it safe to let her say goodbye to him. The sailors forced the lass to board the ship. Once they had set sail she seemed to be resigned to it. She seemed to settle down. Then on the third night, without sight of land, she threw herself into the water and was drowned. Gilbert wrote to me. The captain turned his sail and searched for several days. They did not find her, though.'

Hew shook his head. 'And you believed this?'

'Aye, of course. You cannot think otherwise? Gilbert told me what had happened. He is not . . .'

'A murderer?'

Agnes shuddered. 'That was a mistake. The dyer had provoked him. But he would not harm the girl.'

'What happened to her father?'

'They set him down on foreign shores. Gilbert offered him a place, but he declined it. There are sheep in Holland, are there not?'

Hew did not reply. 'Madam, this dismays me,' he concluded bleakly.

'Aye, it is a tragedy. Gilbert felt it keenly. And we feel for Tom, who looks for Katrin still.'

'Have you not told him?'

'How could I?' she smiled at him faintly. 'I believe he loves her, after all.'

A Blood-colour Coat

'What does it mean,' Hew thought aloud, 'to be caught *red-hand*?'

'Why then,' Giles looked up from his breakfast, 'to be taken in the act.'

'Aye, but *literally*?'

'With bloodied hands.'

'Precisely so. Will Dyer told me it could not be Nicholas that killed his father, though Nicholas was caught red-hand, for he had nothing *on* his hands.'

'Gilbert Strachan killed his father,' his friend reminded him.

'Aye, and *he* wore gloves. And he wore a long green cloak, which protected him from the dye.'

'Which would imply,' suggested Giles, 'he did premeditate the crime.'

'It does imply it. According to Agnes, a single spot of dye had splashed his face, configured like a bruise. What colour is a bruise?'

'Hew, we have lectures at ten.'

'Ah, humour me. This is your field. What colour is a bruise?'

'A bruise may be a rainbow made of yellows, purples, blues . . .'

'A rainbow, aye. Agnes said the dyer had defiled her. She did not mean just the rape. She meant he left his mark upon her like a bruise, a purple stain. I saw it on her wrists. I thought her husband had been cruel to her. But I was mistaken.'

'Where does this lead?' Giles tore off and buttered a fat chunk of bread.

Hew answered with a question. 'Why was Alexander wrapped in wool?'

'No doubt you mean to tell me.'

'I think it was to stop the blood. The murderer had split his skull. Then it would bleed, no doubt.'

'For certain, a good deal,' assented Giles. 'Head wounds bleed profusely. Since he smashed the skull, there would be matter too.' He spoke through a splutter of crumbs.

'It would stain his clothes and his hands.'

'They would be thick with it.'

'I think the murderer used the cloth to wipe his hands and face,' continued Hew, 'and then he wrapped the boy to staunch the blood. There was no water in the shop. He could not wash. Then what were the colour of blood?'

Giles gave up his breakfast and sighed. '*Blood-colour*. I once bought a blood-colour coat. I did not care for it. It showed up all the smears.'

'Tactless, for a man of your profession.'

'Disconcerting, aye.'

'What colour was your coat?'

'It was an ox-blood red, a sort of curdled wine,' Giles answered wistfully.

'And yet it did not mask the spots of blood,' persisted Hew. 'The spirit from the arteries is light red, bright and spouting. Venous blood is dark and coursing, almost black. Dried, it makes a sullen brown.'

'That is correct.'

'Then blood in all those colours marked the killer's clothes as he walked home through the town that Sunday afternoon.'

'But how? It would be seen.'

'No doubt it was.'

At ten o'clock, Hew read his lecture to the magistrands. 'I see that Duncan Stewart remains absent,' he concluded. 'Can he be unwell?'

The students exchanged glances. One of them said, 'I believe Principal Gilchrist has excused him, sir. His father is in town. He will hear the reading-over.'

'He has not mentioned it to me. Pray tell him when you see him there will be no reading-over. Since the rest of you attend, I see no need for it.'

The boy hesitated. 'Is it to be examined, sir?'

'Indeed it is. You may tell him I'll be here tomorrow morning, after six, if he would like to discuss it. But I do not intend to give this lecture again. Now work on quietly, for I have business in the town, and may not return before the dinner hour. This afternoon I will hear you argue on the theme of whether women can have souls. I see you smile. I do assure you, tis no jest. Practise in your pairs. I thank you, gentlemen.'

It had begun to rain. Against the blackened sky, the dyer's cottage seemed more isolated still, more resolutely desolate. The children were playing in the yard, eyes watering in the wind. A smaller girl had taken Jennie's place. Her features were set hard. They threw pebbles at the water butt in some haphazard game, the youngest brother snivelling listlessly. They did not look up from their play.

Inside, the house was quiet, the children's voices fleeting, dropping like the gulls. At first he did not see her though he sensed her watching him. She sat shadowed in the stoor, shrinking in her chair beside the fire. Without recognition, without curiosity, she acknowledged him. 'My sons are gone to market, sir. Come back another day.'

'I do not want your sons.' He pulled up a stool and sat in the midst of it, snatching in his breath amid the thickness of the stench. He wondered she could breathe in it, so close before the fire. Dung-clots of dyestuff clung to the hearth. He smelled the mordant and the lye.

'What do you want?' she whispered.

'We have met before. I came here with my sister on the day your child was born. I'm sorry for your loss.'

She did not reply to this, and he went on, 'I am a man of law, and I make enquiries into your husband's death.'

'Aye?' she asked, uncurious. 'It is resolved. They have the man.'

'Yet it is not resolved. I know who killed your husband. It was not Nicholas Colp.'

Without hope or interest, she said simply, 'Aye?'

'It was Gilbert Strachan.'

He heard her mirthless laughter. Then, 'That's fair enough,' she answered quietly.

'Aye. There was a black deed done. I think you know.'

She shook her head. 'My man is dead.'

'You know that he raped Agnes Ford?'

'There can be no proof of that. Besides, she was a whore.'

He could not read the flatness in her tone. He sensed indifference, resignation, patience, lack of care. 'Why do you protect him still?' he challenged her.

Her eyes were open wide. She watched him pale and colourless, as if convention, like a hand, had moved her face. He saw no feeling there. She spoke complacently. 'I have good sons, who hope to have some standing in the town. Will's an honest lad. How should I condemn their father, when he is not here to answer? Let God judge.'

'But others here must answer, if you will not tell the truth. You told it to your daughter, I believe.'

'Told Nan?' She laughed a little scornfully. 'What should I tell her? She's only a bairn.'

'No, not Nan. You told your daughter Jennie that her father was a wicked man, that he had blackness in his heart.'

'I have no daughter Jennie. She is dead.'

'I have seen her, though,' he contradicted. 'She has spoken to me. Would you not know how she lives?'

'I can imagine how she *lives*,' she answered bitterly. 'She's her father's child. I have no daughter Jennie, for she's dead.'

He rose from the stool and walked to the window, drinking in the air. Standing with his back to her, he proceeded quietly, 'You told her she was like her father. *How* was she like him? And you would not suffer your dead infant to be buried in his grave. You preferred him to lie without Christian burial. Why?'

He felt grateful for the air. In part, he did not want to look upon her face. He sensed a change in her. He knew she held the answer. He was coming close to it. And somewhere, in this house dark-steeped among the lye, would lie the proofs. He knew, and was afraid it might dissolve into the stew. Like Jennie, when he found it, it might disappear. But she was talking still.

'She is like her father. Wicked, bold and lustful. *Whore.*'

He pictured her there, thin and resentful, stirring the ashes, stirring the lye.

'Yet she was not to blame,' he said, just soft enough.

She rose to it. 'He could not help his lusts, for he was moist and hot. But she is cold and dry. She preys on men like him. He could not help himself.'

'Poor Jennie,' he said inwardly. Aloud, he said, 'When you told her what her father was, she did not believe you.'

'Her father dealt in filth. He saw filth where'er he turned. Her father's daughter! Aye, I telt her. She'd have none of it.'

'When was it that you knew?' he asked.

'I knew when Agnes told me. You cannot think he kept me privy to his ain foul filthie secrets. I was full with child.'

'I do not mean the rape. For that did not dismay you. There was something more.'

'My husband an adulterer, a fornicator, not dismay me? How could there be more? If Jennie told you more, she lied to you.' There was uncertainty, a high note marking fear, behind the voice.

He counselled quietly, 'You were not to blame.'

'I don't know what you mean.'

'It was not your fault that he left you while you were with child. That he had to look elsewhere.'

He had gone too far now to retreat. He turned on her. 'Were you *grateful* for it?' he persisted. 'That it was Agnes he forced, and let you be? Agnes was a whore, he told you that. Did she not deserve it, then?'

'He told me nothing,' Janet cried.

'Did you feel responsible? But you were not responsible. Did you feel guilty? Did you feel glad? I imagine you felt both.

You understood his needs. Yet you could not fulfil them. You could condone the rape. It was the other thing that you could not forgive.'

'I don't know what you speak of,' she insisted.

'Then I'll tell you.' He had returned to face her, speaking fast and low. 'When your husband forced his lust on Agnes Ford, it was witnessed by her nephew, Alexander Strachan. He was hiding in the shop. Your husband found him there, and took his life. And when he had killed him, he came home to you. He walked through the marketplace, spattered with blood. But because he was the dyer, he was not remarkable. No one wondered at his clothes. He hid behind the mask that was himself.'

She was shivering. Yet still she answered stubbornly. 'It was the Sabbath day. His clothes were clean.'

'Aye, that's true. He took the risk that those who saw him in the town there would not remark the change. For he was always stained. Even when he wore his Sunday clothes, he could not rid his fingers of the dye. He was despised for it. Men would not shake his hand. Then why would anyone look twice, when he came through the marketplace crusted in gore? And yet to you, who were his wife, it must have seemed irregular. You must have known.'

'I swear I did not know it at the time,' she whispered hopelessly. 'I asked him what had happened to his Sunday coat and he answered he had worn it to the pots. Will was working on a shade and was anxious lest he lost it, and it needed something adding in the afternoon. George had spilled the dye. His coat and breeks were stiff with it. It was not until your sister came with blood upon her sleeve I understood the truth for what it was. My husband, sir, would never stir the pots upon the Sabbath, even to preserve the dye. He did not work on Sundays. He had told a lie.'

'Do you have them still?' Hew demanded urgently. 'The bloodied coat and hose?'

He knew before she spoke it would be hopeless, and before

she shook her head. 'He wore them afterwards for dyeing,' she replied. 'For they were ruined. He was wearing them the day he died. And since his skin was purple and his face . . . It did not seem worth the expense of a fresh suit of clothes, and he was buried in them. It was more than he deserved.'

There was no solace in the truth. He knew the whole. It did not comfort him.

Janet saw it in his face, for she returned complacently, 'There's justice of a sort if Gilbert Strachan killed him.' Then she smiled a little. 'Now I understand that Agnes was protecting him. She wanted me to help her prove the crimes were linked. She begged me to give evidence in court.'

'That served you both,' reflected Hew, 'though neither you nor Agnes realised it. She asked you to swear against Nicholas Colp, because she knew that Gilbert Strachan killed your husband, and you no doubt agreed to it, because you knew your husband had killed Gilbert's Strachan's son.'

'So you say, sir.' Janet shrugged. 'Let the dead lie. What you accuse will never be proved.'

It was almost two o'clock when Hew returned to St Leonard's. The students had dispersed and Gilchrist scowled at him across the lecture room. 'You keep peculiar hours. I looked for you and found your magistrands alone.'

Hew smiled apologetically. 'I left them to rehearse their theme. If I overhear their practising, I find that it inhibits them. I trust you found them working hard?'

'Aye, if a little *animated*.'

'Excellent. It's what I hoped. Though they are diligent enough they seem a little shy of me. It is to be expected. They must miss their regent.'

'I employ you, that they may not miss him,' Gilchrist answered curtly.

'That is my intent.'

'I cannot approve of the theme that you set,' the principal

frowned. '"Does woman have a soul?" You know, of course, that that is spurious?'

'For certain. It was just a trick to exercise their wits. I would have them more at ease with me. In truth, I have felt at a loss as to how to win their confidence. I have come to them so late, and am so inexperienced. Since you think ill of it, I do repent it,' Hew excused himself humbly. 'I am glad of your advice.'

'Well then, we'll let it pass. Your newness vindicates you. If you come up to my rooms tonight, I will show you a list of more proper arguments. But there is another matter I would raise with you, the case of Duncan Stewart.'

Hew nodded. 'He does not come to lectures, sir. I am concerned for him.'

'Yet you will not read them over, is that so?'

'He has not asked me to.'

'*I* am asking you. His father is in college and is anxious to have news of Duncan's progress. You must make report. What will you say?'

'I should say his progress would be greater if his father did not take him to the town, when he ought to be in college.'

'Tsk, you must not say that.'

'No, forgive me. I shall say that Duncan's progress is as steady as expected, and we hope to see him triumph on the black stone in July. Then I shall entrust the bursars with his closer education. They will help him learn his themes. They're clever boys. And for myself, I will come to him in the evenings and read over all the lectures he has missed.'

'Good, that's good,' the principal smiled. 'The father left a present of a longbow. Is the son proficient at the butts?'

Hew looked sceptical. 'I had not noticed it.'

'A pity, that's a pity. It is to be encouraged, don't you think? We have a competition here among the colleges that I had thought to formalise with the provision of a prize. I hoped he might subscribe to it. No matter, you must do your best. This evening you will sup with me. We'll go through the themes, and drink a little wine, for I have something else that I would put to you.'

'I thank you, sir, you are too kind.'

The students were returning from their dinner and Hew had little time to think about the dyer's wife. He spent the afternoon attending to their themes. At last, at six o'clock, his class was dismissed. He returned to St Salvator's to dissect the case with Giles. But Giles Locke was absent from the college. He had not turned up to give the morning lecture, and had not been seen since breakfast. Anxiously, Hew cornered Paul.

'Professor Locke was called away this morning,' the servant reported. 'Your sister sent a message. He has not returned.'

Hew's first fears were for Meg. He cut through the close to the south street, pounding on the Fletts' front door. The house stood locked and bolted with its usual dour contempt for all the street. He hammered with his fists until a servant opened up the shutters, grumbling, 'Whisht, you'll wake them!'

'*Wake* them?'

'Wait, I'll let you through.' She put her fingers to her lips, in a gesture of exaggerated patience, shuffling down the stairs to let him in. 'Be quiet, sir. Ye'll want the doctor. Here he is.'

Giles came down the stair, wiping his hands on a cloth. His cap sat awry and his shirt-cuffs were spattered with blood. Yet he was smiling.

'Meg!' Hew cried out in alarm.

'For goodness sake, you'll wake the dead! They're all asleep!' his sister answered, scolding. She stood behind him in the hall.

'But what has happened?' he stammered.

'Well, I'm done here,' Giles answered calmly. 'Do try to make less noise, Hew. You may write to let your cousin know that he has two fine sons. Lusty and hale as ever I saw.'

'*Two* sons?'

'Aye, it was twins,' confirmed Meg. 'Poor Lucy, and we blamed the sugarplums! Robin will be proud!'

★　　★　　★

Robin Flett, returning home, proved to be ungrateful. The loud and lusty voices of his twins did little to dispel the storm. 'I gave clear instruction that my wife must not have converse at the weaver's house,' he raged at Hew. 'Now she speaks of nought but scandals. Worse, she writes to me that she has been with Agnes, and that Agnes Ford has killed her husband, if you please. Your sister, sir, has led her into this. She is no longer welcome in my house.'

'My sister has been a good friend to her,' objected Hew. 'When your sons were born, she helped to save her life.'

'Lucy says she is indifferent company. Before she lost her wits, she left my wife alone for hours.'

'Meg has not lost her wits,' Hew corrected him. 'She has the falling sickness, as you know.'

'The pair of you, deranged! As I had understood, the sickness was controlled. Now I find it has recurred, and far from bringing comfort to my wife, she turns a pregnant woman from her bed . . .'

'It was Lucy's choice to put her there.'

'. . . has turned her from her bed and sought for comforts, while my wife herself has done without. Physicians calling daily! Without mention of the cost.'

'There is no cost. It is a friend of mine.'

'With no regard to Lucy's feelings.' Flett ignored him. 'Therefore, she must leave. I have found a nursemaid in the town who will serve our purpose well. Return her to her father's house, and say we were deceived in her.'

'I see,' Hew answered coldly. 'Then will she take the monies that my father paid to keep her?'

Robin flushed. 'Well, we were deceived in her. It was she that broke the contract. And the money has been spent.'

'On the *Angel*, I presume,' Hew confided privately to Meg. 'In truth, I could not bear to see you in that house. And Father will be glad to have you home.'

'As to that,' she answered thoughtfully, 'I may not return to him.'

'How so?' he teased. 'He will not have you?'

'I may have another home. My father will be welcome there. Doctor Locke has asked to marry me.'

'Giles?' he echoed, startled, 'asked Father if he may *marry* you?'

'No, Hew,' she said tartly. 'He asked *me*. He wishes me to help him in his practice. He thinks his days are numbered in the college.'

'And you said yes? I thought that you disliked him?'

'Did you, though?' She smiled at him. 'I wonder why.'

Meg was to be married from her father's house. Hew returned on Sunday to collect her things. Lucy Linn was pleased to see him, all ill will forgotten in the light of her most recent acquisitions. The painter had returned at last, a little worse for wear, and had planted two stout cuckoos in the painted nest. Hew was admiring the fat twins, more from politeness than conviction, when Robin burst into the room, crying, 'Scoundrel! Thief!'

'What is it?' Lucy begged him in alarm.

He glared at Hew as if he were responsible. 'We shall be ruined!'

'But what has happened?'

'Gilbert Strachan,' Robin spluttered.

'Gilbert Strachan?' echoed Hew. 'Your friend?'

'He is no friend of mine,' his cousin answered rudely. 'Aye, I'll see him hanged. He took the *Angel*, Lucy! We are ruined!'

'Peace, Robin, for you make no sense,' she scolded. 'The *Angel's* safe in harbour. Gilbert's overseas.'

'Aye, he is *now*, in the *Angel*. He has stolen her.'

'Do you mean to say,' demanded Hew, 'that Gilbert has returned to Scotland?'

'Aye, man, don't you listen? He came here last night. He came secretly, and falsely, and this morning went to the shipmaster and bought out his share. Can you believe, he paid him with *my* money, that I gave to buy *him* out, and has made off with her!'

'It was my father's money,' muttered Hew.

Lucy asked shrewdly. 'Has he taken Agnes?'

'Agnes? Damn it, aye, he did! He has taken the *Angel*, that is the point! He sold his share to me, to buy the other third so that he might steal the whole! And the shipmaster swears that Strachan told him *I* had sold my share to *him*!'

'I am confused,' said Lucy. 'Do not shout. You will disturb the babies.'

'Disturb them? Don't you understand? It's them he robs. It is their future gone. Villain! Treachery!'

'Hush, Robin, do. You'll have another ship. Or Gilbert will return her. He will, won't he, Hew?'

But Hew was staring in astonishment. 'Agnes Ford was right. He did come back for her.'

As the news spread through the town, Hew approached the coroner. 'Now that Agnes and Gilbert have fled,' he petitioned, 'will you not write to the justice clerk, and bid him drop the charge against Nicholas Colp?'

The man shook his head. 'It is not as simple as that.'

'Strachan killed the dyer. Dyer killed the boy. That much is simple.'

'Aye, perhaps. I hear your plea,' the coroner acknowledged. 'But there are no witnesses.'

'There is a twelve-year-old child, Dyer's daughter, who could identify the man who killed her father.'

'A child may not bear witness,' the coroner said patiently.

'If you dredge the Kinness Burn, you'll find his velvet cloak. It's thick with dye.'

'And say we find the cloak, who swears it's his?'

'But still,' persisted Hew, 'unless Agnes and Strachan are to testify, there can be no case against Nicholas.

'I allow they are defaulters. There are charges against them, and they are both denounced as rebels since they do not come to answer them. Agnes is indicted for the murder of her husband,

Strachan for assisting her escape. And Robin Flett has brought a charge of piracy, for the thieving of his ship. Even if they did compear, the court would disallow their evidence against him.'

'Well then, drop the charge.'

'If it were simply murder, then we might. There is a second charge against your friend, of sodomie.'

'Of *sodomie*? How can there be witnesses to that? If Strachan is discounted . . .'

'It was not Strachan who brought the charge.'

'Who, then?' Hew said, baffled.

'It was James Gilchrist, principal of St Leonard's College. He was most emphatic. There were letters and a gown set forth in evidence.'

'Gilchrist? Aye, of course. Yet you must allow that he is not impartial in this case. You have heard him make allegations of the sort before, wild and importunate, and with as little substance. Will the justice not accept his wit's impaired?'

'I have seen him sorely distracted, as you say. I believe he bears a grudge. You and I know his evidence may well be skewed. Yet I doubt the justice clerk would see it in these terms. Gilchrist is a man of some importance in the town. Since he makes the charge, it must be heard.'

'Then how shall we defend it? It's his word against ours.'

'You may not, sir. As you know, it lies to him to prove it, not to you to contradict it. The pity is, the boy is dead.'

That Ye May Nocht Deny

In November came St Andrew's Day, and the last market fair of the year. The harbour saw its last influx of ships before the sleet and ice storms closed its straits. Apples and onions and sacks full of grain were banked against famine like sand against floods. Hew gave his students leave and walked along the shore towards his father's house. He had not meant to come so far. But the house stood reassuringly aloft among the trees, and in the great stone hearth the fire was lit. His father welcomed him.

'We were not expecting you. But I am glad enough to have you here, God knows. Your sister's making wedding plans, and sets my head a-buzzing with her endless inventories. She prates of nothing else but beds and bolsters, silver plate and counterpanes. Should she wear the green silk or the grey? Are there sufficient spices set by for the banquet? Will the Fletts be offensive and drink too much wine?'

'The green, I think,' reflected Hew. 'That will set off the colour of her eyes. And there will be sufficient spice. And for the Fletts, that much is certain. They will be offensive, and will drink too much. You may tell her this, and let her mind be settled.'

'There is no settling of her,' Matthew grumbled. 'I fear she wants her mother, and I am no good to her. Her prattle wears me thin. Had I known that marriage would reduce her wits to pottage then I should never have approved it.'

His grumbling hid a plain delight. His happiness and pride were clear to see.

'Then Giles has been to see you?' Hew deduced.

'Aye, he has. They are to wed next summer, at the end of Whitsun term, for professors at the college are forbidden to take wives.'

'That does not trouble most of them,' his son remarked.

'Aye, for sure. But your friend is a man of principle, who wants to do things properly. He is looking for a house where they may live in openness. And if there are objections then he means to leave his post. He has half a mind to anyway, he says.'

'Aye, *half* a mind,' grinned Hew. 'You have him in a nutshell there. Still, if he resigns, then it will be their loss.'

'He hopes to start a practice in the town,' Matthew went on.

'Aye, so I heard. Will you help him?'

'He does not want my help. And I would not offend him. For all that he prevaricates . . .'

'Ah, you noticed that,' Hew put in dryly.

'. . . For all he does prevaricate,' his father smiled, 'I think he knows his mind.'

Meg came in at that moment, with silks from the market. She shook out the ribbons for them to admire, and Matthew rolled his eyes.

'You see, Hew? Quite addled!' he muttered.

Hew remarked how well she looked. She laughed and kissed them both. 'You'll be sorry when I'm gone.'

'I had thought to be rid of you once,' Matthew retorted, 'now here you are, both of you home again. Now since we are talking of ribands, and other such trifling expenses, you know, my dears, that I begrudge you nothing, and in general terms, you do not overspend. And yet I fear—'

'Giles does not ask for anything,' Meg interrupted quickly, 'and we know the money that you paid to Robin Flett . . .'

Her father shook his head. 'That amounts to nothing,' he assured her. 'I'm ashamed to hear you mention it. And as for Giles, I should gladly give him half of what I have, if he would only take it. Peace, child, I do not mean you. It's your brother I am talking about.'

'I have earned a little money at the college,' Hew protested, startled. 'I admit it is not much. But do you think me profligate?'

'I know not, son. Advise me,' his father said gravely. 'It is not my business to look over your accounts. But there was a bill sent here, instead of to the college, whether by mistake or by design I could not say, and I confess I was perplexed at the amount. And if you have a similar tab at your taverner and tailors, then I fear that you may bankrupt us.'

Hew looked bewildered. 'What bill can you mean?'

'I have it somewhere here.' Matthew fished a piece of crumpled paper from his sleeve. 'Aye, pass me my spectacles – it's from the west port stables, for damage to their premises, and for shoeing, oats and sundries, the sum of five hundred pounds. *Five hundred pounds*, Hew! Is it the king's own light horse you have stabled there?'

Hew was aghast. 'Five hundred pounds? How can that be possible? Are the stables completely destroyed?'

Meg burst out laughing. 'For shame, Father, how can you tease him?' she scolded. 'Don't mind him, Hew! Giles has amused us with tales of Dun Scottis. The bill was for eighty-eight pounds.'

'Eighty-eight pounds, nine shillings and sixpence,' Matthew corrected severely, 'which was more than quite enough. Now, I know you are fond of the horse, and won't have a word said against him, but may I suggest that you stable him here? It will save us both a fortune. And I'll reinforce the fence.'

Hew conceded defeat. 'Aye, if you will. He's a good horse at heart.'

'He's a limmar,' Matthew contradicted, 'through and through. But none the worse for that. Now, here we are together again,' he beamed at them. 'And all is well. There was a time when I feared for you both. Now Meg has recovered and is to be married, and Hew has come home, there's cause to be merry. I'll call for some wine.'

'Yet Hew is unhappy, I think,' Meg said perceptively. 'What is it?' She turned to her brother. 'You barely raise a smile. I think things have not turned out as you hoped.'

Hew stared into the fire. The posset cups shone silver, hanging from the hearth, the plate rubbed worn and clean. There were cushions at his back he knew from childhood, fallow deer embroidered on a scarlet ground.

'Forgive me, Meg. I do not want to spoil your happiness. Yet all the while, I cannot help but think of Nicholas.'

'Nicholas is stronger by the day,' his sister told him gently. 'Giles believes there may be hope.'

'Hope of what?' he answered miserably. 'For you and Giles, I am content. Your outcome is a happy one. But for the rest, I see no hope; I cannot help it, Meg. The days pass. I take my students – Nicholas' students – closer to their end and their examinations. I chase golf balls on the links. I talk of books with Robert Black. And in the afternoons I read to Nicholas or play a game of chess in Giles Locke's rooms, where Nicholas confides that such and such a student may need help with declamations, this one's steady, that one's shy, this one fumbles at the page, and all the while he knows that he must die. I cannot save him. These boys will proceed to their examinations, and the king will come and hear their play, and Gilchrist will speak his smooth lies, and at the end of it all, my friend will hang.

'I have resolved the case, and yet I know not how to fight it. Nicholas is arraigned for trial in May. And though I know who did these crimes, I may not name them. I have proofs; I may not show them. I have witnesses; I may not call them. We are back where we began. All I have is Nicholas, who reeks of guilt, for he is careless of his fate. Against us, Gilchrist and the dead boy's letters seal our ends.' His frustration bordered on despair.

Meg rose without a word and left the room. But shortly she returned, with a jug of wine, a loaf of new-baked bread, and butter on a tray.

'All things are better broken over bread,' she counselled quietly. 'Can you not defend the charge?'

'He may not contradict the charge,' their father said. 'It is the nature of the law.'

'It is unjust,' Hew countered.

Matthew shook his head. 'In practice, it would seem so. There's logic behind it. The burden of the proof lies with the prosecution, not with the defence. If the charge can be proven, it cannot be contradicted, or the act of contradiction would be proof of perjury. If the charge cannot be proven, then there is no cause to contradict it; the accused is not required to give another version of the crime. In consequence, the sole defence depends upon the weakness of the prosecution case. The art lies in the words of the indictment, of the libel writ concluding "*Ye may not deny.*" No charge that is explicit may be answered. The trick to prosecution is to word the accusation tight enough to force out all defence yet loose enough still to be proved. Its weakness lies between the two.

'In this case, it's the proofs themselves that you must contradict. How will they proceed? We may assume the charge will not be proved by confession, for Nicholas has not confessed. Most likely, it will not be proved by exculpation, which is precluded by the wording of the writ. It must be proved by witness, then. Gilchrist and the letters, and your friend's own bloodied gown are proofs that will require corroboration. The word of one man will not be enough. Now, the prosecutor may protest the statements here of Agnes Ford and Gilbert Strachan. You should reject them as irrelevant, which the justice will allow you. Denounce them as rebels. For Gilchrist, you must try to undermine him. He will have to swear he does not speak from hatred. You may call your friends to witness whether this is true. Does he know you are disposed to challenge him?'

'I don't think so,' Hew reflected, 'unless Robert Black has told him so. That I count unlikely. Robert lacks conviction, yet he still has virtue. He was once false to Nicholas, and he repented it. He will not make the same mistake again. These last few weeks in college I have bitten back the words, and Gilchrist seems to trust me well enough. He asks me to his home, and pours me wine. I flatter and dissemble there.'

'Then you are the better placed to discredit him.'

'That will be difficult.' He sighed. 'It will be said he does not bring the charges lightly, since they implicate the college in the crimes. I dare not call Giles, for he is already compromised by his defence of Meg.'

Meg coloured slightly but did not demur as Hew continued, 'Robert will not take the stand. The minister, the man from Holy Trinity, might be prepared to give a true impression of his soul, yet he does not know the facts. Gilchrist will aver it is the crime he hates, and not the man. Which leaves me Nicholas alone to pitch against the devil. And even if he cared to fight, he is no match.'

'There is a last recourse,' said Matthew thoughtfully, 'though it is a desperate one.'

'I'll hear it,' answered Hew.

'You may refuse the trial and plead before the king, to come into his will, and he may pardon him.'

'Why would he do that?'

'The king has come of age. He has a favourite lately come from France, his kinsman the sieur d'Aubigny, an older man who has a wife and child. James has taken him to heart. Too much, his friends protest. There is talk of inwardness, of an improper closeness.'

'How do you hear such things?' Hew teased him.

'Rumour carries even here. I still have friends at court. For my part, I construe it as the fondness of a lonely, love-starved boy, bereft as he has been of family life. Ah, you see my drift. Though he was born a prince, he still was born a child. The king has been in thrall to schoolmasters like Gilchrist and your friend Buchanan.'

'They are *not* alike,' objected Hew.

Matthew went on smoothly, 'And to him, they're tyrants. He is ill-disposed to like them. Now he shakes the chains. If you are careful, you may touch his sympathies. He may read his own heart in the boy's. But do not force the likeness home. He must perceive it for himself. It's hazardous.'

'You need a way,' Meg put in, 'to hold fast the king's atten- tion. To set the case before him, so he understands the whole.'

'Meg, that is genius!' Her brother exclaimed.

'What did I say?'

'Nothing, aye, and everything.' Hew leapt to his feet and began to pace the room. 'I think I see the way. Aye, there will be risk. But still, there's time enough . . .' Suddenly he grinned.

'Could you make some dye? Enough to fill a bathtub? Of a violet shade?'

'I think so,' Meg looked hesitant. 'I know it can be made from watercress. There's plenty to be had here in the burn. But there's other things we need.' She wrinkled up her nose. 'A vat of urine fresh and strong.'

'If reputation counts for aught,' Matthew interjected, 'then we will not want for that.'

'Whatever do you mean?'

He snorted, 'Why, yon bladderskite.'

His children stared at him.

He coughed apologetically. 'I mean the shit horse, Scottis.'

The boy was tired. His mind had begun to make shapes of the words on the paper, no longer letters but patterns. The candle stub had left a smoky film upon the page. He rubbed his eyes.

A sharp knock on the doorframe startled him. He heard a warning cry of '*Salve*', and the door flew upon. The boy stumbled to his feet.

'*Salve, magister*,' he answered anxiously. 'Forgive me, Master Cullan. Do you want for water? I filled the basins after dinner. Was there not enough?'

'Peace, I have not come for water. Where's your roommate?'

'In truth, I know not, sir,' the boy looked away, 'I think perhaps that he is gone to Master Black.'

'For shame, you must not lie for him. No matter, though, it's you I want. I hoped to find you quiet here. But shall we sit?' Hew sat down upon the bed.

'And it please you, sir,' the boy replied unhappily. He tottered on the corner of his stool. The master smiled at him. 'How do you find your studies, Thomas? Do they go well?'

'Yes, sir. Master Black is kind.'

'It is late to be working still. Your candle should be out by nine.'

'Master Black allows a further hour, sir.' The boy hesitated. 'It is hard for me to do what must be done by day. But after dark . . .'

'It is your quiet time?' Hew asked him wryly

'Aye.'

'And who do you work for this quiet hour, Thomas? For yourself, or your truant bedfellow?'

The boy flushed. 'I try to get the theme. I find it hard.'

'For a clever lad like you? I doubt your fellows do not work so hard.'

'They have no cause to, sir,' he answered, close to tears. 'They have more play.'

'For certain,' Hew said kindly, 'they have you. But it's to be commended that you work. I do not come to blame you. I fear you are misused here.'

Thomas shook his head. 'Master Gilchrist says it is an honour, sir, to serve the college and to bed down with an earl.'

'Your roommate? He is not an earl.'

'As good as, Master Gilchrist says.'

'He does not use you cruelly, then?'

'He is not here.'

Hew understood the plea in the boy's voice, and nodded. 'You have your peace in the night while he plays truant in the town, and were his delinquencies checked, it would be worse for you.'

'Yes, sir,' he answered simply.

'Well then, your regent knows him truant?'

'Aye.'

'Then nothing need be said. I am sorry to disturb you in your quiet hour. I have a favour to request of you, which you may think on privately. You know, I doubt, that the king is to come here to visit?'

Thomas answered with a nod, as Hew went on. 'Well then, I am making a play, in Latin, to perform for him, and I would like you to take on a part. I fear it will be work for you, on top of what you have, but I would beg you to consider it.'

'I . . .' the boy stammered, 'a play for the king? But is it not for the magistrands?'

'It is, for the main part, the magistrands' play, and yet I need a young lad, competent in grammar, to play this particular part. I think the role will please the king.'

'But how shall I do it, sir?' Thomas pleaded earnestly. 'How may *I* impress the king? You must ask someone else.'

'I think you will impress him well. The principal also would wish you to do it. He is anxious that the bursars should perform.'

'I could not speak before the king. I should be feart.'

Hew chided mildly, 'No, your training must prepare you to speak before the world. You should know your worth. Besides, the king will like you. You are not so far apart.'

Thomas looked incredulous. He said politely enough, 'I cannot think us further, sir.'

'Nor yet so far. The king beneath his crown is just a boy like you. Besides, the king has been well schooled and has a scholar's ear. Few of our students make verses so sound. Your master schooled you well and your tones are like to please him. And you are a bursar too, which throws a glowing light upon the Crown. There is a world of difference, I grant you, between your life and his, and betwixt the both of you and this sad part I bid you play, and yet beneath it all, you share a common heart.'

'I cannot think it possible,' the boy said doubtfully, 'below the crown there beats a heart like mine. But can a king have feelings like the rest?'

'I know not,' answered Hew, 'in truth, he *should* not. Yet the king is young. I mean to try his feeling, and the play shall be our proof.'

'How so? If he does not like it?'

'He will like it, Thomas. And if he does not, no blame shall come to you. It is a moral tale, and will be most properly and prettily done. If you retain your proper countenance, he will be pleased to see it, I can promise you.'

'Well . . . but tell me,' the boy implored, 'what is the part?'

'If you promise to keep it secret,' Hew confided, 'then I'll tell it. It is a sad tale.

'There are seven persons in the play. The first is a college principal, called Claudus. The second is Mercator, a rich merchant. The third is Adolescens, the merchant's youngest son. The fourth is Tutor, regent in the college. Fifth is Textor, weaver, and the brother of the merchant. Sixth, his wife, is Textrix; and seventh, last, is Tinctor, a dyer most corrupt. I myself shall play the part of Claudus.'

'*Claudus?*' asked the boy, 'why, is he lame?'

'Aye, very lame,' his master smiled. 'Which is to say, he is defective in his morals, and he wavers where his loyalties lie. In truth, you make a point, we'll have him limp, now in this leg, now in that, according to his bent. This Claudus has wines and silks from Mercator, at some expense. He has exquisite tastes. And how does Claudus fund these tastes? He saps the college bursaries, and sells the bursars' places on to rich men's sons, wherefore he profits double for his sins. Now, Mercator, a widower, has such a son, Adolescens, the greenest of youths. Says Mercator to Claudus, "I will give you the finest wines for your cellars and salt for your flesh if you will take into your college my youngest son, unschooled though he is." And Claudus knows the boy has not the wit, yet he promises a master who will school him that he might matriculate as Mercator desires. And they drink to it then, deep of the merchant's red wine, paid for with the bursars' inks, and Claudus congratulates himself that he has done the deal. And does he feel a prick of conscience? If he does, he soon assuages it, for he appoints his poorest regent as master to the boy – we have called him Tutor – his protector. Tutor needs the money, and was himself a bursar. His appointment, reasons Claudus, will redress the balance sheet. So all is well.

'But for the boy, Adolescens, all is not well. He has little grasp of grammar, and he cannot match his father's expectations. His father, in his turn, is blind to this. He has lodged him in the house of his own brother, the weaver Textor, and his wife. The weaver is a bully. He mistreats his wife, and has refused her proper converse now for many years. To his brother, he's a sponging sycophant, but to his nephew he is hectoring and cruel. Mercator comes often, but ignores the boy's distress. He has eyes only for Textrix, whom he has loved most fervently and ardently against the laws of nature and of God. The boy's place in her home allows them to proceed with the affair. It is not, however, without danger, for all the time they are watched by the weaver's friend Tinctor, the dyer, spying and waiting, biding his time.

'As for Adolescens, in his loneliness he finds an unexpected friend in Tutor, who must school him in the path he finds so hard, who nurtures and guides him so patiently, and allows a little gentleness when the burden seems too grave. And in this boy there grows a dark despairing fondness for the master who protects him. He tries to please him, and is left desolate by countless casual kindnesses, dropped careless of the depth of their effect. Then one night, when his uncle the weaver has been particularly cruel to him, he slips out of the house and visits Tutor, asking him to walk with him and give him counsel. Which that good man, seeing his charge in such distress, agrees to do, and they walk by the shore in the moonlight where the callow boy at last gives way to all the stirrings of his heart and tells the master of his love for him. What do you think the tutor does then?'

'I know not, sir.' Thomas was frowning. 'What should he do?'

'Aye, what? Does he strike the boy from him, with bleak and harsh words, for filthiness, corruption, for *presumption*? Does he shudder and recoil?'

'He might,' the boy suggested timidly.

'And though he might, he does not do these things. For he is kind, and he can see into the real hurt in his pupil's heart, and so he tells him gently he is overwrought. He seeks to save him from himself. And seeing the boy standing so desolate there, so fragile on the brink of his despair, he comforts him with a single kiss, and sends him home with promises. He shall not fret. The thing shall be resolved.'

Thomas was silent. Hew went on. 'Think, if you will, what storms were in his heart as he went home. On coming there, he could not go into the house without the notice of the weaver and his wife, and so he went into the shop and crept beneath the counter where at last he fell asleep.

'We may suppose he slept for many hours, his heart wrung to exhaustion, for when he last awoke he heard the sound of voices. I say it poignantly, for that was the *last* time he awoke.'

Thomas remarked to himself that the play was now in the past tense, and become a history. He listened, saying nothing.

'Doubtless he drew himself close into his hiding place. His uncle Textor had gone to the market and was not expected in the shop. And it was Sunday. Who was there? We cannot know how much Adolescens saw or understood of what happened in the shop that day, but we do know what was happening there. His aunt Textrix was there with the dyer, the man we call Tinctor.'

'She was a whore, then?' ventured the lad.

Hew shook his head. 'The dyer had been spying and he came to blackmail her; helplessly, he took her there, the boy beneath the counter all the while. We may suppose that what he did not see he must have heard. He may not have understood. Certainly he heard the sounds of violence and distress. And the last sound that he heard was the slamming of the door into the house, his aunt's sobbing footsteps retreating to silence. Then perhaps did he creep out to find the dyer standing in his hose inflamed still in his anger and his lust. Or perhaps he made a sound, a muffled cry, and was discovered there beneath the counter, cowering in the dust among the threads, and dragged forth by the dyer in his heat to meet his fate. Did he cry and make him promises, begging for his life? God knows. In all events, the dyer murdered him; and with a shuttle of a loom he split his skull and spilt his brains. He wrapped the corpse in cloth and shut it in a closet. And then, cool as you will, he walked home through the town to his wife, where the blood on his hands and his clothes attracted scarce attention from the crowd, for he was Tinctor after all. He wore his stains.'

The boy's eyes opened wide, 'And so he got away with it?'

'Not quite. For Textrix tells the merchant,' they had come back to the play, 'as he weeps for his dead son, about the blackmail and the rape, and he exacts particular revenge. He drowns Tinctor bodily in his own vat, dyeing him deep as the stain on his soul. It's poetic, don't you think?'

The boy said timidly. 'I think that the principal, sir, may mislike your play.'

Hew smiled, 'I grant he may mislike it, though he cannot fault *your* part in it.'

'I cannot . . . I cannot play my part so *forward* as that boy. For I have not been born to it.'

'If you do not play it forwardly, then you will play it well. I bid you catch his innocence. But do you think you can?'

'I think so. It is a striking tale. But, sir . . .' the boy demurred.

'You are unhappy still?'

'No. But is it not a moral tale? I do not see the moral yet. Where does it come?'

'Therein lies the conscience of the play. And I confess, I scarcely know.'

He had not lied to Thomas. It was Gilchrist who suggested it, over claret wine. 'It was Colp's play, after all, and since you take his place, then you must write his play. It's your men that perform it.' Hew had protested he was not a playwright. Gilchrist over-ruled. 'Of course you must.'

There should be a part for the bursars, certainly. The bursars should be seen. The suggestion of a part for the youngest bursar, Thomas Burns, delighted him. He spoke his verses grandly though he was a pauper. Moreover, he was closest to the king in age.

'You must write a part for Duncan Stewart,' he cautioned, 'for his father will expect it.'

'He will not learn his lines,' Hew pointed out.

'One of your bursars will help him. A simple part, not much to say, but prominent, you know. He must be seen.'

'I think I have the part for him.'

'Good man, of course you do.'

From the magistrands, Hew selected five to act before the king. He hid from them the role of Claudus, and rehearsed it privately. The bursars played the Strachans: Mercator and Textor. A slender youth, clear-skinned, was persuaded to play Textrix. For Tutor, he made perfect verse and cast him carefully. He chose a gentle, inward boy. He handed him the script and asked him to consider it. And he had chosen well. The boy had asked him piercingly, 'Do you make this play for Nicholas Colp?'

Hew answered, that he did.

'Then I should like to play this part. The kiss and all.'

'You are determined. Why?' the master asked.

'I like him, sir.'

Was this the boy his friend had loved? Hew could not tell. He looked into his face, upon this simple answer, and read nothing there but sympathy. He spoke his name to Nicholas, who did not blush to hear it said but answered as he always did, 'I know him, he's a constant lad. When first he came, he floundered, yet I think he will do well.'

Only Duncan Stewart, as predicted, found his part a strain. Though he had few lines he laboured hard to learn them. A bursar was assigned to teach him. Presently, the bursar came to Hew and warned him anxiously, 'I do not think he understands the part he is to play, sir.'

'Have you not explained it?'

'I have tried. He does not wish to hear it. Mostly, he snarls at me, "Read out the part," I read the words, and he repeats. He does not understand them. It is the stage direction, sir.'

'Well then, you have tried,' Hew told him kindly. 'You may not be blamed.'

'I fear it, though.' The bursar looked unhappy still.

'If it helps, I'll ask him if he knows his part and if he understands it. Better then, the *principal* shall ask him. If he won't confess he doesn't, then you can't be blamed.'

'I should be grateful for it.'

'Then it will be done. I take it you have learned *your* part?'

'I have.' He hesitated, 'Sir, it is the part of Mercator, the merchant.'

The master smiled indulgently. 'Of course, you are the bowman, chosen for your strength. Then I think you will enjoy it all the more.'

A Guise Before the King

The New Inns of the Abbey, built for Magdalena, wife of James V, overlooked the lawns where Hew proposed to stage his play. Queen Madeleine did not survive the marriage, and it was James' second queen, Mary of Guise, who came at last into her palace in the priory grounds where their wedding vows were blessed in the cathedral. Now the house was opened up and made fair to welcome her grandson. And in the early days of spring in the year 1580, the town prepared to meet its king. Breads were baked, hunts were called; milk lambs were slaughtered, torn from the teat. Stairs were scrubbed and linens laundered; closes were swept and strewn with flowers. All the heavy furniture and trappings of the court came trundling from the harbour, boat by boat, straining through the sea port to the abbey gate. Behind the high walls of the priory, laundry maids beat out the dust and cobwebs in the sun. Their draperies and damasks flagged the worn cathedral stones, where once another king had brought his bride, where bishops, monks and friars once had sung for her. Some recalled the wedding they had witnessed here as children, forty days of feasting, while their church stood proud and tall. And clean and curious at last they lined the hopeful streets to see their king.

Hew did not go among the crowds, but waited with his students in the garden. Beyond the wall, the closes, streets and lanes were choked with people, craning from the window ledges, galleries and stairs. They heard the slow procession turn the corner into the south street, caught in the percussion of the crowd. He sensed the students fidgeting, glancing at the gate, and smiled at them indulgently. 'Aye, then, go and look.'

In a moment they forgot that they were players and were boys again, clambering and fighting for a place upon the wall, mouths agape as all the daftest louns.

'There's the provost.'

'And the minister.'

'Mind, I cannot see!'

'And you jostle like you do, then none of you will see,' Hew observed judiciously. 'Lift Thomas on your shoulders there, and sit him on the wall. No, don't protest, you'll have your turn. They'll be here by and by. But Thomas is the smallest. He can tell us what he sees.'

Grudgingly, they shunted the young bursar to the top of the high wall, where his legs dangled precariously and from which vantage point he was able to look down upon the great procession as it made its way slowly past the kirk towards the New College of St Mary.

'They've been quite around the town. There's Professor Lamb! And he's not been seen for years.'

'Confound Professor Lamb!' a voice came crossly. 'Do you see the king?'

'Aye,' Thomas faltered, 'Aye, I think so.'

'Think so! Can't you tell?'

'There are so many people crowded round. He's sitting on a horse.'

'A *horse*! Of course he is! Come down and let me look!'

'No, it *is* significant,' observed the bursar bowman. 'It is the horse that marks the man. If he's sitting on a *high* horse then he's probably the king.'

Thomas craned his neck. 'His horse is somewhat higher than the rest,' he answered doubtfully.

'Well, what did I tell you? Does he keep his seat?'

'The horse is barely moving. And he has a man to hold it. Still, he rides it well.'

'It's as I thought,' the bowman said approvingly. 'What *colour* is the horse?'

'For pity,' cried a magistrand. 'What signifies the colour of his horse? Describe to us the king! His countenance, his clothes.'

'He is not close enough. I cannot see his face. The professors of St Mary's are presenting him a speech.'

'Poor king,' the boy said rudely. 'Then he may *never* come.'

'It *signifies*,' his bowman friend persisted, 'for the colour indicates the temper of the horse. The temper of the horse reflects his skill as rider. And his skill as rider marks his aptitude as king.'

'Whisht with your horse-whitter! What of the *man*?'

'They're coming to the gate! And there is Master Gilchrist come to greet them.' In his excitement, Thomas lost his grip upon the wall.

'Steady now,' Hew warned. 'Perhaps you should come down.'

'He wears a cap and cloak of gold'

'*Real* gold?'

'Velvet or some such, with a white ruff and cuff of fine lace. And on his cap a plume, above a crimson jewel . . . and a doublet gold and scarlet, all embroidit with gold threads. And now he is dismounting, and he takes the master's hand . . . oh, but . . .' the boy trailed off, confused, 'he does not stand so grand upon the ground. Why then, his gait is strange.'

'And *that* is quite enough,' said Hew, extending up his hand. 'For now you also must dismount, and be prepared to play for him. Come now, and compose yourselves.'

A table was upturned upon the lawn a represent a loom; its broken leg became the weaver's shuttle. Blankets were stripped from the beds and conscripted as rolls of blue cloth. A counter was built from an old wooden chest, and a tub dragged across from the washhouse. As the stage was set, the players grew more nervous. The youngest bursar clung to Hew. 'There's a *woman* in the cloisters.'

'Aye, she's come to help you dress.'

The boy looked scandalised.

'She's my sister, Thomas,' Hew assured him hastily.

'Aye, sir, if you say so.' Thomas turned pink.

'There is a vat of pig's blood by the door,' Meg approached, calling

307

out through a mouthful of pins. I do hope it's pig, for it came from Giles. He thought it would be useful for the dyer's clothes and hands.'

'What does the dyer think to that?' asked Hew.

'He rather likes it, oddly. Has he read his part? He thinks he's playing some sort of soldier. Anyhow, he seemed quite pleased about the blood.'

'A small misunderstanding,' Hew dismissed quickly. 'He'll be happy enough. He's not very bright. Did you remember the gown?'

'Aye, and it fits nicely. Do you think it matters much that Agnes has a beard?'

Hew groaned theatrically. 'I hoped the wretch would shave.'

'I did suggest it, Hew. He says it took him half a year to cultivate, and he will not relinquish it. I thought he seemed a little highly strung.'

'They all are, this morning,' Hew replied soberly. 'And, if they knew it, there's cause. Look, here comes Giles. Where is this blood from?' he hailed.

'Don't ask. A boy has been sick in the courtyard,' Giles remarked briskly. 'I gave him some peppermint water, but I fear he has spoiled the approach.'

Meg started. 'I'll see to him, Hew.'

'He's well enough now. A bit green. But you might attend to Nicholas. He's sitting in the shade.'

'Nicholas is here?' Hew echoed in alarm. 'Do you think that's wise?'

'I think that it's essential,' the doctor answered seriously, 'that he should see the play. For nothing I can do or say appears to bring him peace. Oh, and your father is here.'

'My father? But he has not been to town in years!'

'Perhaps he wanted an occasion,' Giles suggested. 'If you should want him, you will find him over there beneath the trees. He has brought a pile of pillows, which he shares with Nicholas. I half suspect that they are making friends. But don't suppose he's come to see your play. I understand he's keen to see the king.'

Hew broke into a grin. 'Thank you, Giles.'

'Don't mention it. My one regret is that we could not bring your horse. The excitement proved too much for him. He's lying down.'

'Thank God for that,' Hew answered feelingly.

Giles bustled off to join the little group among the trees as Hew turned back towards the stage. The dyer, dripping gore, was chasing Thomas Burns across the lawn. Hew intercepted them. 'Don't daub Thomas with that filth, not yet.' The blood flecks in the boy's bright hair unnerved him. Duncan pulled up sulkily and wiped his hands across his coat. 'Where's Mercator?' he whined. 'He's meant to help me with my lines.'

'Is he not here?' Hew started.

'Looks like it,' the boy said rudely.

Meg was pouring something from a vial into the tub. Hew called out to her. 'Have you seen the merchant? Was he feeling sick?'

'No, that was me,' said a portly youth proudly. 'I spewed in the cabbage bed.' He was playing Archie Strachan.

'I think he went into the chapel,' Thomas ventured timidly, 'to say a prayer.'

'He needs one,' snorted Duncan.

Hew felt his heart stop. 'I will have to go and fetch him, for it's almost time. The rest of you, stand close, and try to learn your parts. No more antic play. For any moment now, the king will walk into those rooms and will look below and see you. Be sure that you are ready. All your life, you will remember this.'

He almost ran into the chapel. As first he did not see the bursar in the darkness. The boy was kneeling on the floor. His head was bowed. Hew urged him softly. 'Come, Sam, quickly now, it's time. We must say our lines together, you and I, for you are Mercator, and I am Claudus. Come, now, quickly, take my hand.'

The boy did not turn, but spoke in a low voice 'I cannot do it, sir. I cannot play the part of Mercator.'

Hew knelt in the dust beside him. 'Of course you can,' he told him kindly. 'This is stage fright, nothing more.'

The bursar shook his head. 'I cannot do it. I am the son of a groom. And Duncan Stewart is the son of a lord. And if I humiliate him in front of the king he will not forgive me. I will be a dead man, sir.'

'The responsibility is mine, not yours,' insisted Hew. 'I'll see you are not blamed.'

'Will you, though?' The boy looked at him tearfully. 'I do not think so. I'm the one who has to strike the blow. There will be reprisals.'

'But you will act the part before the king,' Hew argued. 'Duncan will not dare to touch you.'

'Do you think not? And suppose the king should take his part? And suppose he does not take his part, yet on a dark night will come men to slit my throat. And what will the king do then? Suppose he cares to trace the crime, his father is a lord; my father is a groom. They will pay blood money, aye, a fine at most, and hear the king's displeasure for a day. I am a bursar, sir, my father is proud of me. I know we are ill used, and yet I have the chance to take the laurel wreath. I am a bowman in the college team, and at the butts in June I hope to take the prize.'

'I'm sure you will.' Hew put a hand on his shoulder. 'Forgive me, I should not have asked it.'

'Are you not angry?' The bursar looked up. 'What will you do?'

Hew grinned at him. 'Ah, don't fret. I'll think of something. Your father is a groom, you say.'

The boy nodded. 'An under marschal for the earl of Mar,' he answered with a hint of pride.

'Well, when this is over, I may ask him for advice.'

With heavy heart, Hew left the church and made his way back to the lawn. Meg ran out to greet him. 'Hurry, Hew! The king has just arrived. But where is Mercator?'

'Not coming,' he said flatly.

'What? It's stage fright. I'll go talk to him.'

'No, leave him be.' He took her by the arm. 'He's right. I asked too much.'

'Whatever will you do?'

'I don't know.' He smiled at her bravely. 'There is no one who can take his place, who has Latin, and the strength, and knows the part. I will just have to make something up.'

He walked with leaden footsteps to the centre of the lawn. He was dimly aware of the players behind him. Their shrill boyish voices fell still as they fled to the shadows, awaiting their parts. In the distance he saw Nicholas sitting with his father, blankets around them, under a tree. A hush descended as he looked into the cloudless sky. The birds appeared to pause their song. On the balcony above the lawn he saw the lords assembling, Gilchrist to the right, and in their midst the boy king, James. Hew's throat began to close against the drumming of his heart. He looked up to the window and found that he was staring at the cool gaze of the king. James began to frown. In a moment he would turn his head and walk away. The moment would be gone. Somehow, Hew felt deep and found the words. He heard his own voice shaping, 'Claudus sum.' He had no plan of what might happen next.

And then a shadow fell across the lawn behind him, and a figure in a dark green cloak came striding at his back. The figure dropped his hat and bowed before the king, so low he swept the ground, and a warm familiar voice boomed clear out to the cloisters, 'et ego Mercator.' And it was Giles.

Afterwards, Hew took the lesson, for the students were about to make their final disputations and the coming of a king did not constitute a holiday. Those who had performed sat nervous in the hall. He set them to their task, but they had scarcely begun when the doors were thrown open and the party of the king was announced, James with his cohort of servants and lords, and a flustered Master Gilchrist at the rear.

'Is this a lecture?' asked the king. 'Then we shall stay to hear it.'

Hew bowed low. 'The students are about to make their declamations.'

'We shall hear them. What's the theme?'

'Self-murder, sire.'

'Your Grace, this is the man who made the play,' the lord said at his side.

'I know him. What's his name?'

'Hew Cullan. Sire, the man's a viper. I am most wretchedly deceived in him,' Gilchrist interjected.

'Truly, sir, how so?'

'For his play, his wicked lies, his slanders of the college and myself.'

The king professed astonishment. 'But was that *you*? I had not known. What do you say, d'Aubigny, did you recognise James Gilchrist in the play we saw?'

'Now that you mention it,' his friend replied dryly, 'I perceive a likeness.'

'Morton?'

The earl inclined his head, 'It shall be looked into, your Grace,' he answered stiffly.

'Thank you. I had not observed it,' James revealed to Gilchrist, 'but since you have remarked it, then he must have caught a likeness, don't you think? For ourselves, we liked the play. My lords and I have been discussing your controversies, Hew Cullan, and are entertained by them. We cannot quite agree. Perhaps you will explain them to us when your class is finished. Meanwhile, we shall hear your self-slayers. Peace, Master Gilchrist,' and he waved the man away, 'this interests us. We shall be better exercised in disputations than in listening to more melodies and madrigals.'

The students made their arguments, and most of them acquitted well enough, except for Sam, who had not played the part of Mercator. He stammered blindly through his speech, quite overcome with nerves. But if the king had noticed it, he gave no sign. At last he said. 'I wish to speak with Master Cullan. Is there a chamber close by?'

'The masters' room adjoining, sire.'

'Morton, you may go with Gilchrist and examine his accounts. No, my lord, I pray,' for the earl moved to protest, 'Esme shall accompany us, and the rest will wait outside. Come, Master Cullan, we are private here.'

The door was closed behind them.

'We liked the play,' James went on, 'though we were perplexed as to the meaning. The wickedness of the dyer we found most satisfactorily requited, and the merchant and the woman were well served, and yet we disagreed about the tutor and the boy. According to my regent Morton, their sins were the worst of all, their friendship the most inward and unnatural. But did you mean it so? For myself, and my cousin monsieur d'Aubigny, we perceived their friendship as most virtuous and pure. Morton will assert this marks out my greenness in these matters. Which of us is right?'

'Majestie,' Hew bowed, 'I would suggest that youth has the advantage here, for your eyes remain unclouded by the rheum of his experience. The tutor and the boy are in the play as innocents. Sadly, it is the way of our world that we perceive corruption in the purest heart, and see wickedness where it was never meant.'

The king smiled, satisfied. 'It's as I thought. The earl has lived too long. Whatever is that noise?'

James was startled to his feet, and Esme to his dagger, as the chamber doors flew open to admit Duncan Stewart. Catching sight of the king, he stopped short and let out a whimper before crumpling to his knees.

'Your Grace, I beg forgiveness.' The boy looked close to tears, 'I had not thought to find you here. It was Cullan I was looking for. You see how he has used me, sire.'

It was a rare sight. Duncan had changed his wet clothes, but the drubbings of the laundress and her ash and candle soaps had

had little effect on his face. He was naturally fair, and his hair now darkened to the root stood up in clumps of purple, echoed in the infant wisps of purple-tufted beard.

James suppressed a smile. 'Aye, I do see,' he confessed. 'What say you, Master Cullan?' he enquired, mock-severely. 'You have dyed my cousin, have you not?'

'He played the dyer's part,' shrugged Hew, 'full well.'

'Aye, that he did. But you have made him purple, and he wears it badly.'

'Sire, will you hear me?' Duncan cried, 'I played the part to please you, as it pleased my masters I should play it. Why then would you ridicule me?'

'Peace,' the king said laughing, 'Aye, you played your part. It pleased me well. But what is your complaint? Did your master not instruct you in the part that you were playing? That being the dyer,' he threw back his head, 'being the *dyer*, you should be *dyed*?'

'He did not. When we rehearsed the play, the bath was empty.'

'For certain,' interrupted Hew, 'we could not fill the bath with dye for the rehearsal. For think of it! If you had come into the dye before the play, you would be purple at the start, and being purple at the start, you know, would give the game away. But all this was explained to you.'

'No,' Duncan snivelled, 'I swear to you, sire, that this was not explained. For how should I suffer myself to be *purpled*, had I known?'

'Nor yet to please me?' James answered softly. 'You know, Master Cullan, the man has a point. His father, having influence in court, is likely to bend my ear on this account. I beg you then, account for this: why, for my pleasure, have you made his son violet, without his consent?'

'I know not, sire. It baffles me,' said Hew. 'For it is written in his script, as clear as day, that on the one performance he is dipped into the dye, and he has read the script, and must have seen it there. Moreover, he was asked by myself and by the regent Robert

Black and by our very principal if he had read the script and understood it, and his reply was most emphatically, he had.'

'Is this true, then?' asked the king.

'I would swear to you, sire, I did not,' the purple face blustered. 'It was not in the script.'

'That is easily proven. Bring me a copy.'

The script was found and brought, with Duncan Stewart's name to it, and given to the king, who chuckled as he read.

'Aye, it says here, plain enough. I think you have not read this, or you had not understood.'

'I doubt that may be true,' said Hew regretfully, 'for he is a feeble scholar. We feared the part would tax him. He assured us it would not.'

'I see the whole,' the king said solemnly. 'Come now, Duncan Stewart, I find no cause for complaint. I know you did not learn your part, since you spoke it most indifferently. Your grammar and your diction both were vile. You are, it is plain, a poor sort of scholar. But in our eyes you are redeemed somewhat, for you have made us smile, less competent a scholar than a clown. I regret your loss at court while you wax puce. Tell me, Master Cullan, lest his father make enquiries, shall this colour last?'

'Happily, with scrubbing, twill grow paler by the day. It is the curse of purple dyes, I'm told, to lose their colour with the sun. Within the month he'll fade to plunkett blue.'

'Well then,' smiled the king, 'there's no cause to be despondent. You may lock yourself away about your studies. That, by all accounts, will profit well. And when you come to take your laurel wreath, the shades shall scarcely clash. To plunkett blue? Oh, Duncan, go, or I shall split with laughing. You stand so dismal in your woad. Besides, it is the king's hue you disport so, and I find myself misliking that you wear the shade so flippantly. Take care lest you offend us. Leave us now!'

And waving him away, he laughed until he wept. 'But did you see his face? I could have plucked him like a plum! Did you not *see* him, my lord?'

He changed his tone abruptly.

'Who are you, Master Cullan, who so openly come mocking at the college in your play? You make enemies today of powerful men. Do you dare presume on our protection?'

'I make no presumption,' Hew swallowed. 'The fact is, your Grace, that the play has its root in a history, the truth of which was hidden so deep I saw no other way to make it see the light of day. The people you have seen within the play are real. The merchant and the weaver's wife are fugitive from justice.'

'What then? Was *all* of it true? Not the dyeing of the dyer?'

'Aye, even that.'

'That's better still! But what about the tutor and the boy?'

'That is the worst of it. The tutor is suspected for the murder of the boy. He has been gravely ill these past few months. He is my friend.'

'Then you made your play to reflect the true facts, as you saw them?'

'They are the true facts. I have proof of them. You should know, sire, that the corruption in the college is true also. This regent, the tutor you see in the play, has been persecuted because he did not countenance these deceptions.'

'I see. Then you would have me do what, precisely?'

'I confess, I do not know. I have tried to make the *controversiae*, to set out the rights and the wrongs of the case. But the case is not clear. I do not know where the blame lies. There are several crimes, and three people here accused of capital offences. Are they guilty of them? Should they hang?'

'Well,' the king considered, 'I should think their guilt is clear. The dyer killed the boy, and that is murder. Then the father kills the dyer. And blood for blood, we may forgive.'

'In law, it is no crime to kill a man for killing, or to kill the killer of a son,' conceded Hew. 'But the dyer had not been indicted for the killing of the boy, and the merchant had no cause to have suspected him. He killed him for his threat of blackmail. So it was a crime.'

'I take the point. But nonetheless, because the dyer killed his son, although he did not know it, then I think that I might pardon him the killing of the dyer.'

'Your majestie is gracious.'

'. . . And yet we may not pardon him the converse with his brother's wife, which is, I think, the greater indiscretion. That's adultery and incest too, within his brother's house, which he must answer for.'

'As you say, your Grace. I have pondered this awhile, and I believe that he has answered to a higher court than this, for his collusion with his brother's wife has cost his son.'

'And you think that this atones for it? From what I have seen in your play, he did not think much of his son.'

'You are mistaken, sire. I am assured he prized his son beyond the world. He was the world. And because he was so precious, he had the highest expectations, which the boy could not fulfil. But now without his boy, his world is nothing. He was a rich man. His life and his wealth fall away.'

'You are persuasive. Well then, I may pardon him. But the wife I shall not pardon. She must hang. For incest and adultery, and for the murder of her husband,' the king declared triumphantly.

'In her defence,' insisted Hew, 'she did not mean to kill him.'

'So she *says*,' the king replied. 'She fed him poisons, though.'

'She gave him herbs she was persuaded would provoke him into bed with her. She had been raped. She was with child. What should she do?'

'So you put it in your play. I don't believe it. She killed him for her lover. Doubtless she bewitched her lover, teased him into bed with her and forced him to kill the dyer with her spells. Persuaded would provoke him! How was she persuaded? Who persuaded her?'

'I don't know,' Hew lied uneasily. 'She claimed a cunning woman offered her the herbs, but likely she invented her. Your majestie is sharp.'

'Aye, like as not. For sure, she is a witch, and if she had them from a woman, both of them are witches, Hew, and both of them shall hang. She shall be made to tell.'

'She has fled, sire, with her lover, far across the seas.'

'Has she? Oh.' The king looked disappointed. 'Then we banish her. Well, we have solved your puzzles. What will you do now? I cannot think that you are welcome in your college.'

'No. But I came there by an accident. My training's in the law.'

'I'm not sure you have the mind for it,' the king declared. 'You are too intricate. No matter. I'll remember you, Hew Cullan.'

'I thank you. Majestie, there is the matter of my friend.'

'Your friend? Of course, the tutor. I should like to talk with him.'

This was unexpected, and James saw Hew's hesitation.

'This irks me now. You say he's sick? Tis not contagious?'

'No, sire, not at all.'

'Well, then. Take me there.'

The Majestie's Desire

'You need not stay,' the king advised his retinue. 'Peace, it is a sick man; he can hardly hurt us. Wait here by the door. You too, Hew Cullan.'

He looked at Nicholas. The room was fresh with scented flowers, a sad and sweet tincture of petals and candlewax. A handkerchief, peppered with blood, lay on the bed.

'I pray you, don't get up,' the king remarked.

'I cannot, sire.' The walk back from the priory had exhausted him.

'I see.' Restlessly, he walked round the chamber, fingering a candlestick, leafing through a book.

Nicholas stirred painfully. 'Will you sit, your Grace?'

'I thank you, no.'

Nicholas gave in to a spurt of coughing and fumbled for the handkerchief.

The king returned to walking, and observed him coolly as he shrank back on the bed. At last he said, 'According to your friends, you will not live. And yet the manner of your death may yet be eased. You are accused of crimes, of sodomies, unnatural lusts. Do you deny them?'

Nicholas said nothing.

'I see you do not answer. Would you have me pardon you?' the boy asked earnestly.

'And it please you, your Grace.'

'And it please *me*? Does it please you? Will you not reply?'

Nicholas inclined his head.

His majesty sighed. 'Will you not talk to me, Nicholas Colp?'

'And it please you, sire. What would you have me say?'

'I saw a play this afternoon. It showed a tutor and a boy. Are you that tutor?'

'I believe I was.'

'Then talk with me a little, I would know your secrets. I see how you are broken, and your linen black with blood. I see you catch your breath. You cannot stand. This harm you have done to yourself. I do not think the rack could hurt you more. You need not be afraid of me.'

'I am not afraid.'

The boy was walking once again. It seemed that he could not be still. For Nicholas, it cost him all his strength to lift his head and whisper it.

The king contended still, 'You are regent in the college of St Leonard?'

'Once, I was.'

'Tutor to a murdered boy?'

'Aye, once.'

'Tell me about this boy. What was he like?'

'He was a lad about your age, and almost like yourself.'

'Ah,' the king corrected gently. 'We think not.'

'What would you hear?' His eyes had closed. 'That he was fair, and younger than his years, with milk-white skin and auburn hair, and slender as a girl. That he was like a child, and wept at trials that were too cruel for him, for he was green and artless like a child, and should have been at play.'

'Then not like us at all,' observed the king.

'No, sire, as you say.'

'He formed a passion for you, I believe.'

'For I was kind to him.'

'And you did have more inward thoughts? You loved him?' James moved closer to the bed.

'Aye, perhaps.'

'You admit as much to me?'

'I kissed his head. With that kiss, I sent him home to die.'

'I saw the kiss;' the boy said softly, 'your friend showed it in his play. It was a gentle kiss.'

'I do not ask your pardon, sire.'

'I see that you do not. I pray you find your peace, I cannot help you more. But I counsel you, ask yourself this, were it better he had died *without* the kiss?'

Nicholas opened his eyes. 'I do not know,' he whispered.

'*Ask* it,' urged the king. 'For I myself, I do confess, am thankful for the kiss. He did not die unloved.'

'He is recalcitrant, and not at all subjective. He is a hard man to absolve.'

Hew and Giles exchanged a glance. 'Your Grace, he is not well. His wits . . .'

The king ignored them. 'He does not want my pardon. Nonetheless, I am resolved to pardon him, not for himself, who is beyond redemption, but to thank you for your play, which has amused us well. He will not be brought to trial. I believe he has been misused by his college. St Leonard's shall provide a pension that may make him comfortable while he remains alive. You will arrange it, Doctor Locke? St Leonard's lacks a principal. My lords have found discrepancies in Gilchrist's accounts and have removed him from his post. You may know, Master Cullan, that my counsellors last year denounced the regent system here as open to corruption. Still it is in place. This must be changed.'

Giles and Hew sat on the harbour wall, sharing mutton pastries in a cloth. Giles licked the crumbs from his fingertips, shooing off the gulls. 'When we find a house, we must have an oven.'

'Aye, then, you must.' Hew answered earnestly, 'Did Meg bake these?'

'Aye, can't you tell? The cookshop never baked a crust so light. And spices, Hew!'

'There's other things you like her for, I hope.'

'I love her. In truth, I am amazed she does consent to be my wife.'

'Truly, though?' her brother teased.

321

'Truly. Why not?'

'You do not doubt? Equivocate? You do not *wonder*, Giles?'

'It is not controversial, Hew.' His friend looked hurt. 'I wonder you can't grasp it. It's the oldest theme.'

'Peace, I'm teasing you. I'm glad you are to be my brother.'

'Brother? Now I reconsider, for I had not thought of that.'

Playfully, Hew jolted him, and the last piece of pie-crust fell to the gulls.

'Confound it!' Giles cursed. Mournfully, he shook the crumbs from the cloth. 'It can't be helped. Now, I must return to college. I am late for class.'

'Then you have not resigned the post,' Hew observed as they approached the castle.

Giles shook his head. 'I am persuaded to remain there, for another year at least. There will be changes made. I mean to build a practice, all the same, with Meg. We'll share the work. And yet . . . you never know,' he gave a wink, 'perhaps I'll be an actor, after all.'

'Aye,' Hew grinned. 'Perhaps you should. It still amazes me that you could play the part. You have the poet's knack to rhyme extempore.'

'I knew the thread,' Giles answered modestly. 'And speak Latin well enough. And for the rest, it was but strength, to dip the dyer in. I do confess I quite enjoyed it.'

'I never did say thank you,' Hew said seriously.

'You never needed to.' Giles cleared his throat. 'And what of you? You do not mean to play the regent all your life?'

Hew was silent a moment. He watched a group of students jostle up the hill and turn into the college gates. It was the first fair day of June, and most had spent the dinner hour delinquent on the sands. Presently, he spoke. 'I fear I lack the patience. I am not like Nicholas. I intend to depart at the end of the year. In truth, I'm undecided, though I may return to France.'

'Your father hoped you might continue in the law,' Giles ventured cautiously.

322

Hew laughed. 'I see you have already won his confidence. I detest the law. The law is capricious, contrary and cruel.'

'And yet you did resolve the case,' persisted Giles.

'And could not prove it by the law. If we must resort to kings, it is a tyrant justice after all.'

'Perhaps,' his friend said shrewdly, 'the more you know the law, the better it will serve you. For you have the wit to turn it to your ends.'

'That is what my father says.' Hew sighed. 'I do not know. But for the moment, I must see my students to their declamations. There is no hope, I suppose, that Nicholas may still return?'

The physician paused to consider it. At length he said. 'He will not work again. Yet I observe a change in him. He is more quiet in his mind. I wonder what effected it? Your father has offered him a home at Kenly Green. These strange events have exercised his spirits, and he finds that he is younger than he thought he was. He is resolved, he says, to live a little longer yet.'

'I'm pleased to hear it,' Hew retorted dryly. 'How did Nicholas receive the offer?'

'Gladly, and with grace. Almost, I might say, with *hope*.'

'Then he has changed,' his friend observed. 'Perhaps it was the fear of death that was tormenting him.'

Giles shook his head. 'He's not afraid to die. And yet, I'll vouch, it could not be the king. You heard him, Hew. We were only puppets, dancing in his play. He was disposed to toy with us. It pleased him; he grew bored with it. He did not see the tragedy.'

'Perhaps he did, though,' Hew conjectured, 'and we may not know it. After all, he is the king.'

'Well, it all is settled now. Meg will be sad to see you go. She feels she has not come to know you yet.'

'She should be glad to see the back of me,' Hew answered lightly, 'after what I put her through.'

'Aye, that's the strange thing,' observed Giles. 'She has only seen the back of you. You are a mystery, Hew. You have drawn us all into chaos and disorder, in and out of danger, into peril of our lives, and yet we hardly know you, and you leave a stranger. Stay awhile and show yourself. Else I must think you like the king who sweeps us up and sets us down like pieces on a board but does not really care how he disposes us.'

Hew laughed. 'That's surely harsh. Though I allow I have not made myself well known to Meg, *you* must allow I have been somewhat busy for more social intercourse. But you, Giles, can hardly have felt me a stranger. We have known each other far too well for that, and for far too long.'

'Aye, I concede, I do know a great deal about you,' Giles agreed. 'I know your taste in women and your fondness for French soap, your thoughts on Aristotle and your weakness for your horse. But these things, I protest, though I know well, they are not *you*, for that has been well hidden. Your real self is concealed from us, kept busy by its own distractions. When will we know you, Hew Cullan? When will *your* story be heard?'

'What nonsense!' Hew retorted. But already he had turned his back, and was staring out to sea. At length he added quietly. 'Perhaps it is not finished. Rest assured, it will be told.'

One quiet afternoon before the final disputations, while his students played upon the links, Hew took his walk along the Kinness Burn. And presently beyond the trees he came upon the little house with its single wisp of blue smoke and found the dyer's son at work among the pots. Will raised his cap.

'Good day to you, Master Cullan. We have not seen you here awhile.'

'I heard your mother died. I'm sorry for it.'

'Aye. We buried her beside her bairn. She did not want to share my father's grave. The minister was vexed, but at the last accepted it. It was what she wished.'

'Did she tell you what it was your father did?'

Will shook his head. 'He broke her heart, that's all. What does it matter now? They both are dead. Your sister came to see her at the end. She brought your physician friend Doctor Locke, the grand mediciner, huffing through his handkerchief. He couldna help her, though. They made her comfortable, for which I'm glad.'

'I did not know,' Hew answered awkwardly. 'You're lonely here?'

'We're quiet, aye. My brother took the bairns to town. He's to be married, have you heard, to Tibbie Strachan. Her ma and da gone, the farm and the wool shop are come down to her. Tis good enough for him, he says. They both are orphans now. He wasna one for dyeing.'

'Good, that's good, I'm glad of it. What happened to Tom Begbie?'

'Strachan's death released him from his bonds, and he went off in search of his lass. To the ends of the earth, if he has to.'

'He will not find her,' Hew said sadly.

'No? I feared not.' Will turned his back to him, stirring the pots.

'And your sister Jennie? Have you heard from her?'

'I hear the rumours, sir. I do not heed them. Jennie is a good girl in her heart. Last week the bairns were sent a present of a crate of sugarplums. And for myself, a box of colours, all the way from France. Now, sir,' he cleared his throat. 'I've a dye here quite unlike the rest. I'm sure you'd like a look before you go.'